Christobel
Kent
THE DEAD SEASON

CHRISTOBEL KENT'S previous books include *A Time of Mourning, A Party in San Niccolo, Late Season* and *A Florentine Revenge*. She lives near Cambridge with her husband and five children.

D1634572

For Carrie, brave and kind.

Christobel Kent

THE DEAD SEASON

CORVUS

First published in the UK in 2012 by
Corvus, an imprint of Atlantic Books Ltd.

9 8 7 6 5 4 3 2 1

A CIP catalogue record for this book is available from the British Library.

Hardback ISBN: 978-1-84354-952-9
Trade Paperback ISBN: 978-1-84887-152-6
Ebook ISBN: 978-0-85789-677-3

Printed in Great Britain by the MPG Books Group

Corvus
An imprint of Atlantic Books Ltd
Ormond House
26-27 Boswell Street
London WC1N 3JZ
www.corvus-books.co.uk

THE CITY IS DEAD in August. There is movement, but it's not life.

By day the cruise groups still crawl the streets, slower and slower as the heat intensifies, filing like ants from the Palazzo Vecchio to Santa Croce, their queues snaking around the Duomo and under the arcades of the Uffizi, trying to find shade. The shops beyond the tourist centre are shuttered and silent, the restaurants closed. By day it is bad enough: by night it is a ghost of a place and the tall palaces along the Via dei Bardi, north of the Duomo, and behind Santo Spirito stand even more silent than usual.

There are pockets, on the city's fringes, where those too poor to escape the heat congregate in the shadows, the Senegalese and Nigerian traders, the travellers, the dispossessed. There is the African market, tucked in between the bridge of San Niccolo on the city's eastern edge, the embankment and the green flow of the river below – or there was. Earlier this summer there has been a drive among the city's combined police forces to move the various itinerants along to some other and less visible meeting place; like almost all such moves, its effects will be temporary. The sellers of painted gourds and chipped Nubian heads and tasselled sandals will come back, to sell and to talk, to cook on improvised barbecues and drink sickly canned orange under the scrub oak, the air clouded with mosquitoes from the river below. But for now the place is deserted, or almost.

Where the scrubby trees abut the road, dilapidated crash barriers crowd against oleanders whose crimson flowers look black in the sulphurous streetlighting: even in the hard glare of an August midday, it is hard to see what lies under the densely packed bushes, and by night impossible. Tonight there is a breath of hot wind, a Saharan wind that carries with it tiny particles of sand that will be found the next morning along windscreen wipers. With the wind, the shadows under the trees flicker and shift.

One shadow, though, a low, crumpled shape between oleanders, does not move with the breeze, nor when another set of car headlights briefly illuminates its length beneath the leaves. A silk-socked foot, shoeless; a dark trouser leg, stained darker higher on the leg with a colour that will not be distinguishable against the grey until dawn comes. A battered hand twisted under the body and what should have been a face turned into the dirty scrub.

The flow of August traffic passes on its way out of the city, but no one notices or stops to look. There is no knowing how long he has been there, nor when he will be found.

*

Sandro Cellini was hardly aware of having slept at all, but the luminous dial of the bedside clock told him that it was two-thirteen when he started up in the dark, unable to breathe. Just raising himself from the pillow brought Sandro out in a sweat: he sat against the bedhead and told himself, slow down. It was the heat.

He breathed: slow, shallow, in and out. Sandro knew that if he mentioned this – to his old friend Pietro, heaven forbid to Luisa –

they might suggest, gently, that he talk to someone. A professional. He sat as still as he could, felt the sweat cool on his skin, felt the strong thump of his heart slow to normal.

Beside him, lying on her back, Luisa didn't stir. Her forearms were folded over her chest, protective of its asymmetry under the thin nightgown. On one side a hollowed scar where once there had been a breast; careless of it by day, in her sleep his wife's hands infallibly found their way to the site of the excision. In the slitted light falling through the shutters, Luisa's cheekbones gleamed marble-blue and monumental. A *motorino* whined past, then another and on the street's southern corner twenty metres away a burst of cackling rose from the drunks. This apartment, thought Sandro out of nowhere: this place. I hate this place.

It was the heat.

CHAPTER ONE

Tuesday

ORKING IN THE CITY in August just wasn't civilized.
Climbing the stairs to his office for an eight-thirty
appointment foisted on him by Giuli, his assistant insofar as
anyone was, with a tiny, scalding plastic cup of espresso in his
hand, Sandro reflected glumly on this conclusion. Only the dregs
of society found themselves sitting at a desk in August, only the
driven and desperate and enslaved. Forty degrees in the shade
by day, and at two-thirteen that morning, when Sandro had been
gasping like a fish in the bathroom, it had been thirty-one.

Luisa had not wanted him to buy a thermometer – *Why torture
yourself? What is this obsession with numbers?* – but Sandro had done
it on the sly; it hung just outside the bathroom window. Going in
there in the early hours, as he often needed to do these days, he
could lean out and take a look.

Thirty-one degrees three hours before dawn, and not a breath
of cooler air anywhere in the city. Even the moon, shining perfectly
round and white overhead, seemed to give out heat. During the
day there were distractions but at night, in those long, dead hours
between midnight and dawn when by rights the world should be

cooling, the heat bore down like a weight. The very thought of Florence's tonnes of sun-soaked stone, of the eighty kilometres of baked earth separating them from the coast, of the humidity that rose off the sluggish river and the encircling hills that held it in, was enough to bring on a panic attack.

Which was all it was: panic. The heat.

Luisa had pointed out to him a week ago – when the month had begun not with a bang but with the sigh of departing life: empty parking spaces everywhere, shutters pulled down – that now he was a private investigator, a freelance who could theoretically please himself, whereas when Sandro had been a captain in the Polizia dello Stato, he had been obliged to work in August.

'That was different,' Sandro had said.

Hands on hips, Luisa had not dignified this with a reply, but Sandro could have defended himself if he had had the energy.

It had been different, though: different having one desk of many in a big, air-conditioned building, moving through quiet corridors, everyone being in the same boat, the bar next to the police station staying open all year round – even on the mid-August holiday, *Ferragosto* – not to mention Christmas Day – to cater to the officers. Who after all were providing an essential service. And out in the patrol car, there had always been Pietro to talk to.

Sandro's partner – official or otherwise – for twenty of his thirty years in the Polizia dello Stato, Pietro Cavallaro was a modest, thoughtful man six years his junior, with a round, red-headed wife of permanently sunny disposition and a pretty daughter now coming up to eighteen. (Sandro registered that the big day was tomorrow, wasn't it? He'd arranged to meet Pietro tonight, with their gift for the girl. Damn.) A careful, meticulous man, slow to anger: the perfect complement to Sandro, who had been described as impatient, irascible, impetuous – given to obsessive pursuits but also flashes of insight.

Very occasional flashes, these days, Sandro thought gloomily, gazing out of the window, and no Pietro to bounce them off. He heard a siren, not far away, and by ear he mapped its path around the *viale* from the four-lane modern span of the Ponte alla Vittoria to the choked roundabout of the Porta Romana. A *motorino* crash on one of the bends that the Viale Michelangelo carved through the wooded hillside south of the city, perhaps? There was at least one a week. Lucky if the kid wasn't under a bus. He turned away, telling himself simply to be grateful he wasn't knocking on some parent's door.

If August was a quiet month in the police, there was always something to do: there was paperwork to catch up on; there was drunkenness among tourists, rough sleepers to be moved on, and never mind the domestic squabbles that broke out or the psychiatric patients wandering the streets. People just went nuts in the heat, whether they were already on the edge or not.

And now Sandro was going the same way. 'So take some time off,' said Luisa. The irony was, last year it had been Sandro begging her to take it easy, as she recovered from the cancer treatment.

Sitting down at his desk out of habit, Sandro put a hand to his testicles, just for luck. God willing, Luisa would be two years cancer-free in January. He knew you couldn't breathe again until five had passed, but Luisa was doing a good job: ever practical, she had decided that no purpose was served by thinking about it, so she didn't.

Even Giuli had been away for a week to the seaside. 'On your own?' Luisa had quizzed her straight off, never one for the indirect approach – and on her return, brown as a nut, with a big smile and new fine lines around her eyes ('Skin cancer, yeah, I know, I know. But it does make you feel good, the sun, doesn't it?'), she'd been straight out of the gates with a favour to ask.

'I don't know if she's got any money,' Giuli had pleaded, calling round after her first day back at work at the Women's Centre.

Following it up slyly with, 'But it's not as if you're overrun, is it?'

Standing at the desk with the sweat already beading on his forehead – next year, air-con, vowed Sandro – he could hear her downstairs, the cheerful clatter at the front door, a babble of conversation. She was bringing the client in herself. He downed the thimbleful of coffee, crushed the tiny plastic cup and dropped it in the wastebasket.

'Hey, Giuli,' he called through the open door.

She called back, 'Hey, Babbo.'

'Babbo': Dad. It was only half a joke. Part-time at the Women's Centre – giving free advice on STDs, contraception, pregnancy and the rest for Florence's errant females, of which there were many and various, from middle-class runaways to Roma to illegal immigrants – and part-time receptionist-cum-assistant to Sandro, Giulietta Sarto could be a nightmare, but she was also the closest thing he and Luisa would ever have to a child.

Forty-three this year, if he remembered right, and now three years clean of drugs and booze and bad men. Giuli was an ex-con into the bargain, although no one but the most hard-hearted would have been unmoved by the full story behind her incarceration. Not a trivial matter, murder, but the man whose throat she'd cut had been her abuser and a murderer himself into the bargain, and Giuli, drug-addicted, anorexic and living on the street, had run out of options.

It was taking them longer than he expected to get up the two short flights of stairs, and Sandro found himself listening. To the slow steps, a couple taken, then a pause. To Giuli's voice, cheerful, encouraging, solicitous. Sandro was thinking with pride that she'd turned out to be surprisingly good at compassion, little tough-nut Giuli, with her sharp little face and her spiky aubergine-dyed hair. And still listening, he heard the other voice, apologetic, breathless.

His curiosity overcoming him, Sandro was at the door himself when Giuli pushed it open on him, ushering in his first client of the day – the month. My God, thought Sandro, and he took an awkward step back, suddenly nervous as a cat at the sight that presented itself.

'Sandro,' Giuli said cheerfully, 'this is Anna Niescu.' And fixed him with a frown that said, *Pull yourself together. She's only pregnant.*

And she certainly was.

But somehow more pregnant than anyone he'd ever seen before. Not because Anna Niescu was huge, exactly, although the great thrust of her belly was surely close to a full-term gestation, round as a beachball and tight as a drum under a thin cotton dress. If anything, it was because she herself was so tiny, staggering under the burden of her pregnancy: a sweet, small, heart-shaped face, narrow shoulders, one childlike hand clasping a big, cheap handbag against her stomach. Her black hair, shiny as liquorice, was parted in the centre and drawn back in a tight bun: nothing but a child herself, thought Sandro.

He could feel the unwary emotion rising in him at the sight of her. Stop it, he told himself. He stepped hastily back and, remembering himself, pulled out a chair. 'Please,' he gestured. 'Please. Sit down.'

Giuli stood in the door, arms folded.

'Giuli,' said Sandro, knowing she was about to put her oar in, 'a glass of water, maybe? For Signora – ah – for Anna?'

Rolling her eyes, Giuli turned on her heel.

Watching her lower herself gingerly on to the bentwood chair, one hand behind her for support, Sandro remained standing, his heart heavy. Because it was clear to him, first of all, that Anna Niescu's was an old story and a hopeless one, even clearer that, no, she didn't have any money, and clearest of all that Sandro would have to help her anyway.

'So,' he said gently. 'When are you due?'

CHAPTER TWO

August

I F PEOPLE WEREN'T WHERE you expected them to be, well, no wonder: it was August.

Roxana Delfino sat behind her plexiglas teller's screen in the bank's gloom with nothing better to do and wondered, for example, whether the Carnevale had closed for August this year, because their guy hadn't been in with the porn cinema's takings in a cloth bag, as he had every Tuesday since Roxana'd been there.

In Florence in August you couldn't rely on anything: not the parking regulations, not the market stalls, not the staff of your favourite bar nor the stock of your favourite grocery, supposing they were open at all. A month off in August, that was the tradition, sometimes brought forward and stretched to five weeks if July became unbearable. For Roxana, who liked things the way she liked them, August in the city was a nightmare.

Her mother said it was why she hadn't got a man: had said it again last night. 'You're thirty-three,' she'd said darkly. 'It's a dangerous age. I had three kids by the time I was thirty-three. You're just too fussy, Roxana. You have to have everything – just so.' As if she, Violetta Delfino, was any different.

Roxana had still been grinding her teeth over that when at seven-thirty that morning she had zipped on her silver Vespa down the narrow, high-sided length of the Via Romana, a road that annoyed her every day for its not-quite-straightness, kinked in the middle so she had to ease off halfway down to make the bend. There was – as there always was, even in August – a bus looming behind her, just waiting for her to make a mistake. Not yet eight in the morning and the hot wind had blown on her face like it came straight from a hairdryer.

Roxana had kept her cool, her gloved hands steady on the handlebars; she heard the bus squeal reluctantly to a stop in her wake and she had sailed on.

Then down the Via Maggio, dead straight, stone palaces to either side with their huge eaves projecting so far into the street that they almost met overhead. At ground level the darkened interiors of antique shops, all closed for the month: some with brown cloth blinds down, some with metal shutters, some displaying brocade chaises and heavy wooden frames with patrician disregard for the possibility of a smash and grab. Would anyone have the energy in this heat, Roxana had wondered as she sailed past, to ramraid, to heave all that stuff into a van? The answer, she supposed, was yes: there were always some people desperate enough. Last night a baby had cried somewhere in a nearby house for hours in the heat and eventually a row had interrupted, the child's father shouting at its mother, the mother screeching, *Just do it. Finish me off.*

Three kids, and where were the others, Mamma? she wanted to say, but never did. Got their freedom and left Roxana to look after Ma. Luca in London, twenty-nine and working in a bar, clubbing till dawn most nights, taking God knew what illicit substances – but Luca could do no wrong. Susanna was up north, working in a hotel in Lugano on the Swiss border, with two kids under three and a feckless husband who kept disappearing, but at least she was married, at least she had her family. And Roxana wasn't going to tell Mamma how it really was: and even if Susi called at least once a week to moan about Carlo, sounding worn out and angry, then she'd say, the kids were beautiful, it was worth it. That was always how the call ended: a coded warning not to tell Mamma.

And they *were* beautiful; Roxana had a picture of them at work, stuck under the counter where the customers wouldn't see it. She looked down now, no need to be furtive, the place was as quiet as the grave. Paolino was one and a half and had his dad's dark red hair and a fierce little face; Rosa, three, black-eyed and cherubic, took after her grandmother.

Not that easy though, Mamma. As if she could just nip out of the bank and on to the Via del Corso in her lunch break and nab a man with *I want kids* tattooed on his forehead.

Mamma had this theory that if women lived alone too long – chance would be a fine thing: what she meant was, lived without a man too long – they turned strange and fussy, liked their own little way of doing things too much. They turned into spinsters, and according to Mamma, Roxana was a prime example. 'Sometimes,' she'd pronounce, watching Roxana restack the dishwasher or order the cupboards or check they'd double-locked the door, 'I wonder if you've got that thing. That obsessive–compulsive whatsit.'

Sliding her neat little *motorino* into the space under the embankment wall that was unofficially reserved for it next to Valentino's fat, shiny, show-off Triumph motorbike, Roxana had climbed off gingerly, not wanting to raise a sweat, not before a day's work. She unclipped her helmet, eased off the thin cotton jacket and stowed them away in the pillion box. Removed her handbag and locked the box, fastened the big yellow steel immobilizer and set off for the bank. Even then as she turned off the river into the warren of streets east of the Uffizi, she looked back over her shoulder, to be sure.

The city seemed so empty, bathed in heat and desolate, but there were always thieves: always. Roxana was a Florentine through and through, born in the hospital of Careggi that sat on the hills to the north; she'd been knocked off her *motorino* twice – a broken wrist the first time, a collarbone the second – and mugged seven times. Not in the last couple of years, though: she was careful these days. Her mother's little villa in Galluzzo, where they had both lived since her father had died last year of a heart attack at fifty-eight, had been burgled three times. The thieves came in the early hours, high on something: you woke up in the morning to find wires where the flatscreen TV had been (*My only pleasure, these days,* Ma had wheedled to get her to buy it) and her handbag gone.

Now the revolving security airlock hissed, the mechanical voice instructed the new arrival to turn around and remove all metallic objects from all pockets, as it always did. Only the odd flustered tourist, having strayed off the beaten track, ever complied; the security capsule's early morning occupant stood patiently and waited for the door to open.

Here he is, thought Roxana, almost with disappointment. The bank's most reliable customer, not quite regular as clockwork any more – it was close to ten by now, rather than the usual eight-fifteen – but—

It wasn't him. Signora Martelli, proprietress of the newspaper stand in the tiny Piazza Santa Felicita shuffled through the door, dragging her shopping trolley after her, pale and sweaty with the heat under her habitual full make-up, to deposit her meagre takings. The typical customer: on her last legs, heart trouble, swollen ankles, the summer would probably see her out. Roxana eyed her. She didn't envy the executors of *that* will. The old lady wasn't letting ill health mellow her – she was one of those who had her favourites, Roxana theorized, a working woman who disapproved of other working women. Yet, with a disdainful sniff, she eventually allowed Roxana to investigate the failure of a standing order to pay her water bill. Not quite satisfied by the explanation that an annual review had been specified on the standing order and it had lapsed, she had shuffled off again, leaving the place to return to glum silence, dust motes hanging in the murk.

The last time they'd been burgled, Roxana had been woken by the intruders and she'd got up, bleary with rage, the heavy immobilizer for the Vespa in her hand, only Ma had appeared in her bedroom doorway white with terror and clung on to her. Roxana had had to stand there, stupid big piece of plastic-sheathed metal in her hand, and do absolutely nothing. Nothing but stroke Mamma's hair to calm her. They hadn't even claimed, not wanting the insurance to go higher: Roxana had gone for the cheapest TV she could find this time.

Too many drugs, too many desperate types, too little respect. Easy pickings from the wealthy tourists bred crime as uncleared garbage bred rats.

Obsessive–compulsive? Roxana didn't know where Ma had picked up that little bit of psycho-babble. It was simply that the answer was to be wary, and to pay attention to the detail.

The boss would laugh at her, gently, for this tendency, but then he'd reassure her that this was precisely why he'd employed her. It was why she was such an asset to the bank, with her thoroughness, her conscientiousness.

In the silent interior, Roxana couldn't suppress a sigh. It was also why she was left holding the fort for most of August – that big mummy's boy Valentino Sordi, currently messing about happily with the coffee machine in the little staff room.

The offices behind her were dark and empty: the boss's sanctum – with *Direttore* in big letters on the frosted glass – and that of his deputy Marisa, who could do no wrong as *Gestore, Business e Family* with special responsibilities for bringing in commercial customers. The use of English words in Marisa's title was intended to indicate modernity.

Were they having an affair? Roxana mused, with nothing better to do than indulge in flights of fantasy. Their holidays were more or less coinciding, even if Marisa had been away a day or two longer than him, and since the boss was supposed to be at the seaside with his family, would he even have time for an affair? Not to mention the fact that Marisa, with her designer clothes and her evenings at the Gallery Hotel drinking cocktails, had a wealthy boyfriend already. But still ...

Could Roxana have been appointed *Gestore, Business e Family* if she'd played her cards right? Marisa Goldman, the daughter of a Swiss banker and a Torinese countess, had nothing but good breeding and the right wardrobe, a certain aristocratic way with customers. Whereas despite her degree in economics and accounting, and her thesis on the decline in small-scale manufacturing in rural northern Italy, Roxana was still only a *sportellista*. A teller, a bank clerk, after three years behind the plexiglass, for all the boss's professions of enthusiasm for her attention to detail.

And it wasn't as though the Banca di Toscana Provinciale was one of the big names. No, it was a small, old-fashioned bank, a niche bank, if you wanted to put it kindly, with just ten branches, three of them in Florence. It was her mother's bank, though, which was more or less why she'd ended up here. It had been where her father had brought her to open her own first bank account – now a source of constant frustration to her because the bank was too small, too obscure, and too backward to have its own cash machines anywhere but in the city, so every time she took money out she had to pay some other bank's whopping charge and feel a mug all over again. The Banca di Toscana Provinciale wasn't ready for the modern world, and Roxana had always thought that she was, more than ready. So what was she still doing here?

She stared at a terrible poster, dog-eared on the outside of the boss's office. A man with a white grin and a sharp suit, holding out his hand, and customers queueing in the bank, a dream bubble over each one's head. Kids playing in the garden, a shiny car. *Look ahead!* the man was saying. *Get in line!* Who'd come up with that one? Queue up like a drone, borrow more than you can afford, don't bother to read the small print.

Roxana's friends – friend, really, Maria Grazia, whom she hardly saw now she'd moved to Rome to work in film production – told her, get out, the Cassa di Risparmio di Firenze had vacancies, a big shiny new building in the north of the city; get an apartment up there, there are some great offers on the new developments. Break free.

And she would. Roxana told her – over a snatched coffee the last time she visited, Maria Grazia with that worried look in her eyes – she would, only for the moment, there was that tug at her heart that was Mamma.

'She's only sixty,' Maria Grazia had said in an exasperated outburst. Then hissed, 'She could live another thirty years, Roxi. Getting more cranky and ill every year.'

It was all right for Maria Grazia; her mother, long divorced, was a journalist, she prided herself on being modern, didn't want her kids hanging on to her apron strings until they were forty or married.

Suddenly, unwatched, unsupervised, Roxana felt like calling up Maria Grazia and telling her. Asking her what she thought about the only interesting thing that had happened in the bank for months.

If Maria Grazia was even there. She hadn't been, Roxana had

found with a sense of obscure humiliation, on the last couple of times she'd called – out on location, a kindly, condescending assistant had said. As if the girl knew that Maria Grazia's best friend from school was stuck in a dead-end job while the fledgling production director was hanging out with a film crew in Romania.

And if she was there, she'd think her old friend was losing it. Roxana could imagine the intake of breath, the disbelieving laugh. 'You mean, that's the highlight of your day, Roxi?' she'd say. 'Some old guy failing to turn up to deposit his takings?'

Not old, at least, not very, not much older than Roxana. Deep lines around his eyes, but then working at the Carnevale might have that effect on you. Not her type, even in a different line of work, she'd have to make that clear to Maria Grazia or she'd start matchmaking straight away. Though there was something about him ... Otherwise why would his absence keep nagging at Roxana? Dark hair. Black, black eyes. Not always quite clean, not always close-shaven; there was nevertheless something about the Carnevale's bagman, who no doubt had a name but Roxana had never learned it, that made you think twice. Something that made you wonder, or maybe, as Maria Grazia would undoubtedly say, *You've got a bit too much time on your hands, Roxi, if you're wondering about every customer that comes through the door.* A tendency to daydream: perhaps that was why Roxana had never been promoted.

There was a clatter at the little staff door behind Roxana, and a grunt, and Val was back, a tiny tin tray in his hand with two coffees on it and a ridiculously pleased expression on his big, stupid, handsome face. The coffee smelled good, Roxana had grudgingly to admit. She hadn't felt like breakfast this morning, waking in a sweat after a night of broken sleep, that neighbouring baby crying, the suffocating humidity, Mamma's grumbling still turning over and over in her head, and a bitter taste in her mouth.

'Thanks,' she said, downing the thimbleful and pushing back her chair. 'God,' she sighed, 'I don't remember it being this quiet last year.'

Val shrugged. 'Don't knock it,' he said with indifference, stacking the cups carelessly back on the tray, setting it down on her neat working surface and parking himself beside her. Spinning on the adjustable seat like a child at the barber's. Roxana retrieved one of the cups as it tipped and threatened to spill its dregs. He set his big feet up on the counter in a parody of insolence. Val didn't have a thesis or even a degree; he'd scraped through the Liceo Scientifico with a decent grade thanks to private tuition but had dug his heels in when university was suggested. He was simply too lazy.

Val had got his job at the Banca di Toscana Provinciale because he was connected: his uncle was one of the directors. He might stay a *sportellista* all his life, too, but the thing was, Val didn't really care. His mother – who worked all the hours God sent running a grocery-cum-wine bar – would keep him supplied with money, and business was booming, if Val's appearance was any guide. All Val cared about was how he looked. He would spend the first half an hour of each morning brushing himself down after the ride in on his big Triumph, examining the creases in his sharp wool trousers, adjusting the angle of his tie.

Roxana stood up abruptly, the tray in her hand: she'd wash up. She always did.

'He hasn't been in,' she said, and even as she said it, she experienced a minute, sudden, unexpected nudge of panic. As if shining a light on this small and apparently inconsequential mystery might conjure up a whole world of unforeseen consquences: one tiny thing out of place, one idle, curious question asked.

'Hasn't been in?' repeated Val stupidly. 'Who hasn't been in?'

Dimwit. Val dealt with the bagman just as often as Roxana.

'The Albanian.' To her he was an 'Albian' – he might have been anything Eastern European. 'From the – the cinema, with his cashbag. It's Tuesday, and he hasn't been in.' Then, patiently as if she was talking to a slow child, 'Every Tuesday since I've been here, eight-fifteen – or at least, between eight-twelve and eight-twenty – he comes in to make his deposit. '

Val stared back at her. 'Dunno,' he said, and shrugged, but he was frowning. So maybe it really was odd if it had penetrated Val's thick skull. Or maybe he just didn't know what she was talking about.

'Really,' said Roxana, turning away with the tray but she felt that sharp little tweak of anxiety again. Kept her face impassive, shrugged. 'Maybe it's just that it's August.'

A porn cinema, in this heat. And these days there was the internet. Ugh.

'Yeah,' said Val indifferently. Then, with a child's expression of transparent craftiness, 'How about we bunk off early, then?'

CHAPTER THREE

EVEN LATER AS THE light faded and the heat refused to die in the stifling streets, as Sandro waited on the corner for Pietro, standing awkwardly with the gift in his hands, trailing gold ribbon and all, he couldn't get her out of his head.

Anna Niescu had not been what he expected.

He had felt Giuli's eyes on them every time she came back into the room, on one pretext or another; it had been like being a teacher or a doctor trying to coax a word out of a child, with a pushy parent hovering nearby.

'Giuli,' he'd said in exasperation on something like the fourth interruption – looking for the tax forms, she'd said, as if Giuli had any interest in her own tax code, let alone anyone else's. Anna Niescu had stopped what she was saying and turned to smile that innocent, trustful smile at Giuli as she entered – as she'd done on the previous three occasions. Giuli her protector.

A bit too protective. It was as if Giuli thought she needed an interpreter, as if she didn't trust the girl – woman, Sandro supposed, as he now knew her to be twenty-eight years old, despite appearances – to speak her own mind, or possibly to be able to form a coherent sentence. Sandro himself, he had to admit, had had the impression before Anna Niescu spoke that she might be – simple. Too good for this world, as had used to be said of the backward child of every village; no doubt there was a term in modern psychology for it, but Sandro was quite happy not to know it.

'Giuli tells me you can find him,' Anna Niescu had said, smiling from Giuli to Sandro and back again, apparently unable to see the reluctance in his eyes, the anxiety in Giuli's.

Ironic, Sandro had thought, that these days such trustfulness is assumed to be the symptom of a psychiatric disorder of some kind. Faith. Sandro himself was long past churchgoing: he felt himself to be too dirtied by a life of policing – public servant, then private investigator, and he couldn't have said which was dirtier – to summon up sufficient belief in a benevolent creator. Too much of a sinner himself, too. It wasn't quite the same thing as being an atheist, though.

'Well, I can try,' Sandro had said with extreme wariness.

He had been right about at least one of his assumptions about Anna Niescu. She was indeed looking for the father of her child. She referred to him as her *fidanzato*: her fiancé. Husband, Sandro had thought, would be the appropriate word under the circumstances, but then he was old-fashioned.

'I know four days isn't very long,' she'd said apologetically. 'But he's not answering his phone. I called round at the apartment, on Sunday, then yesterday, and there was no answer.'

She'd given him the address, on a scrap of paper: an apartment block out towards Firenze Sud, a decent neighbourhood, if not exactly picturesque, a place of Holiday Inns and comfortable modern housing and perhaps anonymity. Sandro had contemplated the image of this girl, this child, heavily pregnant, standing in the street in the heat and pressing despairingly on a doorbell. There was something biblical in the scene that Sandro resisted: she was no virgin. Only innocent.

He'd imagined the guy, lying low, waiting for her to go away. Home would not be the place to catch him, would it?

'So when did you last see him?' he'd asked resignedly, overwhelmed by a sense, not unfamiliar to him, of his own uselessness in the face of fate, and women.

'I saw him on Friday, about seven, after he finished work,' she'd replied with bright obedience. 'He came to see me after work as often as he could, with something. A cake, or something, to keep up my strength. He brought me flowers once.'

Today was Tuesday. 'On his way home?' Sandro had asked gently. He had not pointed out to her that it was usual for a couple expecting their first child to be cohabiting, at least.

Anna had smiled, still trusting, and Sandro had felt his gloom grow. 'Yes,' she'd said. 'It's not quite ready yet, you see. The apartment: he's getting everything ready for the baby. And I live in, at the hotel. Since I was eighteen: it's like home to me.'

She was chambermaid and breakfast cook at the Loggiata Hotel. Sandro didn't know it, though it was in San Frediano, not far from the office; he had wondered how much they could be paying her, to shuffle between the tables with brioche and coffee, to take hours over making beds, in her condition. He had returned the girl's open gaze and thought, with a spark of fury: as little as they can get away with. And will she be out on the street, when the baby comes?

A shabby, old-fashioned place, Giuli had said afterwards. 'She might call it home, but you couldn't have a baby there.'

Anna Niescu had been gone an hour by then but the room still seemed to harbour her scent: sweet and spicy, soap and talcum powder and the heat of her skin.

'Will they do anything for her, at the Centre?' Giuli had just shrugged. Meaning, who knows? Meaning, they'll do what they can, but it won't be enough.

'I've got a picture,' Anna Niescu had said, almost the first word she'd spoken, scrabbling in her cheap bag and offering him not a photograph but a mobile phone. As she presented it to him with shy pride, Sandro had identified the phone immediately as a fake – a clone of an expensive make, the numbers beginning to erode, the metal trim peeling away in one corner. 'Josef gave it to me.'

'Josef?' Not an Italian name: that would be Giuseppe.

'Claudio Josef Brunello, but he called himself Josef.' So part-Italian. 'His grandmother was from – somewhere else. He did tell me, I just can't remember it right now—' And she had broken off. Abruptly her eyes had filled with tears and Sandro could imagine her, at eight or nine in school, unable to answer a question.

'I don't suppose it matters,' he'd lied, patting her arm uselessly, trying to suppress the gloom settling over him at her scant knowledge of this man or the world, at her utter guilelessness. He had squinted at the small, indistinct image on the mobile. Almost hopeless: the two faces, hers and his, were pressed together on the tiny screen, the picture of extremely poor quality. All he had been able to tell was that the man had dark hair and eyes and was under fifty years old. He would also have said, from the angle of his head and body, from his slight, uneasy grimace, that, whilst beside him, her cheek against his, Anna was beaming, her fiancé wasn't too happy about being photographed at all.

Then she had looked from the picture to Sandro uncertainly, as if she had only just realized how little she had to go on. 'He's a good man,' she'd said. 'He's educated, he's got a proper job.' Defensive. 'He's high up, in a bank, actually. And expecting a big pay rise, any day now.'

'Really?'

Trying to keep the scepticism out of his voice, Sandro had held the small screen up in front of him. Could this man be – respectable? Could he be for real? He'd tried to persuade himself he could – short-haired, the suit didn't look too cheap – but no. He'd pulled himself up: it was a pipe dream – now these two women had got him at it. Hoping against hope.

He'd handed the mobile back to her. 'Have you got anything more – detailed?' He had spoken as casually as he could manage.

'No,' she'd said, her face falling. 'He um – ah, he didn't like – well.' Then recovering, the smile back: 'I'm sure he would have given me a photo if I'd asked.'

'I'm sure he would.'

They'd looked at each other in silence a moment then; she'd shifted in her chair in some passing discomfort and despite himself Sandro had looked down, at the great round of her belly under the thin cotton. It was too much for her, he'd felt briefly: too big, too portentous, it immobilized her.

And then he'd seen it move under the fabric: like the quick shadow of something, like a shoal of fish under water. It broke the perfect round of stretched flesh with a limb, the knotted curve of a spine; and, with hands suddenly gripping the chair's seat on either side of her, Anna Niescu had looked down too and then up at him, half shy, half delighted.

Now, in the shadow of the brooding statue of Dante outside Santa Croce, Sandro scanned the wide piazza for his old friend. The poet gazed with eyes so darkened now by time and pollution so that they became hooded and sinister, and the statue, the chronicler of the afterlife, more than ever a figure of death. A memory came back to him: of being a boy in the city in the days when this piazza – all the city's piazzas – had been emptier, the occasional car innocently traversing them, when cars were a marvel and not a curse, and tourists had moved through the streets, awestruck and respectful, carefully consulting their red guide books. A memory of running in a gang of boys wheeling like a flock of birds around the city's monuments, trying to dodge the great poet's stern gaze as they headed past him for the market of San Ambrogio.

Anna Niescu, alone, would bring that child not into the world of his childhood but into this new world, where the hawkers and pimps and drug dealers – he could see them even now – stood back in the shadows of palace buttresses around the lovely piazza. She would love the child, that at least was certain, but would it be enough?

'Sandro!'

The hand clapped his shoulder, and the face into which he turned to look was beaming from ear to ear. Sandro was surprised by the gratitude he felt at the sight of his old friend's face, and the happiness he saw there. Pietro Cavallaro, his old friend, his former partner.

It had been too long: they both agreed on that.

'Not here,' Sandro said, taking a look around the big bleached piazza, the gaudy frontages of the cheap leather shops and the souvenir sellers stupefied by the heat.

They ended up in a modest bar in the Piazza San Ambrogio that was still open because the market stayed open through the summer, the butchers and *salumifici* taking it in turns to get away. The place was quiet and old-fashioned, just what Sandro wanted. A bar of speckled mica, an elderly cold cabinet, a listless overhead fan. The middle-aged barman mopped his neck resignedly with a tea towel and moved with extreme slowness to pour them each a *birra media*. The beer at least was nice and cold.

Pietro should have been away on holiday by now. 'A bit of a crisis with personnel,' he said, uncomplaining. 'This flu.'

Oh, yes, the flu, thought Sandro: interesting how someone like Pietro never gets the flu. Flu in August? Bird flu, swine flu – the world really was going crazy: the hysteria and illogic greeting its every new mutated virus a gift to the new breed of freeloader, his eye on the main chance. *I think it might be this new flu, boss.* Don't want to risk my comrades by coming into work, don't want an epidemic.

'Maybe I'll get away by the weekend,' said Pietro, rapping the table with his knuckles, for luck. 'If it's quiet.'

Sandro slid the gift across the table by the door where they sat. 'It's a what-d'you-call-it,' he said. 'One of those music gizmos. Pod, thing.'

Pietro drew his head back in surprise and admiration. 'Sandro,' he said. 'That's generous.'

Sandro smiled faintly. 'You thought I'd give her an apron, or a – a crystal punchbowl?'

Pietro laughed with embarrassment. 'Well,' he said, and stopped.

'I did my homework,' said Sandro. 'Asked Giuli. And Luisa did warn me. Eighteen-year-old girls are different these days, she said.' Of course, he thought with abrupt despondency, she's probably got one already, this pod thing.

'Oh, yeah,' said Pietro, with emphasis.

Another memory came to Sandro unbidden, of Pietro walking his little chubby toddler in her lace socks into the police station, the girl beaming up at each officer as he passed his hands over her red-gold head, trailing her favourite toy through the corridors. Sixteen, seventeen years ago.

The last time he'd seen Chiara, walking with her friends in the Cascine, she'd had her hair dyed black and shorter than a boy's and had been wearing jeans with careful slashes cut across each thigh. When Luisa had been eighteen, thought Sandro, she'd have worn the same clothes as her mother before her, good handmade leather shoes, neat skirts, white blouses. By the time she got to twenty-one they'd been engaged already: walking hand in hand across the Ponte Vecchio and looking at rings. But Chiara had smiled to see him, despite the clothes. He had wanted to get her something nice.

'Well,' said Sandro, clearing his throat. 'And maybe I'm not such an old fart as you think I am.'

'Yes, you are,' said Pietro. 'Nothing to be ashamed of: I am too. How's work, anyway? You going to have room for an unpaid helper, when I'm retired?'

Sandro looked at him sharply and understood that he was joking. Pietro would have plenty to keep him busy on early retirement, otherwise why was he going for it? The wife, the kid, the little holiday house in the mountains. Fishing.

'Work's fine,' he said, hearing the dullness of disappointment in his own voice and making an effort to brighten. 'New client today.'

By the time he finished telling Pietro about Anna Niescu, both their glasses were drained and sticky and the place was empty.

'Oh, dear,' said Pietro, momentarily dejected. 'That's not going to be a happy ending, is it?' Turned the empty glass in his hands. 'Man lets woman down: not a new story, that one. He's the bastard, not the poor unborn kid.' He glanced up at the barman, slumped now on his stool, defeated by the heat. Raised a finger and after a long moment's consideration the man eased himself off his perch.

'This heat.' And they shook their heads in unspoken agreement, on any kind of madness licensed by the inhuman temperatures, the boiling nights, the abandonment of the unborn included.

Pietro tipped his head back. 'Plenty of men run scared, don't they? When it dawns on them. The thought of that responsibility.' He gave Sandro a glance, chewed his lip, knowing that Sandro would have laid down his life for the chance of a child of his own. Sandro just shook his head, almost smiling, and Pietro went on, thoughtfully, 'Or he could have been married already, leading a double life.' Nodded. 'That happens.'

'Yes,' Sandro said frowning. Did that fit? Maybe. She'd seen his apartment only once, she said. Once.

'And what about the bank? That thing about him working in the bank?'

Pietro was still puzzling away at it with that way he had; it was like watching him disentangle his wife's jewellery, no rush, patience itself, until finally with quiet satisfaction he would hold the unknotted chain up to the light. Sandro had to resist a rush of warm feeling: it would be so easy just to settle back in with Pietro, to pretend they were still partners. But that part of his life was over. Pietro was a state policeman, and Sandro would never put his old friend in a compromising situation.

'The Banca di Toscana Provinciale,' he said with a sigh. 'The branch by the station, so he's hardly a big wheel.'

'No,' agreed Pietro. 'Didn't some big bank try to buy it up last year?'

Sandro shrugged; he was having trouble trying to believe any of Anna Niescu's fiancé's story, let alone get a handle on the latest developments in the banking crisis.

He sighed. 'I'm going to talk to her again tomorrow. At the Loggiata, where she works. There's more, I'm sure, she – she just couldn't think straight, she said.'

She'd been flustered, in the office, poor child. As it had dawned on her that her faith might have been misplaced, that Sandro and Giuli were going down a different path than the one she'd envisioned, where her beloved was in a hospital with memory loss from a car accident, perhaps, and when they found him all would be well. Other women might have been frightened, resentful, angry; she was just so certain that he wouldn't want to miss it all. The birth, the uncomplicatedly joyful event. She was so sure that he must want to be found.

Pietro was still musing. 'Responsible job – doesn't fit with the guy who takes fright, does it? To run out on all that?'

Sandro frowned, thinking of the way she'd talked. Telling him about the man who took her for her first prenatal scan and held her hand, the man who came to see her after his day's work, to bring her cakes. 'She really loved him,' he said.

Pietro shook his head, sad but curious. 'To think there are still girls like that around. Where does she come from?'

'She was adopted herself,' said Sandro, gazing out through the window at the shuttered market building. 'Looks as if she's got some Roma blood to me. Found abandoned and adopted by an elderly couple, religious by the sound of it; the old man died before she'd left junior school, and mother when Anna was eighteen. She was devoted to them.'

She'd shown him a dog-eared photograph of the old couple, a pair of *contadini* from a village up in the Apennines. When they'd died she'd gone to the city to look for a job; someone at her school has suggested it, perhaps out of misplaced kindness, knowing the girl would never be academic.

'I've got some savings,' she'd said, looking up at him. 'I can pay you.'

Sandro had just looked at her. 'Let's see how we go,' was all he'd said. Savings: how much could you save living in as a chambermaid at the Loggiata? They probably even deducted her board.

'So, first stop, the bank?' said Pietro. 'Or this apartment he's supposed to be doing up for them, his little family?'

'Yes,' said Sandro, 'I think, the bank.'

And something stirred at last in his sluggish, heat-stupefied veins. The need for action, the chance that maybe tomorrow morning there'd be a breath of air, in the early hours. The Banca di Toscana Provinciale, then, first thing. He stood up.

'I hope you do get away,' he said, anxious suddenly, prey to some foreboding he didn't want to acknowledge.

And at the door he turned back. 'Give Chiara my love,' he said. 'Tell her I remember that day you brought her into the station. Tell her I remember that rabbit she brought with her, trailing around, holding it by the ear.'

And Pietro's expression – the same combination of affection, respect and bewilderment he'd known for twenty years – followed him out on to the street and stayed with him all the way home to Luisa.

Who had a surprise waiting for him.

CHAPTER FOUR

ONE ADVANTAGE OF AUGUST, Roxana had to admit, as she urged her little *motorino* up the Via Senese, between the handsome façades of art-nouveau villas blackened by seventy years of exhaust fumes, was that the traffic was barely non-existent. No rushhour to speak of – even if you still got hassled by the buses; one driver in particular seemed to follow her home every night, serenading her by releasing his brakes with a sharp puff on every bend. Over the houses a ridge of grey-green came into view in the dusk: olive trees, and the beginning of the end of the city.

It had been a strange day, even for August. As the hours had passed, the absence of one particular customer had faded in significance. There could have been any number of reasons; maybe the heat got too much even for Albanians, sometimes.

Someone had phoned for the boss, which might not have been out of the ordinary in the Cassa di Risparmio di Firenze on a sweltering August Tuesday, but here? The phones hardly rang at the best of times.

'No,' she'd heard Val say, loitering behind the boss's desk; had he even had his feet up on it? Pretending to be in charge. A good telephone voice, thoughtful, concerned. 'No, he's not here.'

Sauntering out through the door with a smile to Roxana that perhaps he thought was inscrutable, that certainly was ridiculously superior, as if merely answering the boss's phone was promotion.

She hadn't bothered to go out for lunch, and Val, as usual, had taken advantage. Got back at four. The scream of fire sirens again that had seemed to go on all afternoon, people grilling food outside, even in the heat, and getting careless with matches and accelerants.

And then towards the end of the day there'd been a guy on the pavement outside, idling. White trainers, greased back hair, skinny, hopping from one foot to the other. The police so dozy in the heat the drug dealers could come right out on the streets, was that it?

If anything, it was hotter than yesterday; as the sky turned luminous over the ridge with the setting sun, Roxana, in her thin jacket with a day's sweat and grime under it, didn't know how she was going to stand it. The weather rarely broke before the end of August. Sun, sun, sun, merciless sun. And the tropical thunderheads building over the city to hold the heat in, for another sweltering night.

The road opened briefly after it joined the Via del Gelsomino, a straight stretch with a row of farmhouses along a ridge to the left, the thickly planted cypresses of the cemetery to the right. The green didn't last: beyond the cemetery was a long row of petrol stations, luring holidaymakers and commuters.

Not the prettiest part of Tuscany, that was for sure: the road was generally choked at the end of the day; once, as she hummed past on her *motorino,* Roxana had seen an overheated car burst into flames, a man running out of it holding a baby. Tonight it was quiet; the heat lay over everything like a blanket. The sun was dipping behind the hills now and the electric-blue sky was streaked with neon pink; funny, thought Roxana, allowing herself a brief moment of delight, how a sunset can be so cheesy in art, but never cheesy in real life.

The cluster of modest villas that was Galluzzo stood ahead of her. Roxana's heart dipped and she told herself, not for the first time, that it was no good. She dreaded work and she dreaded getting home again: freedom was this brief moped ride between the two. She could hear Maria Grazia nagging her cheerfully down a telephone line, 'Something's got to change, Roxi.'

It would be fine, she told herself, wheeling the *motorino* in through the gates and under the house. It is what it is. Pushed open the door and called, 'Ma?' And when her mother came slowly through the door from the kitchen, that twisted, rueful smile on her face, the relief behind it probably visible only to Roxana – relief and the lingering trace of a fear that no one might come.

'Hey, Violetta.' She called her mother by her name as often as she remembered to these days, hoping to establish a grown-up relationship, hoping belatedly to bestow on her mother the adulthood she so feared she might lose.

Kissing her mother on the cheek, Roxana smelled face powder, the faint tang of sweat underneath it. No air-conditioning, of course, in the little old-fashioned villa; Dad hadn't wanted it. 'We're practically in the countryside here,' he'd say, brooking no argument. 'I don't want one of those ugly great boxes whirring away on my lovely terrace.' The terrace he hadn't been on in years, which Ma used only to hang out washing, a broom long idle in one corner, old cat-box in the other. A bedraggled plumbago. 'The fan's good enough.'

Dinner was on the table, even though it was barely seven-thirty. Without Roxana's father Violetta Delfino seemed to have lost track of her days, there was so little to fill them. Only Roxana's return from the bank marked a fixed point, and the table was laid to hasten her home.

It was *ribollita*: delicious, under the right conditions – and Roxana knew Ma had made it because it was her favourite – but the most unsuitable dish you could imagine in the heat, thick cabbage and beans.

'My favourite,' she said. 'Sit down, Ma.' Her mother hovered uncertainly.

'Someone called, today,' she said, frowning, anxious. 'For you.'

'Sit down,' said Roxana again, fork in hand. 'I can't eat until you sit down, *cara.*'

It could have been anyone; it was most probably a mobile service provider, wanting to sell her a contract. One conversation with Ma was usually enough to deter cold callers: she'd keep them on the line for hours. Asking advice, what broadband was, whether they thought it might be useful for calling her brother in Argentina. Who had been dead five years, but Ma regularly forgot that, or perhaps didn't want to sound as alone in the world as she actually was. Once Roxana had caught her talking to a timeshare saleswoman about her daughter who had an important job in a big bank. Because to say an unimportant job in a small bank would have been shameful? Or because she had persuaded herself it wasn't so?

'Oh, I was so worried I'd forget,' said Ma, lip trembling.

Roxana took her hand, stilled it. 'Sit down,' she said. 'I'm sure it wasn't important, anyway. Did you drink enough water today?'

Ma had been admitted to hospital for dehydration last summer, just after Dad died. Surprised herself by how urgently she wished him back, Roxana just hadn't been quite on the case; she had tried to make Ma eat, but she hadn't thought it was liquids she needed.

'Yes,' said Ma vaguely.

Roxana poured her a glass, and spooned some of the *ribollita* on to her plate. Took a mouthful herself: it was practically cold, which was a blessing. Roxana thought she detected a rogue ingredient;

Ma's recipes had gone off kilter, too, every meal an adventure now. Mentioning it, though, would lead to Ma telling her she had OCD, again.

The room was dim, shutters closed against the day's heat, and Dad had always used light bulbs of roughly half the wattage necessary. After forty years of marriage Ma couldn't even begin to question his decisions, Roxana understood that. She got up and pushed the shutters open a little: probably a mistake, she thought, feeling the wall of heat that met her. You could almost see it, creeping inside like fog.

Leaving the shutters ajar, she returned to her seat, sweat trickling between her shoulder blades, and her mother looked up at her, helpless. This was worse, she thought, worse than being nagged about her OCD, or her childlessness, or her single status.

'Are you all right, Ma?' she asked, a prickle of anxiety setting up.

Alzheimer's was what she dreaded: she'd tried to broach the subject with her mother's doctor, but he'd brushed her off. 'Grief,' he'd said brusquely. 'If she seems a bit vague, or forgetful, or lost, that's the most likely culprit.' And it could be a killer too, he'd made sure she knew that. She'd taken Ma in on her return from hospital, and had lingered to ask him one or two things she didn't want her mother to hear; his hand on her shoulder as she left, though, had been kindly enough, she knew that. The same doctor who had given her her shots and looked in her ears when she was six years old: he probably still thought of her as a kid.

'And how was your day, dear?' said Ma, the spoon languishing in her bowl, ignoring the question.

'Fine,' said Roxana, staring at her. 'August, you know.' She sighed. 'It's like a ghost town. And Val's driving me mad.' Leaned forward. 'Since when did you ask me about my day, Mamma? Now I know there's something wrong.'

'That Valentino,' said Ma, contemptuous, and Roxana breathed again. Ma had met Val a couple of times and looked down at her nose at his sharp suits, his aftershave – almost everything about him.

'Can't you just imagine him as a child? That kind. Spoiled wouldn't be the word.'

At this point Roxana might normally have mentioned her own younger brother, apple of her mother's eye, but she was so relieved at the return of her mother's sharp tongue that she did not. She concentrated on cleaning her plate scrupulously. It was sage, she decided. Ma had put sage in it. Which wasn't right.

'Yeah,' she said. 'He asked me for a drink after work.'

And laughed. Her mother's expression was a picture: the desire to thrust her daughter into a liaison – any liaison – with a man warring with her absolute disdain for Val.

'It's all right, Ma,' she said. 'He only wanted to manoeuvre me into shutting up early. He's about the laziest man I ever met.'

'But surely you can't do that? I mean – it's a bank!'

'Oh, Mamma,' said Roxana, and sighed. 'We had three customers all day. We closed up five minutes early, that was it.'

'So you did go for a drink with him?' Violetta was looking at her slyly. Perhaps after all she thought Val would be better than nobody.

Roxana folded her arms. 'A drink, yes, Ma.'

Val hadn't meant anything by it. She knew he hadn't. They'd had a nice enough half-hour, though, sitting in a bar just across the river in the Piazza Demidoff. In June and July the place would be so packed you had to walk around the customers in the road; as it was, there'd been a couple of expensive convertibles parked ostentatiously and illegally. Hardly a parking warden about, at this time of year. They'd sat on the terrace under the lime trees outside, though their scent was long gone.

'You don't mind?' he'd said curiously, as the waiter set down their drinks, a cold beer for him, a ruby-red Crodino for her. 'Stuck here in August?' Someone had called over to Val, from another table, asking about the weekend, and leaning back in his chair, he called back an answer, shaking his head ruefully.

He'd turned back to Roxana, sipping his beer. 'Everyone's off to the seaside,' he'd said sourly. 'Elba. Vincenzo's got a place there.' Covertly, Roxana had eyed the man who'd called across: tanned, lazily handsome. She'd shifted in her chair.

'You could go?' She had wondered what he was still here in Florence for.

Val had shrugged. 'I agreed to stick around, didn't I?' he'd said thoughtfully. 'Marisa wouldn't take no for an answer. Very insistent, that she had to get off on the yacht with Paolo.' He leaned back. 'Their perfect life.'

'It's all right for them,' Roxana had said. Marisa'd just assumed, in her case. That she'd comply. 'For the bosses. But just for the weekend?'

'I've got no one to go with,' Val had said, eyeing her. Then drank a little deeper from the beer. 'It's not like it was. You know, the lads, away together for the weekend, the girlfriends come and go. But these days, the girls stick around, wives some of them, by now. It's the lads that disappear.'

It had been the deepest conversation she'd had with Val since she'd known him. Maybe it wasn't all roses, being a man about town.

'Sorry, Val,' she'd said. 'What happened to – what's her name?'

'Lily?' Val had given her a sidelong, sardonic look. 'The American?'

'If you say so.' Roxana had only glimpsed her from a distance, now and again, a rangy blonde with expensive clothes. 'She go back to America?'

'Greece,' Val had said briefly, draining his beer. 'Next stop. On the Grand Tour.'

'Right,' she'd said, giving him what she hoped was a sisterly, consoling smile. He'd laughed and got to his feet. 'Want another?'

Roxana glanced across the table at her mother in the uneven light of the inadequate bulbs. It wasn't as if she'd never had a boyfriend, for God's sake; there'd been Matteo at college, only he'd fancied someone else more; that kind of thing happened when you were twenty-two. And then she'd been too busy working – trying to please the boss, staying late; for a while Violetta had even warned her off, thinking there was something going on, telling her he was a married man and she should be careful. And when next she lifted her head from her desk, all the men her age seemed to be taken.

Can't be helped. Someone will come along. That was Roxana's mantra.

Roxana didn't bother telling Violetta any of this; she'd only get the wrong idea.

Instead she stood up and dutifully began to clear the plates. This kitchen, she thought absently, ugh. The wooden units were thirty-five years old, oppressively Tyrolean in style but still, unfortunately, in excellent condition.

At the sink – no dishwasher, of course – she spoke over her shoulder. 'So what did you get up to today? How far did you get on your walk?'

Violetta was very good about her daily walk, as prescribed – the only thing prescribed, in fact, by the same family doctor. 'Fresh air, exercise,' he'd said briskly. 'Better than antidepressants,' and Roxana had agreed with him. Violetta would walk up around the side of the Certosa, the pale-walled monastery surmounting its hill beyond Galluzzo, and along the lanes into the countryside. She grumbled that she was turning into one of those old widows from her own childhood, bow-legged in black, searching the hedgerows for sorrel and chestnuts. It was doing her good, they both knew that, and she did come back with a bag of something most times, even if it was only nettle heads for risotto.

But now behind Roxana there was a silence, and turning she saw on her mother's face only anxiety and confusion. This was new: she'd been vague, there'd been episodes – but this was another thing.

'Violetta? Ma? I said, how far—'

But her mother's lip was trembling. 'I didn't go out. I – there was the phone call. And then someone came to the door. I didn't have time. It – it looked like rain.' She was practically babbling.

'Looked like rain? What are you talking about?' Roxana could hear her own fear, sounding like anger, and she tried to soften it. 'Sorry, Ma. One thing at a time. Someone phoned.' She came back to the table and sat down; outside a siren wailed, far off in the city, and she reached for her mother's hand. It seemed to hold no warmth, the fingers no more than skin and bone.

'There was a message.' Violetta Delfino stopped.

Roxana smiled steadily into her mother's eyes. 'You wrote it down.'

Her mother returned her look. 'Yes,' she said, hopefully, then with greater certainty, 'Of course.' And made as if to get up, in awkward haste, to fetch the pad they kept by the telephone in the hall. Roxana held fast to her mother's hand.

'But you don't remember who it was?'

Violetta looked around herself, anywhere but at her daughter. 'I'm sure it'll come to me,' she said, and with a sigh Roxana released her.

'Yes,' she said.

Ma stayed where she was, as if she'd forgotten any urgency. 'A woman,' she said. 'It was a woman, I remember that much. I'm not gaga, you know.'

Roxana let out a quick nervous laugh. 'I know,' she said, and got to her feet.

But the pad by the telephone in the hall was blank; it sat there on the perfectly polished table, dead centre on its own lace doily. Behind her in the kitchen doorway her mother stood, nervously moving her hands.

'Oh, Ma,' said Roxana.

*

'So what d'you think?'

Sandro gazed at his wife, who was eyeing him with a certain sceptical amusement, one hand on her hip, the other having just gestured across the dusty tiled floor.

'I think it's a wreck,' he said, paying no attention to the protesting murmur that came from the third figure in the room, a small, bearded young man in a short-sleeved shirt and tie, clutching a briefcase. 'And it's three floors up.'

Luisa had met him on the doorstep, ready to go out. Dark-grey linen dress, a bit of lipstick, her best handbag on her arm. She'd sniffed his breath as she kissed his cheek, good-humoured.

'How was Pietro?' she'd asked cheerfully. 'Amazing, to think of that little girl all grown up.' He'd agreed.

What had been more amazing, although neither of them was going to say as much now, was how Sandro and Luisa themselves had survived, because when Chiara had been born, Luisa had shut herself in her room for a day and a half, emerging pale and monosyllabic. She had given birth to their only child twelve years before Chiara; close to perfect on the outside, the baby had suffered from a syndrome that brought with it major defects in the internal organs; at most a baby born with the syndrome might survive for a month. Luisa and Sandro's daughter had lived a day and a half. There was still no known treatment; these days there were prenatal scans – and abortion. Sandro still sometimes wondered about it all. About what they would have done if they'd been offered that option: would it have changed anything? Their daughter's birth and short life had left them too shell-shocked to approach the possibility of trying again, until it was too late. Would a termination have left them any different? Sandro could not grasp it: it was too big a question.

On their doorstep Luisa hadn't let him go inside to change. 'We've got half an hour,' she'd said. Sandro had just looked at her with faint exasperation, and she'd said, before he could ask, 'It's a surprise.'

The first part of the surprise had been standing on the doorstep of a grubby-stuccoed three-storey villa in the south of the city, on the eastern edge of San Niccolo, twenty minutes on foot from Santa Croce. The young man with the beard, who smelled strongly of aftershave, had greeted them, introducing himself as Sergio Galeotti of Galeotti Immobiliare. An estate agent.

Galeotti's car had been outside, an expensive, low-slung model with a personalized number plate: GALIMM. Even a mid-range Maserati didn't come cheap: Sandro imagined that plenty of backhanders would have come Sergio Galeotti's way. Prices fixed, deals done.

Whatever happened, Sandro'd wanted to say to Luisa, to the old way? Where you went to see a man you knew, who knew a man who knew an apartment that had come free, in a nice area, knock-down price for a quick sale? But glancing at his wife, he'd seen that she knew exactly what he was thinking, because she always did. And he'd known what she'd say, too: that was how we got our flat, the old way, and we've never been happy there.

'Mr Galeotti is handling the sale for a client of mine,' Luisa had said briskly. 'Signora del Conte. You know her.'

It hadn't been a question, but yes, Sandro knew her, one of many devoted clients of his wife's, this one a fierce, beady-eyed, elderly woman. Oh, and startlingly wealthy, too. A hoarder, of shoes and silk blouses and properties, here, there and everywhere, little apartments, garage spaces, a cottage or two in the country. Luisa had spent her whole working life at the same place: Frollini, just off the Piazza Signoria, a shop that over the years had transformed itself from an excellent old-fashioned haberdasher's and ladies' outfitters – all wooden display cabinets, sensible knitwear and lace collars – to one of a chain of sleek palaces of luxury. Luisa, who had enjoyed moving with the times, was now the most senior saleswoman, and their treasure; she had many loyal ladies – not to mention those ladies' daughters and granddaughters – and some of them were extremely well connected.

'She's a very good client,' Luisa had gone on. 'And as a favour to her Mr Galeotti has agreed to waive the buyer's fee.' *Oh, yes,* thought Sandro. The money'll reappear somewhere else, you can bet on that; no such thing as a free lunch. And the old lady certainly had a fat portfolio of properties.

But it was a nice area, even Sandro had grudgingly had to admit that. If pushed, he would have said it was his favourite part of the city: not quite on the tourist track, tucked between the river and the green hills that rose up from it to the Piazzale Michelangelo.

Quiet but not too quiet: they'd walked through a small piazza on their way here, no more than a junction between roads just inside the soft stone of the mediaeval wall, and there'd been the sound of quiet conversation in a bar, the rattle of cutlery being laid in a restaurant, some kids on their mopeds chilling out. No blaring satellite TV, no thumping music, no smashing bottles. It was a nice area, which was why they couldn't afford it.

'We can't afford it,' he'd said flatly before they even went inside. The street had been quiet, a patch of green rose above a low wall opposite the hundred-and-fifty-year-old building; a rusting, wrought-iron balcony ran right along the top floor. The agent had dipped his head discreetly at Sandro's words, leaving Luisa to deal with that particular obstacle.

'You don't know how much it is,' she'd said.

Galeotti had raised his head again. 'I think you'll find my client—' and he had broken off, nodding to Luisa, 'our client, should I say, is open to offers. The apartment does need, ah – some attention.'

And Sandro had sighed, giving in. Then Galeotti had fished from his briefcase a great circular bunch of keys – eight or nine different sets, each tagged – extracted one and they had gone in.

Some attention: well, that had certainly been true. The roof had collapsed in places, and the speckled tile of the floor was heaped with rubble. The window frames were rotten and the shutter-slats half broken; the tiny bathroom blotched with rust and mildew, the kitchen no more than an ancient cooker and a stained sink in one corner of the main living space. But the room was wide and light and spacious and beautiful, with chestnut beams; one set of long French doors let in a rectangle of green hillside, and another a slice of the view, between rooftops, of the smoke-blue layers of the Casentino hills.

'Perhaps you could leave us for ten minutes, to have a look around?' Luisa had said politely to Galeotti, who had appeared unsettled by the request.

'Well, I don't know,' he'd said, chinking the big hoop of keys against his thigh.

'Please,' Luisa had said, and there was something about her tone – Sandro knew it all too well – of precision and firmness and certainty, which demanded compliance.

'I'll be downstairs,' the estate agent had said shortly. 'Ten minutes.'

'I don't like him,' Sandro had said, listening to the man's footsteps on the stairs.

'I think he can tell,' Luisa had said, smiling. The pale soft skin around her dark eyes had crinkled and Sandro had found himself wondering why anyone would want to erase such lines. 'I could never work out how you managed to be such a good policeman,' she'd said, hands on hips. 'You're so bad at pretending.' He had laughed abruptly: wasn't that just like Luisa? Hide a compliment in an insult. Or vice versa.

'Yes,' he'd agreed. 'Do you like him, then?'

And she'd laughed out loud.

A little trace of a breeze had set up, drifting through the long window nearest to them that gave on to the hillside, and it brought with it the smell of hot, dry earth and pine needles. It hadn't rained in five months.

'You love it, don't you?' Luisa had said, and Sandro had nodded, just barely.

'Why did you bring me here, Luisa?' he'd said with a sigh, turning slowly on the spot, taking in the scratched floor tiles, the long streak of reddish-brown stain down one corner, the lovely windows one after another. 'We can't afford it.'

'Come here,' she'd said, and dutifully Sandro had followed his wife. Ahead of him her wide shoulders – finer than they'd been before the chemo, her collarbones pronounced now, but still strong – made him think of Anna Niescu's tiny frame, struggling with its burden. Had her fiancé brought her to a place like this and said, *Imagine, darling? This is where we'll put the nursery.*

'We're too old,' he'd begun, but Luisa's sharp backwards glance had silenced him. She had then taken him into the only other real room in the apartment, the one bedroom. It was big, too, twice the size of anything you'd find in a modernized place. A square, handsome room, with two windows looking down into the nested houses, ornamented with window boxes and washing hung out to dry, that clustered around the old wall.

By now the sun had disappeared behind the dark hump of hillside to the west, but the sky had remained livid blue, and clear. Luisa had been leaning on the windowsill, silhouetted as she gazed out. The hot wind had blown in past her, carrying her scent inside with its load of humidity. She'd turned.

'Do you think I want this for me?' she'd said softly. 'Just for me? Do you think I don't hear you, lying awake, grinding your teeth every time someone smashes a bottle in the street? Pacing the flat at night as if you're in a cage?'

Sandro, suddenly overwhelmed by his own stupidity, had said nothing.

'Too old? No,' Luisa had said. 'Life is too short. You need to make changes, now and again. Not too often, but Sandro, *caro*, once or twice in a lifetime? Is that too often?'

He'd nodded, mute with shame. 'I thought you loved Santa Croce,' he'd mumbled.

'I made the best of things,' she'd said, shrugging. 'We both did. But we don't necessarily have to do that forever.' She'd sighed. 'Yes,' she'd said. 'I don't think it was a bad place. But I like this one much more.'

There was a sound from below, of someone slipping on the crumbling steps, and a muffled curse. And then the agent was with them in the bedroom, examining the dust on his shoes with disgust. 'Seen enough?' he asked brightly, key in hand. 'Ready to go? Sorry to rush you, but there's another viewing in ten minutes.'

'Another viewing?' Luisa said with dismay, and the man shrugged.

'It's a good area,' he said. 'Places like this don't hang around.'

One of the windows hung at a crazy angle, and Galeotti, trying to open it, had pulled a rusting hinge out of the wall. 'Needs some attention,' Sandro had said drily and the man had looked back at him with a trace of sullenness before putting the professional smile back on his face and leaving the rotten window to dangle against the wall.

Now settled in at Nello for a late dinner, they talked around in circles. Could they afford it, how much would they get for the place in Santa Croce, who might they get to do the work? Pietro knew a mason, and there was a good place in Santo Spirito for the windows. Every time Sandro felt excitement bubble up inside him he fought to suppress it – partly because it was his nature, partly because it was only sensible, wasn't it? Because nothing was certain. So dangerous, to make plans: disappointment was the default position in life. But Sandro found himself agreeing to go into the bank, to talk about a loan. He pushed away his plate, the breaded cutlet on it not quite finished. This heat, it had taken away his appetite, too.

'There was a girl came in today,' he said slowly. Talking of plans.

And he was suddenly overcome by the desire for a cigarette, after twenty years without one. But now smoking was banned more or less anywhere but most particularly in the place where it would have been most perfectly enjoyable, in a convivial restaurant after a good meal. Since when, he asked himself, did we become so intolerant? Since when did we start refusing to take even the tiniest risk for another's pleasure? Of course, smoking terraces had sprung up all over the city since the new law, most of them so fully enclosed that effectively people were still smoking inside. But that was the Italian way: keep your head down under authority's demands and then carry on as before.

Fleetingly he wondered: perhaps taking up smoking again would be a change too far even for Luisa.

'A girl?' said Luisa, her curiosity caught by whatever it was he had allowed to slip into his voice. Reluctance, regret.

And for the second time that day Sandro laid out Anna Niescu's story, but the version of it he found himself telling Luisa was different in several particulars, some of it new even to Sandro himself. He talked of the sweetness of the girl's nature, of her conviction that the man needed only to be brought back to her for a happy ending to ensue, her faith. And he even found himself telling Luisa, wonderingly, what he would not have dared describe to her even five years ago: of the moment when he and Anna Niescu had both looked down at the child moving inside her, immanent; untainted perfection waiting to be born.

'It seems like waiting for someone to die,' he said, without even thinking if what he was saying made sense. 'Waiting for a child to be born. You can't – anticipate. You can't know what it's going to be like, until it's there.'

Too late, he heard what he had said. They had waited for their child to die. But Luisa closed her hand over his. 'You'll have to find him, then,' she said. 'The father. If anyone can, you can.'

It had never failed her, not through all the chemo and the surgery, the bruising cannulae, the drips and the hospital wards and the vomiting in the dark. And not for the first time Sandro wondered where Luisa got it from, all that certainty.

CHAPTER FIVE

Wednesday

THE SKY HAD CHANGED overnight; the breath of wind had dropped and, while they slept, it had closed over them like a lid, white-hot. As Roxana climbed off her *motorino* by the river and removed her helmet, it seemed to her that the city was nothing more than a cauldron, and they were boiling in it like the damned.

As soon as he got back from the seaside, she would talk to the boss. *Prioritize*, Maria Grazia had said on the phone last night. Make a list of how you need your life to change, and take it one step at a time.

Leaning over the parapet for a moment, Roxana could still feel the helmet's pressure on the back of her neck and her temples, where it had made her sweat; she knew sweat was designed to lower the body temperature, but it didn't seem to be working.

In the centre of the river, a bleached stick emerged from the clogged green, a crested bird perched on it, head cocked to look down into the water. Roxana thought that surely there could be nothing living in there; like every Florentine with any choice in the matter, the fish would have moved along to cooler, faster waters.

There was time for a coffee this morning; Roxana had left

a good half-hour earlier than usual. Leaving Mamma in the kitchen on her knees in housecoat and rubber gloves, cleaning out cupboards and muttering angrily. Better the fierce, furious, energetic mother she'd always known growing up, than the fearful, gentle, clinging one who increasingly seemed to be taking her over? Roxana thought so.

Last night, for the first time in eight years, Roxana had smoked a cigarette, and not just one, either. When Violetta had finally shuffled upstairs to bed, with a small glass of warm milk, Roxana had gone into the *salotto*, where neither she nor her mother ever went except to put another coat of polish on the huge Biedermeier dining table. As if sleepwalking herself, Roxana had gone straight for the inlaid box where Dad kept American cigarettes for visitors, had taken a handful, dry and light as dead leaves, felt the cool weight of her father's old Zippo in her hand and then she'd stopped. The smell of lavender wax and stale air, the solid pieces of heavy, old-fashioned furniture around her – the sideboard from her grandmother's house, the upholstered chairs, the glass-fronted display cabinet – familiar in every detail even in the dark, the ugly roll-down shutters: it had all suddenly borne down on Roxana like a landslip, and she felt as though she was about to lose her balance. So she backed out, as far as the front door and beyond, out on to the porch, leaning against the dusty plaster and looking into the street. Quiet as the grave.

Lighting up, she'd taken one drag of the stale cigarette, practically coughed up her lungs, and had walked in the hot night down the road to the machine outside the tobacconist's to buy a half-pack of MS. On the way back home, as she'd listened to the trickle of the river – a tributary of the Arno – that ran through the suburb unseen, through bamboo thickets and culverts, the heat if anything had seemed to be intensifying.

She'd stood in the garden and smoked among the feathery branches of a big unwieldy shrub her father had loved. There was bougainvillea too, growing up the back of the house, a moth-eaten banana palm, and a fig tree whose fruit was just ripening. She'd heard a whine and slapped fast and hard at her calf; the river drew the mosquitoes. She'd put out the cigarette then and gone inside to get a moon tiger, the coiled incense burner whose smoke was supposed to keep them away. Listening in the hall she'd heard Ma snoring at last, a soft, regular sound through the door. She'd been exhausted, poor old thing.

Sitting at the table in front of their empty bowls, Roxana had interrogated her mother as gently as she could.

'Was it – one of those people trying to sell you something, Mamma?'

What had been starting to worry Roxana was not the stupid phone call, but Ma's reaction to it, standing there in the gloomy hall in her slippers, about to burst into tears. The forgetfulness, the panic, the disproportionate anxiety over the whole business.

'You know,' Roxana had said, trying not to sound impatient. 'Mobile phone, or internet or something?'

'Oh, no,' Ma had said then, and her face had seemed to clear. 'Oh, no, nothing like that. She was – a friend of yours maybe? She called you by your name—'

'Oh, Ma,' Roxana had said, in despair, 'they all do that. It's a kind of trick. A selling tool.'

'A trick?' Her poor face falling all over again. 'I don't think so. She was upset. She was really upset.'

And now, twelve hours later, Roxana was as far from being ready for work as she'd ever been, her mouth sour from the cigarettes and lack of sleep. She stood outside the only bar near work that was open – the Bar dell'Orafo, an exhausted little tourist dive tucked into a subterranean archway behind the bank – and she considered. Considered how few friends she actually had, friends who would call her if they were upset. Maria Grazia was about it – and she'd spoken to Maria Grazia. Eventually.

Across the street, a garbage truck squealed and hissed into position beside two big dumpsters, the noise alone enough to drown out Roxana's thoughts. The Bar dell'Orafo seemed pretty quiet, and looking through the window Roxana relented: it wasn't such a bad little place. Who didn't serve tourists, in this city? The pastries would be no good – only a handful of *pasticcere* worked through August, just as very few bakers did, and the very thought of those ovens blazing brought Roxana out into another sweat – but the coffee would be fine.

She went inside, ordered a glass of water and a cappuccino, no chocolate on top. Orlando, the wizened, moustachioed barman, made it with ridiculous care, pouring the milk to make an oakleaf shape in the foam. Either oakleaf or heart; if she'd been a different sort of woman she'd have got a heart, maybe, but Roxana liked the leaf better, anyway. Orlando was the middle of seven children, he'd once told her; not much elbow room in his life; perhaps that was why he was working through August, too.

The coffee was excellent, in fact. Someone standing outside the open door was smoking, and for a second Roxana thought, what the hell. The security guard can wait on the door until Val arrives, ten minutes late as he always is. Stay in this little bolthole half an hour, have another, borrow a cigarette, be five, ten minutes late to work. Life's too short. Just for a second.

Maria Grazia had heard her inhale on the phone last night, when she had paused for breath herself in the middle of singing the praises of her Romanian forest and lecturing Roxana on how to take control of her life. And had started shouting down the line at her. *Are you mad? Do you remember that bronchitis*

three years ago? Do you remember how many times you've told me
that giving up was the best thing you ever did?

'Maria,' she'd said, and it might have been the nicotine rush
but it seemed to Roxana that just hearing the words coming out
of her own mouth had made her dizzy, 'I think Violetta – I think
Ma might be losing it. I mean—' taking a deep breath, 'I think she
might be getting dementia.'

Maria Grazia had gone very quiet. When she spoke eventually
Roxana could hear the strained note in her voice. 'Over one phone
call? Forgetting to take a message?'

'It's not just the phone call,' Roxana had said.

And she had unconsciously lowered her voice. Standing in
the garden, with the street barely ten metres away, the nearest
neighbours no closer, Ma fast asleep upstairs, whom did she think
would hear? The pungent smoke from the moon tiger glowing at
her feet spiralled into the still, hot, damp darkness.

'She says there was someone in the garden yesterday. Someone
hiding in the garden, and she didn't dare leave the house all day.'

Damn, damn. It hit Roxana all over again, in the humid coffee-
scented gloom of the Buca dell'Orafo, with Orlando's kindly, tired
eyes on her.

'Your mother still alive, Orlando?' she asked.

He crossed himself. 'Not for twenty-five years,' he said with
genuine sadness. 'God rest her.' Shrugged. 'Worn out. She passed
away in the middle of scrubbing someone's floor.'

And Roxana nodded, thinking of her mother on her knees this
morning. Better to go that way, she thought, though she didn't say it.

Ma hadn't wanted to tell her. Had skirted uncomfortably
around it, unable to tell an outright lie but miserably aware of
what Roxana would think. After twenty minutes of going round
in circles, Roxana had been reduced to taking a tough line,
demanding only yes and no answers.

No, she hadn't gone out. No, it hadn't been because she hadn't been feeling well. Yes, she had run out of bottled water and milk and bread. Yes, the supermarket was open all day even though it was August but she hadn't gone out. Yes, she just hadn't felt like it, would Roxana please just leave her alone? She needed to go to sleep. No, she hadn't seen anyone.

But she had heard someone. He had come to the door.

'A man?'

'I don't know.'

'You said he?'

'I don't know. I – I just thought it was a man. I don't know why.'

'Did he say anything?'

Yes, that was it, the man had called through the door, *Signora Delfino, I know you're in there.*

At the bar Roxana signalled to little Orlando, thumb and forefinger about two centimetres apart, for an espresso. He'd bobbed a tiny bow, a smile toothless behind the big moustache, and busied himself.

She had stared at Ma.

'You couldn't tell,' Roxana had said numbly to Maria Grazia, stubbing out the cigarette. 'From the way she said it, it did sound bad. Like the big bad wolf, or something. With poor old Mamma trembling in the hall. But you couldn't tell, could you? He might just have been a delivery man.'

Maria Grazia had taken her time answering and Roxana's heart had sunk. They'd known each other since *asilo*, when their mothers had collected them from the nursery at lunchtime together; Maria Grazia still called Ma 'Signora Delfino' on her rare visits home.

In the brief silence as Roxana stood in the garden, something rustled in the dark, over towards the wall that divided them from the neighbours, and Roxana felt the creep of the fine hairs rising along her arm. She turned, just a fraction, setting her back against the rough trunk of the banana palm. Was someone hiding in the garden?

Eventually Maria Grazia had sighed. 'Yes,' she'd said. 'Delivery man, postman, yeah.' But she'd sounded – if not worried, then puzzled. 'But they do usually leave a card, don't they? If they've tried to deliver and – and there's no one home?'

Someone had called in the background and Maria Grazia must have put a hand over the receiver to answer because there was the sound of a muffled reply.

I know you're in there, Signora Delfino. Would a FedEx man say such a thing? And what would they be delivering, anyway? Roxana never bought online, and Ma's sister in Pescara mistrusted the post with a vengeance. Would rather make a 400-kilometre round trip by train to deliver a hand-knitted sweater that no one would wear, refusing all offers of a bed for the night.

'Yes,' Roxana had said. 'There wasn't a card.'

He hid round the back, Mamma had said, and then it had all spilled out of her in a quavering torrent, face in her hands with shame. *I waited and waited, I sat in the hall by the door and waited for him to go.*

'Ma said it was at least an hour,' Roxana had told Maria Grazia, 'she said she heard him moving around outside the house. All around, then back again, then into the garden. But she fell asleep in the end so she can't be sure. When she woke up, she thought he was gone but she stayed inside, just to be on the safe side.'

Orlando slid the small shot of coffee with a dash of hot milk across to Roxana. Behind the bar the clock said seven-fifty-five. Roxana smiled at him. Wished she could stay in here all day.

'Did you look around?' Maria Grazia had asked. 'In the garden, for example? To see if there was any sign anyone had been there?'

There had been more noise at her end: raucous, end-of-the-day voices, people perhaps heading off for a drink together.

'It was dark,' Roxana had said, and heard the dull certainty in her voice. 'But there was no delivery man, was there? No stalker, either.'

And Maria Grazia had changed tack then, not wanting to answer. Briskly she had shifted back to her constant refrain.

'Look, get proactive, Roxi. I don't know how you can stand to have that Marisa Goldman promoted over you, to start with, useless piece.'

Marisa and Maria Grazia had history, as they said. Some ex-boyfriend of Marisa's had pulled out of funding one of Maria Grazia's films.

She went on, 'What you need to do is prioritize. Talk to your boss.' As if it was Roxana who was going off the rails. The answer to everything: get ahead. Get your freedom.

You think it's all in my head. That's what Mamma had said, disbelieving, reproachful.

No, Ma. I believe you. It's all right, Ma.

As Roxana set the cup back down on the bar, the door swung open and the sharp-shouldered silhouette of a new customer blocked the doorway, a gust of dirty summer air entering with him: the sour smell left by the morning's bin collection, and the exposed slime of the river bed. It was Val.

He smiled cheerfully. 'You're late,' he said, nodding up at the dusty clock over the bar. 'That's not like you.'

Prioritize.

'You're later,' she said sharply. 'Five minutes, Valentino.'

*

For the first time since as long as Sandro could remember, they had a lie-in.

Luisa wasn't starting till midday, she said, padding back into the bedroom in her nightdress with a tray, a napkin on it, two glasses of water, an espresso for him. He had heard her bustling in the kitchen, had smelled the coffee, and had kept his eyes closed in case it might all be a dream.

It was so unusual for Luisa to start late – her mind was on work the moment she opened her eyes; she was always excited to get into the shop – that it did cross his mind, very briefly, that it wasn't true. That she was regressing, turning into an idle teenager phoning in sick. Not that Luisa had ever, ever been idle.

They drank, set the tray aside, slid back under the sheets to talk, side by side. Luisa was holding his hand, quite unconsciously. It was like being newly-weds. Sandro didn't know if it was due to getting his anxiety over Anna Niescu off his chest and Luisa actually being fine with it – with the discussion of a pregnancy, an imminent birth. Or it could have been the meal at Nello together, just the right amount of wine – his small suggestion of a hangover almost pleasurable in the dim bedroom, a reminder that he wasn't past having fun.

Mostly, Sandro decided, it was the house-hunting. They had both, separately and in silence, lain there as the light crept in around the shutters. Enjoying the tiny breath of dawn cool in the air, seeing with new eyes the familiar lines of the room they'd woken up in together for thirty-five years and wondering whether they really could say goodbye to it.

Yes, was the answer.

'It's down to money, you know,' Sandro said. 'That's all. Down to how much we can get for this place, how much there is in the bank, how much we can borrow.'

There was a pause while they considered what a bank manager might say to a modestly employed couple of sixty-something, thinking of taking out a mortgage.

'I'll make enquiries,' said Sandro.

He tried not to listen to the happy, whispering voices that started up in his head, telling him how good it would be to begin again in a quiet street with a view of a green hillside, how good it would be for Luisa, give her something to think about. Boost her immune system.

'But it's OK, you know, if – if it doesn't come off,' said Luisa, as if she knew what he was thinking. 'This place isn't so bad. Or somewhere else might come up, somewhere cheaper.'

He squeezed her hand and, to forestall the disappointment creeping into the conversation, Sandro sat up. 'OK,' said Luisa, changing the subject obligingly. 'So what's your plan today? This girl, yes? This Anna Niescu.'

'Yes,' said Sandro. He snorted. 'Actually, maybe I could ask her fiancé for a loan. He's supposed to be a bank manager, after all.'

'You think he really is?'

Sandro pondered. 'No,' he said finally. 'She believes it, though.'

Luisa persisted. 'If there was no answer on his mobile, or at this apartment he's supposed to be doing up—' And she paused. 'Well, why didn't she just call him at work?'

Sandro recalled Anna's eyes, round as saucers in response to this very question. 'Oh, no,' she'd said, something of reverence in her voice, and something else too. 'I'd never call him at work, never. Oh, no, I couldn't do that.'

'I think he'd warned her off coming to the bank,' he said warily.

'Well, husbands do,' said Luisa, getting up, tying her robe tight at her waist and setting her hands on her hips. 'Don't they? Not many like the idea of the wife turning up at the office unannounced.'

'I suppose not,' he agreed. 'Particularly if she's pregnant and hasn't been introduced to anyone and isn't even your wife yet.'

Luisa turned towards the kitchen. 'Never an issue with us,' she said cheerfully over her shoulder. 'You out in a patrol car with Pietro half the time, I'd never have known how to find you if I'd wanted to.'

Reluctantly, Sandro got out of the bed, straightened the pillows and smoothed the single sheet under which they'd slept. At the window he pushed open the shutters and heard the rattle and roar of the garbage truck at the end of the street, smelled the stench from the dumpsters as they were upended into the back of it. There was early morning rubbish collection all over the city, he reminded himself; there were drunks and tourists too. A little apartment south of the river wasn't the answer to every problem. He leaned on the windowsill. It was hot, already. Eight o'clock. But for the first time in weeks he'd slept soundly.

'Did you?' he asked absently. 'Ever want to find me?'

Luisa was back beside him, leaning out, wrinkling her nose at the smell. 'Now and again,' she said, with a smile. 'Mostly not. Mostly I didn't want to know what you were up to, cleaning up car wrecks, taking dead junkies to the morgue. Getting shot at by armed robbers. Maybe I should have.'

Sandro tipped his head from side to side, considering the matter. 'No,' he said. 'I don't think so. And I never actually did get shot, did I?'

They both knew that this was an evasion: he'd been shot *at*, during a raid on a warehouse in Prato, but they'd missed. He'd been stabbed three times – once in the arm, once in the thigh and once near a lung; he'd nearly bled to death. An HIV-positive hooker had bit him, twenty years earlier, when no one had known anything about the disease and it had taken nearly a year to have final confirmation that he was clear.

'But one thing's for sure,' he said. 'If her Josef was not the manager of the station branch of the Banca di Toscana Provinciale, he would make damn sure she never turned up there asking for him.'

'Funny bank to choose, if he was just making it up on the spur of the moment,' mused Luisa, head cocked as she looked at him. 'Don't you think? I mean, it's such a dodo. Old-fashioned, obscure – I keep expecting it simply to vanish.'

'That occurred to me, too,' said Sandro thoughtfully. 'And Pietro, for that matter.' He shrugged. 'Maybe he picked it at random, or maybe he has some other connection with the bank we don't know about.'

With the departure of the garbage truck, the street was abruptly, albeit temporarily, deserted. Sandro blocked out the thought of that rusting wrought-iron balcony, on which they might both be sitting now, looking out towards the Casentino. 'Although,' he said, 'the station branch is probably as far away from the Loggiata Hotel as you can get.'

Chin in her hands on the windowsill, Luisa just nodded. 'Uh-huh,' she said. 'But I still think it's strange.' Then she straightened. 'I'm starving,' she announced cheerfully. 'Let's go and get some breakfast.'

CHAPTER SIX

EVEN IN AUGUST, THE Piazza Stazione was never deserted. Nor was it much of a piazza, surmounted by the low, modernist bulk of the Fascist-era station that overlooked a patch of sparse and scrubby grass. The blackened concrete façade of an ugly 1970s hotel to one side, the shabby bus station, a busy roundabout. Not much of a piazza at all.

Where the hell was it? Sandro stood at the taxi rank and pondered. In front of him a group of foreign teenagers lounged on the ground, leaning on their backpacks. One of the girls – pudgy, pale, pretty – had taken off her T-shirt and was sunbathing in a bikini top; Sandro stared, so dispirited by the sight that momentarily he forgot why he was there.

All right. He passed a hand over his sweating forehead. He'd looked up the branches of the Banca di Toscana Provinciale: there were three in the city, three more in the suburbs. The nearest one to the station was in a road called the Vicolo Sant'Angelo, but although he had lived in the city more or less his whole life, Sandro didn't know it. Nor, it turned out, did any of the taxi drivers, but then again, in August, what did you expect? Those left in the city were the no-hopers, half of them probably didn't even have driving licences.

One of the news vendors inside would have a map he could look at; he knew most of them. But for the moment he stood, under the shade of the station's portico, watched another girl from among the backpackers feed a piece of fruit into a boy's mouth, and thought about Giulietta.

He and Luisa had gone for breakfast to one of the big, gleaming, businesslike bars in the Piazza Signoria, a few metres from the shop and therefore very much on Luisa's turf. Never mind that it was expensive, never mind it catered largely to tourists: the bar made its own pastries, it was clean and sparkling – marble, polished glass and yellow cloths – and there was the view. Not even the heat and the querulous voices of tired tourists shuffling past could spoil that: the fine turreted tower of the Palazzo Vecchio silhouetted against the glaring sky, the pale arcades of the Uffizi leading off to the river. Luisa had settled them on a corner of the wide terrace; the waiter had bowed to her because here she was royalty.

Briskly Luisa had given their order: *caffè macchiato*, pastries filled with custard, a *budino* of sweet cooked rice, two glasses of water. Then folded her hands in her lap.

'You know where you're going?' she'd said.

Sandro had glanced sidelong at her and shrugged. 'Of course.'

'You should get one of those new phones,' Luisa had said pensively. 'You just key in an address, or the name of a restaurant – or a bank, for that matter – and *eccolo*! All up on that little screen, telephone numbers, map, everything. I'd like one. Beppe in menswear has one.'

Sandro had snorted explosively. As if he would want to emulate Beppe in menswear. An amiable enough young man, handsome, fit, polite, but interested in nothing but his own reflection in the shop's many mirrors. An airhead, as Giuli would say. Although Giuli had been known to harp on this particular string too: the magic telephone with all the answers. *I know this city already*, was all he'd say to her, or to Luisa come to that. I don't need a map or a telephone directory; there's no substitute for getting out there and talking to people.

And as if on cue had come Luisa's next question; Sandro had begun to suspect her of having a strategy, and that this loving breakfast together was a part of it.

'Are you – um, are you seeing Giuli today?'

The coffee arrived; just from the smell Sandro had been able to tell it was good. These days – well. August. He'd had a really horrible cup on Monday morning in the only bar still open in San Frediano, not his regular place: he'd had to push it back across the bar in disgust.

'She's coming over later,' he'd said warily. He'd been beginning to think that, when she finished at the Women's Centre, he might send her over to the Loggiata to talk to the girl again. 'This afternoon. Why?'

Luisa had carefully dissected the *budino*, looking down at the plate. When it was done, four neat quarters of sticky golden rice and pastry, she had looked up again and said, 'I think she's seeing someone.' Sandro had felt his mouth hang open and Luisa had sighed. 'I want you to talk to her about it.'

'What?'

Why should he be surprised? Giuli was only forty-three. Was she attractive? Hard for Sandro to judge. He'd first encountered her as a damaged teenager, long ago and briefly, then found her again, now a stringy, desperate, drug-addicted hooker, before prison and rehab shook her up and set her straight, or straight enough. She looked pretty good to him these days; every time he looked at the girl he marvelled at the strength of will that had pulled her back. She got her hair done every six weeks, had her clothes dry cleaned, was at work five minutes early. And as Sandro had observed, she had even mastered her quick temper – the long-suppressed rage of a neglected child.

She had begun to care about others, and in a constructive way, too. Giulietta had learned to consider their problems in detail and work towards a solution; Anna Niescu was a case in point.

And now she had a boyfriend?

Sandro had put his face in his hands, feeling Luisa's testing gaze on him. Because with Giulietta Sarto men had always been the biggest problem. If you asked Sandro – not that the psychotherapist ever had, not that Sandro had ever volunteered his opinion either – the self-mutilation, the drink, the anorexia, the drugs, had been the symptoms; men had been the problem.

'It really hadn't occurred to you?' Luisa had asked.

'Why?' he'd replied, despairingly. 'What makes you think she's got – someone?' But even as he'd said it, he knew, there'd been all sorts of clues.

'That week away, last week,' Luisa had said. 'A week camping by Monte Argentario? Do you think she did that alone?'

Slowly Sandro had shaken his head. 'No. No – but—'

'But what?'

'But she might have gone with a girlfriend.' Sandro had stared down at the glaze on his pastry, still warm when it had been set in front of him.

'Might have. But she didn't, did she?'

When she had got back from Castiglione della Pescaia, a pretty fishing village in the shadow of the big forested mountain that ended in the gleaming sea, the last place on earth the old Giuli would have wanted to go to, to be among the happy families and the old couples in their caravans, Giulietta had come straight round to Sandro and Luisa's apartment. She was paying rent on a bedsit in San Frediano now, but their place was home.

It had dawned on Sandro as he'd ushered her inside that this was probably the first time in her life that Giuli had been on holiday; she certainly hadn't had a childhood brightened by family trips to the seaside. It had agreed with her, though; she had looked great. Brown as a nut, a hint of a belly from the good food, wearing some crazy batik wraparound thing she'd bought from a Senegalese on the beach and a smile that had split her sharp little face. She'd given him a bottle of wine from Pitigliano and Luisa a reproduction of an Etruscan statue, plonking them proudly on the kitchen table.

When Luisa had asked her whom she'd gone away with Sandro had turned quickly and gone into the kitchen, so as not to hear her reply. But he had – he'd heard her conspiratorial laugh, too, as she'd answered, *Nobody.* The thought of Giuli getting herself a man was too complicated, and not just because Sandro was her father by default, in the absence of anyone better.

'Just have a word,' Luisa had said. 'Make sure she's – being sensible.'

'Wouldn't it be easier coming from you?' Pathetic, Sandro had thought, hearing the wheedling in his voice.

Luisa hadn't been listening. 'She's forty-three,' she'd said, looking away from him to take in the piazza. A pale, exhausted-looking foreign woman was pushing a buggy diagonally across it, doggedly negotiating a listless cruise-ship group, in off the coast for a sweltering day.

With a sinking heart, Sandro had understood her intonation: remembered Luisa at forty-three. The outer limit of fertility. Had thought of Giuli tenderly shepherding Anna Niescu up the stairs, as the girl's belly preceded them.

'It's a dangerous age,' Luisa had said. 'She—'

'No,' Sandro had said sharply. 'Don't. All right. I'll talk to her.'

Though God knows, he thought now as he surveyed the

bleached piazza, God only knows what I'll say. And turned to hurry inside.

The newspaper kiosk right inside the station's echoing ticket hall was open. The young guy behind the counter – Sandro reflected wryly that he didn't know him, after all, but knew his father, a sign of how things were, these days; next it would be the grandfather you knew – gave him a bit of a sideways look at first but grudgingly shook his hand, thus acknowledging there was sufficient connection between the two of them to permit him to hand over a dog-eared display copy of a city map.

The Vicolo Sant'Angelo wasn't even on the map, nor on being questioned did the boy know where it was at first. But then he brightened and got out his magic phone.

The street turned out to be on the far side of the *viale*, the roaring six-lane ring road behind the station. As Sandro waited patiently for the lights, it seemed to him that everything – traffic, technology, other people – was moving too fast for him.

The walk sign came up but there was a siren approaching from the east and instinctively Sandro hung back; he could tell it was coming fast. The girl beside him, impatient, took a step into the road but he put out a hand and firmly kept her where she was. A pale-blue Polizia dello Stato vehicle hurtled past – too fast to see who was driving it – and an ambulance came in its wake, rocking slightly as it moved between lanes. Sandro waited, watching to see where they went, his hand still on the girl's arm. Heading southeast, towards Fiesole perhaps, or down to the Ponte San Niccolo and Firenze Sud. The girl shook him off, shooting him a resentful look as she hurried across before the lights could change again.

The Vicolo Sant'Angelo was a dingy street that ran between two faceless, traffic-choked, residential boulevards. A mix of big, grimy apartment blocks from the turn of the century – well, thought Sandro, turn of the last century, these days – and a newish, rather ugly residential development, all exposed brick and coloured panelling, already down at heel. Sandwiched between a boarded-up kitchen showroom and the dusty window display of an ancient hardware store, this branch of the Banca di Toscana Provinciale was not a good advertisement for the business.

Standing a moment on the pavement outside, Sandro surveyed the place. The hole-in-the-wall cash dispenser looked as if it had recently been vandalized, and a large, grubby piece of chewing gum was stuck to the screen. The smoked-glass windows of the bank's narrow frontage were dirty. No wonder the guy didn't want his sweet young bride-to-be coming up here. Sandro, thinking of the reverence in her voice, tried not to visualize Anna's small, brave face absorbing the disappointment, turning it around, but the picture was there anyway. He stood at the revolving security door and waited to be admitted.

There was no air-conditioning, and the place was stifling; it was also unkempt, the polished marble of the floor was scuffed and dirty, and the strip lighting blinked and fizzed. A row of four cashiers' desks occupied the rear wall but only one was occupied, by a bored-looking middle-aged woman with a frizz of bleached hair, chin in her hands as she contemplated him without curiosity. Eventually she leaned towards the glass of her screen and tapped it.

'Take a ticket,' she said. And pointed towards a plastic dispenser on the wall, the tongue of a numbered paper ticket protruding limply from it. Sandro looked around in disbelief, in case there might in fact be a small crowd of customers behind whom he would need to wait in line, but the place was still empty. He cleared his throat and stepped gingerly closer.

'I'd like to see the manager,' he said, and the teller pursed her lips, as if offence had been given. Her eyes flicked briefly to a spot over Sandro's shoulder, then back.

'He's not here,' she said, and Sandro sighed. She was lying.

'You're here alone?' he said. She shrugged. Sandro dispensed with respect and walked straight up to her glass screen. He took out his identification and slid it across to her, but she ignored it. 'I'm a private detective,' he said wearily. And before he could stop himself, 'Retired police officer.'

The look she gave him conveyed only indifference. He could smell cigarette smoke on her clothes, even from behind the glass, and he said, keeping his voice pleasant and even, 'What happens when you need – a break, then?' Looked at her name tag. 'Signorina Fano?'

'We're not exactly run off our feet,' she said, eyeing him. 'And it's Signora Fano.' Then finally, abruptly, she relented, nodding over her shoulder and lifting a telephone receiver beside her to punch in three digits. Sandro turned to see a door set with sandblasted glass, with a small plastic nameplate uncertainly attached. *G. Viola Direttore.*

'Someone to see you,' said Signora Fano into the phone.

Not Claudio Josef Brunello, then. There might be an explanation for that; he might be a recent appointment. They might not have got around to changing the sign. But Sandro didn't think so.

'Come,' came a voice from behind the door.

The room he entered was shabby and under-decorated, and Giorgio Viola was not Claudio Josef Brunello; he was not Anna Niescu's husband by another name, nor had he been recently appointed. He was a fat man of sixty-odd, with a heavy salt-and-pepper beard, and he was sweating under his suit. He sat behind the desk at an uncomfortable distance necessitated by the size of his stomach and, despite the initial Santa Claus impression given by his girth and beard, in his eyes there was a sort of helplessness. *How did this happen?* they seemed to be beseeching Sandro as he leaned across and shook his hand tentatively. *How did I end up like this?*

'They're closing this branch down,' he volunteered apologetically.

'That's all right,' said Sandro, acknowledging that this somehow explained everything – Signora Fano, the dirty floor, the chewing gum on the ATM.

Noting that Giorgio Viola seemed entirely unflustered by his presence, exuding no whiff of guilt or discomfort, he told the man why he'd come. Viola was voluble, eager. Perhaps, thought Sandro, if I only had old mother Fano out there to talk to from one end of the day to the other, I'd be pleased to see me, too.

No Claudio Brunello had ever worked there, to the current manager's knowledge.

'But I think,' he said. 'I think – hold on.' He pulled the keyboard of his computer towards him, and looked at Sandro. 'I'm taking early retirement,' he said. 'This branch has never been profitable, too far out of the way. I've got a good package.'

No, thought Sandro absently, I bet it hasn't been profitable. Station branch, indeed: it's close to a kilometre in the wrong direction from the station, whatever the bank's brightly uninformative website said. Anna Niescu's man might just have been guessing, mightn't he? Every bank has an *azienda* near the station, doesn't it? Except a miserable little outfit like this.

Giorgio Viola was leaning over his belly and tapping on the keyboard, absorbed now. His hands, Sandro noticed, were surprisingly elegant for a man so fat: long oval nails, well-shaped fingers.

'How many branches are there, then?' asked Sandro.

'Oh, not many left,' said Viola, vaguely. 'They've closed Scandicci, and Bagno a Ripoli.' Reluctantly his eyes flicked back to Sandro's, and he smiled, apologetic again. 'Old-fashioned values,' he said. 'Local loyalties. Not so important these days.'

He looked back at the screen, grew intent, then poised, clicked on the touchpad. He beamed, briefly triumphant, and for a moment Sandro could see he might have made a convincing Santa Claus after all, given the right incentives. On the desk was a little plastic holder for business cards: Giorgio Viola, *Direttore*. Sandro picked one up absently: they were dog-eared with age.

'Ha,' he said, and turned the screen a little so Sandro could see it. 'Brunello. Via dei Saponai branch.' He glanced from the screen to Sandro. 'Down by the Via dei Neri.'

'I know that,' Sandro snapped. *I know this city*: how many times would that come back to haunt him? Maybe he should just get himself a magic phone and be done with it. He relented. 'Sorry.'

The man gave him that small smile again that said, *And you think I'm a sad case?*

'Sorry,' said Sandro once more, and concentrated on the screen.

'Shouldn't really be showing you this,' said Viola, cheerfully. 'Staff records, you know. But actually – well, there's hardly anything to see.'

Claudio Brunello – no sign of the Josef, but perhaps he'd kept that little ethnic detail quiet – born 1958, handsome in a dark, hollow-cheeked sort of way, although you couldn't tell much from the faintly smiling photobooth shot, glasses, suit, smoothed hair. Joined the bank in 1982, straight out of university.

Could it be him? The dark, nervous man pulling slightly away from Anna Niescu on the fuzzy screen of her mobile phone? It could, just about.

Most people had never heard of the Banca di Toscana Provinciale. Anna's boyfriend had to have some connection with it. But there was something not right.

Sandro continued to gaze, scanning the flat, dull details for something, anything.

Married, two children.

He could hear Giuli's sigh. Same old story. Maybe he did love her, maybe it was some kind of midlife crisis, maybe Brunello saw that sweet little face and thought, why not start all over again?

The image of him and Luisa, going to ask the bank manager for a loan, jumped unbidden into Sandro's head. What are we thinking of?

Maybe he really thought he'd leave his wife. When did the dream end? When did he wake up and smell the coffee and think, no, it'll never work? Was it when she got to the eighth month, those eyes gazing trustfully up at him, that belly a daily reproach? And he thought he could just disappear; he stopped calling. Stopped answering his phone. How did he think he would get away with it?

'Thank you,' he said to Viola. And with an odd gracefulness the fat man inclined his head in acknowledgement as he tilted the screen out of Sandro's line of vision once more, and Brunello was gone.

But he wasn't going to get away with it.

*

'Who was it, then, who called yesterday?' said Roxana.

So far she and Val had been at work for three hours and had only served two customers, both foreigners wanting small amounts exchanged. An American man and a Swedish woman, they'd both had the same look, of helpless, exhausted dismay. Get us out of here, they seemed to plead.

Val had been out for a long coffee, on the understanding that he'd give her the same privilege in the steaming, dead hours of the afternoon, and now he was back, leaning against her desk. An hour till they closed for lunch.

'Yesterday?'

God almighty, thought Roxana, searching the comical blank of Val's handsome face. Give me strength. 'You answered it. To Brunello's office.'

He frowned in a parody of deep thought. 'Oh,' he said eventually, 'a woman, I think.'

'You *think?*' At least Ma had an excuse for not being able to keep anything in her head.

Valentino nodded earnestly, apparently deaf to Roxana's tone. 'Yeah, definitely a woman.' And looked up. 'Why? Does it matter?'

'Oh, I don't know,' Roxana said, losing patience. 'It just seemed – oh, I don't know. Out of the ordinary. God knows, there's little enough going on round here. Didn't it seem funny to you? No one ever phones in August, not on that line. His private line.'

'Would you go out with me, some time?' said Val, without blinking.

Roxana stared at him, and to her fury felt a blush rise. 'Have you even been listening to me?' she asked.

He smiled. 'You wear those glasses the whole time?' he asked. 'Like, if you go out dancing, or anything?'

The blush refused to subside: she thought of last night, at the bar. She'd worked with Val two years. Was he just bored, or what was it?

'I don't go out dancing,' said Roxana bluntly. 'Or anything.'

'Not that I don't like them,' he said, holding her gaze steadily. 'They're nice glasses. Only I wondered what you'd look like without them.'

And in a split-second of weakness Roxana did wonder, *what if*, what if he means it, before she was saved by the sound of the mechanical voice at the security door.

Please remove metallic objects from your pockets. Please remove your headgear. Please exit and try again.

Hastily Val slid off her desk and returned to his own; the new customer, only visible in silhouette, seemed to be completely stuck. Roxana pressed the button under the desk that would open the doors. She turned her head sideways, determined to show Val she hadn't been taken in. 'So she didn't say who she was,' she asked. 'This woman? On the phone?'

Val's smile held a trace of disappointment. He shook his head. 'She wanted the boss.' He frowned. 'I suppose it's funny she didn't give me her name, but she was pretty worked up. Asked over and over if he was here. Had he been in since Saturday.'

Roxana frowned. That seemed quite specific.

The customer stood at the machine that dispensed tickets, clearly an idiot if he couldn't see there was no queue and so no need to take a ticket. Jesus wept.

'She was upset?' That was what Ma had said too. A woman had phoned, upset. 'You didn't ask her name?'

Val shrugged uneasily. 'Hysterical women,' he said. 'You can't talk to them. Might have been anything, might have been her overdraught.' He fished in his pocket for a toothpick and began working at a molar.

It didn't sound like a routine enquiry to Roxana. It sounded like someone trying to track Claudio down. Had Val no curiosity?

'Excuse me,' said the customer, keeping his distance: a stocky man in a crumpled jacket and an ancient hat, quietly polite. Val, typically, turned his head the other way, still busy with his toothpick.

Roxana examined the man. He had not, after all, taken a ticket from the machine, so perhaps he wasn't an idiot. He didn't look like one; what he looked like to Roxana was her father, or at least her father a few years back, before he became ill and tetchy.

'Please,' she said politely, beckoning him, and pressed the button that lit up her desk number, for extra emphasis. The man stepped forward.

'I'm not a customer,' he said, immediately, and slid something under the screen. It was a small plastic card that identified the holder as Sandro Cellini, member of the AIIP or Associazione Italiana Investigatori Privati.

A private detective. Roxana looked at him, not quite surprised, knowing that there was something wrong, after all, that she'd been expecting – something. She felt him scrutinize her: felt him register that shade of hesitation, that part of her that was not in fact surprised to find a private detective at her desk. No, he was not an idiot at all.

'I'm looking for Claudio Brunello,' he said, gruff but respectful. 'He's the manager here, is that right?'

'Yes,' said Roxana from behind the glass, knowing she should, if she wanted to show her mettle, somehow be more guarded with this man, or perhaps even send him packing. Private detectives, after all, were dubious types. What if he was after – money? Or serving some kind of court notice? She felt Val's eyes on them, expectantly – and then the mechanical voice at the door announced the arrival of another customer. Over Sandro Cellini's shoulder she saw the knock-kneed profile of a skinny woman in shorts. Another foreigner.

She rose. 'Just a minute,' she said, nodding towards the boss's empty office. 'In here.'

Because whatever this business was, it was best conducted out of earshot of customers, even if they were foreign. She saw the man gaze around as they walked through the space, registering the sign on Marisa's door, M. Goldman, *Gestore Business e Family*, *Vice-Direttore*.

Gingerly seating herself in the boss's chair, Roxana gestured to the detective to sit down.

'He's not here,' said Sandro with resignation, sitting also. His gaze travelled around the office: taking in the expensive leather desk set, the moulded chairs, the designer filing cabinet. Pausing at the family photograph on the shelf.

'No,' said Roxana, spreading her hands apologetically. 'It's August: he's on holiday.'

'With his family?' Nodding towards the photograph.

'Well, yes,' said Roxana, uncomprehending. Because there could be no harm, could there, in confirming that piece of information?

'And would you mind telling me,' Sandro asked mildly, 'when he left?'

'On Friday afternoon,' said Roxana, the man's diffidence disarming her. It was not privileged information, was it?

'Friday.' Sandro Cellini looked glum.

Roxana felt her insides shift: she knew she shouldn't confide in this man, she had no reason to trust him. But she did; she thought of last night in her own garden, remembered the prickle of fear she had felt. She needed someone she could trust.

'His mother-in-law has a place up in Liguria somewhere,' she said quickly. 'At Monterosso, Le Glicine, the house is called. Overlooking the sea.'

He inclined his head a little, to indicate his gratitude, waiting.

'Are you—?' She stopped, then began again. 'Someone phoned for him. A woman phoned, yesterday, asking if we'd seen him since Saturday.'

'Really?' asked the detective, suddenly quite still, like an animal alerted to a predator – or prey. 'Did she say who she was?'

'You need to talk to Valentino,' said Roxana, pushing back in the wheeled chair to get a look at him through the window. He was counting out notes for the elderly backpacker, frowning with concentration, and Roxana sighed involuntarily. 'Val was the one who talked to her.'

Leaning a little further back to get a better view of the bank floor, she was startled to see the outline of another customer.

'I'd better get back to work,' she said, sliding towards the desk again. As she did so, she noticed that although the screen of Brunello's computer was dark, it was only sleeping: a tiny blinking light on her side of it indicated that it had not been fully shut down when he left on Friday. It was against protocol. All electronic desk equipment had to be shut down every night, for security. Well, he'd been in a hurry.

'Can I talk to him, then?'

'Sure,' she said, hesitating. Deciding against warning him Val wasn't exactly the memory man: that would be mean. 'It's a free country.' She glanced up at the clock; Val wouldn't appreciate her arranging his lunch hour for him. 'We close at six, if you want to come back. I'll tell him.'

'Thank you,' said Sandro Cellini, but didn't move, frowning as if he was trying to make sense of something.

'Why are you here, Mr Cellini?' said Roxana, knowing she should have asked this straight away. 'Is someone looking for him? For Brunello?'

Sandro Cellini returned her gaze warily, and Roxana felt indignation rise. Did he think he couldn't trust *her*?

'Are you the *vice-direttore*?' he asked. 'Are you, ah, Miss Goldman?'

'Sorry,' said Roxana, tight-lipped, glancing back out through the door. Val seemed to have everything under control. 'I'm just a teller. A *sportellista*. That's all. Everyone else is on holiday.'

He leaned back in the chair, and smiled wryly. 'Not much fun, is it?' he said. 'The city in August. I didn't need the *vice-direttore*, I just thought – well. You seem to know what you're doing, I thought you might be the second-in-command.' Roxana frowned at him, but he appeared to be sincere.

'So someone is looking for him.'

Sandro sighed. 'Yes. Someone's looking for him. I suppose I could wait until he's back from the seaside.' His brow creased, he looked genuinely anxious. 'But it's sort of urgent.'

'A woman?'

The private detective stared at his hands. 'I really can't tell you that, Signorina, ah—'

'Roxana Delfino.' But from his expression she could tell. It was a woman. Roxana got to her feet.

As they passed through the banking hall, Val was still occupied with the backpacker; the other customer must have lost patience and gone. Roxana sighed, unable to summon up a great deal of professional guilt: it wasn't as if that one customer had been coming in with his lottery win to be invested, was it? Not in August.

She bypassed the security door to the staff entrance, to let Cellini out, trying to stay coolly polite and maintain the slender authority she had scraped together. But as she shook his hand – warm and dry, despite the humidity that barrelled inside before the door was open more than a crack – she felt suddenly reluctant to let him go.

'D'you have a number or anything?' she said. 'In case I – we need to contact you?'

With a grimace the detective patted himself down, eventually locating a worn card with his contact details in a breast pocket. He handed it to her.

'In case you remember anything?' he supplied. And then Sandro Cellini smiled, a sad, crinkled, kindly smile. 'Thanks, Signorina Delfino,' he said. 'It's been nice talking to you.'

CHAPTER SEVEN

AT THE RECEPTION DESK of the Women's Centre, Giulietta Sarto – Giuli to her friends, but not here – was fifteen minutes from the end of her shift and taking a risk. She sneaked the mobile out of her bag under the counter and peeped at the screen. She smiled.

Mobiles were supposed to be switched off at the door and kept off; if anyone had heard the trill that announced a text message, she would have been reprimanded. But that was because the unspoken rule was: keep the phone on silent. Nobody actually switched them off: not the cleaners, not the doctor on duty, not the nurses, not the security guy. They needed a security guy at the Women's Centre, not because of the women but because of the men that followed them in: the batterers and stabbers, the ones who branded their wives' faces on the stove and the ones who told them they loved them. The ones who wanted to force them to have the kid, the ones who slipped abortion drugs into their coffee.

The heat didn't help, that was for sure, and their clientele couldn't afford a month on a sunlounger at Forte dei Marmi either. August wasn't a quiet month at the Women's Centre. Anna Niescu's problem was by no means as bad as it got; Anna had plenty going for her, compared with most of the deadbeats that came through the door.

The phone bleeped again, and the pale face and lank hair of the doctor on duty appeared at the door of her consulting room. 'Sarto,' she said wearily.

'Turning it off,' said Giuli, smiling shamefacedly, holding the thing up. When the woman's head disappeared, she took a look. But this one was from Sandro.

Lunch?

Sure, she typed, her dark maroon fingernails clicking across the screen, *porta romana midday-ish?* Giuli could text faster than anyone she knew. 'Shows your motor skills are intact at least,' Sandro would say, with wry respect. Because with what she'd put her nervous system through, it was nice to know.

Sandro wanted something: she was supposed to be in the office this afternoon anyway, at two-thirty. He was going to take her along with him to talk to Anna again.

Giuli held her finger on the off button until the little screen dwindled and died. Along the corridor in an examining room a woman cried out in pain, a small, hopeless sound, like a cat in a back alley. Giuli thought of Anna's bright face as she smiled down at that belly. A baby: a joy. The equation was as uncomplicated as that.

Looking down, Giuli realized she had her hand protectively on her own stomach. *As if:* the very thought raised the hairs on the back of her neck. Giuli had never wanted a baby; she wasn't going to start at her age. But the chain of thought, lighting up its path in her brain like the display on an arcade slot machine, was irresistible. Why now – why did Anna Niescu come into her life now? And why did Sandro want to talk to her over lunch?

But before she even pushed through the door to the modest self-service restaurant – open all year round, on the *viale* in the great arched shadow of the Porta Romana – Giuli had a pretty good idea why. She could see him through the glass, sitting in a corner, frowning down at his hands tented on the formica table in front of him, beside his old battered panama hat.

'Luisa's put you up to this, hasn't she?' she said, swinging her bag down beside her, admiring in passing the new brown on her arms, the fine bleached hairs from a week in the sun.

'Let's get something to eat,' said Sandro, starting up. He piled stuff on her tray: Russian salad, *bresaola*, two rolls, a piece of cake.

'And she told you to feed me up while you were at it?' Giuli set down the tray and fastidiously divided the oozing mayonnaise of the salad from the meat.

'You're going to eat it, aren't you?' said Sandro, impatiently.

She forked up a load, pointed it at his plate, where two sweating slices of pecorino lay unadorned beside some small hard pears. 'If you do,' she said, and cheerfully began to chew, hungry after all. Starving, in fact. Sandro eyed her: apparently her appetite was worrying him now, on top of whatever else.

Giuli decided that if he was going to interrogate her about her private life, he'd get no help from her.

'How's it going?' she said. 'Have you tracked him down yet?'

'Maybe,' said Sandro cautiously. 'I think he might be up in Monterosso, you know, in the Cinque Terre, with his family. August, you know; at the bank they said he left on Friday.' Giuli thought she saw a shadow pass over his face as he said it.

'You think?'

'The name's right,' said Sandro. He eyed the cheese on his plate, and gingerly cut off a corner. 'I'm not a hundred per cent sure about the face. Maybe we can get the staff mugshot online, and Anna can take a look.'

'You sickening for something?' said Giuli. Her own plate seemed to be empty, suddenly. She pulled the cake towards her.

'Or maybe we could go up to Monterosso and ambush the guy? It's only a couple of hours on the train.'

The piece of cheese still on his fork, Sandro appeared depressed. 'So it's just the old story,' he said. 'Married man, with a bit on the side. A whole family on the side.'

'Is that worse?' Giuli found herself saying. 'I don't know. I don't know if it's worse. He might have forced her into having an abortion, I think that would have been worse. I think he loves her, even if he is an arsehole.' And she stopped short at the expression on Sandro's face. 'What?' she said defiantly.

'Since when did you believe in love, Giuli?'

She laid down her fork, mouth full of chocolate cake. It was hard to fight back under the circumstances and, besides, he was right. Since when did she believe in love and family?

'All your fault,' she said, swallowing. She wiped her mouth. 'You and your old-fashioned values. Eat your cheese. What would Luisa say, wasting good food?'

'Are you seeing someone, Giuli?' he asked abruptly.

She sighed: that was Sandro. Nowhere to hide. She held up her hands in surrender.

'Yes,' she said. 'Satisfied? Yes, I'm seeing someone.'

Sandro pushed the plate aside. 'Good,' he said. 'That's great, Giuli.'

'Yeah?' Giuli could not have sounded more sceptical. 'No way, Sandro, no way are you going to leave it at that.'

He shrugged. 'It's none of my business,' he said, but he was smiling. Even if it was a funny, twisted, anxious sort of smile.

Giuli relented. 'It's OK,' she said. 'It's serious. I'm not being stupid. I know a bad guy when I see one, these days. Let's face it, if I don't, who does?'

'Well,' said Sandro, 'he's certainly given you your appetite back.'

She eyed him narrowly, and he looked down to examine one of the hard little pears on his plate more closely than was necessary.

'Which is a good thing, right?'

He sighed. 'Yes,' he said.

'So?'

'Where did you meet him?' Sandro's voice was lowered almost to a whisper. And when she didn't answer he said, awkwardly, 'It is a him, right? Not that – I mean,' and she saw something like crafty hope dawn in his eyes and burst out laughing.

'That'd be nice, wouldn't it?' she said. 'Oh, Sandro, I love it, how you're trying to be cool with it. That'd be so easy, you're thinking, actually, wouldn't it? Giuli hooks up with a nice girl, a girl to look after her, make her eat, cosy up in the evenings together. Nice and safe.' Giuli paused, thinking about it. 'Actually, yes. It would be nice, I might even have wondered about it myself – even if I'm not sure girls are as safe as you think they are. After a year at the Women's Centre.' She leaned across the table, right up close, and whispered, 'Only trouble is, I'm not gay.'

Sandro was now looking so sheepish she could have kissed him. 'So where did you meet him?' he mumbled.

He'd asked Anna Niescu that, too. Like a kindly father: it was a key question, Giuli understood now. You wouldn't want your girl hanging out in the wrong places, for a start – *I met him in an S & M bar, Dad.* Or her boyfriend either, one of those men who comes up to girls in the street and tells them they've got beautiful eyes. What had Anna said? She'd looked up at them from her uncomfortable plastic chair, eyes gleaming at the memory, and said, 'He was buying oranges, at the market in Santo Spirito, I was too, for the hotel. Five kilos. He carried them back for me.'

Giuli thought about that market stall. Back in the winter, the stallholder waddling in a padded coat, her stall piled high with black cabbage, artichokes and pyramids of blood oranges from the south. Hard to imagine how cold the city could get, as they all baked and wilted at the other extreme. She thought of Anna's small frame, trying to stagger back to the hotel under five kilos of Sicilian oranges, a man bending down to offer to help.

She sighed: her own story was not so romantic, for a start. 'He's a computer guy,' she said. 'He services the computers at the Centre, once a month, he's always helping me out. Found me an old laptop for twenty euros on eBay, reconditioned it for me.' It wasn't enough for Sandro; she could see that from the set of his mouth. 'Not much of a looker, a couple of years older than me, very shy. Very, very shy.'

If you want reasons, she thought, *why anyone would look twice at me.*

'He's called Enzo. And yes, it was him I went to the seaside with.' And for a second she closed her eyes, remembering the glitter of the sea. 'His dad's a butcher, they used to do the markets selling *porchetta* in summer, when he was a kid, and since he started work as a computer engineer, well, he says someone's got to do it. Someone's got to do emergency cover. He's that kind of guy.'

A bit like you, she wanted to say. Doesn't complain, gets on with it.

Sandro was thinking about it, she could see, mopping his forehead with a handkerchief to buy himself time. Deciding whether or not to be relieved: it didn't come naturally to Sandro, though, relief. She looked at the lines in his forehead from all that worrying; she wouldn't have him any other way. Who else was going to bother?

'Not your problem,' she said gently.

'Maybe not,' said Sandro, signalling for a coffee to the tired middle-aged woman behind the heated display. It might be a self-service restaurant, but coffee was coffee. The woman moved to fill the little hand-held filter, and Sandro turned back to Giuli. 'I don't suppose you're going to bring him over to meet us, then?'

'Might do,' said Giuli warily. 'Eventually.'

The coffee arrived, one mouthful of treacly black for each of them; Giuli was suddenly aware of Sandro watching closely as she downed hers straight off.

'What?' she said. He drank his, looking at her over the top of the tiny cup.

And then she got it: maybe it was that they were both fretting over Anna Niescu and her troubling condition but it seemed like her mind and Sandro's were running on the same track today.

'Oh, no,' she said, 'no way. All that stuff about my appetite. You're checking to see if I've gone off coffee, aren't you?'

Sandro began to make protesting noises but she cut him off.

'Don't bother,' she said, half laughing, half horrified, 'I'm too old for the birds and bees conversation, Babbo.' She shook her head. 'And I'm too old to get pregnant.'

And twenty-five years of drugs and anorexia and not really caring if you live or die, doesn't get your body in shape for a baby, either, she didn't say. And just as well.

'Let's not go there,' she said instead.

There was a sound from Sandro's pocket: his ringtone was the loud jangle of an old-fashioned telephone bell – hardly, she'd pointed out to him more than once, the discreet choice. He fumbled with reading glasses from his top pocket – since when, Giuli wondered, had he needed them? Could he really be getting old? – then peered over them anyway at the little screen. He lifted a finger to stop her talking.

'Sorry,' he mouthed, putting the phone to his ear. 'Hello?' he said. 'Hello? Pietro, is that you?'

There was a clatter from behind the self-service counter, of metal trays being hurled into the sink. Grimacing, Sandro turned away from the sound and put up his hand to block it out from his other ear.

'You've found a what?'

'Go, go outside,' she mouthed, making ushering movements.

Gratefully Sandro took his hat and got to his feet, stopping to extract a handful of crumpled notes from his pocket and push them at her before hurrying for the door.

Giuli sat and watched him go, and from behind the counter the worn-out woman in her blue overalls paused, her arms full of greasy trays, and her eyes fastened on Giuli.

She's wondering, thought Giuli. She thinks he's probably my dad, but she's not sure; for some reason the thought made her heart just a little heavy.

She took a sip from her glass of water, ran it around inside her mouth. The coffee here wasn't much good, she decided. It was bitter, but then, it was August. Nothing tasted the same in August.

CHAPTER EIGHT

THE SMALL CAR STUTTERED, jerked and nearly stalled as Sandro nudged into the traffic coming off the wide ring road and down from the hills that formed the city's southern boundary. Half the road was up, down to one lane. At the big roundabout of the Piazza Ferrucci, south of the bridge of San Niccolo, the lights changed to red.

Is it me? he wondered as he wrestled with the gears. Am I losing it? Surely he couldn't have actually forgotten how to drive, even if it had been a while. The car – an ancient, unfashionable incarnation of Fiat's smallest and most economical model – was dusty and unloved, its roof crusted with pigeon shit and last year's leaves and all the city's airborne filth. It did not inspire respect among his fellow drivers, which was why he was finding himself squeezed out at every junction and traffic light. He should have walked to lunch with Giuli, only the heat had defeated him, together with the thought of trying to have a fatherly chat when sweating into his suit. *Calm*, he thought. Pietro's not going anywhere.

He'd left the restaurant to stand under the huge portal to the city, the massive stone arch at the head of the artery that was the

Via Romana, and tried to understand what Pietro was saying. Would the famous magic phone solve this problem he had of not being able to hear a damn thing on his mobile? Or perhaps he was just going deaf, along with everything else.

'We've got a body,' Pietro had seemed to be saying. 'And I thought you might want a look at it.'

'A body.'

For a moment Sandro had stood very still as the world seemed to whirl on around him, the traffic, the dusty trees along the *viale*, a gang of tourists just brought up under the arch and their guide gesticulating upwards.

In thirty years as a serving police officer in a big metropolis – most of those with Pietro beside him – Sandro had seen bodies before; he'd dealt with murders, but not so many that death meant nothing. That had been some time back, too: six months ago he'd investigated the death of a woman in a car accident, but by the time he'd seen her she'd been cleaned up, put back together and laid out on a refrigerated drawer under a sheet. It had been years – three, or was it four? – since he'd been first to a fatality and had to take the impact of it.

'We're at the scene,' Pietro had said, and from his tone Sandro had known, even down a crackling mobile line with traffic noise in the background, that it was nasty. Pietro had spoken quietly – he'd never heard his old friend raise his voice – but there was just the trace of a shake, of hoarseness in the lower registers, that Sandro knew very well.

'You OK, Peet?' he had said, quietly in his turn. 'Sounds like a bad one.'

'Uh-huh,' Pietro had said, and he had cleared his throat. 'Not pretty. But he's got ID on him, in the name of Claudio Brunello. A staff pass card, too, that says he's the manager of a branch of the Banca di Toscana Provinciale.'

'You remembered the name?' he had said. 'You haven't lost your touch, Pietro.'

'The story stuck,' Pietro had said. 'Sad one.'

And it had looked like a sad ending.

The lights turned green and this time Sandro scraped through on to the roundabout and into more stationary traffic. A people carrier came up alongside, bicycles on the roof-rack, and first a mother's harassed face glanced in his direction, then her child's, smeared and red, turned towards him from a babyseat in the back. Another child, bigger, was reading determinedly on the other side. Sandro shifted his eyes back to the road ahead and the big car moved on past. The rear window was crammed to the roof with stuff: supermarket carrier bags bulging with food, brightly coloured beach towels, the wheels of a folded buggy.

Claudio Brunello. With cold dread Sandro found himself back in that office where a framed photograph of a woman and three children sat on a shelf; where Roxana Delfino had told him her boss was away on holiday, with his family. A place in Monterosso: perhaps the people carrier that had just overtaken him was on its way to somewhere similar.

It pulled away from him, the father changing lanes impatiently; they'd been in the car an hour already and they weren't out of Florence yet. Dangerous, though, to have the rear view blocked like that.

Sandro came up on to the wide bridge. Ahead lay the dusty trees of the African market's sprawl, a splash of red oleanders, and the small tented structure that – unmistakable to Sandro – indicated the presence of a body. They'd cordoned off one lane to accommodate the pale-blue police vehicle parked at the roundabout, and the traffic was a nightmare.

Sandro parked under the forbidding, barbed wire topped wall of the military barracks, on the Viale Amendola, and walked back.

Holiday traffic squeezed into the narrow confines of one lane, and rubberneckers. As he edged on foot between the cars, breathing the oily fumes, Sandro could see the faces. Turned in their seats and pressed to the glass, pointing at the forensic scientist in his long coat and latex gloves standing incongruously beside a busy roundabout like some postmodern civic sculpture, talking to a policeman. Just for a ghoulish moment or two they'd stare as they crept past, then they'd turn away, towards their holiday.

Sandro reached the crash barrier and climbed over, again feeling his age. Pietro, whom he'd observed discreetly monitoring his approach, tipped him a warning nod over the technician's shoulder and Sandro stopped where he was.

As he waited, Sandro looked. It was hard to tell because of the white tent over it, but the body had probably been at least partly shaded by the trees. In these temperatures, he supposed that hardly made a difference; his gaze swung from the white plastic structure to the glittering heat haze above the big bridge. Below it, the river was low and greenish brown, clogged with weed; on the far bank he could see immobile figures sunbathing down where grass and reeds abutted the water.

At his feet the patchy grass between the oleanders was littered with debris from passing cars: cigarette packets, a fast-food carton, flyers from a restaurant. A child's doll lay among the litter, the face smudged, the pink dress greying. No place, he supposed, to stop the car and go back to retrieve that doll, even if the child was howling.

The forensics guy was stripping off his latex gloves, and Pietro was shaking his hand. As the man walked back to his car, he gave Sandro an incurious glance; Sandro didn't recognize him but then he was young, only thirty perhaps.

'Where's your partner?' asked Sandro, trying not to sound surly. 'You've got a partner on this, right?'

'Matteucci,' said Pietro with a weary smile. 'Sent him off to clear his head, get a glass of water. I thought he was going to throw up: he's not used to this. Came from a desk job in Modena.' He loosened his collar. 'And I can do without him breathing down my neck.'

Sandro nodded towards the tent, 'When did you find him?'

Pietro nudged his cap back on his head, his forehead gleaming with sweat; over his shoulder on the barracks wall Sandro could see a tower with the red lights of a digital display, reading forty-one degrees. You could die out here, thought Sandro. He stepped further into the shade of the thin trees, the earth gritty and dusty underfoot. You could hear the river, a sluggish gurgle fifty metres to the south. The air was thick with mosquitoes.

'About ten this morning,' said Pietro wearily. 'A kid in a high vehicle, some kind of people carrier, on their way to the country, he saw it. Seventeen years old. Got completely hysterical, according to the parents; they thought he was imagining it, or making it up, or it was just a drunk sleeping it off. Same thing everyone else obviously thought. But the kid just wouldn't shut up, until they called the police.'

'All right,' said Sandro, thinking. 'Anything yet?' He nodded towards the forensics man, climbing into his car. 'Preliminary findings?' He knew there would be some. 'Time and cause of death?'

Pietro grimaced. 'Cause of death? Well, you'll see.'

'Ah.' Sandro was in no hurry to go in the tent. 'Time?'

'He'd been there a while – I mean, considering. Three days at least.'

Sandro tilted his head back and looked up through the branches at the pale blue-white sky. 'Considering?' he said. 'Ah. You mean, considering he's out here in the open. Thousands of vehicles must have passed him, in three days.'

'Maybe four,' said Pietro.

Sandro stilled his head, searching the sky for cloud – real cloud. A good tower of raincloud building to the west over the Apuan Alps, cumulonimbus, the signal of the blessed summer rainstorm.

'So, Saturday or Sunday,' he said, still staring up. 'No earlier than that?'

'The heat makes it hard to tell,' said Pietro, his voice so low Sandro had to strain to hear. 'That – oh, you know. Accelerates decomposition. Especially in the dirt, and with the humidity.'

'I know,' said Sandro.

'Pathology's coming back to get him, anyway,' said Pietro. 'We'll know more when they've autopsied him. Insect activity should do it. And there'll be a toxicology report.'

'It's OK,' said Sandro. 'It's just – well. My guy was seen Friday night. If it's more than five days, then it isn't him.'

But it's still someone, he thought. It's a husband or father.

'Have you been in touch with the family?' he said.

'Trying to trace them,' said Pietro. 'Got a home address and phone number but there's no one there.'

'Assuming it's his ID, not stolen, then I think they're in Monterosso,' said Sandro, jerking his head north. 'It's in the Cinque Terre. Holiday house. He's supposed to be on holiday. He's not supposed to be here.'

Pietro shook his head, barely perceptibly. 'I think it's his ID,' he said. 'He doesn't look like a mugger: not wearing those shoes. Silk socks too, for that matter.'

The forensics guy's car revved, his hand came out of the window in thanks to a car that was allowing him out, and he was gone. Watching the car disappear into the traffic, Pietro narrowed his eyes. 'Do you want to see the body, then?' he said. 'They'll be here for him soon.'

With reluctance they both approached the tent. A rectangle of the white plastic sheeting that served as a door flapped idly in the air displaced by the cars; there was nothing as merciful as a breeze. Sandro could see something behind the flapping plastic, dark on the grass, and he had to concentrate to keep walking, one step after another. Not good, approaching a body from this end, with all the faces already ranged in your head, the expectant, anxious faces of those who'd loved him, however misguidedly.

He bent and entered. Involuntarily raised a sleeve to block his nose. The smell was horribly familiar, the putrid smell of proteins broken down, of humanity turned to carcass. He moved inside, to the left, allowing Pietro in after him, turning on a battery floodlight as he entered. They squatted beside him: beside the remains of the man.

This was what Pietro had meant about the heat and the time of death. He'd been shielded from the sun by what there was of the foliage, but where it had got to him there was – decomposition. The body discoloured, just beginning to come apart. Sandro looked away.

Identification might be difficult. It depended: some people – some wives – could tell their loved one from the shape of his hands, or his hair. He leaned in.

A devastating injury to the back of the head, was what he saw. Hair black and crusted with dried blood, and a depression in the skull.

He didn't reach out a hand to touch the man, to turn him; that wasn't allowed. He just knelt, an elbow in the dirt, his face hovering a centimetre or so above it and close to the dead man's. He could smell it. More trauma over the temple.

Had he changed to come into the city? Out of the holiday T-shirt, the shorts. The trousers were bloodied too, below the knee, fine grey summer-weight wool. The leg at an odd angle, as though that had also been broken; out of nowhere Sandro had the image of a piece of scaffolding pole held in two hands being brought down to cut the man off at the knees. Where had that come from? Sandro realized with amazement that it had happened to him, years back.

Twenty-five years back, interrupting a robbery in a warehouse. A gorilla of a guy had come around a packing case swinging for him with a metre of steel pole and making animal sounds. Luckily for Sandro the guy'd been so high on amphetamines that he hadn't been able to focus properly, and the glancing blow had only resulted in a three week bruise. Pietro had got him out of that one, neatly cuffing the man as he staggered in the aftermath of the swing while Sandro lay cursing on the floor.

One shoe was off, lying with the sole uppermost: Sandro leaned down close. 'Is that blood too?' he asked. The pale leather was stained. 'Doesn't look like blood.'

'It'll be analysed,' said Pietro. He kneeled, pulled a pair of latex gloves from his pocket, drew them on and applied a finger to the dusty black on the shoe's sole; it left a powdery greyish residue on his fingertip. They both looked at it, staring as if their lives depended on it. For longer than was necessary: to avoid looking somewhere else.

Then Pietro sighed, and raising one knee he bent down and delicately turned the head, just a degree or two. Over the ear Sandro saw something, matted.

'The oleanders would have concealed the body quite effectively,' he said.

Sandro, sitting back on his haunches, nodded.

'Is that why he's here?'

'We're thinking perhaps – hit and run.'

Sandro stared at his old friend.

'Are you serious?'

'It happens,' said Pietro wearily. 'You know it does. The injuries are severe. Consistent with being struck by a car.'

Sandro scratched his head. Rocking back, he raised his upper body a little to peer through the tent flap and over the oleanders. The traffic was moving slowly, the sun glinting off a rooftop.

But he was supposed to be on holiday,' Sandro said. 'Shouldn't have been here.' And stubbornly, 'I don't buy it. I don't buy it at all.'

'Listen,' said Pietro. 'The man was under a lot of pressure, wasn't he? Money troubles? They'd be the least of it.'

'What are you saying?' Sandro felt unreasonable anger rising in him.

'I'm saying,' said Pietro, 'that we should consider the possibility that he – he walked into the traffic. Deliberately, maybe at night, maybe he waited for just the right kind of car, one of those big bastards with tinted windows that's got hit and run all over it.'

Sandro kept staring. 'As a way of killing yourself? With the river right over there? With paracetamol in every pharmacy?'

'Maybe he wanted it to look like an accident,' said Pietro, his turn to sound stubborn. 'You never know,' he went on. 'Suicide – it's like everything. People are scared of doing it one way and not another. A personal thing.'

'And no one stopped.'

'Like I said,' said Pietro. 'We know it happens. At night, no witnesses? They've done surveys, you know. Ninety-five per cent of Italians say they wouldn't report the accidental killing of a house pet on the roads. It's something like fifteen per cent if it's an adult and there are no other witnesses, and you know you can inflate that because some of those who said they would go back and help are lying. Different if it's a kid.' He straightened. 'If he got knocked over the crash barrier and into the trees. Well. Looking back, maybe you could persuade yourself nothing had happened.'

Sandro was still shaking his head. 'If you say so,' he said. 'I still don't buy it. Why here?'

Belligerent, even as he said the words, Sandro thought, I'm too old for this. Too old to be standing in the particularly livid glare of the inside of a forensics tent, a glare that had illuminated his nightmares for the best years of his life, along with that particular smell of fusty plastic and preservatives, and of decomposing humanity. Too old to be picking a fight with his best – his only – friend. And abruptly he pushed his way out through the flapping plastic.

Pietro came out behind him, a gloved hand on his shoulder. Outside, even the gaseous miasma that rose from the overheating traffic seemed like fresh air, compared with the stench inside the tent, and both men took deep gulps until they began to cough. A woman in the passenger seat of a red convertible brought to a temporary standstill, twenty-five perhaps, though made up to look older, turned and stared at them with distaste. The car's driver, a tanned, well-preserved man approaching fifty, looked ahead resolutely through dark glasses.

Sandro turned, one way then another, still thinking it over, suicide or – something else; still: why here? To the east, the blue hills of the Casentino, Pontassieve and beyond, from where you could stop and look back at the city as he and Luisa used to do, picnicking, and see right through the crenellated tower of the Palazzo Vecchio. Hectares and hectares of forested hillside, untended olive groves, silent valleys where a body could rot to nothing unobserved.

'It's madness, isn't it?' Sandro spoke as if to himself. 'Here?' he said. 'Why not – Christ. Why not somewhere less – less—'

'Yes,' said Pietro gently, 'it's a shithole. But we both know that people sometimes take themselves off to places – to terrible places, far away from home. To do this.'

Pietro stood in uneasy silence, waiting for Sandro to come to his senses. A siren whooped once and they both turned towards the sound; a blue light revolved on an unmarked van's roof, stuck in the traffic coming towards them from the city. At the sound the cars began, reluctantly, to edge out of the way.

'That's pathology,' said Sandro flatly.

'Look,' said Pietro quickly, in an undertone. 'If he'd got himself – into a situation. With the wife, and the pregnant girlfriend. Running two homes?' And Pietro shook his head wryly. 'The wife might have been asking questions, the baby about to be born, the money—' And he stopped. 'You can see.'

'Luisa wants us to move,' said Sandro suddenly. 'She's found this apartment. D'you think I could get a loan, at my age?'

Taken aback, Pietro said nothing, but then again, he didn't have to. His expression was enough. 'Sandro—' he began, aghast.

Sandro nodded slowly. 'I see,' he said. 'Suicide because of – the money. It's always the money. Not wanting to let her down.' He'd been stupid, hadn't he? Instincts were sometimes the wrong things to pursue. He'd let Anna's sweet, hopeful little face get between him and the facts. 'Right,' he said slowly.

Pietro was raising a hand to indicate their presence to the pathology van. 'Monterosso, you said?' Sandro gazed back blankly. 'The wife?' said Pietro patiently.

'Yes,' said Sandro. 'Monterosso. He's supposed to be on holiday.' He thought of the weeping woman who would sooner or later emerge from the room in the police morgue that smelled of bleach and preserving agents and the sickly topnote of decay. 'A house called Le Glicine, overlooking the sea. His in-laws.'

'And we'll need your girl, too,' said Pietro. 'The other woman. When the wife's been. She'll need to ID him too.'

'My girl,' said Sandro and for a moment he set his hand before his eyes, wanting darkness. 'Yes.'

CHAPTER NINE

'IT WAS HIS WIFE,' Ma said triumphantly.

'What?'

Roxana was sitting in an expensive new wine bar this side of the Uffizi – ten euros for a plate of sliced meats and a single cold glass of Greco di Tufa – and trying to relax. She didn't usually drink very much, let alone at lunchtime, but today was not like other days. This month, in fact, was not like other months. Today Roxana needed something to click the little worry switch off in her brain, and wine seemed like a reasonable start. She'd just taken the first sip or two, just felt the beginnings of an effect – felt the shoulders drop, started to look around at the other customers, appreciate the sophisticated air-conditioning, because clearly that ten euros had to be paying for something other than two slices of *finocchiona* and three of salt ham – when her phone went.

And it was Ma. 'Hey, Mamma.' She set the glass down. She'd stopped calling her mother by her first name; there'd been enough confusion of roles already.

But Ma sounded her old self, completely: bristling, sharp, certain. 'I've remembered.'

'Remembered what?'

'It was the wife,' she said. 'Yesterday. His wife phoned.'

'What?' This was the old Ma, too, making no concessions to those trying to follow her train of thought. 'Whose wife? You mean the woman who phoned yesterday?'

'Ye-es,' said Ma, exaggeratedly patient. 'I told you I was just tired, you know. You were putting too much pressure on me. That was why I couldn't remember.' A pause. '*And* I found the paper I made a note of her name on.'

'Whose wife, Ma?'

'Well, your boss's wife, of course. That was the confusion. I know she's not exactly a friend of yours but she did ask for you by name.'

'Signora Brunello?'

Roxana knew her, of course. Gracious, pretty, pampered, with the plump little children she tugged behind her impatiently. On holiday in Monterosso, her darling Claudio grilling fish on the barbecue, children splashing in the blue shallows: why on earth would she be calling Roxana at home?

'You're sure?'

'I've told you.' Ma spoke sharply, as though Roxana was seven years old, and the summer holidays stretched for two months ahead of them and her temper was fraying. 'Irene Brunello, wife of your boss, left her number and said, please could you call back when you got home.'

'Damn,' said Roxana. The supercilious girl behind the cold counter looked across at her with vague interest, and Roxana shifted to half-turn her back, her mind working furiously.

Brunello's wife calls. A private detective comes looking for Brunello. Had it been a mistake to talk to that man? Roxana's stomach clenched. But she had trusted him; even now, she trusted him.

'Give me the number, Ma,' she said. Then, hearing the huffy silence, 'Please.'

Violetta Delfino read out the number, in the cut-glass accent that had served her so well for fifteen years as a hospital secretary. Roxana took a gulp of the wine, too recklessly; it made her giddy. How had Irene Brunello got her number? From the book? She was surprised the woman even remembered her name.

'Thanks, Ma,' she said, apologetically. Meaning, *Sorry I doubted you.*

'And there *was* someone in the garden,' said Ma defiantly. As if she knew exactly the way Roxana was thinking. 'I went out there this morning and I saw footprints. I didn't fall asleep and dream it, as I know you were wondering. I'm not—'

'Footprints?' They could have been Roxana's footprints. 'You're not stupid, Ma, I know that.'

'Gaga, I was going to say. Senile. I'm just old, and – and, well. You wait, my girl. You wait. You think you're in charge, you are the one that manages everything. And suddenly it's all different. Suddenly you have to take care, to be afraid. Soon they'll be talking to you like a baby, feeding you mush on a spoon.'

The food hadn't tasted like ten euros' worth, after that, though it had been fine. Roxana had cut her lunch break short by a good twenty minutes, paid up and headed for the door, the pretty girl's eyes on her back. Didn't she have a mother?

Once outside, within a millisecond she regretted leaving the air-conditioned wine bar. The heat was something else. It probably reached its daily maximum at three in the afternoon, especially in the Via dei Saponai. The street of the soapmakers, how illustrious was that, in the great city of the Renaissance? But it led south off the Via dei Neri and the sun shone straight down its length. Fine in the winter; in the summer, though, it was deserted, a scalding thoroughfare to nowhere. No wonder business was bad.

It was hard to marshal your thoughts in this temperature. Brunello's wife was after him and Sandro Cellini, private investigator, was after Brunello. Roxana slowed as it dawned on her: this was something. Not just a rumour, not just a bit of something to be gossiped about – this was her boss. Her job. If Brunello was in trouble – then she stopped.

Even from the end of the street she could see that something was up. The light was on in the bank, but they didn't open up again till four, didn't have to get back inside till three-thirty. Could Val have come back early from his lunch hour, instead of his usual six minutes late, smiling amiably and knowing he'd be forgiven?

But August turned everything on its head; maybe Val had got too lazy to go out in the first place. And for a minute, her thoughts loosened by the wine, Roxana thought again of the man from the cinema with his bag of takings. As they came in with their cash and paying-in books, all those shop assistants and market boys, were they tempted just to do a runner? They must be. August would be the month to do it.

It wasn't Valentino. Marisa Goldman met her at the security door.

Marisa Goldman, straight-nosed, arrogant and beautiful as an Egyptian cat – only not today. She was tanned, her black hair was looped up in the usual tight shiny French knot, but under the superficial effects of the sun she looked sallow and ugly with shock.

'What is it?' said Roxana immediately. 'Aren't you supposed to be on what's his name's yacht? What's happened? Something's happened.'

But Marisa was saying nothing; carefully she closed the door behind Roxana and as they passed from the sweltering street into the tepid gloom of the banking floor she felt a sweat breakout all down her back. Only when they were both in Marisa's neat office, with the leather and steel chairs and the expensive lamp, did she speak.

'It's Claudio,' she said, and her voice shook.

'Claudio,' repeated Roxana stupidly, wanting to ward off the terrible moment. 'What's happened?'

They were both standing. She saw that Marisa was wearing beach clothes, a turquoise silk shirt, no jewellery, sandals. Those little knotted cotton bracelets you could have tied round your wrist by some Chinese girl on the beach.

'She phoned me. Irene Brunello called me ...' She looked at her watch, staring as if her life depended on it. 'A bit more than an hour ago.'

'You got here quick,' said Roxana. An hour? From Elba?

'I took the helicopter,' said Marisa, distractedly.

'She was calling here yesterday,' said Roxana, hearing the foolish eagerness in her voice. 'She even called me at home—' But then she faltered, seeing the look of dull fear on Marisa's face.

'Yesterday?' Marisa sounded bewildered. 'She knew yesterday?'

'Knew what?'

And then Marisa seemed to crumple, with a small sound of distress, her long angular body collapsing into the uncomfortable leather sling of her office chair.

'She's been asked to – they need her to identify—' She stopped, swallowed. 'He's dead,' she said, barely whispering. 'Claudio's dead.'

Roxana stood over her superior, and stared. With one part of her brain all she could think of was that she should take the woman's hand, rub some colour back into her cheeks, fetch a glass of water – but the rest of her head was suddenly filled to painful bursting with that awful word.

'Dead?'

And the flood of images, unstoppable, came: Claudio Brunello giving her a quizzical, serious, calculating look over his screen; the fastidious movement with which he adjusted the sleeves of his jacket; the look – impatient, fond, superstitious – he would shoot at the photograph on his shelf. And more than images: his soft, considered, evasive voice, murmuring behind his closed door; the smell of sandalwood and polished leather that entered a room with him.

Marisa looked up at her and jerked her head in a nod that was more like a spasm.

Abruptly Roxana sat down. 'But what—' And then she stopped. Of course. 'An accident,' she said, almost relieved. How could it have been anything else? 'And she's been trying to get hold of us. Oh, God. In the car?' The boss drove that car so fast, it was so unnecessarily powerful, and the coast road—

Somewhere off beyond the office door there was a noise, the sound of Valentino back from his lunch break, the hiss of the door and his idiotic friendly voice calling out.

But Marisa was shaking her head. Roxana's thoughts whirled – a drowning, the currents up there, a body pulled out of the sea – until at last Marisa spoke, with what seemed like a terrible effort.

'No,' she said. 'It wasn't an accident.'

*

'Anna's on her way,' said the tough, skinny Russian girl on reception at the Loggiata.

She eyed Sandro with deep suspicion, before adjusting it to a look of contempt for Giuli, at his side.

'She's laying up for tomorrow's breakfast. She's a bit slow on her feet these days.' Sarcastic, with it: Sandro just smiled and nodded. A violent death put things in perspective. Like childbirth, no doubt: the surly Russian was the least of their worries.

Outside there was the soundtrack of August: cicadas in the garden below them, starting up as the sun went down, and the sullen banging of builders at work, the crash of falling plaster. They might work at half-speed in August, but the city was full of them. The skies were clear, people were away, businesses shut for a month – so they called in the builders. Scaffolding everywhere, skips and rubble, and that infernal banging.

He turned to Giuli and whispered, 'Thanks for coming.'

She looked at him with weary amusement. 'No problem,' she said.

The Loggiata was, as Pietro had said in what now seemed like another world but was only that tired bar in San Ambrogio last night, an old-fashioned sort of place. If old-fashioned meant it hadn't been redecorated in thirty-five years and smelled of decades of cat. The hotel occupied the top floor of a crumbling *palazzo* behind Santo Spirito, and the foyer opened through a long, glazed door on to the *loggia* that gave it its name. The veneer reception desk was surmounted by a frayed square of orange hessian and the upholstered chairs in which he and Giuli sat were shiny with age. But the foyer was vast, the polished cotto of the floor undulating and ancient and the tall windows were original, with delicate glazing bars and wobbly old glass.

Outside the light was turning yellow and hazy in the late afternoon; the Loggiata had no air-conditioning but relied on the time-honoured methods of fans and shutters and damp cloths hung in strategic places. They sat very still and breathed shallowly in the heat, he and Giuli and the wary Russian, and they waited.

Take your time, Sandro thought. Don't hurry down, little Anna Niescu, don't worry that child you're protecting so carefully, don't raise your heartbeat. Give me time to think about how I'm going to give you this news.

He had waited in a bar in a backstreet, a dirty little place. 'I'll be there in a bit,' Pietro had said, rolling his eyes and dismissing Sandro. 'Wait for me.'

He'd walked in ten minutes later, frowning down at his mobile, and had called right there and then, from the bar. The seedy barman had eyed Pietro as he talked, his voice hushed and careful. Sandro had listened to one half of the conversation – the other half he could reconstruct on his own, from long familiarity and the occasional loud, gasping exclamation audible even from where he stood, a discreet metre from his old friend.

'I'm so sorry,' he'd heard Pietro say, again and again. He was better at this than Sandro ever had been; Pietro had a natural gentleness, where Sandro became gruff and brusque when he felt emotion struggling inside him.

'I'm so sorry, Signora Brunello. Yes, yes – you need to have someone take care of the children, I don't advise – no. Is there any relative you could leave them with? And perhaps someone to accompany you? It can be a very overwhelming experience.'

You can say that again, Sandro had thought. For the police – on nodding acquaintance with the morgue, its smells and sounds, the unmistakable grey pallor of a dead face, the particular lividity of a bruise on dead flesh – it was bad enough. But for most bereaved fathers, wives, mothers, it was the first and only time. For Signora Brunello and those like her, this would be the single worst moment of their lives.

She would come back into the baking city from the fresh salt air of the seaside, she would drive closer and closer, winding her window down to pay the toll that marked her entry into the inferno, and the choking, intolerable heat would roll in like poison gas. Coming back for this.

Pietro had hung up, looking grave.

'Glad I don't have to do that any more,' Sandro had said, to comfort him, before realizing that *that* was just what he would have to do, and soon.

Now the Russian looked up from her magazine, sharp-eared as

a cat, and Sandro turned to follow her glance. Anna Niescu came towards them through the glazed door from the *loggia* lopsidedly carrying a mop-bucket, and the eagerness in her face made Sandro scowl. Giuli, who knew what that scowl meant, nudged him sharply.

'Miss Niescu,' he said, getting to his feet. She set the mop-bucket down, searching his face, and Sandro took her hand in both his. It felt as small as a child's, and hot.

The Russian girl muttered something that sounded like a curse in her own language and hauled the mop-bucket behind the desk. 'Too heavy,' she said in her accented Italian. 'I tell you, I will carry this for you.'

'Can we talk somewhere – private?' asked Sandro, looking from Anna to the receptionist. The Russian nodded towards the door through which Anna had arrived.

'Outside,' she said.

Anna kept looking up at Sandro as they walked, but he couldn't look back. He tried not to think of Claudio Brunello, of the Claudio Brunello he had seen, stiffened and bloodless and insulted by the elements, inhuman behind the soiled oleanders as cars roared past. He pushed open the door to let her through ahead of him.

The open *loggia*, stretching perhaps twenty metres of dusty cotto under its beamed and tiled roof, was set with groupings of old cane chairs and low tables. The furthest of them were laid for tomorrow's breakfast. A table for four and one for two; August was a quiet month, but even so. Six guests were not enough to support a place like this.

'It's cool in the mornings,' said Anna, seeing him looking. 'All of our guests like to have their breakfast here.' She gestured for him to sit, pulled out a chair for him, and he came around behind her and did the same for her. Giuli managed on her own.

And then they were seated, and it had to be said.

'Anna,' he said, as gently as he could, 'I'm afraid there's some bad news.'

She stared, and her soft brown eyes seemed to darken, and there came into them an awful knowingness that perhaps had always been there, the last vestige of the abandoned child she had once been.

'Bad news?' she said quietly, and her small hands sat on either side of her belly, stilling it.

'An accident,' said Sandro, the dreadful deceitfulness of the word sour in his mouth. Giuli leaned across and took Anna's hand, and the girl's head tilted back just a little, her hand came up to cover half her face.

Sandro leaned close, to draw her back to him. 'A man was – the police think he was struck by a car, out – out near the Viale Amendola. The African market: do you know the African market?' He saw her face bleach with fear and confusion. 'We think he may be your fiancé. He had some documentation on him.'

And Anna Niescu let her hand fall and looked into his eyes. Her mouth was trembling and she began to shake her head. 'No,' she said, 'no, I – no. The African market? Why would he be there? On the *viale?*'

And Sandro had nothing to say to that, because she must know by now, mustn't she? That her beloved Josef wasn't what he seemed. Anna Niescu was not stupid. 'I'm sorry,' was all he could think of. And then, 'I'm afraid we will need you – to identify him. To come and make sure.'

And then the hand flew to her mouth to stifle an awful sound, because now she understood. That this was real: there was a body, and she must look at it.

'Yes,' she said, eyes wide, blinking to stifle the tears, but Sandro could see them.

They had talked about this. He and Pietro.

'The wife, first, of course,' Sandro had said, and silently Pietro had compressed his lips in agreement. Not a matter of the law, but of propriety. It wasn't for them to judge the rights and wrongs in Brunello's marriage.

'She said she would probably be able to get here by six,' Pietro had said. 'She's leaving the children in Monterosso, with their grandmother.'

'His mother?'

Sandro had been aghast: first one, then others, the bereaved always multiplied like this. Pietro had shaken his head. 'Hers.'

Was that a mercy? Silently they had agreed that it was.

And then, drily, reluctantly, because it was almost certainly in defiance of protocol, Pietro had said, 'I imagine you would like – to be there?'

And, as reluctantly, Sandro had said that he would. Tried to calculate the horrible logistics of talking to Anna, getting over to the morgue to observe the wife and her reactions, and then bringing Anna herself, the pregnant lover, to take her turn identifying the body.

'Do you want me to come now?' said Anna, and her hands moved, reaching about her pointlessly for something that might aid her: handbag, cardigan.

'Not quite now,' said Sandro. 'There are – procedures first, that the police have to carry out.'

She looked at him blankly, but nodded. Ever obedient. Sandro felt a pang, because it was nonsense, wasn't it? Procedures? Lies, was more like it. Lies and evasions: when would it end? When Brunello's widow came face to face with this girl? Would they be able to avoid that?

Almost certainly they would not. If they wanted to make a case for suicide, then they would have to produce something beyond the happy family, on holiday by the sea, the comfortable job. The expensive car.

Where was it, that car?

'He took the car,' Pietro had said shortly. 'I didn't want – to go too much further. On the phone. But she said, he took the car, she'd been using the little runaround they keep by the sea.'

'Little runaround,' Sandro had repeated. It said everything.

Outside the Loggiata, the builders' noise had started up again, although the light was mellowing as the afternoon wore on. Bang, bang, bang: there was something vicious about it, something sullen and monotonous and horrible. With every report Anna Niescu's shoulders contracted, like an animal drawing into itself under attack.

'I don't think it can be until tomorrow morning,' said Sandro on impulse, seeing a way through those logistics. He knew what it would mean for her, but it was suddenly imperative that Brunello's wife – widow – should be long gone before Anna got there. 'I'm sorry.'

'Tomorrow?' Her voice was an anguished, disbelieving whisper.

'I'll come back for you,' said Sandro. 'You should rest, if you can.'

She looked at him vaguely: she was pale and her skin gleamed with sweat. Sandro was brought up short by the realization that, whatever happened, within a month this child would be giving birth to another. Perhaps sooner than that.

'I'll stay with you,' said Giuli to Anna gently, arm around her shoulders.

'Oh, no,' said Anna quickly, vaguely, 'I've got work to do. The kitchen has to be ready for the morning.'

'Anna,' said Sandro, 'I know you would like to keep busy, perhaps. But think of your baby. Concentrate on your baby:

that's the important thing.' He saw her mouth form a little 'O' as she breathed, saw her place a hand between her breasts to calm herself.

'Yes,' she said. A little colour returned to her face as she stayed very still.

'Let me stay,' said Giuli again. 'Just see how we go. I can help you, in the kitchen, if that's what you want to do.' She darted a glance at Sandro. 'All right?'

He nodded just once, quickly. Giuli took Anna by the wrists gently and held her gaze. 'All right?'

'Yes,' said Anna and, as so often happened, it was the kindness that brought the tears. The bad news shattered them, dried their eyes and mouths, paralysed them, but it was the arm around the shoulder that made them cry.

Below the lovely, crumbling *loggia*, the builders had at last stopped banging; they were slinging scaffolding joints into a barrow instead, on their way out. The three sat without speaking until at last the noise was no more than the echo of the final steel-capped boot. Sandro left the two women there, so close they were almost one, the neat black cap of hair pressed in under Giuli's chin.

As he left, Sandro nodded his brief thanks to the Russian. She looked up, beady-eyed as a bird.

'What is it?' she said. 'Is bad news?' She spoke warily, wanting information, prepared to give nothing away herself.

'Bad news,' said Sandro. 'Yes.'

'She don't deserve it,' said the girl. It was delivered bluntly, but contained within it also the fatalistic recognition that rarely are the good rewarded.

She might have been beautiful, with her thick black brows and her white, white skin, if she didn't seem so angry, angry even before she knew why they were here. What was she angry about?

Being here, in August, being far from home? Perhaps it was just a Russian characteristic. Defiance and anger.

'No,' Sandro said. 'She deserves better.'

Chapter Ten

THERE WAS A SUITE of rooms at the police morgue, for the receiving of family members; one of them had a viewing room behind a one-way mirror. Behind it Sandro sat and watched Pietro as he stood beneath a large and ornate black crucifix, his hands clasped earnestly, talking to Claudio Brunello's wife – widow. Sandro knew they wouldn't let him in the room, although he'd tried.

'Sorry,' Pietro had said, shifting a glance at Matteucci, the northern dolt, who had obstinately refused to understand what Sandro was doing there at all. ('Say that again? He's who?') Pietro had spread his hands. 'Best I can do.'

They had viewed the body.

She'd said six, but Irene Brunello had been there at ten to. From the long window to the small office Pietro shared with half a dozen others and once with Sandro too, they saw her park her small yellow car – a brand-new Punto, so bright, so jaunty, so appropriate for the beach cafés and villas of Monterosso, so grimly wrong for the car park of the big grey police station on the ring road at Porta al Prato.

'We've got the car on CCTV entering the city,' Pietro had said abruptly as they watched. His eyes had been sad although Sandro hadn't known whom his old friend pitied most: Sandro for his stubborn resistance to the obvious, messy explanations, the dead man, or the dead man's wife. 'A silver Audi. Twelve-thirty, he came through the motorway toll at Firenze Nord. The car, the number plate, his face at the wheel.'

'Quick work,' Sandro had said. 'Good work.' He averted his eyes. 'You don't know where the car is now.'

'We'll find it.'

Somehow they had known, he and Pietro and even Matteucci, even before her slim, tanned sandalled foot first touched the ground, her trim, straight-backed figure, that it was Irene Brunello in that little car.

Early forties: a good age for a woman, or should be, the fierce anxieties of youth all done with, the hard work of child-rearing easing off, enough money coming in. Given the right circumstances in life, of course, given health, given family, children, a happy marriage.

To Sandro, far above, and observing her framed in a great window twice as high as he was, Irene Brunello had looked as if she'd had all that, until today.

Sandro had hovered as they'd greeted her sombrely; she had been too distracted to ask who he was. The tears had dried – she seemed a woman of strong character, bound to the proprieties, to not breaking down in public – but they had left their traces. Her handsome face was puffy and the seaside tan, overlaying drawn and anxious features, had the effect of making her look older than her years. This was entirely a grieving widow, he had no doubt. There had been a quick handshake, the exchange of formal greetings that implied condolence but also avoided the word itself, not wanting to make assumptions.

'Let me see him,' she had said, a twist of handkerchief at her mouth.

She knows it's him, Sandro had thought. Some women refused to believe it: *I said goodbye to him only this morning,* they'd say. *It can't be.* Not this wife.

Sandro had stood outside the door, looking in through the square of reinforced glass; he'd seen her head dip as they drew back the sheet. There had been no way of putting that face back together, but there had been enough of it left, so that if it was familiar enough, if you loved it enough – he had seen her nod, twice. He had seen Pietro gesture down towards the hand, with its wedding ring; she had taken the hand between hers.

Damn, he had thought, damn, damn. Her husband was dead, and there was worse to come.

'I'm so sorry,' Pietro had said, leading her into the interview room, motioning gently for her to sit. Now from the door Sandro watched her intently: Irene Brunello didn't cry. She sat very still, dignified; she began to speak before any questions were put to her.

'We have already been at the seaside for a month – the children and I. My mother's house.'

In those dark eyes Sandro thought he saw something and wondered how her husband had got on with his mother-in-law. Whether he felt they should be able to afford a seaside place of their own. Did she reproach him with it?

She was going on, doggedly, 'Claudio always stays on to work until the first weekend in August. Always, he's—' She stopped, staring. 'He was very conscientious. He would come up at weekends, through July. The city's so unbearable—'

She broke off again, looking from one face to another: Pietro, grave and patient, making notes, Matteucci uneasy – what was the point of all this, you could see him thinking, let's get it over with. Sandro grim-faced and invisible behind the mirror.

'It's all right,' said Pietro. 'Take your time.' Turning to Matteucci, 'Could you get Signora Brunello some water, Officer?'

Matteucci left the room, the set of his shoulders saying he didn't care, at least he was out of there.

Pietro turned back to Irene Brunello. 'He came out for weekends?' he prompted.

She nodded, compressing her lips as she looked down at the handkerchief in her lap. 'But once he was out for August, he was out. He wouldn't go back to work, that was it, he was ours.'

Her eyes widened, and in that phrase all that they had lost was encapsulated. The family table, on a shaded terrace overlooking the sea, the mother laying food in front of her husband, the children on his lap. Journey's end: the reward for a year of hard work.

And yet this man had been leading a double life. There were two women mourning him, another family waiting for him.

A double life: was that reason enough for suicide? Two women in love with you, enough money, a child about to come into the world? And Sandro, who thought he had long since ceased to rage against his own childlessness, found a version of that fury rising in him. What laziness, what selfishness. What monstrous ingratitude.

And yet. Something was not right.

Irene Brunello's husband was a good provider, a loving husband and father, a hard and conscientious worker. The man Anna Niescu trusted, whose child she carried – she had thought of him in similar terms, at least in prospect. Would such a man walk into traffic on a busy road to escape his responsibilities? Would he do it this way, would he do it at all? Nonsense. It was nonsense.

'But this weekend?' said Pietro gently.

Irene Brunello straightened on the uncomfortable chair, and when she spoke it was calmly. 'He arrived on Friday night, as he always did, the first Friday of August, at about eleven o'clock in the evening. He'd stopped for something to eat at the bar near work, and the traffic had been bad, he said.'

She was a good witness: she was clear-headed. Sandro found himself nodding, and by instinct stopped himself, as if she could see him through the one-way glass and would know what he was thinking. Eleven o'clock: that would have given him time for close to an hour with Anna Niescu, who'd seen her lover at seven, out of the city by eight. He tried to remember what the traffic had actually been like that evening.

She was still talking. 'He brought some things for the children, as he always did. It was our tradition. A new beach toy – every year it must be a bigger one, this time it was an inflatable crocodile – and a big cake from our favourite *pasticcere*, on the Via dei Mille. Everything was fine. Everything was normal.'

'And then?'

Matteucci came back in with a bottle of water and a plastic cup; he filled the cup and set it on the low table. Irene Brunello didn't even look at it.

'And then on Saturday morning he took the car and said he was going to drive to La Spezia to do a big shop. There's a giant supermarket there, much cheaper.'

'Was that normal?' La Spezia would be an hour's drive, at least, from Monterosso, right at the other end of the Cinque Terre. A long drive on a Saturday morning.

She shrugged, uncomfortable for the first time.

'Not really.'

She fiddled with the handkerchief again, not meeting anyone's eye, then finally she looked up.

'Usually we do our shopping in Monterosso, in little places, you know.' She was talking nervously, trying not to think. 'There's a greengrocer, there's a butcher, they're good people. Or, at most, around the coast to Levanto. The supermarkets are small, they're more expensive, but we're on holiday, you know? But he had mentioned money, the night before. He seemed – preoccupied.

He was saying, perhaps we should think about letting the holiday home next year. My mother's home.

'And the next morning – Saturday morning – I thought I heard the phone ring; he must have answered it, if it did. I was busy with the children. It seemed odd to me – well, when he didn't come back. The phone call, then the supermarket.'

'Odd?' Pietro leaned forward, alert. Even from where he stood, peering, his face close up to the glass, Sandro could see the wounded, bewildered look in the woman's eyes.

'I did ask him. We never use that supermarket. He was distracted. He mentioned money again. He said we had to be careful with money in the – in the current climate, that was what he said.' A trace of painful indignation in her brimming eyes. 'I'm not one of those women – who doesn't think about the expense. I'm careful. Claudio gives me housekeeping—'

And her eyes widened. Sandro could see her thinking, what next? Where will the money come from now?

Claudio Brunello was trying to economize?

'Do you think perhaps he might not have been telling the truth?' Pietro's voice was low. 'Would you have been angry, for example, if he said he had to go back into work? Something like that?'

Irene Brunello stared into his eyes, pale. 'I don't know,' she said. 'I don't know. It was a – a thing of ours. Once on holiday, then no calls from work, nothing.' Sandro could see her absorb it, take the burden of guilt on herself. 'I never meant – he never—'

Don't, thought Sandro, enough.

'All right,' said Pietro, soothing, and Sandro felt a small yet strong pulse of grateful affection, that their minds still seemed to run along the same track. Would they ever work together again, properly? Best not to think about it.

'So,' Pietro continued, doggedly patient. 'On Saturday morning he said he would go to the supermarket.'

She nodded, confusion in her eyes. 'I made him coffee, I went out for pastries from the good baker's. He likes something sweet in the morning.'

Liked.

'And then I took Laila to the beach, leaving him there with our son to have breakfast, that's when I thought I heard the telephone, at about ten. I was putting the beach things in a basket. And after about fifteen minutes he brought Gianni, our son, down, and said he was going to the supermarket.'

'And that was the last time you saw him?'

Sitting on the warm stones of the beach at Monterosso, the turquoise sea behind her, the bright little *condomini* along the front, shading her eyes as she waved him off.

'You didn't report him missing?'

She stared at Pietro with wonder, and Sandro already knew the answer before she gave it. Because once you went to the police, once they started checking the hospitals and the RTAs, you were halfway to widowhood. You were admitting the possibility. She just barely shook her head, clinging to that picture of her husband as she had last seen him, standing in the sun.

'What will we do?' she said, her face turned to Pietro, blank with the immensity of it.

Sandro looked at her, at the mute appeal in her eyes; then at his old friend. You will ask, won't you? he wanted to say, through the glass. Check out her story, talk to the mother, talk to the maid, where's she been all weekend? Because it was at moments like this, when all your sympathy was engaged, when everything leaned one way, towards the grieving widow, that mistakes were made. So many murders were committed by someone close. Even if this was not a murder, but a suicide.

He believed her, even through the one-way glass, he believed her, because he wanted to believe her. Was Pietro being sceptical enough?

She said it again, 'What will we do without him?'

And nobody had any reply.

*

On the porch, listening to the cicadas in the trees and the vague, distracted sounds of her mother in the kitchen, Roxana stared into the warm, scented darkness of the garden and tried to make sense of it.

It wasn't easy. Today at the office had made home – the side of her life usually most resembling a madhouse – look like a haven of order and peace.

'Darling,' Violetta had said as she pushed her way wearily through the door, and had held her arms out. Full of affection, the bringer of comfort – was this new Ma just a new phase? Worn out, Roxana had decided to take it at face value. What the hell.

'Ma,' she said, letting her mother put her arms around her. 'How was your day?'

And Ma, perhaps still buoyed by her newly rediscovered powers of recall, had launched into a story about the Sicilian with his vegetable truck who had been selling watermelons at the end of the road. Where the melons had come from, how she'd known the man since he was a small boy selling with his dad, from the same truck. Roxana had sat down and let her mother talk. She had poured herself a small glass of white wine from the refrigerator, and when the story showed signs of drawing to a close, said, 'I'll be out at the back.'

Sipping the wine – slightly sharp, she couldn't remember how long that bottle had been there – Roxana thought about Marisa Goldman. She'd never seen her like that, Marisa whom nothing could touch, always perfectly composed, every little pretty detail of her life under control. Perhaps there were some things that money and good taste could not solve, after all. Roxana, however, for whom Marisa was a daily itch beneath the skin, found that she could not summon up even the most meagre satisfaction from the image of Marisa's sallow, drawn features.

'What did she say?' In Marisa's immaculate office Roxana had poured her superior a glass of cold water and looked intently into her pale face. 'What exactly did Irene Brunello say?'

And as Marisa had stared back at her dully, it had occurred to Roxana that perhaps she'd taken something too, a tranquillizer. Marisa was always popping pills: vitamins, sleeping pills, homeopathic and not so homeopathic. Perhaps life with the playboy billionaire wasn't that much fun, after all. But eventually she had spilled it all out, except that, it turned out, all hadn't really been that much.

The police had got hold of Irene Brunello at Monterosso. They had found a body with Claudio's ID on it – and Claudio had been gone since Saturday. She was frantic with worry – they all were, said Marisa, almost accusingly.

'But she hasn't identified him yet.' Someone, Roxana had thought, had to be blunt; someone had to resist being frantic.

A tight little shake of the head, no. Marisa's face had been anguished. 'But it doesn't look good.' She'd bitten her lip. 'I offered to go with her, but she said no. I'm going over later, to their apartment.'

Kneeling at Marisa's side, Roxana had sat back on her haunches. 'There's something funny about all this,' she had said, almost to herself.

'All what?' Marisa had spoken sharply and Roxana had hesitated.

'A private detective came looking for him yesterday.'

'What?' Marisa's voice had been a whisper. 'You're kidding, right?'

Roxana hadn't dignified that with a response; she had just continued, 'He's been gone since Saturday? So that's why she was phoning. Why she phoned my home, looking for Claudio.'

'Why would she phone *you?*' A trace of the old haughtiness in Marisa's voice.

Roxana had merely looked at her. 'I don't know, Marisa,' she had said patiently. 'Maybe your phone was off, maybe there was no signal out there on the boat. I mean, clearly I would have been a last resort.' She'd frowned. 'It must have been she who phoned here, at the bank, yesterday. God, Val's a moron.'

And right on cue, the clump of biker boots in the foyer had announced Valentino's arrival. Stiffly, Roxana had got to her feet. 'I'll tell him, shall I?' she'd said.

Marisa had rubbed her face with both hands, shivered even though the air-conditioning was barely making a dent in the temperatures. 'No,' she had said. 'It's all right.' And she had moved to her position of authority behind the desk, the bright turquoise of her shirt incongruous against the steel and leather. 'Send him in.'

'What?' Valentino had said, pulling off his helmet as Roxana walked past him, catching her expression, his eyes following her. She had nodded towards Marisa's office.

'Something's happened, Valentino,' she'd said. 'Go and talk to her.'

*

Inside the house, her mother was singing, some old ballad about laying a table for a wedding meal. She had a good, clear voice, but it was a long time since Roxana had heard her sing like this. Perhaps not since Luca had been a kid, and Ma used to sing him to sleep. On the porch in the dark Roxana leaned back and closed her eyes.

Had she wanted Valentino to be shocked out of that cheerful selfishness of his? Had she wanted to see if there was any more to him? And why should she care in any case?

She'd gone and stood at the big pinboard where notices of whatever new account or savings bond they were promoting were put up, her back to Marisa's office. Ridiculously, all she could think was how tatty it all looked. What a stupid dead end of a dump this bank was and how Maria Grazia was right, she had to go.

There'd been no sound from the office – though the door had been closed and perhaps she wouldn't have heard anything anyway. She had walked slowly around the room, turning on the lights, replenishing the deposit and withdrawal slips, resetting the ticket machine before finally she'd flicked the switches that released the security doors and declared the bank open for the afternoon's business. What there was of it.

If she'd wanted to see Val shaken, then she had had her wish. Turning from the door, she saw him emerge from Marisa's office, and his carefully cultivated stubble stood out dark against the pallor of his face.

'You all right, Val?' she'd said.

'What?'

She'd thought he was going to cry, his staring eyes hardly focused on her. Gently she'd put out her hand, touched his arm. 'It's a shock,' she'd said. 'Take it easy.'

'He's dead,' Valentino had said blankly, and she'd thought, poor guy. Nothing bad had ever happened to Val, he was like a kid encountering death for the first time. Only Val was twenty-nine. She'd felt as if she'd aged ten years herself.

'Yes,' she'd said, and he'd took her hand and held on to it, just for a second but very tight. Then someone had appeared at the door: typical. Barely a handful of customers all month, and again some kid was waiting by the door, hopping on white trainers to be let in, looking at his watch.

*

Sweat bloomed, quite suddenly in the humid darkness, at Roxana's temples, down her spine, the backs of her legs against the plastic of the steamer chair. Was it her imagination, or was it even hotter tonight? And the memory of the day – the awfulness of it, stuck in that airless sweatbox of a bank, trying not to think about Claudio Brunello, even the oblivious customer – that was what had brought her out in a sweat.

It wasn't an accident. Marisa had said that sharply, then almost immediately back-pedalled. 'It sounds – well. Mugged, maybe, out on the *lungarno* near the barracks, the African market.' She'd looked blank, trying to make sense of any of it. 'They weren't saying much according to Irene, she was frantic, of course. She can't believe it.'

'What? What?' It made no sense. None whatsoever. 'In Florence? But he's supposed to be on holiday.'

Roxana, thinking back to that stifling office, the air humming with the terrible reverberations of it, kept her eyes closed, and the sounds sharpened. Ma's singing trailed off as she skipped the words she couldn't remember, but the cicadas were deafening, sawing with rhythmic relentlessness in the big umbrella pine that marked the end of the garden.

What did Marisa know, really?

'So someone – do the police think someone did it? What – hit and run?' Then worse had occurred to her. 'Murder?'

'No!' That had got Marisa up out of her chair. 'Are you insane?' She'd put a hand to her chest, the bare tanned triangle of ribcage, not an ounce of spare flesh on her. 'I don't know what they think.

I – there's a possibility of suicide.'

And suddenly aware of her position – a mere teller, *sportellista* sitting calmly in the office of her superior – Roxana had stopped asking questions. She'd just bobbed her head, sorry, but she'd rather wished for that small grey man, Sandro Cellini, to ask her questions for her.

There was something Marisa Goldman wasn't telling.

Eyes still closed, Roxana sat very still. It was almost as though she could feel the overgrown foliage that surrounded her, hear it too, the banana leaves rustling against each other, a dry loquat leaf falling to earth, could smell the overpowering sweetness of orange blossom.

And there was a crack, very close. The sound of something trodden underfoot and with it Roxana's eyes snapped open, the sweat cooling fast on her forehead.

'Who's that?' She spoke louder than she intended, leaning forward in the lounger, hands braced against the armrests.

From inside Ma's singing stopped. 'Roxana?'

Instinctively Roxana put a finger to her lips.

Then Ma was standing on the threshold to the back porch, her face no more than a pale oval in the dark and any trace of the woman singing over her pans gone. Her mouth moved but no sound came out. Roxana seized her hand to still her and they both turned to look into the overgrown garden.

A rustle. Then the great grey Persian from next door lolloped out from under the banana palm, stepping neatly between the dead leaves, leaping noiselessly up on to the terrace. It looked up at them from the rail with unblinking calm, opened its mouth in a single mew.

'Get away,' said Violetta Delfino with sudden savagery, leaning across Roxana and shoving the animal off its perch. Landing on all four feet, with silent dignity the Persian stalked away, its feathery tail upright in affront, the last of it to disappear back into the undergrowth. Not a sound.

'It wasn't the cat,' said Ma, defensively. 'It wasn't.'

And Roxana knew she wasn't just talking about tonight. Could that ball of fluff, which could turn the right way up in mid-air and land without disturbing a leaf, have snapped a twig? Could Ma have spent all yesterday afternoon hiding from a cat?

'Mamma,' she said, concentrating very hard on keeping her tone steady, reasonable. 'You know Babbo's torch? You remember where he kept it?'

Slowly the dark eyes came into focus, fixed on her and Violetta Delfino nodded.

'Bring it to me.'

In the few moments she was alone again on the porch, Roxana's every sense was alert, tensed against panic. Would she know whether there was someone there, if that someone didn't move a muscle? The cicadas scraped on like buzzsaws in the umbrella pine. Mamma was back, pressing the torch into her hand with trembling fingers.

'Go inside now, Ma,' instructed Roxana, but her mother didn't move. 'Not because there's anything to be afraid of,' she said, as briskly as she could.

Ma stared fiercely into her eyes, as she had when demanding the truth of her as a child, *Tell me. Tell me you didn't stick your finger in the pie.* Even though everyone but Ma knew, it had been Luca who couldn't wait for dinnertime. She felt a sudden little surge of irritable love for her greedy, charming younger brother, a thousand kilometres away under a rainy sky, living it up in a grey northern city while they bickered their lives away.

'There's no one there,' she said patiently, and even believed it. 'I'm going to make sure the back gate's closed.' Fished the small rape alarm whistle from her bag and brandished it. 'You'll know if

I need you.' Smiling to show it was a joke. Mostly.

And at last, with an angry sigh, Ma gave in. 'The dinner'll be cold,' she said.

'Five minutes,' said Roxana. The porch door closed behind Violetta, and Roxana got to her feet.

The wooden stairs down into the garden were rickety, at every step a loud creak, but her noisy movements provoked no answering sound from the undergrowth. *There's no one there.*

It wasn't completely dark. There was a distant glow from the tennis court floodlights a kilometre away, a square of slatted bedroom lamplight from next door, through closed shutters. But as she moved under the great drooping leaves of the banana palm, Roxana turned on the torch, and cursed. God knew when the batteries had last been replaced; it shone with a feeble yellow beam, hardly enough to illuminate her own hand.

Never mind. She switched the torch off, got out the battery and rubbed it between her hands, leaned against the palm trunk, and listened. She could hear the sluggish gurgle of the river, from here, and something else, something dripping. And she thought. Ma had said that yesterday he had come around the back of the house. But that wasn't straightforward. The side door was kept locked. The back gate could be accessed only by an overgrown footpath, and you had to go to the end of the street, round the houses, scout around a bit. She'd have said, you'd have to know the area.

The man had called her Signora Delfino, but if he'd known her, Ma would have recognized his voice.

You'd have to know the area – or be determined. Desperate, perhaps.

Roxana sighed involuntarily: was she really taking this seriously? It would seem that she was. Twenty-four hours ago she'd assumed that Ma had imagined the whole thing. But a great deal had happened in twenty-four hours, a great deal that was no one's imagination. Brunello was dead, his kids were fatherless. Still something dripped in the undergrowth, nagging at her.

She replaced the battery in the torch, turned it back on. The garden was no more than ten metres square, even if it felt like a full-sized jungle in the dark. This was where Roxana had grown up, hide and seek among what had then been stunted shrubs, waist high. The back gate, set in a two-metre fence, had always been kept locked, Ma terrified they'd find their way down to the river and drown. In half a metre of filthy water: it had been known. And an eight-year-old girl had been abducted from the local swimming pool, when Roxana had been twelve, found dead in the river thirty kilometres away a week later. Never, never, never talk to strangers, Ma had scolded, then when it turned out the killer had known his victim, Ma had gone silent and obdurate.

In the dark Roxana moved towards the back gate, knowing she would find it locked and bolted as always and then she could switch off the torch and go inside. Eat dinner and try not to think about Claudio Brunello. As she pushed under the oleander – poisonous, Ma had told them all, over and over, don't even touch it – the dripping was there, louder. It was getting on her nerves, and – ugh. Something squelched underfoot, boggy, wet overrunning her sandals, mud between her toes. Damn. The torch swayed in her hand, and the feeble beam lit up the garden tap, in the back corner, set against the fence. Dripping. A puddle had formed at the base of the pipe. Roxana sighed; removing her sandals, she stepped gingerly around the water and turned the tap to close it tightly.

Tentatively she tested the only ordinary explanation out for size: Ma had been watering the plants. Well, she could ask, though she was fairly sure Ma had not watered anything since Dad's death, which was why half the terracotta pots contained only desiccated twigs.

Had the tap somehow loosened itself? It seemed unlikely, despite the regular fluctuations in water pressure. Or were the next-door neighbours, what, climbing over the fence and stealing water? But as Roxana tried hard to restrict herself to only the most innocuous possibilities, almost despite herself she raised the torch beam so that it shone weakly along the now damp leaf mould at the foot of the fence, nearly, but not quite, reaching the back gate.

What was that?

She kneeled, and the movement seemed to alter some connection in the torch because it blinked and faded, before strengthening again, suddenly too bright. Bright enough for her to see what it was that had caught her eye: some regular, familiar indentations in the damp soil.

Footprints.

They ran along under the fence, a walking pace, even weight distribution, Roxana would have said, as if she knew anything at all about the analysis of prints. *The police* – she considered them briefly, then dismissed the possibility. The police might know about footprints, although she wouldn't have credited any of the ones she'd come across with knowing more about anything than she did. They might have whole labs of technicians, but none of them would be sent out to investigate a nervous old woman's fear of strangers, the dark, loneliness.

The steps stopped, feet planted perhaps ten centimetres apart, the impressions deeper, as if he'd stood here a while.

He?

The footsteps were not large for a man's. But too big to be a woman's, too wide, too deeply set. A heavy woman with big feet? She could picture no such person; next door was a widow built like a bird. A woman Violetta resented, more experienced in her widowhood, not much heavier than her Persian cat, always pacing and hurrying herself into emaciation, never sitting still long enough to eat. Roxana sat back on her haunches in the warm damp, and shone the torch back towards the house. It was still ominously bright. It would die on her, any minute.

As her eyes adjusted, she could see the slatted rectangle of the *salotto*'s French doors, a square of light from the upstairs bathroom. A man could stand here and observe.

He'd gone closer to the house, this man with modestly sized feet: a couple more steps then he'd stopped again, and looked. He had called out to Ma, *I know you're in there, Signora Delfino.*

There was something about that phrase. Had Ma just – made that up, unconsciously? Given a voice to the man and his intentions, turned him into a bogeyman, repeated a line from a story to frighten children, *Little pig, little pig, let me come in?* Might he, after all, have been a perfectly innocent delivery man?

He had not come right up to the house; he had stopped. Something occurred to Roxana and she stood, quickly, and before the torch could expire, turned and took her own, hurried, smaller, lighter steps back to where she'd come, only a few metres to the left, to the fence, along the fence—

To the gate. Which was not locked and bolted, as she had last seen it, as it had been for as long as she could remember, but hung just ajar, crippled and askew with one hinge right off. And the casing that retained the bolt was barely hanging from screws torn out of the soft and rotten wood.

Don't tell Ma, was what ran through her head, as though she and her naughty brother were whispering together in the dark. It might have been an accident. But as she stared, Roxana took in the violence of it, the split and torn wood. This was no accident.

With a last flicker, the torch died.

CHAPTER ELEVEN

*D*AMN, THOUGHT SANDRO. *DAMN. The bank. I forgot to go to the bank.*

He was sitting at the kitchen table, immobile in the heat; he even wished they could turn off the low-hanging light in its stained-glass, *stile liberty* shade. The coloured glow through the glass seemed to be giving out heat.

It came to him as he followed Luisa's slow, deliberate movements around the kitchen, trying, as he seemed often to be doing, to interpret her. Luisa needed interpretation because she was in her way a master strategist, a Machiavelli. She didn't ask anything straight out, she checked the lie of the land. She talked to him over her shoulder as she fiddled with the peeling of an onion, about her own day.

'The shop was full, can you believe it? We had out the autumn collections, boots and sweaters, and people were buying them.' Shook her head in mystification. 'Forty degrees outside.' She chopped. Onion, carrot, celery, garlic. Parsley.

'He knows what he's doing, old Frollini,' said Sandro mildly. Frollini – not much older that Sandro if truth be told – Luisa's suave boss, was a bone of contention between them. Too fond of Luisa for Sandro's comfort, too smooth, too rich. 'The world's changing. People want to shop in August.'

'For ski jackets? For the dregs of last season's things in the sale? Dragging round a city when there are woods and rivers and seaside? It's not changing for the better.'

Sandro smiled to himself: she knew how to soothe him, with her indignation. Luisa could tell even with her back turned what kind of a day he'd had and the way he was this evening; she wouldn't stand in front of him in the doorway and say, *Well? Did you ask about a mortgage?*

And he'd even been in a bank, too. Not, he thought, that he would go to the Toscana Provinciale for money, not even if that clever, watchful girl in the glasses – what had been her name? – was the manager rather than just a *sportellista*. What was she doing in such a place?

With a wrench he tore himself away from his memory of the wary bank teller – Delfino, that was it, DELFINO Roxana on her little badge – unwilling, back to the matter in hand.

'I'm sorry, darling,' he said to Luisa's broad back, as she lit the gas under the chopped vegetables. 'I – it slipped my mind. The bank.' A battered fan stood on the counter beside her, wafting the scent of onions.

She washed her hands under the cold tap, rubbing them over and over, before she turned back to him.

'It's all right,' she said easily, and he saw her look quickly around the room, taking in the old melamine-fronted cabinets, the dent in the stainless-steel sink. It showed all the signs of having been thoroughly cleaned; getting home from work an hour before him, at six-thirty, she must have set to straight away. To reassure herself that, with a quick brush-up, this place wasn't so bad after all, they could stick it out?

Or perhaps the first step towards getting it spruced up for sale.

Probably both: that'd be like his little strategist, to kill two birds with one stone.

'Tough day?' she asked, sitting down and taking a sip of the drink he'd poured her, a glass of Crodino in which the ice had already melted to slivers; she tipped the glass from side to side, to hear them chink.

He nodded, hesitating. Not quite ready to tell it all. Then remembered: he'd done something right.

'I spoke to Giuli, though,' he said.

'And?' Luisa set her hands on her hips.

'And you were right, she's got a boyfriend, and it was him she went to the seaside with. Computer geek, by the sound of it. A technician.'

'Well,' said Luisa drily. 'That's better than – it might be.'

Better than nightclub bouncer or pimp or debt collector or homeless junkie, was what she meant. The choices Giuli had made in her previous life did not bear too much contemplation.

Sandro frowned. Lunch with Giuli seemed a long time ago, eclipsed by the memory of that battered body decaying in the gaseous heat of the ring road. He remembered her saying, *I know a bad guy when I see one.*

'Actually,' he said cautiously, 'I think we should – well, maybe not stay out of it completely, but at least – give her the benefit of the doubt. I think she knows what she's doing.'

Luisa gave him a long look. 'Fine,' she said at last, and he saw her struggle to say it. She sighed, said it again. 'Fine. You're probably right.'

'His name's Enzo,' he said. 'I think she'll bring him over, eventually. For inspection.'

'Right,' said Luisa, and he could see that for the moment, she had decided to be satisfied. 'So tell me,' she said. 'About the bad day. Did you find him?'

'Ah.' Sandro rubbed his eyes, suddenly exhausted, and smelled the day on his hands. Traces that stirred disquiet in him: aftershave and disinfectant, soot and car exhaust and latex gloves. Traces of the old life; him and Pietro shoulder to shoulder, looking down at human remains. 'Well, it's complicated.'

Luisa cocked her head, a gesture he knew of old, that meant, *So tell me.*

And he told her, leaving nothing out. As he described Brunello's wife, dignified in her crumpled linen shift, he saw Luisa's mouth twist. Whose side could you come down on, after all?

'Bring her here,' she said, getting to her feet, rubbing her back. She had grown stiff and sore listening to the story, and the air was rich with the scent of the meat sauce that had cooked while they talked. Luisa crossed to the window and leaned out, looking for a breath of air. 'Bring the girl here, after. I'll take the day off.'

*

The internet café off the wide expanse of the Piazza dell'Carmine was where they usually met, not a glamorous place but it suited Giuli fine. It was one of the things she liked about Enzo, that he didn't notice his surroundings, really. He would sit across the small table and just look at her while he talked, as if nothing else was there. Focused, that was Enzo.

He wasn't late – Enzo was never late. Giuli was early, because she simply felt like being alone a bit. Only ten minutes early, that would be plenty.

Anna Niescu, she had learned, was tougher than she looked. After Sandro had gone, she had stayed, silent, pressed against Giuli on the wide *loggia*, for ten minutes at least, and Giuli had felt how still she was, like an animal hiding from a predator, conserving her strength. And then, as though something had come to a conclusion, she had quite abruptly stood up.

Giuli had followed her, not daring to speak because anything might be the wrong thing to say. In the big, old-fashioned hotel kitchen – a dresser, a wide iron range, a big marble-topped table – she had followed helplessly as Anna wiped surfaces and put bread in a cloth bag, cheese in the fridge. Eventually Giuli had been allowed to put away the scoured pans waiting on the draining board and only because she had not been able to watch as Anna staggered under their weight and had physically removed them from her.

Then at eight Anna had said, 'I go to bed now.' As though she was still living out in the countryside with her *contadini*, and dusk was bedtime.

Giuli had followed her there, too, without being asked. Her room was at the end of a corridor of guests' rooms, and might have been mistaken for a cupboard, its door was so narrow; Giuli had to blink to believe that Anna had managed to slip through it herself. It had one small high window, a single bed, a wardrobe and a wooden chair. Looking at the single bed, Giuli had wondered – not for the first time since she'd met Anna Niescu, and uncomfortably – how she had conceived, this child with her little child's bed. And not so much how – because, she could almost hear Sandro saying wryly, *it would be in the usual way* – but where.

Anna had turned and seen her in the doorway behind her, but hadn't told her to go. She had taken something from under her pillow and gone out, through another door; there had been the brief sound of running water, and cautious, uncertain movements, as though once finding herself alone she had lost all sense of where she was. Giuli had sat down on the wooden chair and waited until Anna came back, in a cotton nightdress with faded flowers, a market-stall thing meant for a woman three times her age that made her look even younger. Without meeting Giuli's eye, she had got into bed.

For a long time neither of them had said anything. Moonlight had come through the long window and fallen on the old tile of the floor, turning the deep waxed red to black. Anna had lain quite still, curled on her side. It had taken her breathing a long time to slow, while Giuli listened. Trying not to think of what would be going through Anna's mind. And then, just as Giuli had thought sleep was overtaking the girl, she had given an awful start. Struggled up on one elbow, as desperately as if she had been drowning, pleading in incoherent half sentences. *No, no,* she had been saying. *No, no, don't go, don't.*

Putting out a hand to quiet her, Giuli had said, softly, 'Anna, shh. Anna.'

Anna had groped blindly for the hand and Giuli had seen from her face, blank in the moonlight, that she had not quite been awake. She'd wanted to say, it's all right, but it would have been a lie. So she had said, 'It's Giuli. I'm here.'

'Giuli,' Anna had repeated, first wonderingly, then with dull realization. She had lowered herself back on to the pillow, but held on to Giuli's hand.

'You've got your baby,' Giuli had said. 'Think of the baby.'

On her side and staring into the darkness Anna had moved her free hand down, across her belly, hesitantly, as though it was new to her, this weight she had been carrying around for eight months.

She had spoken, quietly. 'He said the nursery would be ready in time.'

Giuli had seen that the girl's eyes were open, and that something gleamed on her cheek. Love, she'd thought; Sandro had been right all along. What was I doing, believing in love? And rage had bubbled inside her, at Anna's man and his lying.

'He wouldn't have killed himself.' Anna's voice had not been defensive, or angry, but calm. 'I know he wouldn't. You didn't know him, none of you did. He was – like a boy, when he heard about the baby. He was so happy.'

Giuli had held still, keeping back her anger.

'Where was it?' she had asked softly. 'The apartment? The – the nursery?'

By way of distraction but also because it had niggled at her. Was this bank manager a man so wealthy he could set up another home? Would it be a mistress's penthouse, or would he park Anna, too naive to know any better, in a tenth-floor *monolocale* overlooking a trailer park? She'd said, *like a boy*; boy wasn't a bank manager. And all this talk of a pay rise coming his way? He was into something dodgy, one way or the other.

'I'll show you,' Anna had said, her voice drifting. 'I'll take you there.'

'You sleep,' Giuli had said.

'You could see the hills,' Anna had murmured. 'A beautiful view. Needed some work, he was going to do the work, just to make the nursery, that was all it needed. The bathroom had marble tiles and the bed had a blue cover. He couldn't find the light switch.'

She'd turned a little in the bed, and her grip on Giuli's hand had loosened.

Giuli had wondered if it was wrong to let her go to sleep, dreaming of this house in the hills that would never be. 'Yes,' she had said.

'You can go now,' Anna had said, faraway now. 'You can go, and I'll take you there in the morning. I remember the way.' Her eyes had drooped. 'I remember the way.'

The reception desk had been unattended as Giuli had passed on her way out; she'd found the Russian on the terrace under the *loggia*, smoking. Her eyes were blue as ice under black eyelashes, and she'd still looked angry.

'I'll come back in the morning for her,' Giuli had said.

She'd fished in her pockets for one of Sandro's cards; he'd put her mobile number on it when they had them reprinted at the beginning of the year. She'd held it out, and the Russian had taken it, in the same hand as the cigarette, held it disdainfully between thumb and little finger. She hadn't looked at it.

'Call either one of us, if she – well, if she needs us. If she wakes in the night, or anything.'

The Russian had looked at Giuli levelly. 'My name is Dasha,' she had said. 'I don't have card.'

Despite herself, Giuli had smiled; Dasha hadn't quite smiled back, but almost.

At the rickety lift in the corner of the room Giuli had turned. 'Did you meet him?'

'Him?' Still standing in the door to the *loggia*, Dasha had leaned back to stub out the cigarette on one of the terrace's ashtrays.

'The baby's father.' Giuli had watched her. 'I mean – he's real?' Stupid thing to say. What was this, the immaculate conception? But there was something unreal here.

'Real?' The Russian had looked almost amused. 'I suppose. Not meet him, no. Not an introduction. I see him in the street with her once or twice. Not ghost, if that is what you mean.' And she let out a surprising cackle. 'Not Holy Ghost.'

'He didn't mind being seen?' Giuli had turned right around to face the girl, and she'd been able to hear the lift cranking wheezily up behind her. Dasha had shrugged.

'Not so much, no. On Piazzale Michelangelo, out in open, sure. They were not hiding.'

There had been something in her eyes, though: something. She had shifted, looked away. Hiding something.

The internet café had fierce air-con, and now Giuli shivered, remembering. There was something not right about this, the married bank manager holding hands with his pregnant mistress on the Piazzale Michelangelo, among the thronging tourists. Was that it? Tourists were strangers, here today, gone tomorrow. Or because his wife was safely stowed at the seaside, along with most of his colleagues, no one to catch them? She got out her phone and texted Sandro, quickly. *Shd talk 2 Russian at hotel?*

But the case was closed, wasn't it? Give or take a few loose ends.

Enzo would be here soon, and Giuli was glad. She was hungry, all over again.

In the café's lurid red and green evening lighting, heads bowed intently over computer screens, a couple in a corner, she looked up and there he was, at the door, her sweetheart. She watched his face light up as he saw her; she checked her watch. Ten o'clock, bang on.

*

In her bedroom, Roxana lay very still and listened. This was the room she had slept in for her entire childhood – and now, it felt, most of her adult life too. She should feel safe here, if she felt it anywhere. She knew the sounds – the cicadas, the river, the distant roar of the motorway interchange. She even knew what it sounded like when someone broke through the downstairs bathroom window, and knew what to do. She wasn't stupid, but she wasn't neurotic, whatever Ma said. The trouble was, Ma had gone through her life thinking – knowing – that there was always someone else to deal with stuff like this. There had always been Dad, and now there was Roxana, and Roxana had no one.

A man would be coming out from Prato tomorrow evening to sort out the back gate. Some handyman-cum-locksmith, she'd been all through the Yellow Pages and hadn't been able to find one closer, not at nine at night in August.

Of course, she had had to wait until Violetta was asleep and snoring first; Ma had a bat's ear for panic. Roxana had come back in from the garden with the dead torch, pausing for a long moment on the veranda to collect herself, to put an expression of wry irritation on her face.

'Bloody thing,' she'd said, setting the torch down on the kitchen table. 'My fault, I should have bought batteries.'

Ma had looked at her oddly, as if she had decided to wipe the whole thing from her mind and didn't want to hear otherwise. 'Yes,' she had said, complacently, setting down a bowl of salad with tuna and sweetcorn. And that had been that: they'd eaten stolidly in the heat. Although when a car had backfired a couple of streets away, Ma had looked wild-eyed, just for a second.

'I'll make you a camomile,' Roxana had said, to hasten her to bed, and obediently she had padded upstairs. Roxana had heard the creak of the old fan coming on.

She could hear it now, whirring across the landing, and Ma's soft snore behind it. From somewhere on the slopes below the Certosa, the soft warning hoot of an owl.

She had made herself stay and listen long and hard. Was there someone there? She would not have let Ma think everything was well otherwise; she would, whatever her low opinion of their capabilities, have called the police and not a locksmith if she had had a single doubt. Wouldn't she?

But as she lay stiff in bed under the smooth sheet, she knew she was on full alert: all her senses straining. She had to switch them off, one by one; there were techniques she'd learned, an age ago, when studying for her final exams. Tense, then let go, each muscle, one after the other. The last to go were the fine muscles of the face. She could picture herself frowning fiercely in the dark, brows knitted. She ordered them to relax.

And she lay, her features smoothed out, perfectly still. But

Claudio Brunello was dead. Why?

All was not well, out there in the world. Along the dark highway into town, behind the shuttered glass of the bank, up on the hillside overlooking the sea where Brunello's kids were sleeping. It was all wrong.

There was no reason. Roxana had always believed Claudio Brunello to be a good man, a decent person. People like him did not die like this, suddenly, violently, bizarrely. Either she had been wrong about him or – something else was involved. There were things she didn't know yet, but she would find out, that was all. There were questions to ask Marisa, there were people she needed to find. Against all the odds, Roxana felt the relaxation technique begin to work. She let her mind drift, so as not to fight it.

And so she didn't recognize him, when his face appeared to her, just as she edged over the border between sleep and wakefulness, just an agglomeration of shade and light, like the image of Christ on the Turin Shroud, pale cheekbones and pools of dark for eyes. She didn't know him at first, and by the time she did, it was too late, and she was asleep.

*

On her bed in the moonlight, Anna Niescu came gradually upright, her small hands flat on either side of her belly. She breathed out, slowly, through a mouth set with some indeterminate effort. In the pale, flat light it was hard to tell whether she was awake or asleep as she looked around her, searching the room's shadowy corners for something, or someone. *Don't go*, she murmured. *Don't.*

CHAPTER TWELVE

Thursday

A T THE KITCHEN WINDOW, dressed only in undershorts at six-thirty in the morning, Sandro frowned down at the mobile, handed to him by Luisa.

He had heard her on the landline earlier, which was why he was out of bed.

'What on earth are you up to?' he'd said, padding into the *salotto*, cold as the grave in winter, clammy this morning, but a degree or two cooler, at least, than the bedroom. We should sleep in here, he thought, looking blearily around the good furniture, the shiny silk of the hard sofa and upholstered chairs. Like a dream half remembered, the slideshow image of a balcony and hills seen through a lopsided window came to him, and he had the impulse to junk all this, mirror, uncomfortable chairs, sideboard: the lot. Luisa stood by the small round polished table, her hand on the receiver she had just replaced.

'I'm calling in sick,' she said.

'At this hour?'

'There's an answering machine,' she said, and then he noticed the dark circles under her eyes.

'You're not really sick,' he said, fear ballooning inside him.

His wife folded her arms. 'I said I'd stay home today, didn't I?'

'You look wiped out,' he said. He could feel sweat between his shoulder blades.

And then Luisa sighed. 'I couldn't sleep,' she said. 'That's all.'

'That's all?' He didn't move, daring her to look away.

'Yes,' she said, and the trace of impatience calmed him. 'The heat, you know. And – what you told me. This girl. The father of her child.'

'Hell,' said Sandro, 'I should never have told you.'

He himself had slept for the first night in weeks: accumulated exhaustion, perhaps. Or having a job to do, again. It looked as if he'd managed somehow to shift the fallout directly to Luisa: his better half.

'That was stupid of me,' he said, properly contrite, and she let him put his arms around her briefly. He breathed in the musk smell of her sweat. When she pushed him away, she caught him smiling, foolishly.

Sandro shrugged under her gaze. And she clicked her tongue, turning for the door, but he could see she didn't mind, not too much.

'It's been pinging away,' she said, picking up the phone from the fruit bowl in the kitchen. 'That didn't help, during the night.'

He must have slept like a log. The phone was set to keep bleeping intermittently to let him know he hadn't read a message. He had no idea how to change it, just as he had no idea why it was on that setting in the first place. People got their children to sort stuff like that out – people like him did, anyway. Old farts. He'd ask Giuli.

He frowned down at the message. *Shd talk 2 Russian at hotel.* He had no idea what she was on about.

'Give it here,' said Luisa, reading his thoughts, or some of them. Deftly she moved her thumb over the screen, before giving it back.

'The message was from Giuli,' he said slowly.

'You're meeting her at the hotel,' said Luisa.

Right, thought Sandro, OK. That hotel. That Russian. And the grim day loomed ahead; he sat down at the kitchen table, weary already.

'Yes,' he said. 'She thinks I should talk to the receptionist there.' Perhaps she'd seen them together; but it was too late for all that now. He sighed.

Luisa set two glasses of water on the table and sat next to him. By the sink he could see the remains of the bottle of wine he'd drunk last night; he could feel it behind his eyes, too.

'Want me to come?' she asked.

The light was better in here and he could see that she was all right. She put out a bare arm; the soft skin above the elbow looked vulnerable to him, and for a second he wanted to put his face against it. 'You get some sleep,' he said.

'Rubbish,' said Luisa. 'Me, sleep in the day?'

He smiled at that. Luisa had never even taken a siesta, in all the time they'd been together. Not even when she'd been pregnant. Early to bed, early to rise, but no lying about while the sun was up.

Giuli smiled broadly when she saw it was both of them. They'd arranged to meet at a bar called Ricchi in Santo Spirito. There were barely half a dozen market stalls in the piazza, but the bar was busy enough, just because it was open. It would close next week, announced a sign on the door, until 1 September, but for the moment its metal tables were laid out under the square's dusty elms. A few old ladies sat out there, with hardly enough energy between them to gossip, but gamely trying all the same. Gossip being like coffee or wine: what was the point in breathing if you couldn't indulge in life's pleasures?

Ricchi didn't wait on its tables, so you didn't get charged extra to sit at them, and Giuli was parked in a corner, as far as she could get from the beady-eyed senior citizens.

Her bag on her knee, Luisa ran a finger over the unwiped tabletop, and with a roll of her eyes Giuli went inside to order.

'What?' said Luisa, defensively.

'Give them a break,' said Sandro, smiling. 'It's August. A public service to stay open at all. We can't all have your standards.'

It was because she wasn't working. Luisa got fidgety with nothing to do.

She looked around the square and Sandro saw her take in a big stall selling cheap clothing, Chinese-made, brought in through Osmannoro, where they all lived. The smiling, chunky Chinese girl manning it was exchanging fluent banter with a customer. Two aproned *contadini* dozing behind near-identical displays of oozing figs, knotted onions and ripe, misshapen tomatoes. A trestle with old bits of brassware: there were lampstands, candlesticks and ornate chandeliers.

'Not a bad spot,' Luisa conceded. Sandro knew she was thinking about the flat in Porta San Miniato, and how close it would be. 'Nor's San Ambrogio,' he said. Their own local market, much bigger, more bustling, with a covered meat and fish hall. Luisa pursed her lips.

The biggest pitch was allocated to a fruit and vegetable stall, selling more exotic imported items, olive oil, bottled water and greenhouse lettuce, as well as local produce. Liliana Granchi. Everyone knew purple-haired, handsome Liliana; knew her sullen daughter-in-law, her unruly grandsons, her co-workers on the stall who she sent running here and there with a sharp look. Her soft words were reserved for her little curly-headed poodle, sat perched on his cushion in an orange box. The stall had a pyramid of oranges, even in August.

'That's where they met,' said Sandro, nodding at the oranges. Giuli was at his elbow, with a tray, two cups of coffee, a *spremuta d'arancia*, and a cloth for the table. She set it down.

'Where?' said Luisa, seizing the cloth before Giuli could, and working it into the table's corners. When she'd done she set down the drinks.

'Buying oranges,' said Sandro, nodding at the stall. 'Last November.' He might have talked to Liliana, too, but events had overtaken him. Which reminded him. 'What was that about the Russian?' he asked, taking the mobile out of his pocket and feeling the smooth weight of it in his hand. 'The message you sent me.'

Luisa tutted just barely, at the memory of a broken night. She pushed the orange juice towards Giuli with a frown.

'I don't know,' Giuli replied, despondent. 'Too late now. It's just – well, she saw him. We only had that terrible image on the mobile, and she'd actually seen him.'

'Did you think he might not exist?' He spoke wryly, because they both knew there was evidence that Anna Niescu had had a lover. He felt a pang, at the thought of the big melon-belly, and what effect it might have on Luisa.

'Come on,' said Luisa, knowing what he was thinking. She drained her coffee. 'Let's get this over with.'

At the great wooden street door to the Loggiata, they squabbled, briefly. 'D'you think I – we should wait down here?' said Giuli nervously. 'Just you go up?'

Luisa took charge. 'We're all here now,' she said. 'I don't suppose she's going to be frightened by *us*, under the circumstances.'

And so up they all went, squeezed into the tiny lift. It was eight-thirty.

There was no sign of the Russian receptionist, just an impossibly ancient woman behind the desk, who looked at them with filmy eyes and an unfocused smile. To Sandro's surprise, Luisa immediately greeted her with respectful formality, asking after her health, commiserating over the heat.

Giuli and Sandro sat on hard chairs from the small collection in the corner that served as a foyer, and waited while Luisa talked, working her way around, with the right courtesies, to stating their business. They saw the old woman indicate the door to the *loggia*, Luisa bowing thanks, turning back towards them.

Sandro raised an eyebrow.

'Serafina Capponi. My mother knew her,' Luisa said, settling herself between them. 'She owns this place. She used to shop at Frollini, in the old days. I haven't seen her in years; I'd forgotten about her.'

'She doesn't look as if she's out and about much,' said Giuli.

'I thought they might be exploiting the girl,' he said in an undertone to Luisa.

Luisa frowned. 'I doubt that. It's a funny old place.' She looked around, at the wide foyer's odd combination of dusty magnificence and tat, a vast, gilded mirror set over a cheap veneer table. 'They're all in the same boat in this place, just lame ducks. Just limping along.'

'No children?' Luisa shook her head.

They all looked at the old lady at once then, all with the same thought. *And when she dies?* The Russian, Anna, the other staff, the handful of guests – they'd all be out on the street, while some distant cousins fought over the property. The hotel's owner smiled with vague benevolence at their faces turned towards her, her head almost imperceptibly nodding.

The door to the *loggia* opened and a slow-moving elderly couple emerged. Behind them was Anna Niescu, holding a tray, waiting patiently for them to move along. She saw the three visitors, and stopped.

Sandro watched Luisa's face, but she was too quick for him.

She was on her feet and hurrying, hurrying to get to the girl, and seizing the tray and its cups and saucers and stacked breadbaskets before Anna went over and it all went with her. Because she'd seen in an instant what he saw too late, that this – the sight of them, waiting with their anxious, knowing faces – was almost too much for Anna Niescu. She was close to collapse.

'I'm Sandro's wife,' said Luisa, taking the tray and passing it to Sandro, guiding the girl on to a rickety cane sofa while the old lady looked from them to the lift door in vague panic. 'It's all right.'

And there was something about Luisa – her voice, her solidity, her capable hands – that made it seem almost a possibility. Anna Niescu obediently sat.

'Are – are we all going?' Her eyes went from one of them to the next: at anxious Giuli, grave, unwavering Luisa. At Sandro.

'We didn't want you to feel alone,' he said, not looking at Luisa. 'As you haven't got – anyone.'

Anna didn't protest at that. But a little colour was coming back to her cheeks. 'That's nice of you,' she said. 'That's kind.'

'He's bringing you home with him, after,' said Luisa. 'To us. Until you feel – ready.'

'After,' repeated Anna, with diffuse terror.

Sandro took her hand. 'What do you want?' he asked gently. 'Do you think you'd like us all to come?'

It only occurred to him fractionally too late that he was putting more stress on her, obliging her to make choices. Anna looked at them again: Giuli, Luisa, Sandro. He could see a different variation of anguish in each woman's face.

'You,' she said, stopping at Sandro. 'Just you.'

'Good,' he said, getting to his feet, showing nothing of the sudden terror he felt himself. There was a pinpoint flush on Giuli's cheeks, the shame of a child not chosen at school.

It was nine o'clock. Pietro had said he'd be waiting for them at the pathology lab from nine-thirty. The body had been moved there from the morgue, now that the official identification had been made.

'Do you have a bag?' he asked Anna, refusing to hurry her. 'You go and get your bag. Perhaps a few overnight things, just in case.'

When she was gone, Luisa turned on him. 'You bring her straight back to me,' she said, in an agony of frustration. 'For heaven's sake. Anything could happen. In her condition.'

Giuli was frowning hard. 'All right, Giuli?' he asked.

'It's all wrong,' she burst out. 'It's not fair. I thought you'd find him – I told her you'd find him, and you did, only he's dead. It's like a horrible trick. Why should it be him? You don't know it's him.'

'That's what we're going to find out,' said Sandro, his heart like a stone in his chest. 'That's why I've got to take her.'

Giuli subsided, all the fight gone. 'She was talking, last night. About the place he'd made for her, she said. Like a – a nest, he'd built for her. A view of the hills, she said. Where's she going to live now?'

'I don't know,' said Sandro, feeling Luisa's eyes on him. He knew she was wondering whether they'd have their own view of the hills, from that rusted balcony in the Oltrarno. He thought of something.

'Look, you're right,' he said, lifting his battered briefcase, rummaging in it. It was just a distraction, but who knew? They didn't know anything, really. 'It won't do any harm – to know more about him. It might help her. Even now he's—' And he looked quickly across at the door through which Anna had disappeared. 'Even if he's dead.' He found it: the paper with the address she'd given him. He thrust it at them, and it was Luisa who took it.

'This is it. The apartment's address.'

He saw Luisa frown down at it. Why hadn't he gone straight there? He couldn't remember, only that he'd had his doubts, straight off, about this dream home of theirs. Brunello had taken Anna there only that one time. She'd gone back looking for him when he disappeared, but she hadn't got in.

'What do you want me to do?' asked Giuli slowly. Slowly, her eyes on Luisa.

'I've got the day off,' said Luisa impatiently. 'I'm not going home to twiddle my thumbs.'

'Us, then,' said Giuli, and her eyes were almost bright now. 'What shall we do?'

The door opened in the corner of the room, and turning his head Sandro saw Anna edging through it, encumbered by a small holdall. He got to his feet.

'Well,' he said quickly, 'just go to the apartment, ask a few questions, neighbours, porter if there is one. Look around, see whether anyone knows anything about the man there. Why he might have – done what he did?' He frowned. 'If maybe he was in any trouble. You might even get inside the place.'

Sandro's suggestion had been just to keep them busy, stop them worrying. But then, as he turned to help Anna with her bag, Sandro found his own curiosity stir as he thought about what they might find. And as they stood on the doorstep, Luisa grumbling that he should have brought the car, Sandro responding automatically that there wouldn't be any parking over there and what was wrong with taxis, Anna standing small and quiet between them and thinking God knew what, his curiosity hardened into something else.

Because the family home – the big comfortable apartment that he imagined Claudio Brunello inhabited with his handsome, sensible wife and two children – Sandro knew now that it would hold no secrets, even supposing he had the brass neck and cold ambition to barge in on Irene Brunello in her grief and ask to look around. It was the wife's territory: she went into its corners with her brushes and dusters, she emptied its drawers and its pockets. But the place that Claudio Brunello had bought, or rented, or borrowed, furnished or otherwise, with its nursery being worked on, its neighbours, its views: it seemed to Sandro that *that* might be the place, the place where you'd find answers.

The taxi appeared, edging around the double-parked corner with difficulty, and Sandro had to raise an arm to advertise their presence.

Answers? To what? And quite suddenly it came to Sandro that he didn't believe that Claudio Brunello had committed suicide. Not for a moment.

CHAPTER THIRTEEN

ROXANA WAS EARLY, BUT Marisa Goldman was earlier.
More surprisingly, so was Val. He was in Claudio's office, and two policemen were talking to him.

Marisa came out of her office when she heard Roxana pass through the security doors, and standing in the doorway, she seemed frightened. Pale under the tan, and there were details – tiny things, a crease in the silk shirt, no earrings, a ragged nail on one hand – that if you knew Marisa, gave her away. Because Marisa was always perfect. She'd broken her arm in three places a year ago, riding pillion on her boyfriend's motorbike, and Roxana had heard that when she'd come round from the operation the first thing she'd done was to ask for her make-up bag and her earrings.

'You're next,' she said, turning her head to follow Roxana's gaze with her eyes. 'They've talked to me already.'

Roxana set down her bag: she could see one police officer, leaning forward, hands steepled on the desk, sitting where Claudio would have sat. Late fifties, bags under his eyes. The other she could only see in profile, a younger man with a crew cut, staring from one face to another with dogged intensity. Val had his back to them: he looked like a small boy, sitting very still. As she watched, he nodded, and she could see the tanned back of his neck above the crisp shirt.

Roxana turned back to Marisa, and was shocked all over again.

'Have you been here all night?' she said, aghast. 'You look – um—' She stopped. *You look terrible.* 'What did they ask you?'

Marisa was staring, distant. 'They asked how he had been, that sort of thing. Had there been any unusual stress, had he any reason to – to— ' She faltered, ashen. 'I don't suppose they want us to – to confer,' she said. 'I'm sure they'll ask you what they asked me, and then you'll know.'

'Right.'

'And that's just the beginning,' said Marisa, with what might almost have been grim satisfaction. 'The Guardia di Finanza's called.' The force that policed financial crime. Roxana swallowed: Marisa continued. 'They'll be in when this lot are gone.' She looked at her watch. 'And the manager of another branch to – to liaise with them.'

'What branch?' asked Roxana, curiosity getting the better of her.

'Giorgio Viola, from Sant'Angelo,' said Marisa shortly.

Sant'Angelo: Roxana had been seconded to that branch briefly, just after she started with the bank. Viola: vaguely she recalled a sad, fat man. That's probably him, judging from Marisa's pursed lips and expression of distaste.

'They're closing him down, aren't they?' said Roxana.

'Yes,' said Marisa, rubbing her eyes with a slim hand. 'I believe so.'

'Right,' said Roxana, 'I'll look forward to that, then.'

Looking down her long nose, Marisa seemed at last to focus on Roxana, and her expression. 'I shouldn't worry, Roxana,' she said flatly, 'I mean, they're hardly going to take you for anyone significant, are they? It's not that, anyway, they were perfectly –

perfectly civilized.' Her dismissive tone wasn't entirely convincing. 'I'm – well. It's all been rather stressful.'

'Yes,' said Roxana, startled by any admission of weakness at all, conciliatory. 'Yes, of course, you were – he was – I mean, you knew him very well. Of course.' She could hear herself, sounding like her mother, once upon a time. *There, there.*

The tone was not lost on Marisa: she drew herself up. 'Oh, for God's sake,' she said. 'She's staying with me.' And Roxana got a glimpse of how she'd look when she was old. Grim-faced and gaunt. 'Irene Brunello's at my place. I – we didn't get much sleep.'

Roxana stared. 'Maybe you should take the day off,' she said slowly. 'I mean – you were on holiday anyway, weren't you? We can manage.'

'No,' said Marisa quickly. '*No.*'

Maybe Marisa *had* been having an affair with him; had she and his widow sat up all night, thrashing it out? Maybe she was the woman – but no. The woman who'd phoned was Irene Brunello. Was there another woman, who had hired the private detective? Roxana's head ached with trying to make sense of it, and with the undertow of panic that had woken her at four. Ma, and intruders, and whether anything was safe any more.

'How is she?' Roxana ventured. Then thought about it, the little family smiling in the photograph on Brunello's shelf: stupid question. 'She must be in a terrible state. What about the children?'

Marisa let out a shaky exhalation. 'She didn't stop crying all night. I could hear her. She didn't want to go back to them, she said, back to the children, till she'd got it out of her system. They're with her mother.'

There was a pause, during which Roxana thought about the children, in their happy ignorance, playing on the beach. She could not have guessed what Marisa was thinking.

'She asked if she could stay with me.' Roxana stared – she couldn't imagine Marisa providing comfort. It might be because after his wife, Marisa had known him best – God knows. The idea that Claudio and Marisa might have had an affair grew. Marisa went on. 'What could I do? I couldn't say no.' She moved her head to and fro as if in pain. 'Paolo's stayed on the yacht. I mean, if he was here, it would be different – but I couldn't say no, could I?' Pleading, her eyes met Roxana's. Was she expected to answer?

Irene Brunello would have been better off in Galluzzo, squeezed between Ma and her at the table, prowlers or no prowlers, was all Roxana could think. She'd seen photos – on the iPhone, Marisa showing off their new interior decorator – of her superior's big, cool marble-lined apartment overlooking the city, with gardeners, maids, not a stick of furniture that cost under a thousand euros and none of it comfortable.

'I didn't know you two were even – close,' she said cautiously.

'No,' said Marisa, looking at a point somewhere over Roxana's shoulder. 'She – I don't know. I have the feeling she – she wants something from me.' She shifted her gaze reluctantly to look directly at Roxana.

'Wants something?'

'I think the grief is making her imagine things. I think she thinks I know something. Some explanation of – what has happened.'

'They still think he killed himself? Why would you know anything about that?'

The struggle for patrician reserve on Marisa Goldman's fine-featured face was visible. *Why*, she was asking herself, *why must I talk about this?* The police had made her talk about it, hadn't they, aristocrat or not? It seemed to Roxana that Irene Brunello wanted to stay with Marisa because she'd been her husband's other woman, either professionally, or something else – who knows how grief can hit; you might even find yourself reaching out to Marisa Goldman. 'Do you know anything?' Roxana asked, cautiously. 'Were you and he – was there anything between you?' It would explain the extremity of Marisa's reaction.

'What?' Marisa looked horrified. 'Do you think that's what she thinks?'

'Well,' Roxana spread her hands, trying not to shrug. 'What else?'

Marisa passed a hand over her forehead, and her hair – expensive, tawny, usually not a strand out of place – was ruffled by the unguarded movement, briefly giving her the appearance of a disturbed person. 'For God's sake,' she said. 'What if Paolo hears about this?'

'So you were? Having an affair?'

Would her billionaire kick her out? Marisa, homeless: she could always go back to her mother in Turin. Roxana couldn't be even a tiny bit gleeful. It was all too grim.

'I was *not*,' said Marisa, turning on her. 'No, no, no. That is *not* what I meant. He and I never, ever – there was nothing.'

So all she was worried about was that there should even be such a rumour, was it? Roxana didn't know what to think. If something had ever happened – well. He was too much of a family man not to have regretted it pretty quickly. Expressionless, Roxana stared at her boss, feeling that things had shifted, somehow. That if she were a different person, this might be her chance, to seize power, or at least to take a step towards it.

Behind them in Claudio's office there was a scraping, the sound of chairs pushed back. The clock said eight: they should have opened ten minutes ago. Everything was going to pot.

'We should open up,' Roxana said.

Marisa stared at her uncomprehending, then her expression cleared. 'Yes,' she said. 'Well, I can do that.'

'There's the cash delivery to receive,' Roxana said. 'It should come in fifteen minutes or so, and the ATM's been playing up.'

Marisa's expression hardened, as if she suspected Roxana of twisting the knife. Had she ever had to do anything so menial as signing off a cash delivery?

Beside them, the door opened to Claudio's office and out came Valentino, looking subdued. Nothing like an interview with police officers to help you grow up, Roxana supposed. She smiled tentatively and, clearly anxious, he stared back at her for a long moment. Claudio was dead: it still hadn't sunk in, not for any of them.

'Miss Delfino?'

Roxana straightened, held out a hand.

The older policeman regarded her levelly, unsmiling. 'Might we have a few moments?'

She sat where Valentino had sat, the seat still warm. The crew-cut younger man was on her left, watching her intently, the baggy-eyed policeman across the desk. He appeared to be exhausted. Roxana remembered that she'd wanted to be a police officer once, when she was still a child, as a result of some TV show with female detectives. She hadn't imagined it would be about telling people someone they loved was dead, and not being able to sleep for what you'd seen. But she didn't know whether she felt relieved she'd gone into banking instead.

The older policeman explained in a soft monotone why they were there, as if she didn't know. She gazed at him earnestly, wanting to be helpful.

'There'd been nothing unusual,' she said. 'There was the talk of being bought by the Banca d'Italia a couple of months ago, six months, that made him anxious, made us all anxious but then it blew over. He loved this place.' She realized it was true only as she spoke, and she felt her eyes burn. 'We stayed independent.

It's not the – the highest-flying bank in the world. But he knew his customers, and his staff. He looked after us all.'

Her eyes dropped to her lap. He was the reason she was still there, she wanted to say, even when she shouldn't be: that, too, came to Roxana for the first time. Loyalty, just like her and Ma, a double-edged sword. And now? She could leave.

'Right.'

She thought something softened behind the old policeman's eyes. Beside her the younger man was checking his watch, trying to catch his superior's eye. The older man didn't seem to see.

'Saturday,' he said, thoughtfully.

'Saturday?'

'It seems that on Saturday morning someone telephoned Claudio Brunello at the seaside. And shortly afterwards he came back into the city.'

'Right.'

The day after leaving for his holiday, he had come back. Roxana frowned.

'That surprises you?'

'His holidays were sacrosanct. We weren't even allowed to call him.'

'So the telephone call didn't come from here?' The policeman raised his head, just a fraction, to look beyond her, through the glass and into the bank. 'No one phoned him, on Saturday morning?'

Roxana shook her head, uncertain. 'I didn't. And I'm pretty sure Valentino didn't. Saturday's a short working day and it was busy. A lot of small traders cashing up before the holiday, I suppose. We didn't take a break, not even for a coffee. Valentino sits a metre away from me. There's no signal on the mobile in here, which the bank's fairly pleased about. No time-wasting.' She frowned, trying to think. Something – had there been something? A call? No, she was mixing the days up. That was Tuesday, when a woman phoned for Claudio. 'And there was nothing to call him about, anyway. Nothing out of the ordinary.'

'And Miss Goldman?'

'Marisa?' Roxana didn't understand. 'Marisa wasn't here. She was on some boat somewhere, with her boyfriend.'

'Yes, that's right,' said the policeman. But there was something about the way he said it.

'She went off Thursday night.' Roxana spoke earnestly, as if trying to convince him. 'She was meeting her boyfriend – Paolo he's called – at Piombino or somewhere.'

'Yes. That's what she told us.'

Roxana sat back in her chair, trying to work him out. Marisa must have really rubbed him up the wrong way.

'So.' The weary-looking policeman steepled his fingers again. 'Saturday. You closed up at one.' The younger man shifted in his chair again. 'And afterwards?'

He spoke almost as if he were making conversation. And how did you spend your holidays? Even as she told him – she'd done ten quick lengths at the public pool surrounded by screaming kids, if he must know, before she went home. Then she'd gone to the supermarket, vacuumed the house – all she could think was, why do they want to know? Did they ask Val, did they ask Marisa, how they spent their Saturday afternoons? Schmoozing at the rowing club, drinking cocktails, choosing from a selection of bikinis? No supermarket shopping and housework for them.

'Your colleague – Valentino.' So they had asked him. 'He says you left together, at lunchtime on Saturday?'

'He went to the rowing club. He was wearing his kit.' There was no need for Val to put on that singlet, the one that showed off his biceps, but he had.

'Yes,' said the policeman with the ghost of a smile. 'Well, I'm sure the club will confirm that.'

It wasn't an accident. They thought he'd committed suicide. Was that a crime? Did it require proof, and witnesses? Roxana supposed it did.

And then abruptly it was all over, and Marisa was showing the two police officers out, hurrying them through the still-empty bank, looking tensely around as Roxana watched, hugging herself fiercely. Val was staring from his workstation behind the screen.

'Jesus,' he said as she slid in beside him. 'It's serious, isn't it?'

'Yup,' said Roxana, booting up her screen. She felt suddenly exhausted.

And then it dawned on her: this could be it. The bank – well, she could see it in the policeman's eyes. Struggling to survive as it was, barely fighting off a takeover. This could be the nail in its coffin. First policemen, then the Guardia di Finanza.

The door opened and old Signora Martelli came in, dragging her shopping trolley behind her. 'You,' she said, shaking her finger at Val, already fumbling in her bulging handbag.

'I wish it was all over,' said Val, looking away from the old woman.

'Me, too,' Roxana said.

*

'Are you all right?' asked Giuli. Her eyes were fixed anxiously towards Luisa as they stood on the bleached and empty pavement. They were outside the address written on the piece of paper Sandro had given them. Luisa gave the girl a gimlet stare. 'Giuli,' she said, with barely concealed impatience, 'I didn't sleep much last night. It's nearly forty degrees and I can't get the sight of that poor girl out of my head. I don't suppose you're all right, either.'

And in fact Giuli didn't look that good to Luisa. The cheap briefcase she had brought with her seemed to be weighing her down; her tan was peeling and underneath it her narrow little face was pale and beaded with sweat. 'Not you too,' Giuli said. And Luisa smiled. Allowing herself to forget that it was she who'd set Sandro on to Giuli.

They hadn't mentioned the boyfriend yet. After the sight of Anna Niescu, Luisa had just thought, life's too short. There are worse things than Giuli falling in love.

They'd come out on the bus, one of the small electric ones without air-conditioning; them and a mountainously wheezing old man in a string vest who, Luisa had worried, might be making his own last ride. He'd still been sitting there when they got off, taking tiny breaths and mopping his forehead. But if they thought the bus was hot, stepping out of it was like walking into the Sahara. As Luisa stood on the pavement in the insufficient shade of a spindly cherry tree and watched the bus disappear off down the Viale Europa towards Firenze Sud and the distant hills beyond, she wondered whether that was perhaps the old man's strategy. Perhaps he was just going to ride around until dusk.

They had walked very slowly away from the *viale* and, keeping to the shady side of the street, in among the big apartment buildings, squares of high-maintenance garden courtyard dividing them. This was not a cheap part of town, but Luisa didn't feel particularly at ease. It wasn't, she couldn't quite prevent herself from thinking, like San Niccolo: these blocks were solid and luxurious, no rusting balconies here, but it was lacking something essential.

Luisa looked up at the flowers tumbling down the white concrete, hibiscus and plumbago, purple and scarlet and pale blue; it was all very nice. But none of these people had been born here, had they? These buildings were twenty, thirty years old, maximum. With an uncharacteristic flush of sentiment Luisa thought of Santa Croce, of the old lady opposite them, ninety if she was a day, making her doddery way down the street to the market, six days a week. In Santa Croce there were people – herself among them – who hadn't moved more than five hundred metres their whole lives.

Giuli gestured them across the street, into the sun, to a metal gate with an entry phone at the foot of a twelve-storey block. 'This is it,' she said, coming to a halt.

And Luisa had felt a little thump of panic: was this what she really wanted? San Niccolo was only a couple of kilometres away – but still. And it was her expression that had prompted Giuli's concern.

'We're a pair, aren't we?' Luisa said. Hardly anyone's idea of private detectives, she and Giuli, nagging each other about looking peaky. 'Give me that.' She put out a hand for the paper and frowned down at it. 'Yes, this is it.'

Via Lazaretto 13. Apartment nine, third floor. Luisa was not superstitious at all, ever. But *lazaretto* meant plague hospital, and the significance of the number thirteen, even if you didn't believe in anything at all, couldn't be avoided. And what were they doing here, anyway? Poking about in Claudio Brunello's double life, just to cause Anna Niescu more misery.

There was the solid-looking metal fence, a metre and a half high, the gate with its entryphone, a small, well-kept strip of shrubbery, a wide, smoked-glass door beyond it. From somewhere out of sight came the sound of a masonry hammer, battering rhythmically. Builders: the soundtrack to August.

On the gate there was a numberpad for punching in an entry code, but no code on the piece of paper Anna had given Sandro. Had Brunello never given it to her? Had she not even got past the gate, when she'd come here looking for him? There was a bell, marked *Portiere*. Luisa pressed it and, when nothing happened, pressed it again, holding her finger down five, ten seconds.

Still nothing.

Giuli made a sound of impatience. 'He's probably at the seaside, too,' she said.

They looked up at the façade, wondering whether anyone was at home at all. There were signs of life, here and there: some washing hanging out on a balcony about halfway up, a little dog's paws and snout peering over a balustrade lower down.

And then, as if by some miracle, someone – a youngish man in a suit – brushed past them, swiftly stabbed at the keypad and was through the gate without a word or a backward glance. For a second they gawped, then just in time Giuli put out a hand to stop the gate, and they were inside – inside the garden at least. Ahead, the young man, indifferent to their presence, was through the smoked-glass door before they could catch up with him. The door clicked solidly shut as they reached it.

'Bastard,' muttered Giuli. 'Didn't even look round.'

There was another bell for the porter here, and Luisa pressed it, without conviction. This time she could hear a tinny ring behind the glass, but there was still no response. And then from behind them someone said, in a deep, cigarette-roughened voice, 'Don't bother. He starts on brandy at eleven.'

A weather-beaten woman as wide as she was short – a metre twenty, at Luisa's guess, and sixty or so years old – was behind them on the path, pulling a shopping trolley, a cigarette stuck between her lips, sizing them up unashamedly – and why not? – through smoke-narrowed eyes. As they stared back at her, she looked up and called a gruff endearment, and the little dog began to yelp excitedly in response, straining to see further over his balcony.

'He yours?' asked Luisa.

'No,' said the woman shortly. 'If he was mine I'd take him out for a walk, now and again.'

'Do you live here?'

'Who wants to know?'

Luisa held out a hand. 'Luisa Cellini,' she said. And seeing the woman's eyes shift to Giuli, 'And this is Giulietta Sarto.' She took a deep breath. 'We're trying to trace someone. This is the address we've got for him.' She held out the piece of paper.

Calculation crept into the woman's stolid expression. 'Expectant father, is he?' she said, and Luisa's eyes widened. The woman smiled, just faintly. 'Someone said, there was a pregnant woman hanging on that gate for an hour, a couple of days ago.'

'And no one let her in?'

The woman grunted. 'I'm Giovanna,' she said. 'Baldini. Fourth floor. People – not me, mind, but perhaps you'd worked that out – people keep themselves to themselves out here. I wasn't there – I might have let her in, might not. But I'd have asked her what she wanted, that's for sure. Only I wasn't here. I was out at San Lorenzo for a few days. Cooler out there.' She folded her arms across her broad chest. 'All right?'

'All right,' said Luisa warily. 'So you didn't see the girl. You wouldn't have – recognized her. From a previous visit?' Giovanna Baldini was obviously someone who kept her eyes open, but it was best to proceed with caution.

The woman regarded her. She shook her head. 'I haven't seen any pregnant women calling here. Who was she looking for, then? Who's the father?' She looked through the smoked-glass door after the young suited man, long gone by now. 'Not him. Sixth floor, him. Not to mention gay.'

Luisa shifted her gaze discreetly to the bell-pushes beside the door, each with its own nameplate. There were something like thirty of them, and at first glance she saw no Brunello.

'Well?' said Giovanna Baldini, amused. 'Found him?'

'He's called Claudio Josef Brunello,' said Giuli curtly, clearly not interested in dragging this out.

'Never heard of him,' said Giovanna Baldini promptly. 'But then people do come and go. Some of these nameplates are ten years out of date. Did you say third floor?'

'Can you let us in?' said Giuli.

Luisa began to shake her head at the girl but then Giovanna Baldini laughed abruptly. 'Impatient, huh?' she said. 'I'll let you in, but that's it, you're on your own. See if you can get any sense out of our estimable concierge.'

She fished a key out of her shorts pocket and pushed open the door. As they went through, Luisa paused to study the panel of bell-pushes again. 'How does this system work, then?' she asked. The flats were numbered, but Anna Niescu had written no number on the piece of paper, just as she had no code.

Giovanna Baldini was patient. 'Four flats per floor. Nothing on the ground but the concierge, first is one to four, second five to eight, third nine to twelve. And so on. You get that?'

'I get that,' said Luisa, 'yes.' She scanned the names against apartments nine, ten, eleven, twelve. Names faded and stuck over, but no Brunello.

'Well?' With the woman's face up close, there was suddenly something familiar about Giovanna Baldini. The tiny gold hoop earrings, each with a garnet. 'I was at school with you,' Luisa said, studying the names of the third-floor apartment owners. No Brunello. 'In the Via Colonna. 1961?'

A faint smile appeared on the weatherbeaten face, the ghost of a girl behind it. 'You weren't Cellini then,' she said.

'Venturelli,' supplied Luisa, staring: they might be everywhere, the kids she was at school with, mightn't they? Become invisible with age: you'd have to get right next to them to see any trace of what they once were. And Giovanna Baldini nodded.

'Venturelli. You married a policeman, I heard,' she said. 'Straight out of school.'

'Can we get on with this?' said Giuli with gathering impatience, from the polished marble interior of the dim hallway.

And Giovanna Baldini seemed to take the words as her cue because quite suddenly she had slipped between them and was off, hauling her shopping trolley up the stairs. She paused only when she'd reached the landing, opened her mouth and said, 'Four five nine one. The entry code outside.' And she nodded back down towards a shadowy corridor that led off the hallway, rounded the corner and was gone.

As the rattle of the trolley receded, outside the scuffed doorway at the end of the corridor, Luisa and Giuli looked at each other. Whatever lay behind the door wasn't an alluring prospect.

Luisa rang the bell, a long peal. Then rapped, very sharply, on the wood, barking her knuckles. 'Hello?' she said, in her very sharpest tones. 'Hello there. I need help. Concierge?' She saw a faint smile on Giuli's face. '*Portiere!*' she bellowed.

And finally, there was the sound of slow footsteps, and the door opened.

Concierge was a grand name for it: the man who stood in the doorway – unshaven, balding, in a brown cotton overall half unbuttoned to reveal a grubby vest – was more what Luisa would have called a janitor.

The man made no move to admit them to his rooms, but stood in the doorway, lumpen and immovable. 'What's this all about?' he said, surly. 'All this racket.' He smelled strongly of sweat and cheap spirit. Giovanna Baldini's account of the man was accurate, so far.

He let Luisa talk for some time, listening with a vaguely contemptuous smile as she produced an explanation of their presence in her softest and most reasonable voice. She could smell the staleness of the room behind him, as the door stayed open: the smell of a man unloved and alone. At her side Giuli had a hand covering her mouth and nose; Luisa could feel her itching to take the man by the collar and threaten him, and hoped she would keep her cool.

The porter let her finish, still smiling. 'I cannot give away details of our residents' private circumstances,' he said with a drunk's heavy precision.

'How much?' said Giuli. 'Twenty?'

Luisa saw greed chasing false indignation off the man's face. 'Well,' she said, 'I can see that you might need some – compensation.' She tried not to show her disgust. Was this how Sandro would deal with the man?

'Twenty euros?' he said. 'Hardly.'

Luisa took the coin purse from her pocket; she'd put a few notes in there for the dry cleaning and hoped they weren't fives. Thirty. She handed them to the man, trying to suppress the sinking of her heart as she understood there'd be no repayment of expenses on this job. Anna Niescu probably lived for a week on thirty euros.

But the dry cleaners would probably be closed, anyway. August: hateful month.

The porter still made no move to admit them. 'So what exactly is it you want to know?' he asked, leaning against the doorframe, insultingly at ease.

Giuli opened the briefcase against her knee and brought out a sheet of paper on which a blown-up, pixellated photograph appeared, of Anna Niescu and a man: his face blurred, his body language uneasy. She held it in front of the porter's eyes. Luisa felt a pang of pity at Giuli's determination, her readiness to work, the briefcase whose stitching was already fraying.

'This man,' Giuli said earnestly. 'We – have reason to believe he was renting an apartment on the third floor. Renovating it.'

The concierge took the paper and pretended to scrutinize it. Then snorted. 'His own mother couldn't identify the man from this,' he said. Luisa saw his gaze linger just fractionally on Anna's beaming face, then he shoved the paper back towards Giuli.

'What about her?' Luisa said quickly.

'Never seen either of them before,' said the porter, folding his arms.

'So who does live on the third floor?' said Giuli.

Good girl, thought Luisa. Only then, from her handbag, her phone began to ring. The porter looked on with malicious amusement as she scrabbled to find it. Luisa saw it was Sandro and, not even knowing if it was what she'd meant to do, cut him off.

'Smithson, Grasso, Martelli, de – de something or other,' recited Giuli, ending a little lamely.

'That doesn't mean anything,' said the porter. 'Half the time people don't bother to change the nameplates.'

'Call yourself a porter?' said Luisa. 'You mean you don't know who's up there?' A mistake, she thought almost immediately, but it turned out she was wrong. The porter drew himself up.

'Smithson's long gone, he worked for the British Council,' he said, spite making him sound almost sober. 'They use the flat for visiting artistic types. The last one left two days ago. De Tedesco is a Torinese comes here for business once a month, there've been ten or so tenants since the original Martelli, ditto Grasso, currently – respectively – a fashionable young couple abroad since last September, and an old bitch with a nasty little dog.'

The little dog Giovanna Baldini had been blowing kisses to. Luisa wished she'd followed Giovanna up those stairs instead of standing here inhaling the porter's stink of unwashed clothes and booze.

'Right,' said Giuli with relief. 'Well, that's something,' fumbling in the briefcase for God knew what else. Although she didn't get time to find it.

'Good,' said the porter. 'Because it's all you're getting.' And lurching round, he turned his back on them and slammed the door.

Luisa's phone began to ring again.

'Hold on,' pleaded Giuli, cupping her hands to the closed door. 'Hold on. Which apartment faces the hills?' There was a kick against the door from inside and Giuli stepped back.

Luisa retrieved the phone and this time managed to answer it.

'*Caro*,' she said, and her heart sank as she remembered where he was and what he was doing. 'How is she? Is she all right?'

Sandro's voice was high-pitched but intermittent, and she moved back down the corridor, towards the light.

'Say that again,' she said. 'What is it? What's wrong?' She was at the smoked-glass front door now and she pushed it open, wanting to get out, even into the scalding air. Wanting to get to the light.

Holding the door open, Luisa looked up, looking for the hills as she tried to make sense of the snatches of Sandro's voice. The builder's banging had stopped, thank God. The apartments with a view of the hills would be around the other side of the building and out of sight, at right angles to the balcony where the little dog's paws and snout were still visible. With some instinct for the smallest movement below it, the animal barked, questioningly, just once.

Leaning out, one foot keeping the door open, and Giuli coming towards her from the gloom of the hallway, something about her angle brought her into a clear line with some transmitter or other, no doubt up in those very hills, and Sandro's voice was abruptly as clear as a bell, midway through a sentence.

'... no idea what the hell's going on, now,' he said.

'Say that again,' she said. 'What's happened?'

'I said, this has thrown everything,' said Sandro. 'It's crazy. I practically had to pick her up off the floor, poor kid.' He paused, and she heard exhaustion in the silence. 'Look,' he said. 'I'll have to bring her back with me. Once we've – well, soon. She really needs looking after – I'm worried she might— '

'Hold on,' said Luisa, 'I don't understand.' Her back was aching from the position she was having to maintain, half in, half out of the building. 'What's thrown everything?'

There was a silence, and into it Sandro spoke quietly. 'It's not him,' he said.

'Not him?'

'The body. She says, it's not him.'

And as if on cue, overhead the dog's shrill and desperate yapping began again.

CHAPTER FOURTEEN

THEY WERE SITTING IN someone's office, at the pathology lab, which was where the body had come from the morgue. There were no visitors' rooms here, not really; it wasn't a place for the general public. The room was untidy, with an overstuffed in tray and a dirty coffee cup on the desk, as though it had been abruptly vacated for them.

It was the waiting that had raised Sandro's heart rate, more than the final shock. The waiting and the watching. She looked pale enough now, but while they had waited – forty-five long minutes – to view the body, as he had watched her Sandro had feared for Anna Niescu's health. She had been so silent and staring and blank, her breathing shallow with apprehension. It was as if she had gone into suspended animation, until she received the answer to this one question.

And when at last someone had come – a woman in operating scrubs, mask slung around her neck and a plastic bonnet – and told them to follow her, Sandro had been startled to be shown directly into the autopsy room.

'Is the autopsy completed?' he had asked. 'Are you the pathologist?'

'I'm just a tech,' the woman had said, looking nervous. Her face was clean and very young under the scrubs cap. 'I assist. We're not done yet, no. We've just done the preliminaries. Skin samples, last night.' She had glanced at the clock. 'We're due to get going in half an hour, look—' she had hesitated, 'I was told this was strictly for identification, nothing more. Yes?'

'Yes.'

Sandro knew what strings Pietro would have pulled to get them in here, and he hadn't been surprised at her expression.

The room, its lighting painfully bright, its surfaces coldly reflective, had been dominated by the central steel table, gutters running each side, and the shrouded shape that lay on it. Watching Anna Niescu, as close as he could come without touching her, Sandro had seen her pupils contract against the light: she had taken in the shape, then looked away. He had seen her eyes run around the room, helpless, alighting on one dreadful apparatus after another: an extendable drill, a handsaw, a machine providing suction, a metal tray of instruments. And back to the table, where the technician had then stood, waiting for them. Sandro had put an arm around Anna's shoulders.

'That's him?'

Her voice had been almost inaudible. She had stared. Sandro had nodded, and step by slow step they had approached the table, walked up the shrouded length of the body. The torso had had a diminished look under the sheet. He had hoped Anna didn't notice.

And then the time had come: Anna had put out her own hand to take the sheet off his face but the technician had shown alarm. 'Let me,' she had said.

Beneath his arm Sandro had felt Anna go, collapsing out from under his embrace like a deflated balloon. He had caught her and felt her brace against him, but when he looked down something unexpected had happened. She had duly struggled back up, turning warm and solid again as her weight came to bear on him.

'I knew it,' she had said then, transcendent with relief, searching his face. 'I knew it.'

'Knew what?' Sandro had said, faltering.

'This isn't him,' she had said. 'This isn't my Josef.'

At first he had thought she must have been deluding herself: it would not be the first time. People sometimes don't see what they don't want to see, they hear only what they want to hear; patients with an unequivocally terminal diagnosis leave the consulting room believing there is a cure. Others, Sandro knew, heard only the bad news. Himself, Sandro was one of those.

Sandro's eyes had swung from Anna's face to Claudio Brunello's: was he so mutilated that she might be mistaken? Yes – but his wife had been sure it was him. The trauma to his forehead was unavoidably still there but now that it had been cleaned up, the face did look more human. His eyes had slid to the young technician: had she done this? Cleaned and smoothed and settled the dead body, restoring to it a shred or two of dignity? His gaze went back to Anna. She had been lifting the cloth, focusing on the body.

'You don't believe me,' she had said, eyes down, euphoria evaporating, and Sandro had felt his own certainty ebb. If Claudio Brunello was not Anna's lover – then what?

Taking the sheet from Anna, the technician had made a sound of gentle reproof.

'Can you show me his hands, please?' Anna had asked, a flush on her cheeks. Latex-gloved, the woman withdrew an arm, half-blackened from exposure and decomposition, the right arm, and laid it on the cloth. The hand, upturned, fingers swollen but human.

'Can you turn it over, please?' Anna had asked politely. 'The hand?'

Abrasions on the knuckles and a ring embedded in the flesh. Claudio Brunello had been married twenty years. Sandro supposed they would get it off, somehow, and give it back to his wife. Sandro had seen Anna gaze at it.

'This man was married,' she had said, with innocent earnestness. Sandro and the technician had exchanged glances.

'Yes,' Sandro had begun. 'Brunello was married.' And had stopped.

The flush in Anna's cheeks had deepened at his tone; her eyes had grown wider. 'My Josef was not married,' she had said, and forced herself on, 'he didn't wear a ring, there wasn't even a mark—' and hesitated, flushing, 'and – his skin was different, his skin. He – he—' She had realized they were staring at her and she had grasped for the words that would convince them. She had taken a breath.

Sandro had been able to sense the deep discomfort of the technician at his side; Pietro had said he would come, when he could. Sandro had wished he had been here.

'You think I don't know?' Anna had said, and Sandro had seen a shift in her that he wished he had not seen. A puzzlement, a tiny diminishing in her faith – in them, in the world, in her Josef. She had shaken her head. 'No. This is not his face,' nodding towards the battered, cloth-bound head. 'And this is not his body. My Josef wasn't like this, he had hair – on his – his arms. His chest. Very dark, soft. Like an animal, I said to him. We laughed about it.' Sandro had been aware that he was averting his eyes, the female technician too, both of them staring at the floor as Anna spoke. 'And his hands, on the back of his hands.'

On the spotless white cloth the arm lay between them, discoloured and battered, but the fine hairs visible: none on the back of the hand. Unasked, the woman in her scrubs had gently tucked the arm back beside the body and covered it.

'I'm sorry for him,' Anna had said, turning away. 'And for his wife – his family. I'm sorry to be glad. But this is not Josef.'

The technician had shown them into the stuffy office, then, with its table-top detritus, the smell of powerful disinfectants even in there.

There was a water dispenser in the corner and Sandro had supposed it couldn't matter if they used it. Anna had drunk the first glass greedily, in seconds, then another. Sandro had watched her, listening to his heart pound, led her to a chair and she had sat obediently. 'I've just got to make a call,' he had said.

She had nodded, staring into the distance as the whole thing settled, thinking, *What now? What will they show me next?* Sandro had seen her grasp that it wasn't over.

He had left her there while he went to phone. His instinct had been to dial Luisa first; he had just wanted to hear her voice. It had rung and rung, then the connection had been abruptly terminated, not even going to answerphone.

Then he should have phoned Pietro, but being hung up on like that had started his heart pounding all over again. What if she – what if something had happened? An accident, a mugging, a stranger hanging up. So he had punched in the number again, and this time she had answered, and the world had returned to its normal axis.

Pietro had been a different matter. 'Jesus,' he had said. A long pause, one in which Sandro had been able to hear him calculate the implications of what he'd just heard. 'I'm sorry I wasn't there. I had to talk to Brunello's colleagues. The Guardia wanted a briefing. They've gone over to the bank. Is she all right?'

'Yes,' Sandro had said, not hearing, really. How would he have been sure, if it had been Luisa on a slab? He just would have been. 'It's not him.'

'Ten minutes,' Pietro had said urgently. 'I'll drop Matteucci first.'

Anna had nodded when he explained the situation, obedient as ever. He had thought, when he first met her, that she'd be so easy to fool, a sitting duck. But having seen her under pressure, in the glare of the autopsy room standing beside the body of a man violently killed, having grasped the clarity with which she understood right from wrong, true from false – he wasn't so certain any more.

And now they were waiting. He'd heard it in Pietro's voice. Weariness, fear, adrenaline, in that order, the same old story. Claudio Brunello wasn't the father of Anna Niescu's child.

This changed everything.

*

The weird thing was, Maria Grazia was phoning and asking Roxana the question – the same question that had been buzzing just out of Roxana's reach all morning and had just that moment come into focus.

Maybe it had taken her lunch break, and getting out of the stale gloom of the bank, for Roxana's head to clear.

It had been a slow, slow four hours: eight to midday. Giorgio Viola had turned up at some time after nine and established himself in Claudio Brunello's office, the officers of the Guardia wandering in and out, polite, but acting as if the place was theirs, opening cabinets, standing behind Roxana, looking over her shoulder. In with Marisa too, some of the time, asking her questions while she sat, pale and staring, behind the desk.

And all the time Roxana's headache had grown as she frowned and thought, what was it? What was it bothering her, what was it she was trying to remember?

Eight or nine customers: first old Signora Martelli with her newspaper trolley. Haranguing Val, then asking for a new chequebook. Theirs practically the only bank left issuing chequebooks, their customers the only ones ancient enough to rely on them, but all the same the demand had dwindled, so they held blanks and stamped the number on by hand.

Roxana had had to watch, helpless, as the old woman grumbled and a queue built up and eventually Roxana offered to look for her stamp, unearthing a small stack of correspondence while she did so. Jesus, this place was a mess. Since they had dispensed with secretaries, most of the statements and such were now centrally printed and dispatched. With only cashiers and managers and no one actually to clear the decks, stuff got overlooked. No way to run a business: was that what the Guardia were thinking, too? Behind Brunello's office door Marisa had paced, on the phone as she'd been all morning.

A young Eastern European girl from the leather shop on the corner had come in wanting bags of change. She looked startled at the Guardia uniform that appeared behind Roxana and stood there a moment with his arms crossed. This couldn't go on, thought Roxana. They'd have to close.

The old guy who sold tourist knick-knacks in the Piazza Signoria had deposited his takings, and hadn't batted an eyelid at the presence of officialdom. Surprisingly substantial takings: people were obviously out there, buying tat as if their lives depended on it, stuck in the boiling city. A young couple had come in with a baby, wanting to open a savings account for him. Go somewhere else, Roxana had wanted to say to them. Go to a bank that's still likely to be around for his eighteenth birthday. And take him to the seaside, on a day like this. In a month like this: peering over the counter, she had seen the baby's pale and perfect skin dewy with the heat.

But all she had said was, nodding towards Marisa's office, its door firmly closed, 'Why don't you come back after the holidays, and talk to our *Gestore, Family e Business*? She'll come up with the right account for you.'

The couple beamed down at the little head, nestled in a sling between them, and she understood that, really, they'd just been bringing him out to show him off.

'I expect it's hard to keep him cool, this weather,' she'd said, then regretted it as they fell over each other to reassure her, they had air-conditioning, they'd read all the books, damp flannels to cool him, one thin sheet at night. If only they had anywhere else to go. They had all agreed it was too much, this heat, ninety-eight per cent humidity, it said in the paper.

There had been a tiny paragraph in the paper, about Claudio Brunello's death. Strange to see it there, so discreet a mention, with so little detail. *The body of a man. The family have been informed.* And then: *The police are actively seeking anyone who might have been a witness to the accident, which is believed to have occurred between midday on Saturday and Sunday night.*

The bank closed at one p.m. on Saturday. Roxana now tried to bring the day back, to get more detail than she'd come up with for the police, but it was fuzzy. A phone ringing, early. Locking up, Val hurrying away to the river in his rowing vest, smiling up at the sun, the weekend awaiting them. The heat.

Things had settled: the Guardia went into Claudio's office to talk to sad, fat Giorgio Viola for half an hour that turned into an hour, then more. Weren't they going to ask her any questions? Any real questions, not just, 'where's the coffee?' It would appear not. Her headache had grown.

Ma had called mid-morning, during a lull, fortunately. 'There's a man,' she had complained, 'phoned. He says he's coming to fix the gate and can he come a bit later? He telephoned.' She didn't sound even slightly anxious about *this* man: Roxana sighed. Just when she thought she'd worked out what Ma's problem was, it seemed to turn into something else.

'Yes, I arranged it,' she had said. 'It needs a bit of TLC, that's all. I'll deal with it.'

Listened to Ma grumble on a bit more; those footprints by the broken back gate came into focus as she half listened. She'd put them out of her mind, overnight; something that had seemed alarming in the dark would turn out to be innocent enough by daylight. Only she couldn't quite think of an innocent explanation.

'I won't be late,' she had finished: too many things competing for her attention.

Not only the horrible fact of Brunello's body, lying there two, three days in the heat – but something more amorphous that came with it. The feeling, something invisible as gas that had crept in here with the news and settled in corners, that things weren't what she'd thought. That this place she came to every day – suffocatingly dull and reliable as clockwork – had secrets these men were trying to root out. And it had changed, in subtle and frightening ways that she couldn't even put her finger on.

Roxana had stood up the next time Marisa appeared.

'What are they doing?' she had hissed. 'This can't go on, can it? They'll have to close us for a bit.'

And at some movement beyond the door she had looked out to the street; you could never quite make out who it was out there, until you got up close. She had seen a flash of white trainers: kids.

'It's not good for business, is it? Having those guys here.'

'They're just doing their job,' Marisa had said stiffly. 'There's nothing to worry about.' Roxana had eyed her flatly: she was worried all right.

'Have they found anything?' They had both turned their heads towards the closed door that the three men hadn't opened in some time.

'They wouldn't tell me if they had,' Marisa had said, arms folded across her body and hugging herself. 'I'm sure there's nothing to find. You knew Claudio. Claudio wasn't dishonest.' She had sounded like she was trying to keep up her own morale.

'Are we going to – what's going to happen to us? Are we going to lose our jobs?' Roxana had been surprised by how little she cared.

Marisa's face had frozen. 'I don't think it's appropriate – ah – that kind of talk isn't appropriate, under the circumstances.' She had drawn herself up. 'Of course not. This is routine.'

As if he'd heard, or sensed, what they were talking about, Val had suddenly appeared in the doorway, at Roxana's shoulder, hands in his pockets.

'You'll be all right, Roxi,' he had said. 'Girl like you.' He had been leaning his head against the door jamb looking at Marisa, and the look she had given him back had been startlingly hostile.

'You tell her, Marisa,' he'd gone on. 'She's employable anywhere. She's a grafter. Work ethic.'

Roxana had stared at him. He'd seemed to mean it.

'Unlike you?' Marisa had said, steely.

'If you like,' Val had said.

Roxana hadn't been able to work out what was going on, exactly: a kind of face-off. They had glared at each other a long moment and in the end, it was Marisa who had blinked first. 'Back to your desk,' she had said to Val. 'This is a bank, remember?' He had smiled and turned on his heel.

'You can take an early lunch,' Marisa had said peremptorily, turning to Roxana. 'Thank you. Thank you.'

Which was as close as she was going to get, Roxana had thought, to saying anything nice at all.

The phone went within minutes of her getting out of there, walking away from the bank towards the river and just as the heat, shocking at first and then overwhelming, brought a sudden sweat to every pore of her body. Roxana stopped, dripping now with the effort of rummaging through her bag, overtaken by a stupid panic that was about nothing and everything. What had she spent all morning trying to put her finger on? What was she trying to remember? What was wrong, what was different? Was she losing it?

This must be what it was like for Ma was the thought that came to her just before she saw the phone, glowing in the portable rubbish dump that was her handbag.

'Maria Grazia.'

She exhaled with sudden relief, her back against the warm flank of the nearest building, in the shade, looking down the length of a filthy, sunlit alley, the blank and crumbling façade of a church halfway down it, the lopsided sign of a boarded-up grocery. Just out of sight at the end of that alley was the porn cinema, one street back from the river. And then it came to her.

'He turned up, then?' Maria Grazia asked, her voice crackling and distant, people shouting in the background. 'Your boyfriend with his cashbag? Or has he done a runner with the takings?'

For a moment Roxana didn't know what to say, so abrupt was the coincidence. Then she said, 'No.' She pressed her forearm against her forehead: could she seriously go back to work like this? She was drenched. 'I mean, no, he never turned up.'

'Well, if it was a movie,' Maria Grazia said cheerfully, 'he'd have done a runner with the takings.'

'Life's not like a movie,' Roxana said automatically: an old joke between them, she the bank teller, her friend in the glamorous business of films. And besides, what takings? A couple of hundred euros on a good week.

'Where are you, anyway?' she went on.

'Oh, just work,' said Maria Grazia, sounding uncharacteristically vague. There was a pause. 'I was a bit worried about you, to tell the truth. Are you OK? You don't really sound OK.'

Roxana sighed, reluctant, suddenly, to go into the whole horrible mess. 'I'm hot. The city's a nightmare in August.'

Maria Grazia's voice sharpened. 'Come on,' she said. 'It's more than that.'

'Brunello's dead,' said Roxana abruptly. 'My boss. They found him dead. The Guardia's in the bank, looking at the books.'

'What?' An intake of breath. 'What does that mean, they found him dead? What – suicide?'

Roxana found herself shaking her head. Why was that everyone's assumption? Because it was more probable than – the alternative? Or more acceptable?

'An accident?' Maria Grazia corrected herself.

'They don't know.' Roxana heard the dullness in her voice. 'Looks like he was hit by a car – or something. Look, I don't know the details, I – I—' And then she couldn't help herself. 'It's – it's scary, to tell the truth.' She didn't even know it, until she said it.

There was a silence: she could almost hear Maria Grazia thinking. 'Yes,' she said eventually. 'I can imagine.'

'The branch is all over the place, uniforms looking at everything, shut in his office and telling no one anything. We get a private detective in one day, looking for Claudio – next thing we know, he's dead and the Guardia are turning the place upside down.'

'Hold on,' said Maria Grazia. 'What private detective?'

Roxana sighed as her thoughts settled on the man who reminded her of her dad. A nice guy, in all this. He'd given her his card. Could a private detective really be a good guy? Other than in the movies.

'He was looking for Claudio.' She frowned. 'Someone – some client was trying to track him down. I had the impression it might be a woman, though he didn't say that. It doesn't seem – maybe it was just a coincidence.' His name came to her. 'He was called Sandro Cellini. The private detective, I mean, though, God knows, that's the least of our troubles, if Claudio was having an affair.'

'Wow,' said Maria Grazia reverently. 'And I always thought that place was so sleepy.'

Roxana went on, 'No one knows what's going to happen next, I'm even feeling sorry for Val, you know? And Marisa looks freaked. Completely terrified.'

Maria Grazia snorted, unsympathetically. 'Well,' she said. 'Well, her.' As if that said it all.

Roxana sighed. 'I know. You'd have thought Val and I would have more to worry about, it's not as if she needs the money. I was beginning to wonder—' And she stopped.

'Doesn't need the money? I don't know about that. What were you beginning to wonder?' And something in her old friend's voice alerted Roxana.

'She's got money, though? That Torinese countess business.'

'Oh, come on,' said Maria Grazia wearily. 'Her family's got a stuffy old apartment in the Piazza Carlo Felice. Very nice, been in the family donkey's years, but that's it. No country house, no private income. Why d'you think she hangs on for dear life to any man with money that comes near her?' An explosive sound. 'Why d'you think she works in that dump?'

Right, thought Roxana.

'Sorry,' said Maria Grazia, reading her mind. 'I just – I just don't like women like Marisa.'

'I was beginning to wonder if *she* was having an affair with Claudio. Claudio – Brunello, that is, the boss. She was so upset.

Upset in a weird way, as if it was going to reflect on her somehow. Frightened.'

There was a long pause. 'I see,' said Maria Grazia slowly. 'D'you know, I don't think that's how she works. It's not like he's going to keep her in the style she wants, is it? A bank branch manager.'

'Was,' said Roxana sadly. 'He's not going to keep anyone now, is he? There's his family.'

Roxana stayed there after Maria Grazia had hung up, leaning against the wall. Lunchtime now, she should eat, but she had no appetite. This heat. The alley in front of her shimmered in the sun, the bent figure of old Signora Martelli, still dragging her trolley, stepped out into it from the side door of the church. Roxana wondered how she – and all the other old people stuck here – could stand it: the air shiny with pollution and humidity, the smell of the dumpsters practically palpable. It occurred to her that church might well be the best place to be, dark and cool.

The old church, cheek by jowl with the porn cinema: how did that work? Did the customers call in on their way home to their wives? Was it even a sin? Impure thoughts: that was the one that came to mind.

The porn cinema, the Albanian with his bag of takings: it was him, all morning – never mind the Guardia, they'd just been a distraction – he was what had been haunting Roxana. Gone missing. She'd taken his money on occasion, and had let her eyes slide over the scribbled and indecipherable signature, but she couldn't even remember the account name. Something anonymous, as you'd expect of a backstreet porn cinema, a set of initials. A regular was a regular, you didn't make the usual checks, and it wasn't as if he was putting in thousands, which would require them – not that they always did – to ask their provenance under money-laundering legislation. A few euros, a modest deposit, and porn cinemas were legal, even if they were not to

Roxana's taste. Was he her responsibility? In some obscure way, Roxana couldn't get rid of the feeling that he was.

'Done a runner with the takings,' Maria Grazia had said. He wouldn't get far on the takings from the Carnevale, that was for sure. Unless he'd been creaming it off for years; unless something else was going on. Pushing herself away from the wall, Roxana stood stock-still on the pavement and felt the sweat cool on the back of her neck. Unless it was all connected.

What was bugging her was that she'd never known his name, and the person she wanted to ask was Claudio Brunello. Serious-faced Brunello, frowning down at the figures, watchful Brunello, who had a word for all his customers: *How is your son getting on at university? Have you managed to find a buyer for your apartment yet? How's business?* He would have known, had Roxana asked, *What's happened to the Albanian with his cashbag from the – um – cinema? You know the one. What's his name again?*

But Claudio Brunello would never be walking back into the bank with a kindly smile, would never prop his umbrella carefully in the corner and straighten his tie before sitting down. And the more she thought about that, the harder it was for Roxana to get rid of the idea, however foolish it might seem, that there was a connection. Between Claudio Brunello and the Albanian. Two disappearances.

The security guard from the bank rounded the corner in his little car, parked it illegally up on the pavement. He shielded his eyes and then, recognizing her, raised his hand.

Reflexively returning his greeting, Roxana registered a hesitation in the man's stance when, instead of heading for the cool wine bar for a little plate of something daintily presented, Roxana stepped off the pavement and into the dumpster-choked alley.

CHAPTER FIFTEEN

I T HAD SEEMED TO take Anna Niescu an age to climb the two flights of stairs to the flat, time for Sandro to reflect, with increasing desperation, on a number of things. On how long Anna had before she gave birth to this baby, and on all that had happened to worsen her situation since he had sat in his office and listened to Giuli helping her up the stairway with kindness and encouragement. Now the roles were reversed: Giuli was waiting upstairs with Luisa, and Sandro wasn't doing half as good a job at easing poor Anna's burden.

'Nearly there,' he had said under his breath. Beside him Anna had paused and in the half darkness he saw her face. Dark-browed, intent; as closed-off and alone as an icon.

They hadn't really been able to talk in front of Anna, he and Pietro, and Sandro just couldn't bring himself to leave her on her own in that horrible place. He knew all too well what Luisa would have said to the suggestion.

Besides, his duty was only to his client; he wasn't a police officer any more, nor an impartial seeker after truth. That was the theory, anyway, and even if most people would laugh long and hard at the thought of the Polizia dello Stato as truthseekers, at least Pietro fitted the bill. A good man.

'He's a good man,' was just what he'd said to Anna earnestly as she had flinched at the uniformed figure coming through the door. 'You can trust Pietro. I mean, really.' Thinking, as the gust of disinfectant and the decay it was supposed to mask entered the room with Pietro, *I've got to get her out of this place.*

Pietro hadn't disappointed: perhaps he'd looked at Anna Niescu and seen his own daughter's sunny features somewhere in the little oval face, the shiny black hair. He'd taken her hands in his and spoken gently.

She was sure, had been all Anna would say, over and over, absolutely sure it wasn't him, and in the end Sandro could see that Pietro had believed her. His old friend had sat back in his chair, musing.

They had both been thinking the same thing, Sandro had felt it. That it couldn't just be coincidence. That there must be some connection.

'When did your fiancé tell you his name?' Sandro had asked gently. 'Do you remember? When he first told you.'

'Oh, straight away,' Anna had said, and he had seen her brighten, just fractionally, before fading again abruptly. Had Sandro been glad that she was learning to be wary of hoping for the best? All he had felt was a leaden sort of guilt. She had gone on, looking down into her lap, 'As we were walking home from the fruit stall, that first time. He shook my hand and everything.'

Liliana, Sandro had thought. I should talk to Liliana, who sold them those oranges.

'And?' Pietro had asked.

'Well, he said, I'm Josef,' she had said, faltering. 'I suppose it was only later he told me – that was his middle name. The name his mother called him.'

'He told her his mother was foreign,' Sandro had said, by way of explanation.

'French, sounds like,' Pietro had said, 'or North African,' and Sandro had nodded; the way she had said it sounded French, the accent on the second syllable. There were so many nationalities, washing around the city. English, American, French. And now Albanian, Somali, Korean, Ukrainian, Chinese. To begin with it had been hard to tell them apart; an Englishman could turn out to be from New Zealand, a dark-skinned Romanian might be mistaken for a North African. Names helped.

'And later?' Sandro had prompted. 'When did he tell you – his full name?'

She had frowned effortfully. 'The third time, I think. If the oranges was the first time. He came to find me at the hotel the second time, two days later, but I think perhaps he wasn't made very welcome.'

Sandro had pursed his lips judiciously, thinking of the desiccated old lady at the reception desk. Had she been looking after Anna's interests, or protecting her investment, her cheap labour supply? Both, perhaps; he had made a mental note, *send Luisa back there. Get her to talk to the woman.*

'We went for a meal together.' He had seen a fierce blush beginning, at the base of her neck. 'And then he gave me a telephone, my telephone, so that we could – so that he didn't have to call the hotel.'

'And the third time you met?' The blush had been building, and Sandro made his voice as soft as he could.

'It wasn't the third time, it was the fourth. We were walking in Fiesole, he told me. He told me he worked in a bank, his name was Claudio Josef Brunello, he had a good job.'

She had bobbed her head down, and Sandro had seen the glow of her cheek, her mouth set. Had it been the third meeting, or the fourth, or the fifth, when the child had been conceived? This was what she had been waiting for them to ask, and this, he could tell, was the first time it had occurred to Anna Niescu to feel shame.

Had her Josef been lying to impress her into bed – or had the deed been done, and he desperate not to lose her?

'You've done nothing wrong, Anna,' he had said in an undertone.

Behind him, Pietro had cleared his throat.

'You've been through a terrible experience,' Pietro had said, leaning forward, both of their heads close to hers now. 'I'm so sorry that we had to bring you here.' She had been stilled, head down and thinking. 'But this man,' and Sandro hadn't known Pietro could speak so softly, 'this dead man you just saw. He had a family. It seems, he was a good man, and at this moment there is no explanation for his death.'

Anna had raised her head to look at him suddenly, the flush already cooling on her cheeks. Pietro had gone on. 'There may be a connection. That's all. There may be – what you tell us may help us to find – to find out what happened.'

She had shifted her gaze to Sandro, then back, looking from one weary, anxious face to the other. 'A connection?' Then a hand had come up to her mouth. 'You think this man—' Her eyes flew to the door, then back. 'You think it wasn't an accident?'

They had just looked at her sorrowfully, and her eyes had widened.

'Do you think my Josef – what do you mean, a connection?' She'd sat forward, rigid, hands either side of her on the chair and the hard mound of her stomach in her lap like a boulder she couldn't shift. 'Is he in danger? You must tell me. Is Josef in danger?'

The extremity of her anguish had frightened Sandro; he could only think of the child crammed inside her, the panic transmitting itself, a flood of chemicals. 'Shh,' he had said, desperately searching for calm. 'Please, don't worry. We don't know anything at the moment. There's no reason to think that – your fiancé is in danger. We're just trying to understand. That's all.'

He had turned to Pietro. 'Not now,' he'd said. 'This isn't helping. There may be no connection at all.' And brusquely Pietro had nodded, knowing that the words were principally for Anna's benefit.

'Go with Sandro, now,' Pietro had said, searching the girl's face. 'He'll look after you.'

He hadn't needed to say to Sandro, *I'll call you later*. He'd known enough to say nothing more. But at the door they had exchanged a look over her head. There was plenty to talk about.

Pietro had called them a taxi. 'Oh,' he had said, almost an afterthought. 'I – we were in the bank this morning. His bank. A chat – with the colleagues.'

'Right,' Sandro had said. 'And?'

Pietro had shaken his head. 'We took statements,' he had said. 'None of them thought he was suicidal. Terrible shock to all of them. All came up with stories as to what they were up to that weekend. Actually, they looked scared stiff, all three.'

'I liked the girl,' Sandro had said.

'The girl,' Pietro had said, pondering. 'The younger woman, you mean?'

Sandro had allowed himself a smile. 'They're all girls to me. But yes. Roxana Delfino. I spoke to her – when I thought my guy was your guy.'

Pietro had nodded, distant. 'What a set-up,' he had said. 'That place is on the way out.' Sandro grunted agreement.

Pietro had gone on, 'The Guardia di Finanza's on the case. In there, in the bank this morning, I hear. Just after we left.'

'Really? That was quick.' And Sandro had felt a pang, for Signorina Roxana Delfino.

'Yeah,' Pietro had said, avoiding his gaze. And at his expression Sandro had felt a small pulse start in some distant part of what was once his policeman's brain: the beginnings of a trail, like a porcupine quill in the woods. There was something Pietro hadn't told him. Yet.

'They closing the place down, or what? The Guardia, shutting the bank down, I mean?'

Pietro still wasn't quite looking at him. 'Who knows?' he had said. 'They said they'd have a look. Could mean anything, couldn't it, with those guys? Tape across the door and frozen assets, or just a coffee and a chat, or something in between. They said they'd keep us – what did they say? In the loop. It's a suspicious death, after all, that's our territory.'

'Suspicious death now? What happened to suicide?'

And Pietro had sighed. 'Well. All right.' Still sounding cagey. 'So he didn't get the girl pregnant, he isn't her guy. We were kind of going down that road, as motive for suicide.'

'I never went along with that,' Sandro had pointed out.

'No,' Pietro had said. 'OK. But he was a bank manager. If the Guardia see fit to talk to us about the state of that bank ... He might have got himself into all sorts of trouble, and this seemed like the only way out.'

Sandro had grunted. That kind of information might take its time getting through, to say the least. 'Anything new? Anything at all? The injuries: I don't see how it could have been a hit and run. I just don't see it. How about DNA?'

His old friend had shifted uneasily. 'There are – difficulties, just now. It doesn't quite add up.' He had stopped, and Sandro had taken pity.

'It's OK,' he had said. 'I know, I've got no uniform, no right to know. Plus, this isn't even my guy we're talking about. It's OK.'

And they had both looked away, anywhere but at each other,

over at Anna sitting in the corner patiently, at the dust motes on the unwashed windows, the car park, the traffic moving snail-slow on the motorway a hundred metres away.

'I'd give you a ride,' Pietro had said, breaking the silence eventually, nodding down to the patrol car sitting in the laboratory's car park. 'But I'm pushing things as it is. Matteucci's started grumbling. Who are you, to get all this attention? Abuse of privilege, blah, blah.'

'Bastard,' Sandro had said reflexively. He'd have to wait, then, for Pietro to decide to tell him whatever it was. Pietro had just grunted again.

In the cab home, though, Anna sitting beside him, clinging to the side of the car as they bumped over the flagstones of the city's empty backstreets, Sandro had grown anxious. Was Pietro telling him to back off? Was he pushing his luck? The last thing he wanted was to get Pietro into trouble – serious trouble – just as he was thinking about taking early retirement. He had caught the driver eyeing them curiously in his rearview mirror, putting it all together: police call, pick-up from the pathology lab, pregnant girl, man old enough to be her father. What sense could it make to him?

In the doorway Luisa had said nothing, just clucked despairingly at the sight of Anna, pale and exhausted, and shushed her into the bedroom, closing the door softly behind them.

Sandro had heard tentative sounds from the kitchen: Giuli trying to make herself useful, nervous of putting things away in the wrong place. But he hadn't gone in, he had stood in the dim hall, between the coats hanging along one wall and the ugly landscape Luisa's mother had given them at their wedding on the other, for the moment not ready to move.

There was information in his head but unfortunately it hadn't come in the shape of facts arranged in useful, neat columns:

more like a swarm of wasps, circling and scattering, forming and reforming.

In no particular order: Liliana, seller of oranges; the old woman behind the reception desk at the Loggiata; the Russian girl; Josef: Albanian, Moroccan, Tunisian, Romanian – which was he? Did it even matter? The apartment he was planning for his little family, with its nursery. How had he got his hands on such a place?

And, incidentally, the apartment with a long, rusted balcony and a view of the hills that he and Luisa (too old to be newly-weds) would almost certainly never move into. And the more impossible it seemed, the more angry it made Sandro, that he was such a failure, that he had not provided for this eventuality.

The Banca di Toscana Provinciale too. Why had Anna's fiancé chosen that bank of all banks? How had he come up with that name, Claudio Brunello?

And apropos of nothing, apropos of the dead man in the morgue who no longer had anything to do with Sandro, now that he turned out not to be the father of Anna's baby, he had thought of a smear on a man's pale-leather shoe, in the white glare of a forensics tent in the August sun. He thought of the dusty earth under the trees.

What was the connection?

Now Sandro dialled Pietro's number, and it went straight to answerphone. Damn: was he being screened out? Or being paranoid? Slowly he hung up. Think.

Folding his arms, Sandro frowned, remembering the bank's gloomy interior, Claudio Brunello's bank. The dusty marble flooring. And that faded, cheesy poster on the wall: a man in a suit holding out his hand and in the background a cartoon of people in a bank queue, dreaming of a house with a garden. *Look ahead! Get in line!* It was something from another age.

'Sandro?' Giuli called from the kitchen, her voice high and anxious.

'Coming,' he said.

She was standing behind a chair, hands resting on its back.

Sandro's frown deepened. 'What is it?'

'Nothing,' she said, fidgeting. 'Just – wondered what you were up to out there.'

'Something's up,' he said.

'It's just the heat,' Giuli said, and let out a sigh.

'It's not the boyfriend? He hasn't – let you down, or anything?'

To his relief she smiled, broadly. 'No. No! He's great. Enzo's great. Luisa said she wants him to come over.' She opened her mouth to say more, then closed it again. She smiled.

Sandro pulled out a chair and sat, heavily. Giuli was right: everything seemed more of an effort in this heat, even sitting down. 'Wants to inspect him, you mean. Sure he's ready for that?'

Still she looked relaxed. Not that, then.

'So, what?'

She pulled out another chair and sat. Sandro could see food ranged along the kitchen counter, a Russian salad, some cold fried veal cutlets, peperonata. He realized he didn't even know what time it was: the clock said one-forty. They must have stopped at the *rosticceria* en route for this stuff.

'She should eat,' said Giuli, and the anxiety was back on her face.

'Luisa?' Sandro felt a lurch. Had she looked ill?

'Well, her.' She caught his expression. 'No, no, not Luisa. You should have seen her out there this morning, she's a killer. Knocking on doors. Giving them hell.'

Sandro smiled faintly. His Luisa, a killer.

Giuli went on earnestly, 'But Anna, I meant. Doesn't she have to eat?'

The heat gathered in the room, stealthily. Sandro could see the oppressive afternoon hours awaiting them; any kind of activity, even animated discussion of anything seemed inadvisable, lest it raise the temperature. Sandro put his hands through his hair, feeling the sweat at his temples, and leaned back.

'I'm no expert,' he said. 'I think she needs rest, more than food. She needs peace and quiet and nothing to worry about.' He grimaced. 'Fat chance.'

Giuli nodded thoughtfully. 'Tell you what,' she said, 'I can get down to the Loggiata. Tell them she needs looking after, she can't do their beds any more. Well,' and she compromised, seeing him pull a doubting face, 'for the time being.'

Something occurred to Sandro. 'Pass us a plate,' he said, nodding towards the side.

'We're not waiting for Luisa?'

'Well, we can lay things out, can't we? We can manage that.'

Giuli smiled, impish. Meaning, not even that.

As they were putting the plates out, wondering why they didn't look right, Sandro said, 'And you could have a word. While you're over there.'

'With the Russian. Dasha.'

'Her, yes. But how long's she been there? Was she there when Josef first came on the scene?'

Giuli frowned. 'Maybe not.'

'Could you maybe talk to the old lady, too? The owner.'

Luisa appeared in the door, looking weary. She puffed her cheeks and sighed. 'Poor kid,' she said. Then frowned at the table. 'You two,' she said, gently shoving Giuli aside and going round, straightening, setting mats, getting out napkins. She laid an extra place, for Anna.

'So she knows she's welcome,' she said, when Sandro looked at her. 'So she knows she's staying.'

'Have you two been talking about this?' He shook his head in mock disapproval. 'She's moving in, is she?' It was the only thing to do: he could see that. Luisa had got there first, as usual.

'There's the spare room,' said Luisa.

'Just as well we're not living on a building site in San Niccolo yet,' he said. She said nothing, but he knew she'd noticed that 'yet'.

'I'll ask,' he said. 'About a loan. I will.'

'OK,' said Luisa comfortably. Not pushing it. 'And what was that you two were plotting when I came in? Something about the old lady?'

'The old lady at the Loggiata. Your mother's pal. Apparently, she didn't make Anna's beau too welcome, when he first put in an appearance. That's what Anna said.'

Luisa pursed her lips, pulling out a chair, and as she sat down Sandro saw her shoot a glance at Giuli.

'Just being protective, perhaps,' she said. 'Looking out for her kid's interests. It sounds like she more or less took that girl in when she had nowhere else to go.'

Sandro nodded. 'She's not – it wouldn't be that he might not be Italian?'

'Is that what you're thinking?'

'It's a theory,' said Sandro cautiously. 'In that he told her his name was Josef, to begin with. Does that sound Italian to you?'

'And the old lady not welcoming him with open arms would confirm that, because she'd be likely to – have her prejudices?' Luisa seemed merely interested. 'Well, I don't know. I would guess that, like any older person – like us maybe,' giving him a sharp glance, 'she probably wishes that everything was as it was when she was young. But to be honest, I don't know her that well, she might be a – a member of the Greens, for all I know. She was just one of Mamma's friends.'

'I don't see any harm in Giuli talking to her, anyway,' said Sandro warily. 'Asking her what she thought of him. Old ladies – you know. They have sharp eyes.'

'And sharper tongues,' said Luisa. 'I'll come too.'

'I can manage.' At the sound of her voice – quiet, calm – they both turned to look at Giuli. 'I can talk to her, Luisa. I'll say you sent me, if you like. But you should stay here.' Sandro saw her eyes shift to him. 'What if Anna wakes up, and there's no one here? She needs you.'

Luisa looked from one to the other, knowing when she was beaten. Set two hands on the table, indicating the places laid to either side of her. 'Well,' she said. 'This veal doesn't look bad, for August. Are you going to eat, or not?'

And it was when they'd sat down, obedient at last, that she got to it. Her eyes were on Giuli first, who was lifting a forkful of salad to her lips, a look that meant something and the fork stopping in mid-air.

'Giuli's got something to tell us,' she said. 'Well, something to tell you.'

'Oh, yes?' said Sandro. Oh, no, was what he was thinking.

'Yes,' said Luisa, and she raised her water glass. 'Giuli's got some good news.'

*

The city glittered under the late-afternoon sun.

He parked up under some trees, his preferred spot, known only to the select few. A neatly kept row of mulberry trees on a ridge overlooking Scandicci, a stone bench. Someone could be bothered to tend the trees but he never saw them do it: he never saw anyone here, perhaps because the view – below, the sprawling suburb's tower blocks baking in the heat, the distant industrial profile of the Pisan plain fell far short of Tuscan perfection. But the trees' big, glossy leaves and heavy canopies gave excellent shade, and the ridge got a nice breeze.

Not that the breeze touched him today. He sat with the engine running and the air-con going full blast. Top-of-the-range climate control: this car had everything: WiFi, Bluetooth, seats that remembered your shape and massaged you in just the right places, two months old and his pride and joy. He could have gone back to the office – but he liked his car better. The furnishings were more tasteful – and there was no one in his car to tell him where he should be, no interfering menial to ask him had he called so-and-so yet, frown at him every time he stepped outside for a cigarette.

A cigarette, that was it. That was what was lacking. He felt in his breast pocket: the pack of Marlboro Lights was reassuringly full. Save it. He wouldn't smoke in the car: save it, luxuriate in the delicious blast of cold air a while longer.

August. He shouldn't be working in August anyway. Did anyone? No one but losers, and he wasn't a loser. Could sell ice cream to a Sicilian, snow to an Eskimo. There was no one to sell anything to, though, in August. Only losers, who didn't have the money for what he was selling anyway. Go away, he should have told them, you can't afford it. It would have been a mistake to have kept the office open if there hadn't been the one big sale that would justify it.

He put two fingers inside his shirt collar to ease it. Trouble? Maybe. The single glass of Friulian Chardonnay glowed comfortably in his stomach, complementing the salade niçoise. His favourite, on a hot day: he'd choose a nice salad niçoise over a *bistecca fiorentina* as his last meal, any day of the week, not to mention salad was better for the maintenance of the six-pack. Any day. A *ristretto* with a shot of grappa, and all it needed was that cigarette to top it off. He could almost taste it now. His last meal.

Turning up the stereo, he settled back, dreaming. *Search for the hero inside yourself.*

Just as well he had sidelines, he didn't rely on the office. There were ways of making money in this business. If you knew what you were doing. He'd have this car paid off in no time at all: no time. Might even trade up, for the real thing, the big red beast with its leaping horse. He felt for the pack of cigarettes again, sat up, rubbed his eyes.

Even with the breeze, was he ready for the heat, out there? It was just right in here, the suit sat comfortably on him in this temperature, the shirt crisp, collars sharp. Two minutes out there and he'd be sweating into a thousand-euro suit. He pictured himself, blowing smoke rings under the trees. The music slowed, coming to the end of a track. He heard something.

Outside, something.

What? A stone displaced? He turned his head, squinting into the sun back along the road, but all he saw were the thick, rough-barked trunks of the mulberries, the dry seedheads along the verge, further off the squat shapes of a couple of ugly semi-detached villas. Nothing. No one. The sun bleached the road out to nothing.

It unsettled him: this was his place. He didn't want to have to find somewhere new for his illicit afternoons, when he was supposed to be with clients. He almost started the car up to head back to the office after all. Just to show the girl: he liked to pull up alongside it, slowly, the gleaming length of the car, the music booming. But it was the cigarette that did it. He took out the pack with his right hand and with his left tugged on the door handle, listening, without knowing he was doing it, in pleasurable anticipation of the central locking system's heavy, expensive click at his command. *Open Sesame.*

But he never heard it.

He thought for an instant that the sound he heard instead might stop his heart, the horrible sledgehammer crunch of metal on metal, of irresistible force meeting the beautiful immovable object that was his pristine company car. He whirled his head, thinking, *What the fuck?* thinking someone had rammed him, but there was no car behind him. But it wasn't the sound that stopped his heart.

Someone was there all the same, at the driver's window now, he just got a glimpse of dark midriff at eye level, a centimetre of tattoo as the door was pulled from his grasp. Then a blinding pain as the door was swiftly slammed back, trapping his left hand; he twisted against its upholstery, trying to see up and out of the window, trying to work out what was going on. *Oh, shit,* he thought, as the door, pulled sharply open again, gave way beneath him and, now freed, he fell heavily to the gravel, head first. A glimpse of white trainers. *Oh, shit.* And someone's foot stamped hard on his ear, fracturing his skull, and his last living thought, profane, astonished, disbelieving, was just that. *Oh, shit.*

White wine, olives, tuna, *lattuga romana.* Consumed approximately one and a half hours before death. His last meal.

CHAPTER SIXTEEN

GOOD NEWS. WELL, HE'D be the judge of that.

Sandro mopped his brow, walking more slowly than he had thought possible so as to keep the clammy heat at bay. Without success: the Banca di Toscana Provinciale was in sight but he still had to stop.

For the second time that day, Sandro had found himself rolling his eyes in a frustrated attempt to communicate silently with one of the only two people he had ever been able to trust. First Pietro, when Anna Niescu's presence had prevented them getting down to the important question as to why, if Claudio Brunello was not Anna's lover, her lover was using his name? And then Luisa, her eyes boring into him and commanding him to keep silent as Giuli beamed up at them like a child taking a bow at the school play. Bursting with pride.

'You're what?' Sandro had said, modifying his tone only just in time from appalled to merely startled.

'Engaged,' Giuli had said. And she had put out her right hand, on the ring finger a diamond so modest he had had to resist the impulse to pull her fingers up to his face to squint at it.

'Isn't that lovely?' Luisa had said, a warning note in her voice.

He had looked from one of them to the other, knowing when he was beaten. *Lovely?* What was this Enzo after? He had to be after something.

He hadn't listened as they started murmuring on about how long it would be till the wedding, what his family thought, what Giuli would wear.

'Not white,' Giuli had said – he'd heard that much.

Sandro had just needed to get Luisa on her own. And then Pietro. But instead he'd said, 'I think I might just get off down to the bank.'

'But they won't be open,' Luisa had said, giving him a hard stare. He wasn't lying either: he just wasn't going to *his* bank, to ask *his* manager if they'd consider him for a loan, but to Claudio Brunello's bank. If he couldn't rely on Pietro to give him the inside track on the sudden appearance of the Guardia di Finanza, then he'd better do some detecting on his own.

'I've got an appointment,' he had said defiantly, although Luisa had clearly not believed him.

The Banca di Toscana Provinciale looked very shut indeed. Sandro's heart sank. He took out his mobile and looked at it, pointlessly; he'd tried Pietro on the way down but no answer. All it told him now was that it was almost three o'clock. He peered through the window, a hand shielding his eyes against the smoked glass. He could see two people in there, a tall woman, a man. He moved to the door: opening time was four. He peered in again, and saw the two heads turn to look at him. The taller of the two held up a finger, no.

There was no sign of the woman he'd spoken to yesterday, and his heart dipped. Because she was his only in; and because he'd liked her. She'd been straight, which was rare, in Sandro's experience. Wary, but honest; she'd trusted him.

What was he going to do in there? In his briefcase – which

was beginning to make him feel stupid, carrying it around like a man who's lost his job and needs to convince the wife he's still got something important to do – he had the out-of-focus picture of Anna Niescu's fiancé.

Fiancé: an untrustworthy word. Engagement wasn't marriage; it was a promise worth no more than air. Every girl coming gossiping out of senior school for her lunch break was engaged, but not many of them were actually going to get married any time soon.

And now Giuli had a fiancé too.

Not that he and Luisa had needed to say it out loud to know what they were thinking. *Surely she's not.* But why else did people get engaged? Why had Anna Niescu got engaged? Because they wanted to set up home. Make a family.

Isn't Giuli too old – for all that?

Inside the bank it looked dead. The three figures had gone further into the interior somewhere. He straightened. On the corner an overweight man in a security guard's uniform was leaning against a small, cheaply armoured van, lighting up a cigarette in leisurely fashion. Illegally parked. They obviously didn't go for the premium service at the Banca di Toscana Provinciale.

In his pocket the phone rang. He held the screen up to his face and saw that the call was from Pietro. Slowly he raised it to his ear: since when had his heart sunk at the prospect of talking to his oldest friend?

'Sorry, mate,' came the familiar voice down the crackling line. Cheerful, straightforward. Traffic noise in the background. 'I had to have the phone off, I was getting the preliminary findings. On Brunello's body.'

'And?'

'Well, one or two things.' Now Pietro's voice was wary. 'Look, we need to talk, don't we?'

'And his apartment? Been there?' He was aware of being pushy, but somehow could do nothing about it.

A whistling sigh. 'Clean.' Sandro detected a lowering of his old friend's voice. 'Unless you count two tumblers washed and upside down on the draining board.'

'Two. His wife away at the seaside.' A silence. Could be anything, or nothing: a neighbour round, an old friend, or they could have been there a week, no wife around to put them away.

'Matteucci there?' A grunt. 'Hold on a second.' Muffled talking as at the other end Pietro, his hand over the receiver, told someone – Matteucci – to go get himself a coffee, something to eat. And then he was back, loud and clear.

'Jesus,' said Pietro cheerfully, 'sticks like glue, that guy. Sometimes I wonder if he's been sent down here with a mission.'

'A mission?' That little prick of anxiety again: he mustn't get Pietro into trouble. 'What mission?'

'A mission to wind me up,' said Pietro cheerfully. 'It's OK. He'll learn. I guess it's just that he wants to know everything about everything, and he wants to know it now. He's young.'

'You were saying,' said Sandro. 'We need to talk.'

Pietro sighed. 'Impossible to say anything with the girl there,' he said. 'Poor kid. Didn't realize she was so far gone. So pregnant, I mean.'

Sandro grunted. He didn't want to think about what would happen when Anna Niescu's time came.

'At least it wasn't him on the slab,' he said. 'That's all she was thinking. Could have been worse.'

'Well,' said Pietro, hesitating.

'I know,' said Sandro. 'You're thinking, can't be just a coincidence, right?' He turned and peered into the bank's gloomy interior: a strip light blinked on. They must be close to opening.

'No,' said Pietro with finality. 'Why did he choose that name, of all names?'

'And this dozy little bank,' added Sandro. 'It's hardly a household name.' He hesitated. 'He's got to have some connection with the bank. A customer? A – a neighbour? And perhaps with Brunello himself.'

'With Brunello himself,' repeated Pietro. 'With – his death too. Perhaps.'

'All Anna can think is that he's in danger,' said Sandro thoughtfully. 'It hasn't occurred to her that he might have—'

'Might have had something to do with Brunello's death.'

'Yes,' said Sandro, without thinking. But there was something in Pietro's voice. 'What? Hold on. Preliminary findings, you said?'

Pietro sighed. 'Looks like some of the injuries were post-mortem. Plus there's the angle of trajectory— ' He broke off, irritable. 'Injuries not consistent with being struck by a car, after all. There'd have had to be a lot more force than is consistent with the trauma, particularly if a car managed to propel him over the crash barrier. There'd have been more in the way of scratching – I don't know. The geeks presumably know what they're talking about.'

Sandro said nothing: he knew what it was like, to have a theory demolished. 'You've talked to his wife,' he said.

'Up to a point,' said Pietro wearily. 'I told her we're still not sure, about whether it was an accident after all or – or something else. She's staying with the woman, his colleague from the bank.' Pietro sounded thoughtful.

'Really?' said Sandro. He could almost hear Pietro's shrug.

'She wants to keep the children – out of it, for the moment.'

'Yes,' said Sandro, trying not to think of the children. 'So he – ah – he died somewhere else. Anything on time of death?'

'He hadn't eaten in four hours at least, and probably died in the afternoon or early evening of Saturday.' Pietro cleared his throat. 'They can work it out from the insect activity.'

Sandro felt his stomach clench even at the memory of the pathology lab. He had grown soft, that was for sure, away from the smell of formaldehyde and carbolic and latex, the bonesaw, the tilted slab and the ceramic trough for bodily fluids draining from the body.

'Any sign of the car yet?' he asked.

'Not yet,' said Pietro. 'But we'll find it.' They would, too, even if it was burnt-out or sunk in a reservoir. 'I'll let you know.'

Catching the resignation in his old friend's voice, Sandro had his shoulder against the hot wall in the shade, feeling his cheeks and forehead bathed in sweat. He loosened his tie. *Jesus*, he thought. To be out of here.

'I'm sorry,' he said softly.

'No,' said Pietro. 'It's all right. It's – well. Complicated enough already. The wife, the kids – I just don't want to be the one tells her he was on the make.'

'Is that what the Guardia think?'

'Who knows what they think?' For a moment Pietro sounded angry, then he sighed. 'They're being tight-lipped bastards just now. But it's obvious. When a bank manager dies in unexplained circumstances – well. He might have been on the make – or someone wanted information out of him. That's what I'd look for first.'

Sandro pursed his lips and said nothing: he knew what Pietro meant. There'd been a case only a month or so back, a bank employee and his wife abducted and tortured by an Eastern European gang for security details, a whole wall of safety deposit boxes plundered before the bodies were found the next morning. He peered inside: no sign of panic in there. No sign of violence, or ransacking, and however sleepy the security guard looked, surely he'd have noticed?

He could say to Pietro, I'm right here, I'm on the spot. Want me to ask a few questions? But he didn't, because he didn't want to hear that tone in Pietro's voice again. And what could he do, anyway? Without the technical support to make sense of what would be encoded and computerized and secured beyond the reach of intruders, legitimate or otherwise.

In the background Sandro heard the bleep and crackle of Pietro's police radio, and wiped his forehead. 'You need to go?' he said softly, but Pietro was already on it, talking in that familiar urgent and muffled tone into the radio. Then he was back.

'Sorry,' he said, and Sandro could tell his mind was already elsewhere. He wished he could ask what had come through on that radio message but he kept silent.

'Something's come up,' and from his guarded tone Sandro realized Pietro knew what thoughts had gone through his old partner's head.

'I understand,' said Sandro. 'You go.'

'There was something else,' said Pietro, hurriedly. 'The forensic examination. The post-mortem injuries – there were some marks – small abrasions – on his wrists, something like a friction burn across his back. And there was a lesion on his leg. Long, oval-shaped mark, on the inside of his leg.'

'A lesion?'

'Like a deep graze, or a burn.'

'And that stuff on his shoe, that was ash, right?' Sandro ran his tongue over his teeth, thinking. His mouth was sour. That was the heat too, and last night's wine. 'A fire?' He puzzled over it, thinking aloud. 'But he wasn't seriously burned.'

'No, no,' said Pietro, distant, not quite answering. 'They're analysing the ash. It's something unusual. Cellulose, celluloid, something like that.'

'Pietro,' said Sandro, losing his cool just a bit. 'Look. Is this a problem? I know he's not my guy. I know it's not my case. I know all that. I'm just trying to be thorough.' He sighed. 'I just wish we could – I don't know. Sit down and chew this over. Face to face.'

There was a long silence, and Sandro resigned himself to failure. He had no leverage: he couldn't ask, he could only wait, and patience wasn't his strong point.

Then Pietro breathed out explosively. 'All right,' he said. 'I know. It's just delicate, you know? With the Guardia and all. All right. There was some – DNA evidence.' Again Sandro waited. 'That blood – it wasn't all his. We're checking it against what we've got registered. You never know.'

All right. Sandro was keenly aware that Pietro hadn't told him not to worry, this was fine. But still.

You never knew. There was no national DNA database yet; the legislation was still being wrangled over. So presenting it as evidence was far from being a guarantee of results, unless things were absolutely cut and dried. But there was an embryonic resource, and some regional forces and some individuals were becoming enthusiastic about collecting samples. They could get lucky.

'I'll let you know.' And again that resignation.

'Thanks,' said Sandro humbly, staring down at the pavement.

'Chiara loved the present,' said Pietro, out of the blue, then hurriedly, 'I trust you. You won't let me down on this.' And he hung up.

It was a warning.

Sandro turned and once again he looked inside the bank. Time to grow some balls, he thought, and rapped on the window; when those inside turned towards him, he took out his badge and held it up against the glass.

*

Why didn't anyone tell me? This was the thought that ran stupidly through Roxana's head as she stared at what was left of the Carnevale.

Stupid, because why would anyone? *Oh, by the way, Roxi,* she could just hear Maria Grazia say, *the old porn cinema's closed down, thought you'd be interested.* Not.

It was hardly dramatic, either. They'd only got around to mounting the board halfway round the frontage. The signage – a vertical strip of coloured neon letters spelling out the name, 1950s vintage – was intact. Gaudy once, never tasteful, maybe they'd even be re-used now that kitsch was in again. When the building became whatever it was going to become, people would walk past, they'd shop there, maybe they'd even live there, and they'd be oblivious to the fact it had once been a porn cinema.

Roxana had never seen a porn movie in her life, nor had she the intention of ever doing so. She came closer to the boarded-up façade, unaccountably depressed. Why? It was a horrible little place. The dark glass, the mealy-mouthed notices forbidding minors entry and, inside, the dirty, dog-eared posters of thonged backsides and plastic breasts – clearly visible to those minors, undiscouraged, who would have had their noses pressed against the glass.

All on computers now. It had to be worse. Millions of images, each one a hundred, a thousand times worse than anything they ever showed in here, and no one to police who saw what. At least with the old cinema in the backstreet there'd always be some old dear leaning out of her window to see whose husband might have been paying a sneaky visit.

There was a door fitted in the hoarding. Roxana stepped closer and out of the shade, feeling a wave of heat rise from the stone.

So this was why the dark-eyed man with his cashbag hadn't been in: his job was gone. Had whoever owned the cinema found a place for him somewhere else? For some reason, that mattered to Roxana. What would he do? He'd always been so polite. Waited obediently, let old ladies go ahead of him, never grumbled if there was a queue.

You didn't think customers made any impression, not really, just the same old thing day in, day out, but there they were, the details, they stacked up over the years. Maybe it was the same for someone working in a porn cinema. The shade of lipstick, the dog always tied up outside, the car parked illegally, the particular brand of aftershave. Ma would say it was the OCD. 'You shouldn't fill your head with all that stuff,' she'd say. 'All those little tiny bits and pieces, a waste of space. Only so much room in your brain.'

And then, 'You're just like your father.' With his labelled jars and drawers in the shed, his tools laid a certain way in the box, his folding and refolding of shirts.

She should have gone and got that toolbox and fixed the gate herself, shouldn't she? Roxana realized she was dreading going home, talking to the handyman about the gate. What if he wasn't trustworthy? What if he preyed on vulnerable women?

Stop it.

Roxana looked up at the building: like the signage, it dated from the 1950s, and it was drab and filthy. It would have sprung up after the war; this close to the Ponte Vecchio, a lot of buildings were just as ugly, the originals having been blown up by the retreating Germans. The plaster was black with decades of grime and exhaust fumes. The windows were thick with dust, inside and out. There was a sign up, too high for her to read: an artist's impression of balconied apartments and people – those blissfully ignorant people – walking by. Redevelopment: of course. The only mystery was that it had taken until now.

How long since she last walked down here? How long had it been boarded up like this? The man had brought in takings only ten days ago. She moved closer to look at the pine boarding: it was still tacky with resin and smelled of the forest. Then she put her hand against the door that had been cut into the tongue and groove, and it swung open under her hand. Without thinking, she stepped through, and the door banged shut behind her.

She stood on the pavement, hidden by the boarding from the street. The steel fishnet security shutters were still intact. Stepping up, she peered through. Between the shutters and the smoked-glass doors, the floor was ankle-deep in a slurry of junk mail and other flotsam: Roxana could see the polystyrene of a fast-food container, with the shrivelled remains of its contents. A number of envelopes she recognized, the little paned ones with the mark of the bank's franking machine, then she turned her head sideways to see better. MM Holdings: that was the name of the addressee. No surprise there: the company was a customer of the bank.

One of the darkened glass doors was ajar behind the shutters and with some displacement of air, from inside or out, perhaps even the delayed effect of her own entrance, a gust of something reached her. It was not clearly identifiable, that smell: it was some combination of dark things, of staleness and damp, rotting carpet, the sharp stink of urine and something chemical too, something sulphurous, but Roxana, even having grown up in the city with its overflowing dumpsters and leaking drains, found herself putting a hand to her mouth and nose and holding it there.

There was a sound from behind her. The flimsy door wrenched open and as she turned a voice, deep, angry and suspicious, and not quite Italian.

'What the hell d'you think you're doing?'

A man in a torn T-shirt under overalls, wiry and unshaven. He carried a hammer.

'Sorry,' said Roxana, 'I'm sorry,' and saw him looking her up and down in silence, the shirt and jacket and tights. She didn't belong here.

'I – I was looking for someone,' she stammered, and his stare hardened.

'There's no one here,' he said curtly. He was from the East, she thought, Romanian or Polish or Bosnian, one of those. 'The place is empty. We'll be getting guard dogs in next week; you're lucky you didn't come looking then.'

'I'm sorry,' she said again. 'The door wasn't locked, I just thought – he might still be here.'

'Who?' said the man, folding his arms aggressively.

Roxana darted a glance over her shoulder into the dim, fetid interior beyond the wire shuttering. 'He used to work here,' she said. 'That's all. He just – just disappeared. I wanted to know where he'd gone.'

Something dawned behind the man's eyes, no more than a crafty glimmer. 'Right,' he said. 'What d'you want him for, exactly? Girl like you.'

Roxana swallowed: she didn't like being called a girl, suddenly.

'Nothing,' she said, involuntarily taking a step backwards, feeling the stinking dark behind her. 'It's all right, it doesn't matter.'

'Let me tell you,' said the builder, and a smile widened, without warmth. As he uncrossed his arms, she saw the veined flexing of biceps, despite his leanness. 'It was disgusting in there. Whoever he was – he didn't live like a king. That little hole of his.'

She couldn't stop herself; incredulously she blurted, 'He *lived* in there?'

The man with his hammer grunted, rocking on his heels. 'You can call it living,' he said. 'This city,' and he smiled again. 'You seen them? It's not all rich, with the swimming pool and the garage. In the basement, in the attic, they live like rats, no one can see.' And the arm with the hammer relaxed and the hand swung down loose at his side. 'Should have got started months ago,' he said. 'Come looking in September, no more pigsty. You find someone your type.'

'It – it was a business matter,' Roxana improvised, wanting to shut him up, wipe that smile off his face, wanting to push past him and run.

'Business?' and he cocked his head, suddenly quite still: it was as if the word had sent an alert somewhere. 'What kind of business?' And then, pushing his angry face close to hers so she could see the trace of white in his stubble and smell the cigarettes on his breath. 'You tell me your name, please.' And his hand was on the strap of her handbag, and holding.

'Roxi?'

And she felt her knees almost buckle with relief at his voice, coming from the other side of the tongue and groove boarding. High-pitched, a bit panicky, a bit useless, but she'd never been so happy to hear it in her life.

'Are you in there? The security guard said – Roxi?'

It was Val, come to find her.

CHAPTER SEVENTEEN

S HE APPEARED IN THE kitchen doorway, padding on bare feet, pale but not sick, not any more. The ghost of colour in her cheeks.

From the kitchen table Luisa smiled at Anna tentatively. The tabletop was scattered with pages of notes: Sandro's notes. She hastily pushed them into a pile and pulled out a chair beside her. Moving gingerly under her own weight, Anna lowered herself obediently into the seat.

Without asking, Luisa put water on to boil. Camomile tea, the answer to everything and nothing. Sweet biscuits: she wished she had something better than the plain ones she kept as a last resort. She would buy something with chocolate, Luisa decided. She should also get something more tempting and began to wonder where she might get a decent chicken in August; chicken would be good for the baby.

Telling herself not to be daft, that Anna Niescu would probably have fled before she got back from the butcher's, Luisa turned from the stove to see the girl studying a page covered in Sandro's scrawl. He'd written down what they told him about the apartment. It was headed, *Via del Lazaretto*. It was about the only thing on the page that was legible, but it was enough. Anna turned her head sideways to meet Luisa's gaze.

'You went there?' she said, and at the trace of pride in the girl's voice, Luisa's heart sank. 'Did you see it? Did you see our apartment?'

Carefully, Luisa set the cup in front of her and the plate of biscuits. She sat down.

'It's a lovely area,' she said. 'Close to the countryside, isn't it? Very nice.'

Anna set her chin in her hands and gazed off into the distance. 'You think I'm an idiot,' she said simply. 'You think he deceived me.' She sat up and looked into Luisa's face, hands folded on top of her belly. She didn't even glance at the biscuits.

'I don't know,' said Luisa, and it was the truth. However bad it looked, she still clung to the belief that the man had at least loved Anna Niescu. What kind of human being could deceive this child, in that way? If Sandro were here, he would tell her, *Plenty. There are plenty of them out there.* Luisa knew as much herself, if she was being sensible, only she wasn't being particularly sensible at the moment. Going to see that apartment with the balconies in San Niccolo had only been the start of Luisa not being sensible.

'We couldn't get inside the apartment,' she said with a sigh and pushed the plate closer to Anna. 'Eat. For the baby.'

Anna contemplated the biscuits, which Luisa had arranged in a star shape, and picked one up. 'No,' she said, nibbling, the food held in her little paw of a hand. 'I couldn't get inside either. No one would let me in. That porter knew I was there but he hid from me.'

'Did you see him when you went there with your – with Josef?' asked Luisa. 'The porter?'

'He spied on us,' said Anna, still nibbling, to Luisa's satisfaction. 'I saw that the door was open a crack.'

'But he didn't come out? He didn't speak to you?'

Anna shook her head and laid the biscuit down. It looked as if a mouse had been at it. Luisa gestured towards the tea and Anna drank. Luisa waited; Anna was defensive enough as it was. If there was doubt in her mind, somehow it seemed important to Luisa that she realize it for herself.

Eventually Anna spoke. 'Josef had the keys.' She frowned. 'Three or four keys on a keyring: a big Ferrari keyring, red with the horse. A small one for the front gate, a medium-sized one for the front door, a long one for the apartment door, a tiny one for the postbox.'

She was observant. That hadn't really occurred to Luisa before. 'Did he look in the postbox?' she asked, more out of idle interest than anything else. It was the first thing she would do herself, on returning home.

Anna frowned at the question, then hesitantly shook her head. 'We went straight up,' she said, smiling a little. 'In the lift. I like to take the stairs, it's good for me, I said, but he made me take the lift.'

Luisa tried to visualize the apartment building's lobby. Lift facing as you came through the doors. She hadn't seen the stairs. They must be round at the back.

'And then?' she asked softly. 'I expect you were excited, weren't you?'

'Well, he said, don't expect too much. He said, it needs work. He tried to keep my hopes down, I think. But I was excited. I haven't ever had a place of my own.'

Luisa nodded. She knew how that felt. She and Sandro had lived with her mother for three, nearly four years before they got their own place; they'd moved out when she was pregnant. That had been how it was done. And when the baby died, thirty-six hours after she was born, Luisa remembered how that felt too, coming back to the empty apartment, too big for just the two of them.

'And when you saw it? What did you think?'

Anna turned her head a little, a distant look in her eyes. 'I don't know. It was – a bit dusty. I think it had been empty for a long time. Josef kept apologizing for everything, when he couldn't make the light come on.'

'Was the flat furnished?' There was something about Anna's account that made Luisa uneasily curious.

Anna chewed her lip. 'There were beds and a couch and a very old kitchen. You could sleep there.' Luisa saw her glance quickly around herself. 'Much older than this one, I mean, more like the one at the Loggiata. It would have been fine, of course. I am used to old things. I told Josef, there was no need to change it.'

'And how was he?'

Anna set her lips together, a small line appearing between her eyebrows. 'He was – agitated. A bit.'

Luisa nodded. Her unease was not diminishing.

Anna went on, concentrating as she tried to be precise, 'He – he was excited like me, when we opened the door. Then he grew more – anxious, as we walked around. I think he was worried that I didn't like it. I kept telling him I liked it.'

'And did you?'

'Of course,' said Anna, still frowning, looking down at her hands. 'I would have made it our home.' She looked up. 'As you said, it is a very nice part of the city. Very quiet, very green.'

Quiet, thought Luisa. Remembering the hum of the motorway as they had exited the bus on the ring road, a different sort of sound, low and constant. She preferred the sounds inside the city. People talking in the street.

The suburbs were an uneasy place to Luisa. A view of the hills was one thing, although you could get a similar, more distant version of that from the city centre if you were high enough. She pondered the slopes of the Mugello that would have comprised the view from that apartment, and below the picture-postcard view, the remains of old farm buildings slowly eroded by the advance of the city. Shacks and old fridges and woodstacks in the lee of the motorway, old lives disintegrating on the dirty verges and beside slip roads.

'Of course,' she said gently. 'Very good for children, especially.' Anna brightened, and cautiously Luisa proceeded.

'Did you meet the neighbours?'

'Not really,' said Anna, and Luisa heard a defensive note in her voice. 'I would have liked to. I suppose perhaps people keep themselves to themselves in those places. Do you think so?'

Luisa shrugged. 'Some do,' she said cautiously. Thought of Giovanna Baldini. 'Some don't. Maybe it was the wrong time of day,' she went on. 'People at work.'

'Maybe,' said Anna. 'We didn't stay long.' Her head bobbed down. 'A night. Then later, when I – when I was pregnant. We thought about where we would put the nursery. Two nights. Both times he had to get to work, early. I had to also.'

Luisa nodded, Anna looking away, not wanting to say any more. Two nights together, one to get pregnant, the second to make a home. Decide where to put the baby's cot. What had they said at the Loggiata, when their little Anna stopped out all night?

'I have one day off,' Anna said, her small chin jutting defiantly as if she knew what Luisa was thinking. 'Monday off.' Luisa began to murmur something non-committal, only Anna took hold of her hand and with sudden and surprising determination held her eyes. 'Where is he?' she said. 'Where?'

Looking back at her, Luisa waited a moment, concentrating on keeping her expression, her movements, her voice, quite calm. 'We don't know yet,' she said. 'We will, though.' Uncertainly Anna nodded, not turning away, and then Luisa asked her, 'You noticed something, didn't you?' she said. 'When you went to that flat with him. You knew something was wrong, then, didn't you? You knew even then.'

And keeping her eyes fixed on Luisa, slowly Anna nodded.

*

'I don't know who he is,' said the woman called Marisa Goldman, glancing down at the crumpled paper with a cold stare. 'No. But it's a ridiculous question.'

The officers of the financial police might, to Sandro's relief, have gone out on their lunch break – Sandro had no desire for a run-in with unfriendly authority – but someone was in Claudio Brunello's office.

The door was firmly closed, but as Goldman had ushered him into her own room, at once impatient and reluctant, he had seen a large head bent over a desk next door. The head had been raised at the sound of Sandro's entrance, and even though the computer screen on the desk had blocked all but the eyes and a bulky outline from view, there had been something about those eyes, the big rounded shoulders that, had Marisa Goldman not practically shoved him ahead of her into her office, he'd have liked a closer look at. Something familiar.

Sandro knew her type. *Bella figura* was all she cared about: keeping it together and looking good. Wearing the right kind of shoes. Luisa had a thousand customers like Miss Marisa Goldman, with long brown legs, long aristocratic necks, long noses to look down, women she'd clothed since they were fifteen but who wouldn't deign to recognize her in the street. Empty-headed, self-absorbed, narcissistic people – they were everywhere – people who regarded things and labels as if they were more important than the human beings holding them out for inspection.

There were two photographs in heavy, discreet frames on the

shelf: one of Marisa Goldman somewhere like Scotland, looking charming in a tweed outfit beside a heavy-set, glowering man, gun carelessly over her shoulder. In the other she was on a horse. More of the same: those sports that didn't mean sport but status.

He kept his smile.

'I know it's an awful picture,' he said patiently.

She thrust it back at him. 'You're right,' she said. 'It's an awful picture,' and he heard weariness in her voice. Perhaps he'd misjudged her. 'And it's a bad time,' she said.

'I am aware of that,' said Sandro earnestly. 'Please.'

She'd only agreed to talk to him because he'd invoked Pietro and the investigation into Brunello's death. With arms folded on the other side of the smoked glass, she'd glared at him stony-faced as he pleaded. 'Call the Polizia dello Stato,' he'd mouthed. 'Ask for Pietro, Officer Cavallaro. He'll tell you.'

'So this man—' She gestured at the paper now folded in Sandro's hand. 'He was passing himself off as Claudio.' She shook her head tiredly. 'I don't understand. Why? Was it – fraud? Was he trying to – make money in some way?'

Sandro was struck by the fact that he had not considered that possibility; he really hadn't. It was only at this moment that he thought of what Anna Niescu had said about her adoptive parents leaving her their savings: a few hundred, maybe at a pinch a few thousand, in the bank. A sum, from which Sandro had no intention of taking a penny himself. She was going to need it. But there were plenty of people out there who mugged and murdered for less. Was Josef going to suggest he invest it for her? He cursed himself: it took a money person to ask the money question.

'I don't know,' he said, aware how lame this sounded. Then sat upright. 'At least, I believe he only passed himself off as Claudio Brunello to one person. A limited deception.'

So far that was true, but then again he had not so far tracked down another human being who had been introduced formally to Anna Niescu's fiancé. His spirits sagged further: so what if he was only thirty-six hours into this investigation? He'd got nowhere.

The young – well, youngish – man put his head around the door. Sandro had glimpsed him on the way in. The male version of Miss Goldman, perhaps, glossy hair, crisp collar.

They'd been in the middle of something when he'd knocked at the window, no doubt prompted by the Guardia di Finanza's disappearance for lunch, and after reluctantly allowing him in, Marisa Goldman had concluded their talk without reference to Sandro, who was standing there like a fool. It had turned out to be nothing to do with officialdom, as far as he could tell – more like the usual office bitching.

'It's too much,' Marisa Goldman had been saying. 'If her mother needs – care, well, she should organize that. If she wants to be a professional. Calling her at work, God knows how many times a day, saying her mobile's engaged and where is she? Rabbiting on to me about God knows what. Intruders? Delivery men?'

This woman, this Marisa Goldman, obviously had no time for mothers. Had she not had one of her own? Sandro had stayed silent, trying not to think about what would happen to his country if old women, old mothers, were no longer given respect.

The young man, retreating behind his cash desk, had looked pained, to his credit: had tried to defend whoever it was needed defending. Sandro saw a photograph of a motorbike pinned up behind the boy's workstation. That was what they called them, workstations. The word made Sandro feel ill. He was beyond it now, wasn't he? He'd never be able to knuckle down to office life again.

'We've got ten minutes,' the young man said now, looking earnestly at his boss. 'Then I'll open up, right? Do you – um – need me in here?'

And the penny dropped: Sandro remembered. This was the guy he was going to talk to when he got back from his lunch break, the one Roxana Delfino said spoke to a woman calling for Claudio Brunello. What was his name?

'No, Valentino,' said Marisa Goldman impatiently. Val, Roxana Delfino had called him. That would be him. Sandro eyed him covertly. 'We don't need you.'

'Well, I—'

Sandro interrupted diffidently. 'There was a phone call, wasn't there? Miss, ah, Miss Delfino said you took a call.'

'A call?'

Slowly something dawned in Valentino's eyes. Could this boy be as dozy as he looked? Sadly, Sandro suspected that he could. Pampered kid: if you rated witnesses on a scale of one to ten, well-bred young men would be about a one and a half. They could hardly see further than the shine on their own shoes. Mean old ladies: now, they'd be up in the nines.

'A call,' he repeated patiently. 'On Monday? From a woman?'

'Yeah, that was stupid,' Valentino said, almost but not quite shamefaced. You could say that, thought Sandro. How come this guy has a job? It occurred to Sandro that there might be circumstances in which you would need your employees not to notice stuff.

'I guess it was his wife, trying to track him down,' Valentino faltered. 'Poor lady.' He grimaced.

'You guess?' Marisa Goldman looked at the limits of her patience, staring at Valentino.

'Well, she was pretty over the top. *Is Claudio there? Just tell me if Claudio's there,* she kept saying. She didn't actually say who she was before she hung up. I suppose maybe she thought I knew.'

Sandro looked at him. Trying to decide whether anyone could really be so dumb, or so uninterested. And found that the thing he didn't want to think about was that calm and dignified woman, screaming down the phone.

Marisa Goldman turned to Sandro. 'It was his wife. Irene Brunello is staying with me, now. She told me that she was phoning all over the place to try to track him down.' She spoke stiffly.

'She's staying with you?' Sandro could not stop himself raising his eyebrows at that. But Marisa Goldman was frowning as if already regretting saying anything at all, turning away from Sandro to the door.

'Valentino, go and find Roxana, will you? We can't open like this. Where on earth has she got to?'

The head withdrew, the door closing smartly behind him. And there was the poster again: *Look ahead! Get in line!* Sandro remembered with a sinking heart that he had still to ask his own bank manager about a mortgage.

'Perhaps I could talk to him when he gets back,' said Sandro, almost to himself.

'Perhaps,' said Marisa Goldman. 'But perhaps he will be otherwise engaged.'

'Miss Delfino was exceptionally helpful,' said Sandro and immediately regretted it when Marisa Goldman's eyes narrowed. Was she wondering how many of the bank's secrets her colleague might have given away? 'Look,' he heard himself pleading now. 'I understand this is a difficult time. Of course I am acting in my client's interests but –' and he held up a hand as she opened her mouth to protest '– but it is possible there may be a connection. With your boss's death. It may help the police if we can trace this man. Don't you see?'

'You think he has something to do with Claudio's death?' Marisa Goldman's whole stance had changed, become stilled, intent. Arms on the desk, she leaned forwards, closer to him.

'Who is your client?'

'I – I don't think—'

'Look,' said Marisa Goldman, speaking carefully. 'If you want me to respond to your questions –' and she darted a glance at the office next door '– now of all the moments to choose, you must at least answer mine.'

Sandro regarded her, thinking furiously. 'There is such a thing as client confidentiality,' he said.

'Like with doctors?' Marisa Goldman replied, raising her eyebrows sardonically. This was better than her coldness, but Sandro still couldn't bring himself to like her.

'That kind of thing,' he said. Then sighed. 'Look, I can't tell you her name. But I can tell you that it's to do with a personal situation. She's trying to find this man for private reasons. It is not a financial investigation.'

Marisa Goldman sat back in her chair, and he didn't like her expression at all. Something like satisfaction, something like disdain. 'Oh, I see,' she said.

'Did your boss have affairs?' he asked, before he could stop himself, ask himself where he was going with this. Just wanted to wipe that look off her face, probably.

'My boss has nothing to do with you,' she said levelly.

Yes, thought Sandro, and just from the look she gave him, a whole history unfolded. Yes: he improvised. You and Brunello had a small thing, a few years back, no doubt you engineered it while his wife was pregnant or something, and he regretted it, he wasn't that kind of man, and you bullied him into giving you this job out of guilt. That's how it was. Sandro couldn't have said how he knew it just from the cold flash in her eye, but he did. Sometimes a small gesture told a big story.

'You're right,' he said. 'I'm sorry.' And when she turned her gaze away he knew that she knew that he knew.

And Irene Brunello probably had a pretty good idea too: that woman wasn't a fool. Did Marisa Goldman offer to take her in after her husband's body was found, or was she asked? When men died, wives and mistresses often got together, to mourn or to scream at each other, or both. Not these two, though; he could picture them circling, dropping hints, evading, coldly polite. Irene Brunello would get to the truth in the end, he was fairly sure of that; he was also sure he didn't want to come between them.

Marisa Goldman was watching him; she wasn't telling him to get out. 'Show me the piece of paper again,' she said.

The bank settled into silence around them as she gave the picture another, closer look. She even went so far as to switch on a small anglepoise on her desk and hold the paper under it. Sandro shifted on his chair: he didn't like it in here. The air seemed thick and sluggish in the heat, the gloom was oppressive, and the outside world, dimly visible through the smoked glass and security doors, far off and inaccessible. It was like being locked in a cave. He pulled at his tie to loosen it.

'I don't know,' said Goldman slowly. 'I don't know.' But there was something in her voice, more doubt than before. Sandro gave her time: his eye roving the room's neat, minimal decor. Not like her boss's, no family pictures, just those ones of her, polished and posing.

He noticed that she had a small stack of papers to her left, on the desk. She'd been doing some work. He tilted his head just a degree to get a look. The top page was printed with two colour photographs, a shuttered façade, a garden with some white chairs. His eye travelled to the letterhead: something Immobiliare, it said. Not work then? Galeotti Immobiliare. His head jerked up and he caught her watching him. Galeotti was the name of the estate agent who had shown them the apartment in San Niccolo. Small world.

He smiled.

'How would I go about getting a loan?' he asked, just idly, nodding towards the poster on the wall. 'If it was me, I mean? What would I have to do to get, say, thirty thousand euros?'

Marisa Goldman eyed him narrowly. 'Proof of earnings, bank statements, credit history,' she recited distractedly, her eyes once again on the paper, held between both hands now. 'You'd have to have an interview with our – with. Well ...' She looked back at Sandro, as though he was finally coming into focus. 'You would have had to talk to Claudio,' she said. 'Some banks wouldn't require that, but he was very hands-on.' Compressed her lips. 'And with older customers – it's more complicated.'

'Thanks for that,' said Sandro drily.

She looked down again. 'Do you think he might be a customer?' she said. 'This man you're after? I really see customers only by appointment. Valentino and Roxana – Miss Delfino – they – ah – they have most of the routine customer interaction.'

Hands-on. Routine customer interaction. Proof of earnings. How could Sandro even contemplate asking to borrow money, here or anywhere else? They didn't speak his language. But Marisa Goldman was looking at him, calculating.

'But I might have seen him.' She spoke stiffly. Was she finally beginning to see the point of them: the human beings who came in and out of here asking for help, asking for money, asking for sympathy? People in trouble.

The sheet of A4 paper was folded now, on her desk. 'Yes,' said Marisa Goldman. 'I think I saw him in with Claudio, in his office. A month ago perhaps? Perhaps more.'

'So he's a customer.'

'It would seem so,' said Marisa Goldman. 'I imagine he was asking for a loan. When you mentioned – well. That is generally what people want, here.'

And he saw her eyes shift, professional, cool, to look past him, and she got to her feet. Turning his head, Sandro saw them standing there, just inside the door through which he'd been admitted, Roxana Delfino and the boy who'd been sent to find her. They seemed almost out of breath.

'Did he appear – this man you saw? Did you notice anything about him? Anything at all?'

'Notice anything? No,' she said. 'People asking for money all look the same. They want to please you, they are a little nervous perhaps. They don't know: in the end it's all down to the figures.' She compressed her lips. 'He wasn't our sort of – well. Claudio let him down gently, told him, "here's my card, let me know if anything changes." You know the sort of thing.' She flicked her hair back. She'd have shown no such civility. The smile she turned on him was chilly. 'Look, if you'll excuse me now. We've got to open up.'

And she was brushing past him, out into the bank's foyer. Feeling himself dismissed, Sandro followed her.

'Roxana, your mother called.' Marisa Goldman had already moved on, and as he edged around her to the door, she was talking to the Delfino girl in a tone that set Sandro's teeth on edge. 'Several times. I would like to remind you that this is your place of work.'

'I—' Roxana Delfino looked very pale. 'My mother?'

Sandro hesitated at the door. His phone bleeped in his pocket and surreptitiously he stole a look at it. Three missed calls, it said, one from Pietro, two from Luisa.

'It's all right,' said Valentino, darting a glance from Roxana to Sandro and back. 'I'll get opened up.' And he hurried to a panel beside the security door.

Sandro felt Roxana Delfino's eyes on him. 'Miss Delfino,' he said.

'You're back,' she said, distractedly. She didn't look as though her lunch break had done her much good. 'Maybe you're what we need,' she said, trying to smile. 'Maybe my mother needs a private detective, not a carer.' Her troubled expression intensified.

'Is everything all right?' he asked, feeling his hand curl around the mobile, wanting to look at it, but something about Roxana Delfino detaining him.

'Roxana,' said Marisa Goldman sharply.

'Back to work,' said Roxana, meeting his gaze directly. 'I'm fine, thank you, Mr Cellini.'

She remembered my name, he thought as he passed out through the security door, its strident mechanical voice lecturing him, unheeded. *Please step back and remove all metallic objects.* Well, that's something. She remembered my name.

Out on the street, Sandro had to walk quickly away from the bank's window as it was in full sun, the suffocating heat of a long afternoon hitting him like a wall. This could go on another month – that would kill him.

There was no sign of the returning Guardia di Finanza. Walking as far as the river, Sandro found some decent shade before he dialled the familiar number. As it rang, Sandro realized he'd left the picture of Anna Niescu and her Josef behind on Marisa Goldman's desk. The only image of the man whose name they still didn't know, a sheet of crumpled A4. Of course, it still existed, in theory. It was on the phone, they could print another off, it existed – digitally. But Sandro didn't like digital, Sandro liked the real thing, even if the real thing was only a blurred image on cheap paper. He felt uneasy.

Looking along the river with the phone to his ear, down to where the grassy terrace of the city's prestigious rowing club glowed in the late-afternoon light, Sandro saw a man in a singlet, with the deep tan and air of ease of the very wealthy, lifting the long fibreglass hull of a boat into the green water.

The voice answered, and not as wearily as the last time they'd spoken.

'Pietro,' said Sandro. 'What's new?'

CHAPTER EIGHTEEN

WALKING HAD SEEMED A good idea when Giuli left the apartment – no more than a kilometre; the Via dei Serragli was being dug up so she'd have had to make a long detour on the moped – but by the time she reached the vast and peeling front door of the Loggiata, she was exhausted. The heat thickened the air, somehow, so even moving through it seemed to use up extra energy. What was wrong with her? Getting old, old and heavy and slow, and her stomach bothering her to boot. Wouldn't it be typical if she turned out to have some new type of hepatitis, or something, after all this time, after cleaning up? They'd had her tested for one or two things when she'd gone to prison and she'd been so surprised that she cared at all when she'd been clear. No HIV, no Hep C.

This heat.

And it wasn't only her moving slowly today, it turned out. It took a good ten minutes before Giuli got an answer through the intercom, and another lengthy pause before the buzzer sounded and the latch clicked to allow her in.

Behind the door, the entrance hall – wide, dark and cool – was so deliciously refreshing that for a moment Giuli was tempted to just stay there a while, leaning against the crumbling plaster. But she went on up.

The grey ghost of a cat slunk noiselessly away at the opening of the hotel's door, squeezing through the glass doors that stood ajar and gave on to the long *loggia*. At the reception desk Dasha hardly glanced up. She was reading a fat, cheap paperback, its spine cracked ruinously.

'Ciao,' said Giuli, cursing herself for sounding ingratiating. 'How you doing?'

'You again,' said the girl, elbows on the desk, settling her chin in her cupped hands and looking at Giuli. 'Kidnap, is it?'

'What d'you mean?' Giuli looked at her, expressionless.

'You have our girl. Who do you think is doing the work, the chambermaid? Have you come for – for ransom?' It was her idea of a joke, delivered without any more malice than usual, but it put an idea in Giuli's head that she didn't like.

'Well, had anyone thought about what was going to happen when the baby came?' she said, and thought, hark at me. Giuli the responsible, the foresighted, as if she hadn't misspent her own youth more comprehensively than anyone she'd ever met. More than Dasha, whose eyes had returned to her book.

'Not my problem,' she said, chewing ruminatively as she turned a page.

Giuli gazed around. 'And it's not as if you're busy, is it? Have you got any customers at all?' She thought of something: two birds with one stone. 'Is the old lady around?'

'No,' said Dasha, still not looking up. Giuli crossed over to the desk and placed her hand on the pages. Dangerously, Dasha raised her head, stared Giuli in the eye.

'No to what?' said Giuli, politely, meeting her black-lashed blue gaze. And Dasha laughed, unexpectedly.

'You are like me,' she said. 'I don't know there are any

Italian girls like me.'

'I'm older than you,' said Giuli, stony-faced. Then cracked a smile. 'And there's a few like us. No to what?'

'No customers,' said Dasha, and stretching a thin pale arm over her head, she yawned. 'And the old woman is not here either; she is asleep.' Jerked her head. 'Upstairs. Siesta she call it. Looks like she is practising for being dead, to me.' She closed the book. 'So what do you want?' she said.

'You've seen him, haven't you?' said Giuli, because then it came to her, what Dasha had been hiding, that last time. The girl's smile faded and she was stilled, watching. She said nothing.

Giuli persisted. 'I mean, since, you've seen him since he was supposed to have disappeared. Since Anna last saw him.'

She held her breath. Dasha looked around as if someone might suddenly materialize in the dead and silent space. She said nothing.

Giuli shrugged. 'People aren't as clever as they think they are,' she said. 'I knew something was bothering you. Why didn't you tell me?'

The dark-blue eyes narrowed, the pale pretty face turned stubborn. 'She's better without him,' she said, and folded her arms. Something in Dasha's set jawline told Giuli to work around to it slowly. Not barge straight in there.

'Anna is – better off without him?'

Dasha nodded, her mouth set in a line.

'Why? What do you know about him?'

'She don't like him,' said Dasha, her eyes flicking up to the floor above.

'She. The old lady?' It seemed to Giuli that Dasha was prevaricating. 'And she's always right about people, is she? About – foreigners, for example? About you?'

'She's – what you say – she is racist, yes,' said Dasha equably, as if she was saying, she's vegetarian. 'She don't like foreigners too much, but I am cheap. She even say I am clean, like usually Russians are not.' Her smile didn't reach her eyes.

'That's the only reason she doesn't like him, that he's foreign?'

'Not only reason. She says he has a dirty job.'

Giuli sat back, looking up at the ceiling, thinking of the old woman lying like a corpse up there, chewing over ancient hatreds. 'A dirty job. You know what his job is?'

Stiffly Dasha shook her head. Giuli leaned towards her, feeling queasiness stir low in her gut, feeling a little sweat break on her upper lip. A tiny frown appeared on Dasha's face as if to say, don't ask for sympathy. Don't ask for sympathy from me.

'Where did you see him?' Giuli hadn't intended to whisper, but a hoarse whisper was what came out.

'You all right?' asked Dasha warily.

'This heat,' said Giuli. It passed. 'Where did you see him, Dasha? Did he come here? When?'

Abruptly Dasha stood up, paced to the glass doors leading on to the wide *loggia* and pushed through them. After a moment's indecision Giuli followed her.

It was better outside; they both felt it. The *loggia* faced north-east and was in shade. It was probably hotter than inside but less stifling, the air less still. Dasha rested her forearms on the waist-high parapet and looked down into the street, Giuli beside her. Her phone blipped: damn. She took it out, glanced at the screen, turned it off. Damn: she waited a moment for the silence to re-establish itself.

'Did he come here?' she said, nodding at the narrow pavement below.

The girl said nothing, just stared down.

'He wanted to see her.' Still nothing. 'You didn't tell her.'

She took the girl's silence for agreement. It was true: she was the same kind of animal Giuli had once been herself, hiding and watching, her survival dependent on never trusting anyone. Giuli couldn't tell her, when you find someone you can trust, the world changes. Better to know whom you couldn't trust, first. She said nothing.

'That your boss on the phone?' said Dasha, changing the subject, Giuli suspected deliberately. 'You can look at the *telefonino*, if you want. You can turn back on.'

At the rough kindness in the girl's voice Giuli shook her head. 'Not my boss,' she said. 'My boyfriend.'

She didn't use the word *fidanzato*. She wouldn't even have used the word 'boyfriend', wouldn't have surrendered any information at all a year ago. She was getting soft: it was asking for scorn, from someone like Dasha.

'How you get your job?' was all Dasha said and, holding the phone out, watching the screen illuminate, seeing two missed calls and a message, Giuli tore herself away from it to look into the girl's eyes. What had she asked?

'How did I get my job?' she said. 'That's a long story.'

'So you going now,' said Dasha defiantly, arms folded. 'Now I tell you?'

'You told me nothing,' said Giuli reasonably.

'He's hiding somewhere,' said Dasha. 'Scared of something. You want her involved in that? I see her looking at her phone, waiting for him to call, but he doesn't call. I'm telling you, it is best for her without him. We can look after her.' Cocked her head to one side. 'Or you going to find your boyfriend?'

She eyed Giuli narrowly and indeed Giuli had been thinking, with tenderness, of Enzo, of maybe a snatched coffee with Enzo, to tell him what she'd learned, to show off just a little bit.

The look that Dasha gave her was so complicated, though, envious, a little malicious, a little suspicious, that it stopped Giuli in her tracks. This was business, this was serious.

'No,' she said. 'First off, I find my boss. He's not far away.'

She'd passed the pharmacy on the Via Romana on the way, and it was still open on the way back, and this time, without thinking, without knowing what she wanted, Giuli went in. It was an old-fashioned establishment, with little gilded drawers and glass urns behind the counter. Even as she crossed the threshold, the thought came into Giuli's head that, if she was right, then this place might mean something to her for the rest of her life. She wouldn't be able to walk past it without thinking, *there.*

She asked for what she now knew she wanted; she tolerated the long, curious look from the pharmacist – a thin man, blue-chinned and prematurely old; Giuli had known his domineering blonde mother before him. He was involved, now; he was her accomplice, whatever the outcome.

Giuli felt slightly stunned as she walked out and back into the heat.

She stashed it right down in her handbag, wrapped tight, although if you looked hard enough, you could read the lettering through the thin plastic bag. Two minutes, it said, find out today in only two minutes. You could read that quietly, soberly, or ecstatically, depending. On how you felt about it. The trouble was, Giuli didn't know how she felt about it.

*

Sandro had phoned home, after he'd talked to Pietro, but there'd been no answer. He hadn't let it ring too long, though, thinking perhaps they were both asleep, in this heat, and he hadn't tried Luisa's mobile for the same reason. Nothing more infuriating than an over-anxious, needy husband when peace and quiet was what you were after. He wanted someone to talk to, though. So he'd called Giuli instead and left a message when she didn't answer either.

'There's a bit of a park,' Sandro said into the phone, leaning on the parapet by the river and looking across at it as he spoke. 'Between the Ponte Alle Grazie and the Ponte San Niccolo, south side, some trees and a bar right over the water, one of those summer bars.' He was rambling, he could hear himself, so he cut it short. 'Meet me over there, if you can? I'll wait. No need to call back.'

In the event, at least to Sandro, it seemed to take a good half an hour just to walk across the wide, deserted, sunlit bridge of the Ponte Alle Grazie. The heat was like a sledgehammer, out there in the open, and there wasn't a scrap of shade. People only congregated on the bridges at night-time in August, gulping anything that felt like fresh air; now, there was barely a soul to be seen. Anyone with any sense hid in cool bars or shuttered apartments until the sun set, or merely stayed in the shade of the biggest, gloomiest *palazzi* in the narrowest streets.

While he waited for Guili, Sandro drank iced tea. He didn't like it; it wasn't cold enough, despite the name, and it was too sweet, but the look in the surly, underaged waiter's eyes had told him ordering water wouldn't do. Why had he chosen the place? Erected every July on this stubby forested outcrop of the embankment, the bar existed only for stranded tourists; it was packed up at the end of the summer and gone. Below it, on the green riverbank, a kind of beach set-up had been conjured out of grass huts and sunloungers on the sparse grass, and one or two diehard sunbathers were there, staked out.

The sun was low in the sky, and Sandro thought that soon, mercifully, the Guardia di Finanza would pack up and leave that dismal little bank for the day, and those haunted, fearful employees would scatter back to their homes, waiting in the shadow of the axe.

There was supposed to be co-operation between the services – the Guardia di Finanza, the Polizia dello Stato, the Carabinieri, even the Polizia Stradale – that was the theory, anyway. In the real world, though, people were jealous of their territory, they wanted the freedom to work over a job before they went public with it. In the real world, there wasn't a cat's chance in hell Sandro would get anything from the horse's mouth – the horse in question being the Guardia – and even Pietro would be lucky to get the full picture.

Setting his glass down on the sticky table, leaving his briefcase there on the aluminium chair, Sandro wandered to the edge of the abutment, stood under a skinny acacia and surveyed the length of the Arno. A little further down the parapet, a small man with an enormous camera was photographing something down below. Following the angle of the huge zoom, Sandro saw the elegant, snow-white shape of an ibis, its long beak poised to plunge into the green water.

There would be more evidence to gather. God knows how much – or how little – of it would be useful, under the circumstances. Dust full of scraps of cellophane and dead lighters, single shoes and old newspapers, a hundred thousand footprints and DNA traces and a whole lot of them rogue, from unregistered, unmonitored populations, immigrant or otherwise off the radar.

DNA: Pietro had mentioned it in a hurry, knowing full well he shouldn't be saying anything. A DNA match. As Sandro turned his partner's words over in his head, something on the far bank caught his eye. A blockish figure walking, just head and shoulders visible, from the direction of the Uffizi and, for that matter, the Banca di Toscana Provinciale. Sandro held a hand up to shade his eyes – there was something about the figure, its size, the shambling walk – and hurriedly he turned to the birdwatcher beside him, who looked alarmed at the abruptness of his approach.

'Could I borrow that a moment?' Sandro asked, as polite as he could without allowing any possibility of a refusal, already holding his hand out for the camera and its hefty telephoto lens. And the small man handed it to him, looking bewildered at his own compliance, unable to restrain a small intake of breath as Sandro raised a hand to adjust the focus.

Yes, thought Sandro. Coming into sharp definition, and moving with the slowness of the seriously overweight on the opposite side of the river in the direction of the African market, was Giorgio Viola, the manager of the first branch of the Banca Provinciale di Toscana that Sandro had visited, the station branch in the Vicolo Sant'Angelo that was soon to be closed.

Those were the eyes he'd seen above the computer screen in the office adjoining Marisa Goldman's, the eyes he had recognized but hadn't been able to identify before Goldman led him away, anxious, brown and buried in flesh like the sultanas in *pane del pescatore*.

Slowly he handed the camera back to the birdwatcher, who immediately took out a soft cloth from the camera pack on his back and began polishing and adjusting, emitting small sounds of distress as he did so. Sandro kept looking, calculating, even as Giorgio Viola turned away from the river and disappeared.

What had he been doing there? Helping the Guardia with their enquiries, Sandro assumed, helping Marisa Goldman, offering a semi-objective eye on the whole sorry business. Sandro rocked back on his heels. It was something worth filing away. He remembered the look of appeal in Viola's eyes in his own dismal, run-down bank; the man's willingness to help; the understanding of how little he had to lose. The Guardia might not give Sandro the time of day, but Viola probably would.

He turned to the birdwatcher again. The man looked at him now with undisguised apprehension. 'You come here at night?' Sandro asked. The apprehension turned to alarm. 'No,' said Sandro, wearily. 'I mean, owls, that kind of thing? Night photography?'

'Now and again,' said the birdwatcher cautiously. 'There are owls, yeah, mostly up there.' Nodding towards the southern hillside behind San Niccolo, beginning to be defensive now. 'No law against it, as far as I know.'

'No, no,' said Sandro. 'I'm sure there isn't, I didn't mean – sorry to have bothered you. Thanks.'

He raised a hand and hurried back to the table. To his mild surprise, his briefcase was still there. Owls. He'd been told by someone, hadn't he, that there were owls, below the Piazzale Michelangelo; suddenly he was overcome by a desire to hear them. To hear them every night, from that apartment with its long, rusted balcony, to sit there with Luisa and listen to them. Taking his mobile out of the briefcase, Sandro dialled Galeotti Immobiliare.

When Guili arrived, Sandro was gazing through the trees in a deliberate attempt to set aside the many frustrations and obstacles of his life just now and get on with the job. He was looking across at the far bank and calculating how far it was from Claudio Brunello's bank to the place his body was found. Two kilometres, perhaps, not even that. A straight line along the river. He heard a sound at his shoulder and there was Giuli.

She didn't look well.

Sandro jumped up, consternation tugging at him. Selfish old bastard, he could hear the voice in his head reproaching him, leaning on these women.

'Giuli?' he said, and at the concern in his voice her eyes flashed, but it was only a shadow of the indignation he would have expected. 'Sit down, girl.' He pulled out a chair and practically forced her into it.

'The heat,' she said wearily. 'It's just the heat.' She'd barely set down her bag and the boy – 'waiter' was too dignified for him – was there at her elbow, with his insolent face.

'Water,' she said brusquely. 'From the tap will do fine.'

The boy turned with contempt back to the stupid, flimsy, pine-built bar, and the moment he was out of earshot Giuli said, 'He's alive.'

For a moment Sandro found himself unable to process what she meant. 'He – he—'

'Anna's fiancé,' she said calmly, refusing to acknowledge the idiocy of the title *fidanzato*. 'Josef.'

Sandro sat back, and for a moment all the things he had to talk over with Giuli found themselves shoved into a heap at the back of his mind. 'He's alive,' he said blankly. 'How do you know?'

She told him: not much information, more guesswork.

'Dasha. She said he was scared. That's all, then she clammed up, wants Anna to think he's dead and gone. It's obvious to me he came looking for Anna at the Loggiata, and Dasha saw him off.'

'Scared,' he said thoughtfully. 'She said he was scared. Dasha. She saw him all right.'

'Maybe Dasha was right,' said Giuli. 'To send him packing. Anna – in her condition. Best out of it.'

Sandro pondered, studying his hands. 'Maybe he just wanted – God. I don't know. Not to talk to her. To know she was all right.' Why did he persist in the belief that Josef had to be the good guy, with so much evidence mounting against him? But he did. 'I would. If I was in trouble.'

And something stirred, a certainty. He looked up, met Giuli's eye. 'He's in trouble. In danger.'

'Yes,' said Giuli, and the tough set of her mouth softened into something more uncertain. More frightened.

Sandro buried his face in his hands, thinking. Josef was alive. And all he felt was afraid.

'I don't know,' he said uneasily, raising his eyes and glancing across the river. 'I don't know about all this.'

'No,' agreed Giuli, frowning. Then, 'What? What else has happened?'

'The Guardia's in there, in the bank.'

'The Guardia?' Her expression was blank. 'Investigating them? And that might be connected to our case – how? Brunello's not our client, you know, nor his wife.'

Sandro shifted uneasily, wishing he had Luisa here. 'Shall we get back to the apartment?' he said.

Giuli compressed her lips, reading his mind. 'I'm not good enough, now you've got me here?' she said. Then relented. 'Anna's at the apartment,' she said. 'Tricky to talk to Luisa with her there.'

Sandro sighed. 'Yes.'

Painful, too, having Anna under his roof: painful both to have to contemplate her big belly, and to see Luisa take on another lame duck. Not that Giuli had turned out too badly.

The waiter returned with a greasy glass of water, setting it down in front of Giuli without a word.

'Thanks,' said Sandro. 'That's kind.' He held the boy's gaze until, uneasily, he turned and hurried away.

'I'll take her back to the Loggiata this evening,' said Giuli, 'and then you can talk. She's tougher than she looks.' She watched him, waiting. 'So?' she said. 'The connection? Between the Guardia and Anna's missing guy?'

'All right,' said Sandro, 'all right.'

Suddenly he felt impatient with himself, letting all this get to him, the heat, the guilt, the shame. It came to him that he couldn't go on like this, apologizing for himself, telling himself how low he'd sunk. There had to be a way of being a private detective that he could live with. He set his hands flat on the table.

'Josef didn't choose Claudio Brunello's name at random,' Sandro said. 'His real name – well. He has a connection with that bank, and I think if we find out how Brunello died we might be an awful lot closer to finding Josef.'

'Fine,' said Giuli warily. 'Agreed. And if the bank's being investigated – fine.' She sat back with arms folded. She knew he hadn't told her what he knew yet.

Sandro rubbed the back of his neck, his thoughts returning at last to Pietro. They were in it together now, like it or not. He should never have put his old partner in that situation.

It must have been a million to one, Sandro had thought when Pietro said it, what were the odds? 'I think we've got a DNA sample that matches the blood,' he'd said. Sandro had almost heard him shifting from foot to foot, his unease palpable. 'Not admissible in court, not officially held – well, you know the deal. They were swabbing a gypsy encampment for DNA a few years ago, just north of Rome.'

They. Sandro could have asked which force they were talking about, but he knew Pietro might clam up. And Carabinieri or Polizia dello Stato, did it matter which? It could even have been some agency in between, some covert operation. The samples would certainly have been obtained under dubious circumstances and should have been destroyed.

They could have had a discussion about it, he and Pietro, if they weren't both now implicated. The gypsy populations were a significant pain in the backside, but you couldn't just take their prints for nothing. Because what would be next? Concentration camps and forced sterilization?

Sandro knew they were mostly good guys, Pietro and the rest. Sandro himself, when he'd been a serving officer.

'Pietro called,' he said. 'It's difficult for him, you know? To tell me stuff. There's this new guy—' He stopped.

Giuli just nodded, took a sip of her water. 'I guess,' she said, waiting for him to go on.

Sandro sighed. 'He told me that some of the blood Brunello was soaked in wasn't his own.'

'Blood,' repeated Giuli blankly.

She did look pale; Sandro leaned across to her and took her damp, warm hand. 'And they've found a DNA match.'

'He's got a criminal record?' She looked shaken. 'Her fiancé?'

'The blood belonged to someone called Josef Cynaricz who was living in a gyspy camp north of Rome a couple of years ago,' he said. 'Eastern European, sounds like, somewhere along the line.'

'Josef,' she said slowly. 'Doesn't mean – doesn't have to be him.'

Slowly Sandro shook his head. They both knew. 'I think it's him,' said Sandro carefully.

'But how did they have his – what did they have? Prints? DNA – how did they know then? If he isn't a criminal?' Giuli, straight to the point, looked down at Sandro's hand holding hers. 'I'm fine,' she said, and he took his hand away.

'Just the usual,' Pietro had said evasively when Sandro had asked more or less the same question, 'a bit of panhandling,' and then, 'No, nothing proven. No outcome, just some routine evidence-gathering.' He hadn't been able to say much more. 'That's it, honestly,' he'd said, and Sandro had believed him. 'There's another case come in, I've got to get down south of the river.'

And Sandro hadn't been able to help himself. 'South?'

'Beyond Bellosguardo, that hill. Fatal mugging, looks like, possible attempted carjack. Fancy car. Got to go.' And had hung up hurriedly.

Now Giuli was still looking at him. 'Well?' she said. 'Do the police have anything on him, this Josef?'

'No,' said Sandro sheepishly. 'Not as far as I know. Just – a fluke they held on to the DNA.'

'Mistaken identity.' Giuli eyed him. 'Coincidence.' Her arms remained tightly folded across her body.

'The DNA record will be destroyed,' said Sandro. 'Eventually. It can't be used in court. And in the meantime, it's helped us.'

'How much, though?' said Giuli, relaxing just a little, leaning forward. 'Can it tell us where he is now?'

'It's a name,' said Pietro. 'There's a family somewhere. There might be a mugshot, a decent photo somewhere on record; he might even be legal. An address.'

Giuli regarded him with deep scepticism. 'Legal? A Roma? And what are the odds that family's long-gone from whatever filthy camp your guys had them cooped up in?'

'Not my guys,' said Sandro, putting up some resistance. He set his jaw. 'All right, so it doesn't get us much further. But we have a name.'

The sun was now low on the horizon, the sky glowing apricot through the arches of the Ponte Vecchio. It would soon be sinking, out in the silver sea off Viareggio. Where was he hiding, this Josef Cynaricz, whose blood had been on Brunello's dead body, and from whom or from what was he hiding?

And then he felt it, the first pulse of adrenaline, as unmistakable as love. They were on to him, at last. They had a name, a profile.

'I know she's your friend,' he said. 'I know. He's alive. He's alive, and Brunello's dead; that's not necessarily good news, is it? Just think about it. It might be better for her if – if he doesn't come back. That might turn out to be our job, to keep him away from her.'

'To turn him in?' said Giuli, fierce but not pulling away. Sandro could feel the waiter's eyes on them, and let go. 'Are you going to tell Pietro that he's been seen? That he's alive? And scared?'

'His blood was on Brunello's body,' he said slowly. Was he going to tell Pietro? Whose side was he on, exactly?

'She said that,' said Giuli, half turning her head away from him to hide her expression.

'Who said what?' said Sandro, his head thick with it all. Like a swarm of bees, like a caffeine hangover, too much adrenaline combined with too much new information.

'The Russian girl,' Giuli spoke slowly. 'When she said Anna was better off without him – she said he had a dirty job.'

'Did she say what kind?' He didn't ask how the Russian girl knew: girls like that, living on the margins, they knew more than most about dirty jobs.

Giuli shook her head.

'The kind that involves violence? Intimidation?'

Sandro was beginning to get that sick feeling in his stomach, the churning that arrived at the stage in any case when you began to wonder about how much you'd been fooling yourself. He really had begun to believe in Anna's version of her guy: he'd convinced himself she'd know if he was – capable of doing what had been done to Claudio Brunello. But he'd seen sentimental drug dealers showing around pictures of their kids, known hitmen who were kind to animals, men whose wives knew nothing – or chose to know nothing – about what they did. But why would he have chosen Anna, if he was that kind of guy?

It could be as simple as the fact that she was easy to fool. He could feel Giuli's eyes on him, taking in his expression. Then she looked past him.

'Does this place have a bathroom?'

She sounded tired. Sandro looked around helplessly. The bar was no more than a wooden counter made out of wine boxes. Bathroom?

'Of course it doesn't,' Giuli answered for him. 'Let's go home, shall we?'

'OK,' he said. Giuli needed a bathroom, and he needed Luisa.

But when they got there, the flat was dark, and neither Luisa nor Anna was there.

CHAPTER NINETEEN

'**S**HE SAID WHAT?'
'Marisa asked me if I'd come out to her apartment,' said Roxana. 'To – um, pay my respects. To Irene Brunello.' She was almost enjoying Val's disbelief.

'It's on my way home,' she went on, shrugging. 'I don't mind.' Pursed her lips, thinking. 'It's got to be tough,' she said. 'Having her there.'

She got out her mobile. She'd called Ma to tell her she'd be a bit late home. Told her not to worry, for the umpteenth time: the handyman would keep her company, fixing the gate. Infuriatingly, Ma had reacted almost with amusement, as if it was all Roxana's invention, her panic attack.

'Oh, you enjoy yourself, dear,' she'd said. Enjoy myself?

The mobile was almost out of battery. Roxana reached up into the overhead cupboard where she kept a charger.

They were in the tiny bright kitchenette at the back of the bank, and no one could hear them, but Val and Roxana were whispering anyway. It was half an hour from closing time and the Guardia and Giorgio Viola had just left for the day. They often came here in the closing hours of a working day when there were no customers.

Each took it in turns to take a breather from the dusty gloom of the bank, a shot of natural light. It had been easier when there was no Marisa, mind.

Val shook his head, watching her fiddle to get the charger into the phone. Gently he took it from her and with a single deft movement plugged it in. 'Better not let Madam catch you,' he said, sliding it out of sight behind the coffee machine. 'That's company electricity you're consuming.'

She watched him, thinking about Irene Brunello and Marisa. 'It's just – it's not like Marisa. I mean, it almost counts as asking for help, doesn't it?' Val pulled a long face. 'With her. With Signora Brunello.' Still shaking his head slowly, chastened. It was almost endearing to see him strain to understand.

He was right: it wasn't like Marisa. She'd called Roxana into her office, about halfway through the afternoon. Roxana had thought it would be to do with the private detective – *her* private detective, was how she thought of him, Sandro Cellini. But Marisa hadn't mentioned him.

Nothing to stop me calling him. The thought had barely had time to settle, then Marisa had said, 'It's Irene.'

The conversation had been stilted and odd, and Marisa had not been herself: stumbling, hesitant, awkward. Had it been something the private detective had said? Or was it the weirdness of the situation generally? Marisa having to be a shoulder for anyone to cry on was crazy.

'I – um – well, I know you don't know her. But I'm at my wits' end, really.' Marisa hadn't seemed able to hold eye contact. 'I don't know when she's planning to go, you see. Last night – well. The – the crying was awful. I didn't know whether to go in.'

Roxana had just stood there, hands clasped tight, not even daring to sit down. Not knowing what to say.

'I've got to get home before too late,' she had begun, hedging. 'My mother's – well, there's someone coming round. There was – some damage to our fence, a man's coming to fix it.'

Marisa had made a gesture, almost impatient. 'Your mother,' she had said, irritably. Then frowned. 'Did you say there was an intruder?'

'Not exactly,' Roxana had said, hesitating, finding herself reluctant to give out any more detail. 'Look, it doesn't matter, he's not coming till seven-thirty or something.'

'Anyway,' Marisa had said. 'She can't stay forever, can she?'

Roxana had looked at her blankly. 'Ma?' she had said.

'No,' Marisa had replied, clicking her tongue. 'Irene Brunello.'

Roxana had contemplated Marisa's expression, and pitied Claudio Brunello's widow even more than she had when she heard the news. 'She'll have to go home and tell her children some time,' she had ventured, faltering at the thought.

And then Marisa's head had swivelled, and for a second her eyes had met Roxana's. 'Yes,' she had said. 'That's it, she will, won't she?'

There was guilt somewhere deep down in Marisa, Roxana could have sworn there was, but a ferocious instinct for self-preservation had been wrestling it into silence. 'She did say that's why she couldn't face going back. Something about holidays, not wanting to ruin the holidays.'

'No.'

Looking into Marisa's face, Roxana had seen she was not interested in thinking about Claudio Brunello's children; it would be too complicated or too unpleasant, or too pointless, that was what she'd been telling herself.

'I'll come,' she had said quietly. 'I'd like to give her my – my best wishes, anyway. He was a – a nice man. A good guy.' And Marisa's eyes had swivelled away.

Now in the little back room with Val, there was a silence. Roxana frowned and rubbed at the circular mark left by a coffee cup. How many afternoons had she come in here, desperate for a quick shot of caffeine to get her to the end of the day?

'What's she got to feel guilty about?' she said, hardly even aware of saying it out loud.

'What?' said Val. 'Who?'

She turned and looked at Val. 'Marisa. Did she – did she and Claudio have a – have something going on?'

He looked at her levelly. 'Is that what you think?'

'Oh, I don't know,' said Roxana and found herself suddenly overwhelmed by the desire to cry quietly somewhere. Poor Claudio. What did it matter, an affair? Poor Claudio, his poor wife. 'Did she tell you what the private detective came back for?'

Val shook his head.

'You didn't *ask*?' she said, hearing the unshed tears coming into her voice. 'Aren't you even curious?'

'Roxi,' said Val, his voice strained. He never called her that – it sounded strange. 'Listen. Are you all right, really?' Roxana felt herself stiffen at his concern. 'I mean,' he went on, 'this thing with your mother. This stalker thing.'

'It was just her imagination,' Roxana said, a little too sharply. Feeling that tug: other people had someone to share their troubles with. All this worry, about getting old. Was that what Val was offering, a shoulder to cry on?

Then they heard her call, from beyond the door. Marisa: impatient, querulous, that *You'd better not make me have to come and find you* note in her voice.

'You're feeling sorry for her, aren't you?' Val said.

'Am I?'

'You're too soft, Roxi.'

'She's a ballbreaker, I know,' Roxana began.

'Oh, yeah, and the rest,' Val sounded almost bored. 'Ball-breaker, marriage wrecker. You know she was supposed to have gone straight to the yacht with Paolo after work, Thursday? Well, let me tell you, she was still in the city on Friday evening. Still here because I saw her on the doorstep of Claudio's building in Campo di Marte, talking into the intercom. I saw the door open, and she went in.'

'Did she see you? You were on the bike?' The shiny red Triumph: Val was hardly inconspicuous.

'Not sure.' He shrugged. 'She might have done.'

'Did you tell the police?'

Valentino looked uneasy. 'Well – not exactly,' he said. 'I mean, it's not like she—' He stopped, looking genuinely puzzled. 'I didn't want to get her into trouble. I mean, that's serious trouble, right? Lying to the police? Telling you – that's not the same. Because's she's behaving like such a bitch.'

Roxana returned his uncertain smile. Who knew what was the right thing to do?

'I guess they'll find out, in the end,' she said slowly.

'Both of you,' called Marisa, imperious, and Roxana practically ran out of the room. Val followed, sauntering.

They shuffled into Marisa's office like schoolchildren. Erase it from your mind, Roxana told herself. It's gossip. She didn't even look at Val.

Marisa looked pale, but calm, setting things straight on her desk, sliding papers into her briefcase. Papers the Guardia might have wanted to see, wondered Roxana? Marisa's expression challenged her to say anything.

She set the briefcase on the floor. 'They're – ah – the Guardia have asked that we should temporarily suspend business,' she said, her voice steady. 'They've been called to another case tomorrow and they think – they want things left as they are. It's temporary.

Perhaps only twenty-four, forty-eight hours.'

Val was pale under his tan, and staring. 'What about the customers?' he said.

'The other branches will be unaffected.' She fiddled with a pen.

No one said anything. It was hardly worth pointing out that the Banca di Toscana Provinciale had now, with the temporary closure of the Via dei Saponai branch, contracted by one-sixth.

There was a folded piece of paper on the desk and Marisa picked it up, more as a distraction than anything else, Roxana would have said, to avoid meeting their shocked looks. Marisa unfolded it and stared down at it, unfocused, and without thinking Roxana followed her gaze. From upside down, it seemed to be a photographic image of poor quality, a blow-up of the head and shoulders of two figures. Roxana tilted her head to get a better look and as she did so Marisa crumpled the page into a ball and swivelled on her chair to locate her wastepaper bin.

Out of the corner of her eye Roxana felt Val turn his head, questioning, towards her.

'Hold on,' she said to Marisa, putting out a hand to stop her. 'Hold on. What's that? Who was that?'

Marisa looked at the ball of paper as if it was nothing to do with her.

'In the picture?' Roxana persisted. 'Who was it?'

'That private detective,' said Marisa, with an angry edge to her voice. 'And his bloody questions. Why should we help him now?'

'Can I see?' Roxana held out her hand, palm open. Marisa glanced at it, and Roxana could see she was considering refusal. She placed the ball of paper in Roxana's open palm and sighed.

'The detective,' she said with cold reluctance. 'He was looking for this man. The man was passing himself off as Claudio, and now he has disappeared. He thinks – oh, heaven knows what he thinks. That perhaps he has something to do with Claudio's –

with his—' And she stopped short, as if the word had escaped her. Death. Was that the word?

Careful not to tear the paper, Roxana prised it open, laying it on the desk, and smoothed it flat. The image had been distorted further now, but she could see enough. She went on smoothing, but there it was. She felt Val come close to look over her shoulder, she could smell his aftershave.

'It's him,' she said and she realized that Val, like a child, was repeating it just fractionally late over her shoulder.

'It's him.'

She turned and looked at him, not feeling like laughing.

'Who?' said Marisa: she spoke sharply, like a teacher suspecting her pupils of insubordination. 'It's who?'

*

'What?' said Luisa to Anna Niescu, taking her arm. 'What's that expression mean?'

The girl was leaning against the fence outside the apartment block, the bougainvillea behind it tumbling over her small shoulder like a bridal wreath. She had one hand against the side of her belly and the other holding on to the railing.

Luisa hadn't wanted her to come. It was half an hour on the bus, they ran erratically at the best of times, let alone in August. And she hadn't even wanted to look at that ridiculous thermometer Sandro had installed on the bathroom windowsill. They said the weather was going to break tomorrow. Thunder, coming down from the Alps.

Anna's face was intent, and she didn't seem willing to move or speak.

'Does it hurt?' asked Luisa. The girl shook her head minutely, and slowly her expression cleared.

'It's fine,' she said. 'They told me at the clinic, these are just normal, it all goes hard for a few moments, the muscles are squeezing. Not contractions, just – just something else. Preliminary.'

'Preliminary?' said Luisa, not liking the sound of the word. She glanced at the dark lobby of the apartment block and saw that the glass door had been propped open by a builder's ladder. A builder's van was parked on the street: August.

'For the last few months. Look,' said Anna, and gestured down as if Luisa would be able to see. 'Not squeezing any more. Not tight.'

She reached for Luisa's hand and, before she could protest, set it against her stomach. Firm and warm and strong, was how it felt, then against her hand something pushed, the knobbed protrusion of a joint, a heel or an elbow. Anna's eyes met Luisa's for just a second, then Luisa took her hand away.

'Are you sure you want to do this?' she said.

'It's better already,' said Anna. 'Better than the last time. When I was alone, and no one would let me in.' She looked up at the building's façade. 'It's around there,' she said. 'The other side. With the view of the hills.'

They stood at the gate and looked, both suddenly hesitant. Then Luisa punched in the code Giovanna Baldini had given her, skirted the ladder and they were inside. Standing in the darkened hallway, they didn't know what to do next.

They'd had to come: Anna had insisted. 'I won't know until I'm there,' she had said. 'I – there. Inside the apartment, then I'll know what it was that bothered me.'

But now that they were here, she seemed to have run out of steam.

'I don't like this place,' she said, her face moon-pale in the gloom. 'I would never have wanted to live here.'

'No,' agreed Luisa absently, glancing down the side hall to the concierge's door. Then recovered herself, 'I mean, it's a perfectly good neighbourhood, good for children ...' She tailed off. She frowned at Anna. 'You never said that before. That you didn't like it.'

'I didn't think that before,' said Anna, her mouth downturned. 'When he showed it to me, he was so proud of it. So pleased – he was trying to see it in the best light. So I tried too. I could have told him, I have some money, we can find somewhere better.'

Luisa squeezed her hand, thinking of Anna's tiny savings. 'Did he – did you ever tell him you had money?' The girl shook her head. Luisa nodded approvingly. 'Good girl,' she said, and Anna's head jerked up, defiant.

'He wouldn't have taken my money,' she said in a clear voice. 'Everything was going well for him, he said. Soon everything would be done, everything would be ready, just another few days. He was so excited.'

'Like he had a secret?'

'Something like that,' said Anna. 'That's why – well, when I didn't hear from him at the weekend, but actually weekends are anyway his busy time – I just thought, Monday, he's busy with – whatever it is.' Her eyes were dark. 'I just thought, he's got everything ready for the baby.' And she looked up the stairwell, towards the light. The walls were scuffed and dirty.

'Yes,' said Luisa, stroking her shoulder. 'Wait here a minute.'

Reluctantly, she tiptoed down the dark side-corridor to the door. There was that sour smell of alcohol breath and unwashed linen. She knocked. Called. Cupped her hands against the door and shouted. Nothing. From upstairs, some banging.

Luisa's heart sank: what next? She hadn't thought this through. Why would either of them be any more likely to get into the place this time?

All right. 'Let's go up,' she said, returning to Anna, trying to sound as though she knew what she was doing. 'There's – ah, someone I know lives upstairs.'

They pressed the button for the lift but nothing happened. Perhaps that was what the builders were here for. They took the stairs. Anna moved steadily, stopping for breath at the top of each flight. It had been relatively cool at the bottom but with every upward step it grew warmer.

On the third floor – her floor – Anna stopped again, but this time she looked as though she didn't want to go on. There were four doors, of flimsy-looking veneer, each with a spyhole. Watching Anna, Luisa shifted from foot to foot: something was sticking to her leather soles. The floor was gritty underfoot.

Sounds were coming from behind the furthest door: scraping. A thump. Men's voices, in a foreign language.

'That one,' said Anna, nodding towards the furthest door as if she didn't want to get any closer to it.

'It's all right,' said Luisa, glancing up towards the light filtering down from the top of the building. None of the stairway lights seemed to be working – another job for the builders. It was hard to see what the concierge was paid for. Perhaps they'd actually laid him off. 'Giovanna's on the next floor up. Let's see if she's in.'

Another flight of stairs was asking more than she'd anticipated, though: as Anna walked ahead of her with painful slowness, Luisa cursed herself for not calling Giovanna before they left, or buzzing her bell at the gate to confirm she would be in, after all this.

'They said, take exercise,' said Anna, out of breath, catching sight of Luisa's expression. 'Good exercise, climbing stairs. I can't just lie in bed forever.'

'When was your last check-up?' said Luisa grimly, holding her under the arm as they took the last step together. Stupid, stupid, stupid: how could I have been *so stupid? Eight months pregnant and*

I've got her climbing stairs. 'Stop,' she commanded, and examined the girl's face. Pink, but better, actually, better in the light, better one floor higher.

'Monday,' said Anna, 'at the Women's Centre, it's every week now. They say I'm doing well. They say the baby's big.'

They both looked down and Luisa felt the coolness of fear, like a shadow falling across her. Anna was so small.

'Do you have any children?' asked Anna, frowning up at her. Then, 'Oh, Giuli said – said something—'

'My baby didn't live,' said Luisa, and with the words she felt breathless. She tried to smile, heard herself stammer. 'There was something the matter with her – in those days, there wasn't the ... the information.' Anna's eyes were on her, intent. 'It wasn't anything to do with the birth.' And Luisa found she could hardly think of another word to say. 'You mustn't worry,' she managed, eventually. She paused, collected herself. 'So your last appointment was on Monday.'

Anna searched her face, then looked down at her belly again. 'That was when I asked Giuli.' She bit her lip. 'She saw me crying, because I hadn't heard from Josef, because they'd said maybe a scan to see how big the baby was and I tried to call him to tell him and he wasn't answering and I really got frightened then.'

'All right,' said Luisa, taking her hand, alarmed by her sudden distress. 'It's going to be OK.'

'She'd told me what she did when she wasn't working at the Centre, a while back. Told me about Sandro. What a nice man he is.'

'Yes,' said Luisa, looking away, turning to watch the stairwell.

'I thought he'd be able to help.' Anna's breathing was better now; Luisa concentrated on that.

If only being a good man solved everything. There was a sound from upstairs, a door opening tentatively, and from somewhere else in the building a dog began to yap.

'Come on,' said Luisa quickly. 'Can you make another flight?'

They saw her feet first, and Luisa knew it was Giovanna Baldini, in grubby slippers, standing behind a door open not much more than a crack. When she saw them, she opened it wider.

'Thought it was you,' she said. And leaned aside to get a better look at Anna, half hidden behind Luisa. 'And you brought the girl.'

Anna came alongside Luisa on the landing and looked at Giovanna, serious under her dark brows.

'Not much of a girl any more,' she said with dignity.

Giovanna Baldini stood aside and let them in.

'It's the same,' said Anna under her breath, stopping short in the hallway. 'It's the same as his.'

'Right above it,' said Giovanna straight away, ushering them on. The apartment was cluttered and warm, but it smelled clean. Luisa sometimes wondered if smell was the most developed of her senses, and she had a particular response to the way an old woman's flat could smell – as she approached being an old woman herself, it was becoming a kind of paranoia. Food kept too long, that was the best of it. Giovanna was watching her with a half-smile.

'You're wondering, do we let ourselves go earlier, single women?' Luisa smiled the same half-smile back. 'I'm hanging on,' said Giovanna comfortably.

They watched Anna, moving through the apartment, looking into one room then another, towards the lighter room they could both see ahead of them down the central hallway.

Coming into that room – a living room, by the look of a low sofa piled with mismatched cushions – Luisa saw Anna put up a hand to her left, feeling for something. A light switch.

Anna turned back to look down the corridor at them.

'That was one thing,' she said. 'He didn't know where the light switches were.' She stood silhouetted in the doorway, almost all belly. 'He didn't know where anything was. It was – as if he'd never been there before.'

She turned away again, and Luisa and Giovanna followed her into the room. It was wide, with one glazed door opening on to a long balcony, one window further along. Both were shuttered against the setting sun, but light leaked through.

They watched as, alert, Anna walked around the space. 'Bigger,' she said. 'This room is bigger. Than downstairs.'

'Some have them divided off, they make another room,' said Giovanna. 'I didn't need to do that. It's just me here.'

Anna looked at her, unseeing. 'That was going to be the nursery,' she said in a stifled voice, and held out both arms as if taking the room's measurements. 'Can I go out?' she asked abruptly. 'On to the balcony?'

Giovanna crossed to the glazed doors and pushed them open; the light that fell inside was soft and yellow. It must be getting late. 'Let me get you a glass of water,' she said.

'Yes,' said Luisa.

Anna smiled faintly. As if water will solve my problems, she seemed to be saying. But 'Thank you' was all she said. She stepped through the doors, and for a second as she disappeared Luisa felt a great surge of panic. What if – what if she—?

But hurrying out on to the balcony all she saw was Anna standing there, solid in the evening sun, her feet set wide apart to give her balance and both hands on the concrete parapet. Giovanna appeared beside them with the glass of water.

'Have you remembered,' said Luisa, 'what it was? What was wrong, when you came here with him?'

Anna was looking at the view: a slice of view at any rate, between another apartment block and some abandoned farm buildings that no doubt would soon become more apartments. A view, not perfect, but good enough, of hills to the south-west, darkening as the sun set behind them, the motorway just audible and intermittently visible. She wondered whether Anna had even heard what she said but then the girl turned her head.

'I think so,' she said, the sun glowing apricot on her face. She took the glass of water that Giovanna held out and sipped.

'Something was wrong?' said Giovanna. She looked at Luisa questioningly.

'When her ... fiancé brought Anna here to see their apartment,' she replied.

'It might be nothing,' said Anna.

'What?' said Luisa.

Anna drained the glass and handed it back. 'The keys,' she said. 'The keys to the apartment.' She frowned. 'They weren't right. He said they were his keys, but—'

'The keys?' Luisa tried to remember what Anna had told her about the keys. There'd been something. 'The – the Ferrari keyfob? Was it that?'

'That,' said Anna, nodding. 'That – he would never have had such a keyring, he wasn't interested in cars, not at all. He didn't even have a car, said he didn't see why you would need one in a city.'

'Right,' said Luisa, waiting.

'There was a label on the keys,' said Anna carefully.

'A label? What kind of label?'

'A little card, tied with cotton, like you might have in a shop, you know, a little price tag.'

Luisa frowned, head on one side, trying to picture it, knowing there was something about this picture she would recognize, eventually – only Giovanna got there first.

'Well,' she said, 'that would be the agent, wouldn't it? The estate agent's tag, they put a tag on the key when they're selling a property, telling you who it belongs to? What property it belongs to. So they don't get them mixed up.'

'But it was his place,' said Anna, and her lower lip stuck out, like a stubborn child's. 'He said it was his.'

The older women looked at her.

'He didn't know where anything was,' said Luisa softly.

'They've been trying to sell it for years,' Giovanna added, her head on one side as she watched Anna. 'It's on the market.'

'Maybe he bought it,' said Anna defiantly. 'Maybe he was renting it.' There was a silence, in which Luisa tried to think how to soften this.

'He ... it's possible he just ... he was just ... borrowing it,' she said at last.

Just as he borrowed Claudio Brunello's identity. Buying time.

From below them there was a dull thud and an explosion of fine debris blew out through a window, dusting the trees. All three women leaned down to look, and the powder-white face of a man in overalls looked back up at them.

'Hi,' said Giovanna breezily.

He raised a hand tentatively and said something guttural in a language none of them understood.

'Got the builders in,' said Giovanna. 'Maybe they've sold the place at last.' She looked from Luisa to Anna, then back. 'Come on,' she said. 'You want to know what's going on down there? Come on, then.'

BY THE TIME LUISA walked back through her door on the Via dei Macci, it was dark outside.

Giuli had been making excuses for Luisa while they waited. 'You know there's hardly any phone coverage,' she'd said. 'Inside an apartment building, for example, or in a particular street. The Via dei Bardi, for example, that's a killer. San Niccolo in general, tucked in under the hillside there ...'

Sandro had let her talk, fretting silently, barely even picking up on her mention of San Niccolo and what an undesirable place it could be to live.

'They'll be fine,' she had finished up, uncertainly.

'So why didn't she leave a note?'

'You know Luisa,' Giuli had said, and that was the end of that conversation.

And all Luisa had said when she did return was, 'Don't be daft. It's a Thursday in August, there aren't even any cars, what were you worried about? That I'd be run over by a watermelon seller?'

Giuli had stood there in that stance again, arms tightly folded against her body, and a frown etched on her face.

'Not you too?' said Luisa. 'Come on.'

It was bravado, though. Sandro knew her too well.

'It might be August,' he said, 'but people seem to still be getting murdered. For nothing, some of them.'

'People?' Luisa pulled out a chair and sat with weary resignation. Reluctantly, Giuli let her arms drop and sat down next to her. They looked at him warily.

Sandro wished he could take it back now. 'Oh, nothing. A mugging, carjacking or something on the south side, Pietro mentioned it.' Luisa nodded, her face betraying nothing.

'Where's Anna?' asked Giuli.

'She wanted to go home,' said Luisa, then let out a dry, small laugh. 'Home.' She shook her head. 'Poor kid. That dismal old place.'

'It took three hours?' said Sandro. 'Just taking her over to Santo Spirito?'

'Can you get me a glass of water?' said Luisa mildly. 'I'm parched.'

And she waited for him to turn his back, he knew, before she said, 'We went over to the apartment in Firenze Sud. His apartment, supposedly, the one they were going to move into.'

'All that way on the bus?' Sandro set down the water and the glass. Sighed and poured.

Luisa's mouth turned down, just a little. 'I know,' she said eventually. 'Yes, I know. She wanted to go. She wanted to show it to me.'

'Oh, I tried the estate agent,' said Sandro, absently. Luisa looked at him. 'Sorry,' he said. 'He wasn't back from lunch, they said. Running late, they said he'd call me back. Galeotti. Go on.'

He visualized the man, his flash car. And clients like Marisa Goldman on his books, the agency's letterhead on her desk at the bank. No wonder he didn't have time for Sandro. Was Marisa Goldman moving house?

'He never called, though.'

Luisa sighed.

'Anyway,' she said. 'Giovanna Baldini – I told you about her, right? She was at school with me.' Sandro nodded, waiting. 'She lives in the flat above. We went in. We talked to her.' Luisa took a sip of the water and mopped at her forehead, pale and damp with sweat. 'She knew a bit about the flat – and – and in the end she got the concierge to talk to us.'

'The drunk you talked about?' said Sandro. 'And?'

'All right,' she said. 'So it turns out, the flat wasn't his at all.'

Sandro looked at her and realized he had never really believed in Anna's apartment with its nursery in the first place. What had he thought? That she'd imagined it? Or that her fiancé had? But it did exist.

'No,' he said. 'So?'

'So it's been on the market, half furnished, in a terrible state, for years.' She wrinkled her nose. 'The builders had been sent in, just today.'

'Sent in by whom?' Sandro stared at her, trying to work it out. The timing. When had Josef taken Anna to see this flat?

'The new owners.' Luisa sighed. 'It wasn't easy. You don't understand, getting information out of these people.' She pursed her lips. 'The concierge took twenty minutes of Giovanna bellowing through his keyhole to even come to the door, then he didn't want us to come in.' She shifted in her seat. 'I thought poor Anna was going to throw up in there. I had to make her sit outside in the end.'

'Is she all right?' said Giuli. 'Anna?'

Sandro saw Luisa's expression, remorse and apprehension mingled. 'I think so,' she said wearily. 'I tried to get her to come here, but she said home was the Loggiata, that's where he'd come to find her. She's stubborn.'

You're all bloody stubborn, thought Sandro, looking from one woman to the other. 'What did the concierge say?'

'Well, he blustered,' said Luisa. 'I think he spends too much of the day out of it to know a lot. Said the agent had been round last week with two yuppie types. He didn't know if they'd agreed a price. So we went up and tried to talk to the builders. Only they were Moroccan and none of us speaks French even, let alone the other language they were speaking.'

'Berber,' supplied Giuli. Sandro looked at her. 'What?' she said. 'It's one of the Moroccan languages. Hassan at the Montecarla, that bar, he speaks it.' Sandro looked back at Luisa, outdone.

'She's an asset,' said Luisa, smiling wearily at Giuli, who now almost blushed. At least, Sandro thought, it was a considerable improvement on the pallor she'd had since she turned up at the riverside bar. And why had she spent so much time in the bathroom?

'Agreed,' said Sandro, temporarily putting his anxiety about Giuli to one side. 'So. The builders?'

'And it turns out they got asked to do the work this weekend; the deal went through end of last week. That's all the builders knew, but the yuppies put down a deposit in cash on Monday and they were in.'

Sandro sat. 'The concierge,' he said slowly. 'You told me he was a drunk – but what kind was he? I mean, just a bit of a slob, or all day every day drunk? So he wouldn't notice if Anna's fiancé was squatting in one of his apartments?'

'I talked to Giovanna about that,' said Luisa. 'He might be drunk – and she said he usually is out of it – but *she*'s sharp as a tack. Said she'd definitely have known if someone was living in the flat. But the heating and water were off, for a start. She grumbled about it because it meant she had to turn up the heating in her place to compensate over the winter. It wasn't habitable.' She sighed. 'Giovanna walks past the door a couple of times a day, and she'd never seen Josef.'

But if there was one thing Sandro had learned about the man, he was good at keeping a low profile. It wasn't easy to fall off the radar like that, just the one sighting. As far as they knew he'd broken cover just the once, at the Loggiata, trying to get to Anna? That told Sandro that he was desperate, and scared. Where had he been hiding?

'You showed her a picture?'

'Anna had her phone,' said Luisa, rubbing her eyes. 'She showed Giovanna.' Her voice was muffled.

She raised her head, and looked so tired Sandro said gently, 'All right, angel. You need some rest.'

'It's not much of a mugshot,' said Luisa, ignoring him. 'But Giovanna was pretty certain. She told Anna off for losing weight since the picture, so she could tell that much.'

'She has lost weight,' Giuli put in, frowning. 'Off her face, for sure.'

Patiently Sandro looked at the two of them, and waited for them to return to the point.

'So he wasn't living there,' he prompted eventually. 'But he got the keys – from somewhere, for at least two visits, with Anna, maybe more.'

They looked at him, and Sandro got up and went to the window, pushing back the shutters. They thought it was hot inside, but the air that entered was as humid, hot and stagnant as if he'd opened the door on a Turkish bath.

'Who owned the place, then? Who sold it to the yuppies?' He looked down along the dirty street, where the lights were beginning to blink yellow. They were beginning to congregate, on the corner: three dreadlocked kids, one dog. As he watched, one of them dropped a can to the pavement and stamped on it with a crack. Not too many yuppies here.

'Some old couple, years back,' Luisa said promptly. 'Bought as an investment, hardly lived in recently, she's widowed.'

She was watching him. For a moment, the pale, attentive oval of her face looked like a painting to Sandro in the circle of light falling from the wide, low shade.

'Can't see an old couple being anything but suspicious of a young Roma,' he said thoughtfully. Thinking of the old lady at the Loggiata. Reading his mind, Giuli grunted agreement. 'So how'd he get the keys?' said Sandro.

'The keys,' said Luisa, sitting up straighter, a hand on the table and tapping as she did when she was thinking hard. 'They were what worried her. Worried Anna. They were wrong.'

'Maybe he stole them,' said Giuli.

'Maybe they were lent to him,' said Luisa thoughtfully.

Sandro crossed from the window and leaned down over the table, feeling something take shape.

'By the owner?'

Luisa shook her head slowly. 'The keys he had weren't the owners' set, were they? A Ferrari keyfob? For an old widow?'

Sandro thought of Galeotti showing them round the flat in San Niccolo. His personalized number plate. His Maserati.

Giuli butted in. 'I've heard stories,' she said.

'Stories?' said Sandro.

'Stories about estate agents,' she said. 'And what they get up to in those empty apartments they're selling.'

'Yes,' said Sandro, more tetchily than he meant. 'We've all heard those stories. But what's the connection with Josef? Where's he been hiding? And what has he done?'

*

Bitch, thought Roxana, following her superior's customized Cinquecento – stripes from end to end, red on white – through the automatic gate. Where did Marisa Goldman get off? *Bitch*.

It had had Val shaking his head all over again; Marisa was a weird one, all right. It was as if she had no need to make people like her, she was above all that. Even if Maria Grazia was right and she wasn't as wealthy as she wanted people to think, she certainly acted like it. *Entitled*, that was the word for the way Marisa acted.

And here was Roxana, doing her a favour, regardless.

'No,' Marisa had said, watching Roxana and Val.

'But it's him,' Roxana had said.

'Yeah, it is,' Val had said, looking at Marisa curiously. 'It's Gio. Josef, from the Carnevale.'

Roxana had felt her brain whir as she said it. *I knew it*, a small voice was insisting, *I knew there was a connection*. But the rest of it was just crazy static. It didn't make sense.

'Seems like it,' Val had said. He had shrugged. 'Weird, huh?' Giving every impression of not understanding the weirdness of it at all.

'We should call him,' Roxana had said decisively, and that was when Marisa had been galvanized into action. 'Cellini. I have his number somewhere.'

'No,' she'd said. 'No way, not on company time, not on company phones.'

'But it's him,' Roxana had said.

'You didn't recognize him?' Val had been looking curiously at Marisa.

Marisa's jaw had set. 'A guy from the porn cinema,' she had said, her voice flat and cold, not even a raised eyebrow.

'I didn't mean—' Val had looked alarmed. 'No, I just meant, he's in once a week, you must have seen him.'

'I don't give a damn,' she had said. 'He could be Il Cavaliere, Berlusconi, for all I care. I've given that detective enough of my time; I told him I might have seen him in with Claudio. Is it going to help the bank, looking for this – this guy? No.'

'He was pretending to be Claudio,' Roxana had said, to herself, her eyes on the picture. There was something about it – so cheap, so poorly reproduced – that had made her sorry. The girl's face, she looked so happy hanging on to this – fake. Pretending to be Claudio? It didn't make sense.

'I guess maybe it's this girl that's looking for him,' she had said slowly. 'Although he didn't say it. Sandro Cellini.' She felt in her jacket pocket: was that where she'd put his card?

Staring each other down like cat and dog, Marisa and Val had paid her no attention.

'All right,' Roxana had said. 'I'll call him when work finishes.'

Reluctantly, Marisa had shifted her gaze and nodded stiffly. 'Only an hour to go,' she'd said, the expensive gold watch sliding down her smooth brown forearm as she raised her slim wrist to look at the dial. 'You can follow me on your Vespa. To my place. '

I can, can I?

Now the automated gates swung smoothly closed behind them as Roxana dismounted on to the gravel path. The air up here was different. It was different for the rich, all right. It smelled of roses and wet grass; a sprinkler was rotating beside the big, square villa, a glittering rainbow behind the flowerbeds.

There were two cars parked against the villa: the Cinquecento and a little canary-yellow Punto. The other inhabitants of the villa must be away for the summer, as Marisa would have been if Claudio hadn't been so inconveniently killed. Or inconveniently killed himself.

Marisa was still in the car, tapping something into her mobile. As Roxana watched, she climbed out and briefly her long-legged frame stuck in the car's low-slung door; she looked uncomfortable, wrong, awkward. And for a second Roxana wondered whether it was all made up, all an illusion. She hadn't gone with Paolo on Thursday, Val had said. What if this wasn't really her place and Marisa was housesitting, she was squatting, her boyfriend and his yacht didn't really exist at all, it was borrowed, all borrowed? What next? She'd got her tan at a campsite, her clothes from a discount outlet?

Marisa put the phone away. 'Paolo,' she said briefly. 'He's in Elba.' And strode past Roxana towards the villa's vast door.

Sweetly Val had whispered to her as they'd left Marisa's office, 'I'll call him. The private detective guy.'

And he'd quickly gone to the spot by the door where you got the best signal and dialled the number, while Roxana had looked from her counter at Val hunched over his phone, then at the closed door to Marisa's office, and back again at Val. Urging him on.

It had been almost a relief when he'd hung up, shaking his head, and hurried back to his post. 'Engaged,' he hissed, sliding back into his seat. 'Busy guy.'

Roxana had realized she wanted to talk to Sandro Cellini herself, anyway. Not here, though, not in the toxic gloom of the bank, where everyone could hear everything she said.

Why was that? she asked herself, hurrying across the gravel after Marisa, who was impatiently holding open the heavy door. The scent of roses and jasmine was almost too much, along with the hypnotic motion of the sprinkler and the sense that there were servants, discreet and well-trained, hovering just out of sight.

Why did she want to talk to Sandro Cellini? There'd been something in the man's eyes, something of her father's look as he stood in the *cantina* by his jars of nails, turning some part of machinery over in his oil-stained hands and working out what it did and how to fix it.

Damn, thought Roxana, and in a moment of panic she stuffed her hands in her pockets, looking for it. Had she given it to Val? Cellini's card. Would he be in the phone book? Roxana was in the phone book, sensible ordinary people didn't have any problem with being in the phone book – and then there it was, dog-eared but intact, in her shirt pocket.

'Coming,' she said. 'Sorry.' And slipped inside.

Marisa had the ground floor of the villa: cool, even in weather like this. They came into a wide, dim hallway, pale flagstones on the floor, two sets of double doors on either side of it. There was a smell of polish, of wood and leather and cold stone: all seemed chill, clean, empty of life.

'Hello?' Marisa called out, her voice high-pitched and strained. Roxana saw her look down and as her eyes adjusted she noticed that a small neat suitcase stood beside a console table. Marisa's shoulders relaxed just a little. 'Ah, Irene?'

The doors on their left opened. 'Hello, Marisa.' Irene Brunello stood there a moment, looking from Marisa to Roxana with weary doubt. She seemed much smaller than Roxana remembered from her occasional visits to the bank, sometimes with a young child in tow. Smaller and more uncertain, but dignified.

'You remember Roxana?' said Marisa with a stiff gesture. 'She wanted – she just wanted –'

'I wanted to say I'm sorry,' said Roxana, taking a step towards Irene Brunello then stopping abruptly. 'I'm so sorry.'

Irene Brunello stepped back hurriedly, disappearing into the room, leaving the doors open behind her. There was a quick intake of breath – surely not impatience? – then Marisa went in after her. After a moment's hesitation Roxana followed. This was a mistake.

Irene Brunello was blowing her nose, and pulling on a jacket.

'Thank you,' she said, not looking anyone in the eye. 'Miss Delfino, Roxana, I didn't mean to – thank you. It's just that I haven't got used to – to this, yet. My mother keeps calling me. The police keep calling me.' She sat down abruptly on the sofa.

Marisa seemed rooted to the spot.

'Can I get you anything?' Roxana asked desperately. 'A glass of water? A glass of – anything? Brandy?'

'I'm driving,' said Irene Brunello, pushing her handkerchief into her pocket. 'I – it's time for me to go back to the children. I can't make arrangements for the – for the – for Claudio's funeral, they say I can't do that yet. I have to tell the children.'

Roxana sat beside her and took her hand. It felt cold. 'Your mother's with them?' she said.

Irene nodded. 'At the seaside,' she said, with such desperate mournfulness that Roxana felt like crying herself.

'You don't mind if I have one?' said Marisa, her back to them. Roxana heard something clink and smelled whisky.

'They'll be all right, for a bit,' said Roxana. 'They'll be asleep by the time you get back, won't they?'

Irene looked at her, struggling to regain composure.

'You can't tell them at night,' said Roxana, knowing she was right. 'You have to do it in the morning.'

Irene frowned. 'No,' she said. 'You're right.'

Marisa came over and sat on the opposite sofa, nursing a large tumbler of amber liquid on her narrow knees.

'The police called?' she said, her tone made careless by the whisky.

'They came by,' said Irene, sitting there with her hands in her lap clasped so tight the knuckles were white. 'I went with them to our apartment. There was nothing, I told them, nothing was out of place, everything was normal.' There was a tremor then to her voice. 'The gas and the water were switched off, just as we always leave them, there was no sign that anyone had been there, but they took things from his desk, anyway.'

'Things?' said Marisa distantly. 'Do they know anything yet?'

Roxana tensed: the question seemed so brutal. Irene Brunello looked at Marisa curiously, as if she didn't know her. 'I don't think they do,' she said, trying to keep her voice steady. 'They just ask me questions. More questions. They never answer any.'

'What questions?' Marisa took another slug from her tumbler, and Roxana stared at her, willing her to shut up. Saw the greedy expression in her eyes and it occurred to her that Marisa was a drunk. Maybe she usually had it under control, maybe she was just good at hiding it.

'It's all right,' she said, keeping hold of Irene Brunello's hand. 'You don't need to go over it again.'

Irene showed no sign of having heard, staring at the long window open on to the grass and the rainbow shed by those sprinklers spinning to and fro. 'I don't think I would like to live here,' she said and turned to look Marisa in the eye. 'It's too quiet. I need to hear – something. To hear other people. The children.'

Marisa looked away from her, down into her glass. She could pretend to be embarrassed by the non sequitur, but Irene was right. It *was* too quiet out here.

Detaching her hand gently from Roxana's, Irene sat up very straight. 'The questions didn't make sense to me,' she said. 'They asked me if we had money worries, then if we'd had a windfall recently. They asked me if the bank was in trouble. They asked me how Claudio was behaving when there was talk of a takeover of the bank, a few months ago.'

She shook her head. 'I said, we were careful with money, always: that didn't change. I said, Claudio dealt with all the money matters. I said, Claudio took everything seriously.' She was sitting very still and Roxana saw that it was becoming harder and harder for her, not breaking down. 'He was honest. He was an honest man.

'It wasn't the normal thing, to go to the big supermarket in La Spezia, because it was cheaper. Only I think now that was an excuse. He never went to the supermarket, he was coming to Florence to meet someone, and he knew I would be angry, so he told a lie. He was coming to Florence all the time.' The words came out in a rush. Roxana saw Marisa was very careful not to raise her head.

'They said that?' asked Roxana gently.

Irene shook her head. 'They said they'd been in contact with the mobile phone company and at ten o'clock someone had called Claudio's mobile, from Florence, on a prepaid phone, bought God knows where, not registered. They asked me if I recognized the number.'

'Did you?' Marisa's eyes were fixed intently on Irene now, and Roxana wondered for a second whether she'd been brought out here to play the part of good cop in Marisa's planned interrogation.

'I know it wasn't your number, Marisa,' said Irene. 'It's all right.' The two looked at each other with a strange sort of calm. Irene turned back to Roxana.

'I didn't recognize it,' she said dully. 'But I don't have a good memory for numbers. When all you have to do is press a button on the phone, you don't need to remember a number any more.'

She looked at Roxana. 'I wonder,' and as she said this she tilted her head stiffly as if to relieve some pain. 'Did I leave too much to him? Would a good wife have known all about bank accounts and mobile phones and takeovers?'

'You did know,' said Roxana gently, not knowing where the words were coming from. 'You knew your husband inside out, he relied on you for everything. You were a good wife. You are a good mother.'

On the far sofa Marisa made a stifled sound and got to her feet, stalking back to the liquor cabinet on her long legs.

Irene didn't even turn her head.

'I don't know,' she said in a whisper. 'I don't know anything any more. How could this happen to us?'

'Terrible things do happen,' said Marisa, leaning back against the cabinet with her newly filled glass in her hand. 'We manage not to think about them, that's all.' But her voice was cool and distant.

Irene Brunello did turn her head then and looked at Marisa for a long moment, before getting to her feet, smoothing her skirt carefully, buttoning her jacket. When she spoke her voice was steady again. 'I should go,' she said. 'If I leave now, I will be – will be home by nine. At the sea, I mean. By nine.' She smiled tentatively down at Roxana. 'Thank you for coming,' she said. 'It was good of you.'

Roxana stood too. 'You know how to get hold of me,' she said. 'If you – if you need – if I can help.'

'I know how to get hold of you?'

'You called my home. When ... ' And Roxana saw Irene Brunello's face crumple.

'I did,' she said, 'oh, I did.' Catching a sob in her throat. 'When I didn't know where he was, I was desperate.' She passed a hand over her face. 'What was I thinking of? I called Inquiries for numbers all over the place, anyone I could think of.' Her hand stopped at her mouth, covering it. 'God. I talked to your mother.'

'It's all right,' said Roxana, wishing she hadn't said anything. 'Of course you phoned. We would all have done the same.'

She didn't even bother to look over at Marisa to recruit her. Marisa wouldn't have called anyone. Irene's shoulders dropped, as if she was close to exhaustion.

Gently, Roxana put a hand under her elbow, guiding her

towards the door, edging her out, Marisa watching their every step without moving until they were out in the hall. Then Roxana heard the heavy clunk of the tumbler put back down on the sideboard, and at the front door Marisa appeared beside them. Irene picked up her bag.

While they'd been inside, the light had faded and in the dusk the roses glowed against the luminous green of the grass, the sprinklers only audible as the faintest rhythmic swish.

'Goodbye, Irene,' said Marisa lightly, and leaned forward just slightly as to accept a formal kiss.

Irene came no closer, only held out her hand. 'Goodbye, Marisa,' she said and Roxana wondered if they would ever see each other again, these two. At a memorial service, at the funeral? Perhaps the police would never solve this thing: perhaps they'd never release the body. Claudio would stay in a police morgue forever. Marisa stepped back, her eyes very black.

'He liked you,' said Irene, turning to Roxana. 'Claudio did. He worried about you.'

Roxana didn't even know what to say. Worried about me? And knowing that if she opened her mouth she would burst into tears, she just bobbed her head, except that she could feel the tears anyway. Irene leaned in and pressed her cheek against Roxana's. 'It never meant anything, you know. She never meant anything to him.'

Roxana froze. Claudio. She was talking about Claudio?

Irene drew her head back, just a fraction, her face so close she might have been about to kiss Roxana. 'She was here,' she whispered. 'The maid – she has a maid, the girl doesn't like her – told me, before she went. Here all the weekend. Her boyfriend – her boyfriend with his yacht. He has told her to leave. But I can't even be pleased about that.' And then abruptly she stepped back and straightened her shoulders.

The little yellow car waited on the gravel and Irene made her precise, determined way towards it, but halfway there something stopped her.

Irene Brunello set her handbag down on the gravel and knelt beside it, looking inside, then peering, then scrabbling. Roxana could hear her hurried, shallow breaths, and then the high tinkle of a phone from somewhere in the jumbled contents of the bag. She could feel her own hands clenched into fists as she willed Irene to stay calm.

He's dead, she wanted to say, nothing's going to bring him back. The worst has already happened.

Irene straightened, got to her feet, the mobile in her hand and half the contents of her bag on the gravel. 'Hello,' she said, breathlessly, 'hello?' Then, dully, 'Oh. Oh, it's you. Yes.'

Roxana hurried across to help gather up the contents of the bag while there was still light. Fumbling about on her knees, she couldn't help hearing the conversation – or one side of it – being conducted over her head. Then she stood, holding out the bag.

'Who?' Irene was saying, sounding tormented. 'No, no. I've no idea who that is. No, we weren't buying property, no. I don't know this man.' She was holding one hand over her ear, and she swung round to look into Roxana's face with incomprehension. 'How much?' Her voice went up a note in panic. 'No. I don't know anything about it, he didn't tell me anything about it. Please.'

Over Irene's shoulder, Roxana could see Marisa on the doorstep, four, five metres away, arms folded and the tumbler in one hand, her face sallow in the dusk. She could hear the urgent crackle of a voice talking to Irene and wanted to say, shut up, leave her alone. He was a good man. He was.

'I can't talk to you about this now,' Irene said, with a desperate attempt to sound calm. 'I don't know this man and I have to go home to my children now.' And she clicked the phone shut.

Still holding out the handbag, Roxana said nothing. Irene took it, dropped the mobile inside, slung it over her shoulder and walked in silence to the car but at the door, as she climbed in, she looked up at Roxana. 'I don't know what they meant,' she said. 'The policeman said another man was dead and there may be some connection.'

'Another man?'

There was a sudden silence, except for the evening song of the birds in the trees, thousands of them, it seemed to Roxana, in all this luxurious expanse of garden and trees and shrubs, filling the air.

'A man, a man,' said Irene, her face upturned. 'Found dead at Bellosguardo beside his car, they thought a mugging at first. He had the cutting in his pocket, from the paper. Where Claudio's death was reported.' She was very pale, the thought of another death, another family bereaved, making her face a blank of fear. 'An estate agent.'

'A coincidence,' said Roxana, trying to think. Trying to make sense of it. 'Surely it could be just – I don't know.'

Did people cut out random pieces from the paper? But Irene's expression suggested that there was no room for the possibility of coincidence – that this was bad news, and everything was horribly connected.

'They asked if we were buying a property,' she said as though talking to herself. 'The police. They said Claudio had – they said he had – the Guardia di Finanza said—' And she stopped. 'I can't,' she said. 'I can't think about it.'

'It's all right,' said Roxana, taking hold of her arm. 'Call me later. Call me tomorrow. Call me any time, Irene. This will be all right.'

'He said that,' said Irene Brunello, and Roxana knew she wouldn't call. 'He said that. But I don't know if it can be all right.'

Roxana stepped back and Irene pulled the door closed, wound down the window. 'Goodbye, Roxana,' she said.

Who told her it would be all right? Watching the slow movement of the automated gates opening, the blink of the tail-lights as the car disappeared, Roxana could only think, ridiculously, of Sandro Cellini.

'Don't,' she called back to Marisa, her hand poised over the button that would close the gates again. 'Leave them. I'm going too.' Going home to see Ma, to pay the handyman, to sit a while in the dark until she felt safe again. To call Sandro Cellini.

'As you wish,' said Marisa, arms folded across her body again in that pose of hers that said, *Come no closer*. 'That could have been worse,' she said with a stiff smile as Roxana leaned down to pick up her helmet.

'You think?' said Roxana, pulling on the helmet, horribly uncomfortable in the heat; for a second she longed for the *motorino* rides of her early teenage years, hair flying in the wind along the coast road, arms round some boy.

Could it really be true, what Irene had said about Marisa's boyfriend? Was it some way of – lashing out? Or had Roxana just imagined it, had she misheard? One thing was for certain, she wasn't going to ask Marisa.

Would she even say thank you? Thank you for coming, for talking to the bereaved woman, for diluting the grief? Of course she wouldn't.

'Thank you,' said Marisa. Roxana gawped.

'She hates me,' said Marisa.

It was the whisky talking. Marisa drained the glass.

'You could do worse than Val, you know,' she said then, looking down her nose. Her languid voice was only slightly slurred. 'It's all about family, you see, about connections. He's got his own apartment, all he needs is a wife, and he likes you, I can tell. He told me today he'd sold the motorbike, can you imagine that? Growing up: this has made him grow up.' She paused, her huge eyes gleaming as she gazed up to the darkening sky. 'You've got nothing,' she said, 'no security, if your family's not connected, that's how things are. Particularly now.'

Roxana stared at her: there was too much to argue with in this little speech for her even to get started on it. Particularly now – what? Particularly now we're all out of a job? *He likes me?* She hadn't even thought about that. And looking at Marisa she thought, you're probably not even my boss any more, I don't need to be polite to you. But she found she didn't want to be rude either.

'I don't need Val,' she said, swinging a leg over her Vespa. 'I've got a family.'

'I'll let you know when we re-open,' called Marisa, 'keep in touch,' as the gates began to close behind Roxana. She raised a hand in acknowledgement and turned her head just slightly. Marisa stood there on the porch of the villa that wasn't hers and seemed in that moment to Roxana to be absolutely alone.

CHAPTER TWENTY-ONE

IT WAS IRONIC, THOUGHT Luisa, lying in the dark, that when her baby had died she had thought briefly in the dreadful, mad, dark months that followed – the only time in her life when she'd lain in bed, day after day, this very bed – that it had been the lack of a maternal instinct in her that had caused her baby to die. Even though the doctors had explained their daughter's syndrome to her, more than once, even though they'd told her it was nothing to do with her, it was a fluke, still she'd thought it was because even though she'd waited and waited she'd never at any stage of her pregnancy really felt like a mother.

Ironic, because now she was lying awake fretting over two younger women, neither blood relations, as though she were indeed their mother. Anna Niescu and Giulietta Sarto: the one waiting, passive and hopeful, for her baby, and the other, who had spent her life turning away from normal family life, deciding now at the very last moment that a family might be what she wanted after all. Was ironic the word, or should it be tragic?

Next to her Sandro shifted. She could tell from his breathing that he was a long way from falling asleep.

'You know I'm working tomorrow?' she said. He grunted.

Fine, was what the grunt meant.

They were past that, both of them; Sandro was past being jealous of every moment she spent in the shop, and Luisa was past throwing herself into work so that she didn't have to think about the cancer. It now seemed like a crazy phase. She'd even been to New York. Her boss Frollini had taken her for the collections, no doubt just a misguided attempt on his part to cheer her up, to tell her he needed her, she wasn't on the scrapheap yet. It had caused trouble for a bit, but they were past that now too.

Over thirty-five years Luisa had learned to interpret her husband, who was a man of few words. Fine, was what the grunt meant: fine, let's not talk. He would be thinking, behind the closed eyelids; the occasional impatient exhalation, the movement of the arm, on top of the sheet, then back by his side, told her that much. And they both had plenty to think about.

Of course, they had no idea what was going through Giuli's head, not for sure: Giuli was as tight-lipped as she had ever been about her private life. Work, she could do, scrubbing floors, sorting out the computer, answering phones, taking histories from her clients, either for Sandro or at the Women's Centre. She thought she was playing it close to her chest, but Luisa could see. Something was happening in there: she was pale, she was fidgety, she was distracted. Then there was the tenderness she showed around Anna, the softness in her voice when she talked about Enzo, the engagement, making things formal for the first time in her chaotic life. For God's sake, she must have thought, *could* it happen? Am I too old?

Luisa shifted on to her side. Sandro exhaled.

Or was this just Luisa superimposing her own fears, her own regrets on the poor kid? That would be the look she'd see in Sandro's eyes if she did nudge him awake, turn on the light in the humid room, and say, actually, not fine at all, actually, let's talk. Giuli's a tough cookie, he'd say, wearily rubbing his eyes and blinking at the clock on his side of the bed. Giuli knows what she's doing.

Luisa lay still. Maybe. Maybe she does.

Anna Niescu, on the other hand. Luisa wished she could believe the girl knew what was coming. The birth was one thing – and Luisa found herself squeezing her eyes shut in the dark in an effort not to remember any detail of how that felt – getting that baby out safely was one thing. Dealing with whatever was waiting out there for her to learn about her beloved fiancé was another.

The three of them had sat there under the light as it grew dark outside, Sandro's scrawled pages of notes between them, shuffled around the table like cards. Each of them thinking silently about Anna, whose fate they were deciding, moving slowly around the old-fashioned kitchen of the Loggiata, trying to get comfortable in her narrow bed.

By nine they still hadn't eaten anything, so Luisa had sorted out a plate of good market ham, some bread turning hard in the heat, a jar of pickled vegetables, even though no one had asked for food. Sandro had doggedly forked his way through a plateful, only pausing to ask, halfway through, 'Did they have figs at the market? The black ones?' Luisa had said she'd get him some tomorrow in her lunch break; they'd eaten those figs when they went away on their honeymoon, and August always reminded him of them. A short season, a week or so, a short life – twelve hours, barely enough to get them to the market before they dissolved into their own juices.

Giuli had only picked at the food, but Luisa had said nothing.

Sandro had set it out for them while they listened in silence, both their hearts sinking, Luisa could tell by looking at Giuli's face. Anna's fiancé Josef was not a bank manager, of course he wasn't.

'We know his name now,' he'd said.

Anna's beloved was Josef Cynaricz, a Roma who'd started life in southern Poland and passed through a transit camp outside Ostia three years ago, a gypsy boy whose DNA the police had on file. No one's idea of the perfect son-in-law. Someone was keeping him quiet with the loan – or promise – of the apartment at Firenze Sud. What was he keeping quiet about?

'Not for any good reason,' Sandro had said, frowning. 'The DNA. There was no evidence of criminal activity, none.'

She'd never known him take issue before, seriously take issue, with some of the sleight of hand carried out by what he'd always thought of as his force, the Polizia dello Stato, one to which, despite the fact it had forced him into early retirement, he had always remained fiercely loyal.

Now, it seemed, his loyalties were beginning to shift.

'I don't think she's stupid,' Sandro had said stubbornly. 'He might be a traveller but nothing she's said about him makes him sound like some fly-by-night, love 'em and leave 'em type.' He had slapped a hand on the table, surprisingly loud. 'He'd be long gone if he was. He stuck around till the eighth month, for God's sake. Why go now?'

'Oh, Sandro,' Luisa had said. 'Don't you read the papers? Men do it all the time. They don't know how to get out of it, they pretend to themselves it'll be fine, then she gets bigger and bigger and suddenly the due date's next week – and they jump. It happens. He'd told lies and he was going to get found out.'

But she hadn't thought simple Anna was stupid, either.

'What if they weren't lies?'

'What d'you mean? That really Josef and Claudio Brunello are one and the same after all?' Luisa had shaken her head. 'Let's hope not.'

Sandro had shifted, uneasy, but when he had spoken, Luisa had found herself listening.

'I don't mean that,' he had said slowly. 'I just meant – there was something innocent about it. He didn't think it would matter, telling a small lie. Maybe he had always looked up to Brunello; say he's a customer in the bank, say he comes in now and again, say Brunello's treated him well, because the guy sounds like a thoughtful sort of man. Sometimes – well, there are situations, however honest you are, however well intentioned – sometimes you want something so badly that you fool yourself. Sometimes the thing you want – or the person – seems so necessary to your life that nothing else matters, and the means justify the ends.'

And then he had clamped his mouth shut, speech over, and Luisa and Giuli had just stared at him, Giuli as if she was going to burst into tears.

'Right,' Luisa had said, clearing her throat.

'I mean,' Sandro had said, suddenly weary, as if the speech had drained him, 'it's not as if anyone with an ounce of knowledge of the world would have believed that Josef was a respected bank manager, not for five minutes. And there's no evidence he was properly trying to – to con anyone. Not even Anna, not really.'

'And the apartment?' Giuli's voice had been tentative.

They'd talked about it: Giuli had put forward her theory already. 'They're known for it,' she'd said, 'aren't they? Estate agents have the keys to all sorts of places, wrecks, sure, tenanted places, sure, but also show-homes, model houses, fully furnished empty apartments. They let their married friends use them. For—'

'Yes,' Sandro had said, frowning furiously. 'I know what for. Affairs. Assignations. But there's no evidence – not any more – that Josef was – is – married, is there? None.' They hadn't said anything: he couldn't have been interrupted. 'He didn't take her there to – I don't think that was what it was about.'

'Um, she did get pregnant, though,' Giuli had said, not meeting his eye. 'So that must have been what it was about. At some point.'

'All right, all right,' Sandro had said, sitting down but not admitting defeat, not yet. 'But if that was what you wanted – only that – would you choose Anna? Of all girls? I think he loved her. I think he sincerely believed he would be getting that apartment. The stuck-up woman manager saw him talking to Brunello. What if he was asking about a loan?'

'They'd never have given him a loan,' Luisa had said quietly, and Sandro had pushed his chair away from the table in frustration, letting his clenched fist fall on to the mess of papers, then letting the fingers uncurl.

'No,' he'd said.

Then the phone had rung.

Clearing away the plates, Luisa had listened to Sandro answer it in the hall. She could tell it was a woman, even though she could hear nothing of the voice on the other end of the line. And that Sandro was talking to a woman he liked.

'Right,' she had heard him say, and heard the alertness in his voice. 'You're sure? And not since – when? Right.'

The conversation had lasted perhaps twenty minutes. The woman was asking him questions, too, about Josef, and about Anna. Sandro must have trusted her because, by the time they'd finished, whoever was on the other end of the line had known more or less everything she and Giuli knew about Josef's disappearance.

There'd been a moment when his voice had changed, and he'd turned his back, instinctively, as if to keep this part of the conversation particularly private.

'Really? Really?' she had heard him say. 'Miss Goldman was here? All weekend. I see. Well, yes. The police should be told. Yes, I will, yes – I'll be, I hope I'll be communicating with them in the morning.'

Delfino had been her name; hanging up, Sandro had said it. 'Thank you, Miss Delfino. Roxana.'

As he had walked back into the room, Luisa had felt a tiny little prick of something at the sight of his face, alive, intent, a kind of pleasure in it. Not jealousy, but edging towards it. Sandro had caught her expression and almost smiled.

'The girl at the bank,' he had said, reaching up to the top cupboard for the grappa, a single-grape variety given to them by Pietro at Christmas and reserved for special occasions. Sandro had then fetched one of the liqueur glasses they'd received as a wedding present from the cabinet and sat down. Luisa had cocked her head and stared: he had become a different man. The defeat that had been beginning to settle on his shoulders before they'd heard the phone ring had now evaporated.

'Roxana Delfino. She knows Josef, and she knows where he works.' Sandro had sipped the tiny glass of clear liquid. 'Worked, I should say; it's closed down, since the weekend, and she noticed he'd disappeared. A sharp-eyed girl.' Another appreciative sip. 'He worked at the Carnevale.'

A porn cinema. Luisa and Giuli had looked at each other: this didn't get any better, did it? A man who spent his life sitting in the little glass booth at a porn cinema, taking money, giving tickets, watching the customers shuffle out again into the daylight. Some of them, no doubt, giving every appearance of being upright citizens.

'No wonder he pretended to be something else,' she'd said. And Sandro had nodded.

'I was thinking, can't be much money in porn cinemas these days, what with the internet.' His face had clouded a little.

Luisa had shifted uneasily at that. What did Sandro know about the internet?

'Glad to be out of all that,' he'd said as if in answer. 'Major part of police work, web porn. Sifting through images, no thanks.' He had chewed his lip. 'But that place – well. That huge place, bang in the centre of town and, she said, his takings were less than a hundred euros some weeks. The girl at the bank said. A trickle.' His face had still been dark, troubled. 'It's being redeveloped now, she said. Builders. A mess inside.'

'Roxana Delfino,' Luisa had said very quietly, and he'd looked at her, still distracted, taken in her expression and then quite suddenly he'd laughed out loud, leaned across and put his arm around her shoulders, warm and close. She could smell the liquorice smell of the grappa on his breath and despite herself she had smiled back. Across the table Giuli, frowning into her lap at the thought of Josef working in a porn cinema, had looked up, bemused.

'I think I know the name,' Luisa had said, only partly to deflect them. 'Delfino? I think the mother used to shop with us. In the old days.'

'I knew she'd come up trumps,' Sandro had said, 'first time I saw her.' He had poured himself another glass, small but brimming, and knocked it back. Luisa had given him a sidelong glance, and suddenly they had both been laughing at her.

'Not jealous, darling?' Sandro had said, a look close to pure delight on his face.

And Luisa had not known what to say for a second or two. She had never been jealous in her life.

In the bed now she shifted again, and Sandro turned in unison, and his hand came out to hers, the fingers meeting so precisely in the dark it was like a magic trick, and resting entwined.

She felt herself begin to drift off then, with his touch, and something Sandro had said settled in her cooling brain: *all that space there in the centre of town.* The Carnevale's façade appeared as she first had seen it, the coloured lettering of its name, modish then when it had first opened, in 1950-something. Her mother ushering her to the other side of the street and muttering as they passed, Luisa of an impressionable age, thirteen or so, in her school pinafore. *All that space*, and as she drifted into sleep, the old cinema's features, the ugly concrete of its façade, the faded letters of its sign, the smoked glass that spanned the entrance, all erased themselves and left only that: a dark space, a black hole.

The phone rang again but she barely heard it; it was too late, Luisa had slipped over the edge into sleep. She might reflexively have put her hand out after him, feeling the fingers slipping away as he left the bed, but by the time he had softly closed the door behind him, picked up the phone and spoken softly, quickly into it, she didn't hear what he said.

'There's something I'd like you to find out for me.' Then *Yes* like an endearment, like a secret assignation, *Yes, tomorrow, yes. Early. I understand: I know where.*

*

In her own bed, sleepless and alone, Giuli lay and stared at the ceiling in the dark.

She had shot home on the *motorino*; enough of walking – what had she been walking for? She'd sped through the hot, dark streets, down to the river, along the Arno, the city not quite empty, people walking like ghosts, in silence, but desolate, it seemed to her. Desolate as she'd passed the African market, the tattered police ribbon still in place, desolate as she followed the embankment, looking at the necklace of lights reflected in the water. The surface was clogged with waterweed, brought to the surface by the heat, and Giuli had turned her face away so as not to think of the pale-blue sea she and Enzo had lain beside and stared at from their campsite under the umbrella pines, not much more than a week ago.

Giuli had missed a text from Enzo as she'd been leaving Sandro and Luisa's building. She'd stared briefly at its contents, then climbed on to her moped. She'd known him nearly a year – longer if you counted seeing him, liking him, before exchanging a word – and she had never failed to respond to even a missed call. But what would she say to him? The sense that she was on the point of making a terrible fool of herself – engaged? At her age? – engulfed her, and Giuli had clicked the phone shut, pulled on her helmet and started the moped's engine.

She'd let herself into the silent building on the Via della Chiesa: even from this quiet, run-down corner of the city people were gone, to the hills or the sea. The stairwell smelled stale, the heat rose with her as she climbed. Key in the door, Giuli forced herself to think of Anna.

Estate agents and their games. She'd known a hooker – once, long ago, in a former life – who'd done it, thought it was all a great game, sneering through a show apartment, posing on the bed. Poor Anna; this was exactly what Giuli had wanted to shield her from, the people who'd think she'd done a dirty thing. How many times had it taken? Anna was young, and innocent; in Giuli's mind that had somehow made it easier for her to fall pregnant. It might have been just once. It might have been the first time.

'Did you get the name of the estate agent? For the apartment in the Via del Lazaretto?'

Sandro had asked the question thoughtfully, and Luisa had shaken her head; she hadn't thought to ask, she'd ask in the morning, and then Sandro had laid a hand on her shoulder and she'd smiled up at him, both of them remembering that precious moment when he'd caught her, jealous of the girl in the bank. Watching them, Giuli had thought only of the impossibilities that lay between her and a future like that, a kitchen of their own and no need to say anything to be understood.

Taking off her clothes, she brushed her teeth and lay down

under clean sheets and, closing her eyes, tried to picture Enzo's face but could not.

Could it really all turn so quickly? But Giuli knew this was what she'd expected all along, that it hadn't been real, that she'd allowed herself to imagine things that would never happen. Enzo didn't really want her, wouldn't really want her. She turned over in the bed, then turned back.

What did it matter? She could live without him, as Anna would live without her Josef. What had she been thinking of? And she lay, staring into the dark until she thought at last of Anna's baby, the only thing in the end that mattered in all this, and the small cooling wind that came no more than an hour before dawn finally lulled her to sleep.

CHAPTER TWENTY-TWO

Friday

WAKING EARLY AND DISORIENTATED, Roxana lay with her eyes closed and tried to work out what was different.

At first she could hear nothing, nothing but a little sparse birdsong in the dawn light, not a breath of wind to spur on the defeated chorus. It was no cooler – even swinging her legs off the bed brought a sweat to Roxana's upper lip – so that wasn't exactly it, but close. Weather. The light falling through the slats of Roxana's roller shutters was dull and grey: that was a change. And the air – the air was different. Smelled different.

Someone was moving around, downstairs. Roxana felt light-headed, a little panicky, she held her breath.

'Roxi?'

It was her mother. Roxana breathed out, slowly, and the situation came back to her. No work today. And last night—

Ma had the ears of a bat, sometimes, she could hear her daughter's bare feet touch the floor as if Roxana was still a teenager and she was listening for her key in the lock late at night. 'Roxana?'

'Coming, Ma.' Roxana could hear the sleep still in her voice.

Last night.

It had been purple dusk, not quite dark, when she had parked up and come through the front door under the jasmine: eight o'clock perhaps. Her mind had been on other things than home, all the way; on Irene Brunello walking proudly out of Marisa's front door; Marisa drunk and lonely in her borrowed life of luxury, telling her Val was a good bet for marriage.

Maybe he was. Maybe she really had been being too picky all these years. And thinking of him, his hopeful face, untroubled as a child's – maybe they could be a team. Maybe she needed someone like that, to lighten her up. One thing was for sure, she wasn't going to mention Valentino to Ma.

It had turned out that Ma had too many things of her own to tell, though. She'd had a busy day.

'He's gone,' she had said complacently, silhouetted in the doorway to the parlour. 'The handyman. I dealt with it.'

Setting her bag down wearily, inhaling the powerful scent of the evening flowers, the jasmine and nicotiana coming in at every window and through the open door behind her, Roxana had been on the point of scolding her. For heaven's sake. Couldn't you have told him to wait? But she didn't. She stared at Ma, in a belted, pale-blue summer dress she hadn't seen in years, fine tights, the Ferragamo sandals Roxana's father had bought her for her fiftieth, good as new because almost never worn.

'Ma,' had been all she said, before she'd stopped.

'Well, I went to the doctor's first,' Ma had said, shushing Roxana out through the *salotto* – had it been dusted? There was a smell of polish – on to the veranda at the back. 'This morning.'

She'd wanted to clear a few things up, she had said. Do it on her own: there was no point in just sitting at home fretting over whether she was losing her grip, was there? There were tests.

They'd both sat down. 'And?' Roxana had still been holding

her helmet, she had realized. Gently she had set it down beside her, and pulled off her jacket.

'Well, it takes time,' Ma had said, smoothing the cloth on the little table. Refocusing, Roxana had seen that there was a Martini glass with an olive in it, and a small empty beer bottle.

'I had to offer him something,' Ma had said, seeing where she was looking. 'Coming out here, in August. Nice man. The handyman.'

'Right,' Roxana had said, trying to remember when she'd last seen Ma drink a Martini. Dad had made them once in a while, for special occasions. The bottles must have been gathering dust for a decade. But alcohol didn't spoil, did it? 'The doctor?' she had said. 'The tests?'

'Well,' Ma had said comfortably. 'Like I said, it takes time. They do tests, then do them again, to measure deterioration.'

Roxana had stared at her. So had it taken that day Ma had spent hiding, frightened, in the hall, for her to gather her wits and see what the truth of the matter was? She had imagined Ma getting dressed so carefully, for the visit, and felt a sudden burning shame, mingled with respect. 'So?' she had managed.

'He says, he can't say.' Violetta Delfino's eyes had been bright. 'But right now, it seems I have the appropriate level of – cognition, or something – for a person my age. No evidence of progressive disease – although, of course, he will do the tests again to monitor that. He says, his belief is that I have been depressed.' Pressing her lips together in an expression familiar to Roxana. 'I told him, nonsense.'

'Right, Ma,' Roxana had said, expressionless. She hadn't known whether to cry or to hug her mother. Neither response, she had guessed, would be greeted with anything but impatience.

'They say the weather's going to break,' Ma had said then, getting to her feet. 'I had a Martini.' A week, a day ago, the non sequitur would have panicked Roxana. 'Would you like one?'

There had been no scent of dinner from the kitchen; things, it seemed, had changed today. 'Fine,' Roxana had found herself saying.

The alcohol had been warm and oily but had tasted surprisingly clean. Roxana had let it burn her throat and as it did so, she'd felt her shoulders drop. Ma hadn't had another: at least Roxana didn't have to worry about her turning to drink. The beer bottle had gone.

Ma had settled herself into her chair, smoothing her dress. She had looked perhaps ten years younger; why, the doctor had asked, hadn't they done this test months ago? Roxana had supposed it would have always had to be Ma who requested any such test.

'So what did the handyman say?' Roxana had sat up straight, suddenly flustered and reaching around her for her handbag, 'Oh, for heaven's sake. How did you pay him?'

'He's sending his bill,' Ma had said. 'He said he'd bring it round in a day or so, actually. A nice young man.'

Roxana had subsided, waiting.

Ma had set her hands on the table. 'He said, we should talk to the police because it was criminal damage, not wear and tear. He said, it looked like someone had been – almost camped out there. Recently.'

She had spoken complacently, without the terror that Roxana would have expected, that Ma had herself experienced looking at the damage. It had come to Roxana that she felt justified, happier in some way that the whole affair of the mysterious caller at the house had been a real threat rather than an imagined one.

'Fancied himself as something of a detective, if you ask me,' Ma had said confidentially. 'Talking about footprints, showing me, "Look, there's this set here, lots of those, then someone else, here."'

Roxana had shifted uneasily in her chair. 'Two sets of footprints?' She had tried not to sound alarmed: did she want Ma too scared to leave the house all over again? No. She had got to her feet, and leaned on the balustrade, looking out into the garden. 'I should have got back sooner,' she had said.

But Ma had gone on blithely, 'He put on a very good strong bolt, and a new lock, he pieced in some wood where it had been pulled away. Safe as houses now, he said. He was concerned, that was all. Thorough. Quite insistent, about the police, doing things properly.'

Roxana had tried to remember the man's voice on the phone. Had he sounded young? He had sounded, to her, like a man such as her father, or perhaps she'd merely imposed that on him, poor guy, just as she'd done to Sandro Cellini.

It had come to her that Ma would like Sandro Cellini.

'Well then, perhaps we should,' she had ventured. 'Contact the police. Or someone.'

'Yes,' Ma had said. A silence. 'Tomorrow.' Her face had looked completely serene in the soft light falling through the door. 'He said we should talk to old Carlotta next door. She might have seen something, he said.'

Still leaning on the balustrade, Roxana had turned her head and found herself listening for the grey Persian, nodding absently. The police. Two sets of footprints.

'I thought we might have a bite out, tonight,' Ma had said, standing to brush down her shirtwaister fastidiously as if she hadn't spent the last two years barely even bothering to look in a mirror. 'When you've finished your drink? The place on the corner's open.'

'Leave the lights on,' Roxana had said as they left. Ma had looked at her, enquiring. 'So we're not fumbling about when we get back.' And it'll look like there's someone home. 'We'll only be out an hour.'

It had been a bit more than that, in the end: it had been close to eleven. The trattoria – a decent place, if basic – had been very busy as there were so few places open this time of year; the clientele a mixture of campsite tourists and locals, and no air-conditioning, a waitress with a sheen of sweat hurrying between tables. So it wasn't till eleven that she had started to look for her mobile, to phone Sandro Cellini.

She should have realized earlier; what was wrong with her? The overheated trattoria, its doors open to the steamy dark and the sound of frogs in the trickling river, fireflies on the far bank, a good meal of the old-fashioned kind they used to go out for, when Dad was alive, when Luca was home. The thought of a handyman she'd picked at random out of the Yellow Pages who could be bothered to worry about Ma, and a glass or two of wine on top of the Martini; that was what had been wrong with her. Lulled into thinking, *Life isn't so bad. Things will get back to normal.*

The phone hadn't been in her bag. Fumbling at the restaurant, she hadn't been able to find it, had told herself she'd check when she got home because she was beginning to attract attention as she flung the bag's contents around: Cellini's business card, then her keys landing on the table with a clatter that caused heads to turn.

Must have left it at home. Though she had known she hadn't taken it out. Knew. And when it hadn't been there – the house otherwise just as they'd left it, though in her rush to get back through the door Roxana had barely had time even to worry about footprints and all of that – and Ma had been standing over her in the hall and beginning to look anxious at last, Roxana had made herself stop. She was worse than Ma, panicking over nothing.

'It's only a phone,' she had said, with forced breeziness. 'Must have left it at Marisa's.'

Ma's mouth had pursed. Just as Roxana had been thinking she doesn't like Marisa any more than Maria Grazia, Ma had said, 'Oh!' Startled, pleased with herself. 'Maria Grazia phoned.'

'My Maria Grazia?' Like an idiot. 'Phoned here?'

'Yes,' Ma had said with exaggerated patience. 'Here. At about six. Because you weren't answering your mobile. She was worried about you. She was on a train.'

I'm worried about me, Roxana had thought, feeling the stupid panic rise, pushing it down. What will I do without my mobile? *It's not safe.* She had taken a deep breath, stop it. Twenty, thirty years ago, nobody had had mobiles. We coped. Not safe? Don't be stupid. She had put her hands to her temples.

'Six.' She'd been on the pavement outside the bank at six, if Maria Grazia had called, she'd have heard it ring – oh. Oh. And she'd exhaled. 'It's all right,' she had said. 'I know where it is.'

Standing now, the morning after, at the window in her bare feet, Roxana pulled up the roller shutters with a rattle and looked out over the thick vegetation of the garden to the fence at the back, the path that led along behind the houses; had she always known you could see it from here? She left her shutters closed, as a rule, to keep the room cool. And most mornings she was at work, not gazing out of her bedroom window.

Ma had been right about the weather breaking. The sky was low and grey and the light glared, flat and scalding, turning the green foliage dull and lifeless. It was always the worst before the storm came, and it could take days to break. The air was so dense with humidity that Roxana could hardly breathe, and the light hurt her eyes. And when she remembered where the phone was, she felt a dull throb of dread. It was plugged in, in the bank's little kitchen, tucked behind the toaster, and charging at the bank's expense.

Stupid to feel dread: this was the place where she'd gone to work for the past two, three years. Was it suddenly a hellhole? But standing here, she suddenly felt the most tremendous unwillingness to go back in there, ever. She felt the weight of all those mornings, pulling on her helmet, parking up by the river, letting herself in, booting up the computer screen and settling at her workstation, and realized, she understood that she hated every minute of it. Every minute of it.

At the window, Roxana exhaled, wow. Where did that come from? Her face, she noticed putting a hand to it, was filmed with sweat. Stop it, she told herself. Stop it. Everyone has bad days, no one loves their job all of the time.

Somewhere far off under the low sky, somewhere to the south there was a rumble. Below Roxana and to the right, Carlotta came slowly out on to her rear balcony, which was identical to Violetta Delfino's, and began to pull laundry off a wire rack. In her nightgown, with bare old arms, with that look of clammy exhaustion from too many sleepless nights in the heat.

Seen from above like this, they were so close, so similar, the lives of Ma and old Carlotta, that it was almost comical that they barely exchanged a word from one end of the year to the next. Roxana thought of the imagined slights and hostilities that might stem from a sidelong glance or an overheard word, from the behaviour of the cat, some piece of untamed vegetation or the hanging out of inappropriate garments in full view.

Carlotta looked up.

Roxana waved.

Carlotta hurried back into the house as if scalded, and Roxana had to laugh at the expression of sheer affront on the old lady's face. She pulled the shutters back down, went inside and got in the shower.

As the water ran, lukewarm because it never got properly cold once the summer was here, the heat settling everywhere, even into the stone-cold earth, Roxana pondered. She had already spent longer on the phone to Sandro Cellini than was strictly necessary, she knew that, but he hadn't seemed to mind. Actually – and Roxana felt a little pulse of satisfaction as she remembered it – it seemed as though she had actually made a difference.

So all it had needed was the sound of Sandro Cellini's voice – weary, attentive, kind – as he answered his phone late last night, and she had ended up telling him everything. Rambling on, Ma would have called it, and does he really need to know what you think about this man, this Josef? Does he really need to know that, in fact, you liked him, you'd been suspicious at first because he was a foreigner, and poor, but seeing him once a week, registering his patience and unassuming respectfulness, you had got a feeling about him? Just a sense that he was, in some central part of himself, a decent man, even though you barely exchanged a word. Roxana had told Cellini about her visit to the Carnevale, too.

'They've boarded it up,' she had said. 'I think they're starting work next week, properly, it's been a long time in the pipeline, apparently. He said they're getting dogs – the man who was putting up the boards. Said it was horrible inside.'

'Horrible.' She heard him turn the word over. 'And no sign of him? The builders, or whoever this man was, had seen no sign of Josef, or anybody?'

'Well, I did ask,' Roxana had said. 'That was why I went there, I had a feeling, about Josef.'

She'd sat down then, feeling in the dark for the uncomfortable little upholstered chair that sat by the phone table. Uneasy, because she had known it was going to sound mad.

'I thought there was a connection, you see, I don't know why. When – when Claudio died, and Josef hadn't come in the day before, when he always came in. Stupid, I know.'

There'd been a silence, then Cellini had cleared his throat. 'Not stupid, as it turns out,' he had said. 'Given that Josef was calling himself by Claudio Brunello's name.' He had paused, and he had heard women's voices, soft, in the background. 'So you asked?'

'He said the place was empty.' And she had frowned, trying to remember. There'd been something, though. 'He said, it wasn't pretty, or something like that. There was some kind of mess, left behind.'

'Right.' Cellini had sounded thoughtful. 'When does the work start? Did you say, they were putting dogs in there?'

'That's what he said. Well, he was putting a sign up, too, warning, guard dogs.'

The sound Cellini made had been sceptical. 'Might get down there, anyway,' he had said. 'Have a look around.'

'Will you tell the police?'

'I used to be a police officer,' he had said, distant for a moment, and, in Roxana's opinion, not answering the question at all. Then he had said, 'I will tell them, yes. Of course. It's just that I'd like a look myself first. It's my client, you see. I have to think of her. I have to – act in her interests. The police barging in and digging things up and drawing their own conclusions – well, that might not be in her interest.'

Her. 'Your client.' Roxana couldn't very well ask who she was. But he had told her anyway. 'Josef's – ah – his fiancée,' he had said, and his sigh spoke volumes. 'She's looking for him, too.'

'Fiancée.'

With a flush of obscure shame Roxana had realized that, of course, she knew nothing about him, that narrow-faced, polite man with his takings; she had never seen him in the street, he was one of those people who knew how to make themselves invisible. She only knew he was from the Carnevale because Val had told her, or maybe Claudio. So the bagman *had* had a girlfriend – more than that. A fiancée was more than a girlfriend. 'Is she – they were going to get married. Is she pregnant?'

There had been a hint of reproof in Sandro Cellini's reply. 'I can't say,' he had said. 'Obviously.'

'I'm sorry.' And Roxana had felt sorry, she had felt crass and nosy and thoughtless, almost tearful. 'None of my business.'

She hadn't known what to think then, either. She'd liked Josef, but he'd got a girl pregnant, lied to her, and disappeared. Open and shut case, if you weren't being daft and sentimental.

'You think he's just – a bad guy.' Roxana had heard the flatness in her voice.

'You don't?'

'I told you,' she had said. Hadn't he been listening? 'I told you what I thought, I liked him. There was – I don't know. Mutual respect: he was respectful.'

'He trusted you,' said Cellini. And she could hear him pondering that. 'Trusted Brunello.' He cleared his throat at the end of the line.

'Yes,' said Roxana: it hadn't occurred to her before. 'I didn't even know I liked him until he disappeared, but I did.'

There had been another thoughtful silence. 'I don't discount that, Miss Delfino,' Sandro Cellini had said.

And with that dry, considered sentence, Roxana had known. She could trust him; he might only be a private detective as opposed to a police officer, but she knew she could trust him.

'Roxana,' she had said. 'You can call me Roxana.'

'If you like,' he had said. 'I'm Sandro.'

It hadn't been in her mind to tell him about Marisa. He wasn't investigating Claudio's death, was he? He was looking for Josef.

'I think there's a connection, too,' he had said abruptly, just as she was wondering what was the right thing to do. Did she really want to snitch on Marisa? 'A connection between Josef disappearing and your boss's murder.'

Murder. 'That's what they think it was? Not a – a suicide?'

'They're coming round to it.'

There'd been a pause, then she had spoken. 'The thing is,' she had said carefully, 'it's my boss. My other boss, Marisa.'

'Miss Goldman.' He had waited. Patient, courteous. Like – like someone else. Like Josef.

'Yes. Miss Goldman. The thing is, she told the police – she told everyone, she was away, from Thursday afternoon, away at the seaside with her boyfriend Paolo, on his yacht. Only someone told me she wasn't.'

'Someone.'

'Valentino,' she had said. 'My colleague. Saw her being let into the building where Claudio lives, early on Friday evening.' Paused. 'But it's not just Valentino.' And she had told him what Irene Brunello had said, about the maid at Marisa's house.

'So it looks like she was here in Florence all the time,' he had said. 'Why would she lie about that?'

'I don't know,' Roxana had said uncomfortably. 'She hasn't told the police,' she had added, belatedly. 'Irene hasn't. I don't know why.'

And she had pondered that a moment. Had she been biding her time? Had Irene wanted to have something of her own over Marisa, some secret advantage to hold in reserve for future use?

'Should I tell them that too? Only I don't know – is it the Guardia? Or that Pietro Cavallaro, from the Polizia dello Stato?'

She'd felt sick, then. Telling the police would make it official. They'd arrest Marisa, or something. Call her in for questioning. And sitting there in the dark, she had pictured Marisa on her doorstep, whisky in hand, waiting for the axe to fall.

'It's all right,' Sandro had said wearily. 'I'll tell them.'

And the burden had passed, from her to him. Then Roxana had heard Ma moving slowly upstairs in her bedroom, she had smelled the frangipani and tobacco plants and jasmine. 'Thank you,' she'd said.

Now she stepped out of the shower and stood a second, feeling the brief moment of cool already ebbing as the water dried. She hadn't told him about the footprints. The stalker. Well, she thought, never mind. She wrapped herself in her towel and went to the window, hair still wet, and looked down, next door.

'Carlotta,' she said, and the old lady looked up, alert, suspicious, waiting to disapprove. 'Can I have a word?'

CHAPTER TWENTY-THREE

'**E**ARLY,' PIETRO HAD SAID on the phone. 'I'm on at ten, it'll have to be early.'

'As early as you like,' Sandro had said in an undertone, feeling a flood of gratitude as he sat on the edge of the bed in the dark and listened with half an ear for Luisa's breathing behind him as it slowed and evened. It was late, but the exhaustion in his old friend's voice spoke of more than just late nights.

'Does it have to be about something?' Pietro had said when Sandro had asked him. Of course it had to be about something: they both knew it was this damned case that had them entangled, conjoined twins fighting to be free. But Sandro had believed him when he had gone on, 'I just thought I should see you. Face to face, like you said. Enough of this – this phone crap.'

Only now, slipping out of the house at six-thirty to walk across town to where he'd agreed to meet Pietro, did he wonder. Face to face: for breaking bad news? *Listen, this is it, you're pushing our friendship too far.*

It was probably an hour on foot, but Sandro wouldn't take the car. Climbing into their dusty little Fiat suffocated him, parking was a nightmare and he used the car so little that he had a tendency to forget where he'd left it, but it wasn't just that. There was something about a walking pace that suited him, gave him time to think: that said it all, didn't it? There were detectives who operated at the speed of a high-performance car, no doubt, but not Sandro.

Besides, he liked walking and, more than anything, walking in the early morning. He could nod to his surroundings, his city. He could register the gargoyles on a fourteenth-century palace, a fig tree in heavy fruit leaning over a garden wall; he could see where the junkies were sleeping these days, who'd shut up shop and who was clinging on, who was up early with a guilty conscience or something else. Old widows leaning out of their windows after another sleepless night in the heat, surprised by their loneliness after a lifetime of grumbling at their husbands. Too poor to get out of the city, their children grown and gone, just putting up with it.

Closing the door behind him, Sandro lifted a hand to Signora Kraskinsky leaning on her folded arms, in the building opposite. She simply pursed her lips in response, and he moved on, wanting to shake his head at her comical misanthropy but thinking better of it.

Down the quiet street towards Santa Croce. Quiet but not silent, behind him Sandro could hear the distant clatter of the *furgoni* being unloaded at the market of San Ambrogio. The baker talking sleepily behind his shuttered shopfront; he'd be closed by the weekend – August was no time to be sticking your head into a furnace, and who needed bread, in the heat? Ahead, a Filipina in a pink overall hurried around a corner and into the street ahead of him, carrying a bucket filled with cleaning products. Out they came at this hour, the illegals, the immigrant workers who lived in basements and windowless rooms, without so much as a fan.

Like Josef Cynaricz, in the city somewhere, with no one he could trust, scared. Scared of what? Of the police, for a start, regardless of whether he had or hadn't killed Brunello. Because who would be easier to pin it on, if it turned out he'd been in the wrong place at the wrong time?

And could he be scared of Marisa Goldman? She was supposed to have been long gone on some yacht, but was not. Sandro thought of the woman, looking down her long nose at him. Why had she lied?

But then again, if Josef had killed Brunello, battered that handsome cropped head into a pulp in some deranged frenzy – of what? Jealousy of the man's life, hatred, greed? – not only would he not be the man Anna Niescu had fallen in love with, but he'd have disappeared into some Roma camp hundreds, maybe thousands, of kilometres away, he'd be buried away down in Campania or up in Trieste, across the Brenner and into Austria, or on a boat to Dubrovnik. But he was still here, in the city somewhere; he was looking out for his girl.

She hadn't been wrong about him: Sandro clung to that. He'd thought Anna Niescu was a kind of holy simpleton when he'd first met her, like one of those country saints, but she wasn't. She was flesh and blood, and she wasn't stupid.

Where had he been, since whatever happened on Saturday afternoon? Who would have given him shelter?

Not Anna: he hadn't asked her to help him, to hide him. He hadn't contacted her directly. He was protecting her. From what? Not the police, because in fact it wasn't the police he was afraid of.

The edifice built itself in Sandro's head: wobbly, imprecise, a lopsided building of a theory, precariously balanced on a single assumption, of Anna's instinct for a good man.

As he skirted the arcaded golden stone of Santa Croce's northern flank, in his head Sandro mapped a route. He checked his watch: he had time, too. There were things he wanted to see along the way. He came out into the piazza and slowed as the heat hit him like a wall. Six-thirty-five, and he was sweating, the sweat that comes before the weather breaks. Overhead the sky was low and purplish-grey with cloud, a thick blanket smothering the city. He crossed the piazza – empty but for a couple of motionless figures on the stone benches – in a slow, precise diagonal, heading for the newspaper stand on the far corner.

Three streets fanned out from the Piazza Santa Croce's western side, beyond them and overhead stood the crenulated tower of the Palazzo Communale, and there was something faintly surreal about the perspective, something puzzling to the eye in this heat. As he walked – almost swam in the terrible, humid air – in the wide empty space under the lidded sky, Sandro was for a moment assailed by the most awful feeling of being alone. And not only alone, but walking into a day he might never walk out of, walking to his own death, alone. The feeling was so powerful that if he hadn't been more than halfway across, he might almost have turned and gone back, home to Luisa still mounded under the covers, and reached under for her warm hand, and stayed there.

But his feet continued as if he had no say in the matter, one in front of the other, and then the newspaper stand was in view and he could even read the day's headlines on the placard the *edicolaio* was kneeling to fit into its wire frame.

ESTATE AGENT SLAIN IN BEAUTY SPOT
LOCAL MAN SOUGHT
CRIME RATE A SCANDAL, COUNCILLOR SAYS

His brain focused on the headlines, his feet kept moving and the streets leading off the square at an angle somehow regularized themselves. Sandro felt as though he had managed to fight off a kind of madness by purely mechanical means. By keeping on walking. At the *edicola* he reached over, the coin ready in his hand,

and picked up an early edition of *La Nazione*. He crossed the road, his eyes on the paper.

The story was on the front page. He stopped. Someone hooted, someone else shouted. Sandro looked up, blinked, saw a guy on a *motorino* shaking his fist, and walked on. Reaching the pavement, he leaned against the nearest wall.

He hadn't even read the words: the photograph had done it. A sleek Maserati – not quite so sleek as when he'd last seen it parked up under the city wall in San Niccolo. It was pictured at the side of what looked like a country lane, the low, square shape of a farmhouse some way off and out of focus, a verge of long, dry grass and seedheads, a neatly trimmed mulberry tree. And a vicious dent in the rear-wheel arch, very much as if someone had slammed it with a tyre lever. The personalized number plate: GALiMM.

Beside the open driver's door, a forensics nylon tarpaulin covered an elongated, body-sized shape, almost but not quite out of the car. A dark stain not quite covered by the sheet, where the tarmac met the summer verge. And one shoe.

Slowly, Sandro pushed himself away from the wall, folded the paper and stuck it in his battered briefcase. He took the nearest exit from the piazza, which turned out to be the Borgo de' Greci, then turned off to the left down a narrower street whose name he didn't know. His general direction was fine, for the moment anyway, he was heading for the Carnevale, even if all thoughts as to what he might do when he got there had temporarily deserted him.

That little, sharp-faced, chiselling estate agent, Galeotti, impatient while they looked around the flat in San Niccolo. For a brief, mad moment Sandro thought, does this mean we don't get a deal on that place? The man Sandro hadn't trusted for a minute, with his goatee and his constant glancing at his watch and his flash car. Flash car: the keys to the flat in Via del Lazaretto,

Sandro recalled instantly, had had a Ferrari fob, but he already knew, he had known from his first glance at the photograph, that when Luisa spoke to her old school friend in the condominium, she'd confirm as much. That Galeotti Immobiliare was the agency selling the Via del Lazaretto flat.

Coffee: that was what Sandro's body instructed him. Before you open that newspaper again, you need a kick-start. He passed at least three bars that were shuttered up, scraps of paper posted on their doors carrying cheerful messages about when the *direzione* would be back from the seaside, and by the time he found one that was open, he was a street away from the Via dei Saponai, the bank and the Carnevale.

A dim little place under an archway, a tiny barman with a big handlebar moustache whom Sandro vaguely recognized: Orlando, was that the name? He didn't ask, because if he knew Orlando from somewhere, then Orlando might know him. If they didn't trust you when you were a policeman, they trusted you even less when you'd been kicked off the force. He got a coffee – *lungho macchiato*, he specified after a brief struggle with his conscience; less coffee, Luisa had said, think of your heart, consider a camomile now and then – and moved off to one of a handful of high, zinc-topped tables. He downed the coffee in one and when it kicked in, he felt the smooth acceleration behind his chest wall as something entirely health-giving and pleasurable.

Life was too short.

He hadn't liked the estate agent, he hadn't trusted him, but the sight of the end of a man's life, even that of a venal, greedy man with a fussy little beard, was a sad thing. It couldn't help but turn your mind to how it would look when it was your turn.

Claudio Brunello's death hadn't been any prettier. He'd been chucked like a bit of rubbish over a steel crash barrier to lie among fast-food wrappers in the dirt. That had been different, though. It came to Sandro that he'd never believed that the African market was where Brunello had died. It didn't smell like it, didn't feel like it, and after thirty years' experience, you knew. This – and he opened the paper, shook it flat, looked at another photograph – this crime scene held the traces of this man's last moments. The battered rear end of his car, his body half out of its seat. It was clear where Galeotti had died. But where had Brunello's last moments come? It mattered. Not just to find his killer, but to reconstruct the man, the manner of his death, to find out *why*.

They were talking, at the bar: Orlando with a squat man in a road sweeper's fluorescent overalls with his back to Sandro. About the weather, first.

'My luck,' the barman was saying, 'looks like it's going to break today, you only have to look at the sky. And I'm closing up tomorrow.'

Was tomorrow Saturday? It was. A week since Brunello was killed.

'Looks like the end of the world,' said the road sweeper, nodding out through the glass door. He lifted a small glass of something dark red to his lips and tipped his head back.

And that was what it had felt like to Sandro, crossing the endless suffocating expanse of the Piazza Santa Croce as overhead an apocalyptic sky pressed down on him. Turning dark at dawn instead of light.

He looked back at the paper again. Bellosguardo, it said; that was where the man had been found. Not out in some country village. And Bellosguardo was where Sandro was going to meet Pietro – with a little detour to the Carnevale on the way.

LOCAL MAN SOUGHT. Sandro scanned the piece – a double-page spread – in search of the sub-headline, found it, but was not much the wiser. *Police have identified a suspect known to have been in the immediate vicinity at the time of the killing. The man is local to the area and has a previous history of violent crime. His name will be released later today.* Sandro stared.

Could that mean Josef? Was he a local man? Previous history of violent crime – that would still be speculation, wouldn't it, about Claudio Brunello's murder? Was that what Pietro was thinking? He hadn't said that last night.

He tucked the paper under his arm and slapped his coin on the bar, turning to leave.

'Not many going to cry over the loss of Galeotti,' said Orlando, and Sandro stopped. He removed the newspaper from under his arm and held it with one hand, tapping it in the open palm of the other.

'No?' he said mildly. Frowned down at the headline.

'He was a crook,' Orlando said. He folded his short, weathered arms across his apron and eyed Sandro.

'You knew him?' Sandro asked.

Orlando gave a faint shrug. 'A lot of people did,' he said.

'I suppose I did, too,' Sandro replied.

'Well, then,' Orlando said. 'You can tell.'

'A customer,' Sandro said.

'Now and then.' Orlando was eyeing him narrowly now, and Sandro knew when to change tack.

'It's the way of the world,' he said. 'Bankers, estate agents. It's the working man who pays.' Sandro meant it as a vague gesture towards solidarity that might prompt information, but the barman seemed to take it differently.

'Galeotti was more of a crook than most.' Orlando turned his head a little to one side, as if listening for something. 'And what have bankers got to do with anything?'

Sandro shrugged, watching him.

The barman set wrinkled elbows on the bar. 'Claudio Brunello wasn't a crook. If that's who you mean. Drank his coffee in here every morning, *macchiato in vetro* and a *budino*, wouldn't have anything else if there were no *budini*.'

There was a pause, in which they both reflected on Claudio Brunello's taste in breakfast, his restraint, his discriminating tastes.

'A good man, didn't line his own pocket, always left a few *centesimi* on the bar. I've seen the Guardia in that bank of his – and I've seen you. Asking questions. A good man, whatever they say.'

How, wondered Sandro, did we get on to Brunello? 'No,' he said, 'I meant – I meant the big guys, the Banca d'Italia, those American banks. I didn't mean – the Toscana Provinciale's not going to bring the sky down on us all, is it? Small-time stuff.'

The barman was watching him.

'Did he know Galeotti?' Sandro asked. 'Claudio Brunello, I mean?'

The moustache turned down. 'Wouldn't have given him the time of day,' he said, 'I wouldn't have thought.' He raised a hand to the road sweeper, trudging out through the door. 'See you in September,' he said.

The barman turned back to Sandro; his face seemed somehow to have smoothed, his expression now bland and incurious.

'Forget it,' he said. 'Shouldn't speak ill of the dead.' And he touched a thumb to his lower lip, superstitiously.

Sandro nodded, watching him as he took Sandro's cup and stacked it in the dishwasher basket behind the bar. Sandro slid the road sweeper's sticky shot glass along the bar top, and Orlando took that too, and Sandro headed for the door once more.

'He was a crook, though, dead or not,' said Orlando to his back, and in the doorway, feeling the heat outside, Sandro paused.

Behind him, Orlando spoke deliberately. 'Galeotti had some big deal going down lately. A lot of money involved. And then he gets mugged and killed? Some coincidence.' And then turned his back, the conversation finally over.

For a moment Sandro stayed there in the doorway. Something had happened to the air, the light. For a moment, in the narrow street, he didn't recognize it, then he understood that it had been lightning.

Sandro stepped off the pavement, listening for thunder, to gauge the storm's proximity. None came. To his left was the Via dei Saponai, and the bank.

So Galeotti'd had a big deal going down. Not the flat in San Niccolo; not the apartment in the Via del Lazaretto: they'd be small enough potatoes. Who'd kill a man over a run-down apartment in a condo in Firenze Sud? Unless the secret it was being loaned out for was a big one.

And he went the other way, towards the crumbling brick façade of the church, knowing that the alley beyond it would lead him to the Carnevale. And it was as he turned into the alley that he heard it, an ominous low rumble somewhere far off to the north-west, and over the church the sky darkened perceptibly.

From somewhere a cool breeze came, curling round his ankles, blowing dust in the gutters, then it was gone. Ahead of him was the Carnevale, boarded up in bright pine, half the letters of its vertical neon name already dismantled: '—nevale', it read. Sandro stopped. It was a good-sized building, four storeys, a row of five blind, dirty windows. And as he stared Sandro found himself thinking of those paltry hundred or so euros Josef Cynaricz banked every week and imagining the dusty rooms behind that blind façade.

What was it that Roxana Delfino had said? What had the builder told her, putting up the hoarding? *Not a pretty sight, in there.* There was no sign of any activity today, but Sandro felt a strange reluctance to go any closer. And then he nearly jumped out of his skin as a steel shutter rattled up, shockingly loud, at the foot of one of the buildings between him and the Carnevale. As he watched, a small, two-stroke Ape van of the kind used to transport almost anything almost anywhere in his benighted, low-tech country, edged out, neatly reversing to face him in the narrow alley. Sandro peered through the dusty windscreen, trying to make out who was driving – and then she jumped out. It was Liliana, from the vegetable stall, and she gave him a wary glance on her way round to the back of the van. Sandro hurried towards her, ridiculously pleased to find her here.

Seeing him approach, she stopped, in the middle of fastening down some crates of zucchini-flowers, the delicate furled petals, yellow tinged with green, in neat rows.

'Liliana,' he said, and she raised an eyebrow.

'Sandro Cellini,' she said. 'How's Luisa?' Everyone always asked him that.

'She's good,' he said.

Beyond Liliana, who stood examining him curiously with folded arms, was the cinema's blackened, ugly façade, waiting for him. It was as though fate had put Liliana between him and the horrible old place. Only he didn't believe in fate.

'Listen,' he said. She cocked her head. 'You know little Anna, right? Who works at the Loggiata. Little dark-haired Anna, who's pregnant? Likes her oranges.'

'I know her.' Liliana's expression darkened a shade. 'Sweet kid.'

'And—' He hesitated. 'You know her guy. Josef.' She stiffened, just perceptibly. He persisted. 'You know he's disappeared, then?' Liliana pursed her lips.

'Disappeared,' she said. 'Right.' Giving nothing away.

'I'm trying to find him for her. I'm a private detective now, you knew that, right?'

'I knew that,' said Liliana, with the faintest sympathetic edge to her voice.

'There are people,' said Sandro cautiously, 'people who think she's better off without him.'

Liliana gave him a quick, hard look before turning away abruptly, reaching up for the roll-down shutter to her lock-up. Following the movement, Sandro saw the flash of a big shiny padlock and, as the shutter came down, a broad scrape across the articulated metal slats above the lock. He noticed that although she pulled the shutter down, she didn't secure it.

'That could be true,' she said. 'All things considered. But that doesn't mean he's a bad guy.'

Sandro took a step to the side, leaned down to peer behind her at the shutter again.

'Have you seen him?' he asked quietly. 'You've seen him, haven't you?'

Liliana stood, and tugged at the door of the Ape. She climbed inside, but left the driver's door open. She'd had a husband once. He helped on the stall. An old drunk; everyone thought she was well rid of him when he died, everyone except Liliana. She kept going without him, as you do.

'You can't tell her,' she said, steely. 'If I tell you. He said, look after her. Keep her out of it.'

'Out of what?'

'Out of whatever shit he's in. Up to his neck.'

'But he's a good guy,' said Sandro. 'That's what you said.'

She sighed. 'What do you know about him? Josef? That he worked here?' Nodding towards the cinema. 'That he worked hard, taking the money, projecting the films, sweeping up after, getting the takings to the bank? That he had no one, until he met the girl? That job was the only security he had, the only family, the only home.'

And now the job was gone, the home was gone. 'You knew him. You talked to him.'

She shrugged. 'I don't know,' she said. 'Maybe I'm a soft touch.'

Sandro snorted. Nothing could be further from the impression Liliana generally gave to the outside world.

'The lock-up's here,' she went on, eyes distant. 'He came to my stall for fruit, then now and again I saw him here. He helped me with the crates a time or two. I don't think people talked to him, he was so clearly a Roma, and usually they come with baggage, family. He was trying to make it on his own.'

'You know he told her he worked in a bank?'

Liliana's eyes slid away, her hand moved down to the key in the ignition but she didn't turn it.

'I – I got some of that, yes. She mentioned it on the stall one day.'

'And you didn't set her straight?' Sandro could just picture Liliana, raising an eyebrow, in the middle of throwing oranges into a bag. 'How did he think he'd get away with it?'

'Look,' said Liliana, 'he doesn't have – friends. Doesn't have family. Just like her. He loves her. Sometimes people are meant for each other. Sometimes they deserve a break. He'd have told her eventually.' She frowned fiercely. 'He had a plan.'

Sandro remembered Anna saying something of the sort.

'I see.' Sandro leaned back against the shutter, looking at the Carnevale. 'So you gave him the benefit of the doubt, then. And now you think she's better off without him? What kind of shit is it you think he's up to his neck in, and why?'

In the Carnevale's façade a window stood open, the ragged tail of a curtain flapping through it. Sandro shifted his gaze back to Liliana, and he saw her calculating. Judging something about him. She took her hand from the ignition key and leaned back in her seat.

'See that?' she said, nodding down at the metal shutter he was leaning against.

He followed her gaze to the deep bright scrape on the metal, and looked back at Liliana.

'Tuesday morning, I come here to find the lock's been forced. I thought – well. Junkies. People don't thieve from vegetable lock-ups. I pulled up the shutter expecting some little scumbag sleeping it off, and there he was. Jumped out at me looking like—' And she shivered, just a little. 'Looking like nothing I've ever seen before. Like he'd been – been beaten half to death, or hit by a car. Blood in his hair. One hand all broken, and marks on him.'

'Did he tell you what had happened?'

She shook her head. 'He tried, but I didn't really get it. He was shaking so hard, I could hardly understand him. He said he had to get out of sight before they found out. Found him gone. He did say over and over, don't tell Anna. I'll sort it out myself, he said, don't tell her. Keep her out of it.'

'Right.' Protecting her. That was what Giuli and Luisa had thought.

'He asked me for clothes, and I gave him the old man's overalls, I keep them in the back. I gave him bananas. He wolfed them down, then he asked me for my mobile.' Her voice went flat.

Sandro frowned. 'You gave him your phone?'

Liliana looked away. 'I – no. I kind of flipped out a bit. I thought, oh, that was all he was all along. Small-time rip-off merchant, only chats to me because he wants something, I – I don't know what got into me. I'd had a bad night, sometimes – this heat. I don't sleep, thinking.' Sandro nodded. 'I got angry,' she went on, flatly. 'I told him to get out of there. And then he just ran off.'

'That's why you haven't locked up, just now?'

She shrugged. 'He might still need somewhere.'

'But you haven't seen him since?'

She shook her head.

There was a silence. Sandro was thinking. 'Tuesday morning.

The bruises – purple, green?'

Liliana frowned. 'Purple going yellow.'

'You weren't here Saturday, were you?'

'The usual,' she said. 'Six in the morning, then three in the afternoon putting the stuff away.'

'Anything going on? Here?'

She shook her head slowly, still frowning.

'Not that I can remember.'

'Nothing unusual?'

'I'd have to think,' she said, her mouth set. 'I've got to go, Sandro,' she said. 'I've the stall to set up and I'm running late already.'

'If you remember anything,' said Sandro, stepping back from the little van's window as she turned the key and the shrill engine spluttered into life.

'Say hello to Luisa,' she called as she moved off.

He watched her disappear around the corner in a blue haze of exhaust, and felt something, a spot of rain on his cheek. Then nothing. He looked up at the purpling sky. Not yet.

Claudio Brunello, battered and dumped in the African market; Galeotti, his skull fractured, his body half out of his car at the roadside. Josef bruised and bloodstained – what had Liliana said? – as if he'd been hit by a car.

Suddenly decisive, Sandro turned and hurried towards the Carnevale.

*

In the stifling shuttered darkness of her room off the Via della Chiesa, Giuli lay on the bed with barely the will to move. She didn't even know whether she could get it together to call in sick, but then again, did it really matter? If she didn't call in, they'd just chalk it up to experience, another mistake, another lazy, backsliding ex-con who couldn't hack it in the real world, without the drugs.

If you asked her, she'd have said she hadn't thought about it at all, not her whole life. Who wanted a baby, this day and age? She hadn't thought it would feel like this. Slowly she rolled over and faced the wall, pulled her arms in between her thin breasts. It didn't matter. Nothing mattered.

CHAPTER TWENTY-FOUR

IT TURNED OUT TO be surprisingly easy to get Carlotta to talk. Almost as if all she'd needed was to be asked. A slight show of surprise, suspicion, then she jumped at the chance.

The house inside was identical in layout to Ma's, only the smells were different. She was older, of course, and lonelier. She had a son but he didn't live with her, hadn't done so for years, not since he'd married an Abruzzese. No one to cook or clean for, so it was fustier, sourer. A smell of cat. But everything was neat and dusted, and she led Roxana straight on to the back porch.

'Oh, yes,' she said immediately with relish, standing with her wiry old arms folded as Roxana squeezed herself on to a chair beside the clothes airer. 'I saw him all right. Or them, I should say.' And narrowed her eyes to observe Roxana's reaction.

Another one like Ma: all fuddlement and slow steps on the outside, but inside things were working perfectly.

'Them?'

Carlotta craned her neck to look over into their garden next door. 'Where's your mother?' she asked. 'How come she doesn't ask?'

'Oh, Carlotta,' said Roxana, 'you know Ma.'

And the old woman just raised her sharp chin in acknow-ledgement. They both turned to look out across the garden.

Carlotta's little patch was much neater, more cut back than Ma's. Her son came out to do it once in a while. Three rows of tomatoes growing against the left-hand wall, some sparse flowerbeds edged in decorative terracotta, an abundance of hideous ornaments. Cherubs with watering cans, miniature wooden houses, that kind of thing. But nothing tall, not like Ma's loquat and banana palm, to block out the world and the view. You could see straight to the back fence, and beyond it.

'We talking about Tuesday?' Carlotta said. She leaned on the veranda's balustrade with both stringy arms. 'Mid-morning, I heard the doorbell go. So of course I went to the front and looked. Didn't get much of a look, but I could see his shoulder.' She frowned. 'Some kind of boiler suit, he was wearing. Overalls. Too big for him.'

'Like a delivery man?'

Decisively Carlotta shook her head. 'More like – a mechanic, kind of thing your Dad would have put on, to tinker with the car.' She gave Roxana a quick, sly glance. 'Anyway. His voice. I listened. He was pleading. He sounded—' She shook her head. 'Sounded funny.' She was frowning fiercely.

'Funny?'

'Well. Foreign. And – not normal. I thought – well, drugs, you know.'

'Foreign,' Roxana said slowly. 'But you didn't get a look at him.'

'Oh, I did, later,' Carlotta said, folding her arms. 'That's when I sent him packing.'

'Hold on,' Roxana said. 'So what happened, exactly?'

'He stayed at the front door a while, just talking to her in this voice, through the door. Soft, begging her.' Pursed her lips. 'Sounded like he knew her. Or knew you. '

'You just listened.'

Of course she did. Roxana tried to moderate her resentment, thinking of Ma behind her door, frightened. Tried to remind herself that Carlotta was scared, too. Carlotta just shot her a glance that said, *What did you want me to do?*

'Then he came round the back,' she said. 'He disappeared, then came round the back, in the alley. Couldn't see him, but I knew he was there.'

Two terrified old women.

'He called Ma by name?'

'I thought he was saying, *Signorina* Delfino.'

Roxana inhaled, holding it.

'A small man, dark. Dark eyes. Like a Roma. A gypsy.' She spoke slowly. Carlotta was staring at her.

'Josef,' Roxana said.

He came looking for me. She heard Sandro Cellini's words: he trusted you. A bad feeling, a worse feeling than the one she'd had when she first saw the smashed back gate, rose in her.

'You said you sent him packing.'

'He was there all day. I heard him.' Ma had said the same thing, and Roxana had disbelieved her. 'Making sounds, at the back gate, like he was trying to get through.'

'You didn't call the police.'

Carlotta gave her a look – stubborn, suspicious, weary – that conveyed all Roxana needed to know about being a lonely old woman.

'I wanted a look at him,' she said. 'That was what I was waiting for. I went to the back of the garden, very quiet. He'd got in, he was inside, watching, crouched down, I think, and he stood up suddenly and he was right there. Face to face.' Carlotta's woman's face was alive at the memory, her old mouth quivering. 'I shouted at him then, *I'm calling the police!*'

'He scared you.'

Carlotta refocused on her, and Roxana saw her relive it. 'He was – it was his face. It wasn't even human. Looked like he'd been beaten half to death.' She pursed her lips. 'It was a shock.'

Roxana didn't say anything, didn't suggest the man might have needed help. She could hear Carlotta's angry guilt in her next words. 'He ran off, then.' The old woman turned back to her stubbornly. 'Well, what was I to do?'

Roxana nodded, not listening. Josef Cynaricz had come to her for help. She looked up. Or had he come after her? Was he a victim, or – had Claudio fought back? There was a connection. Absently she felt in her pockets, thinking, I must tell Sandro Cellini this, where's that mobile? Then she remembered where it was. Call him now, from the house phone. Or go and get the mobile? What if – what if people had been trying to get hold of her? *What people?* She could hear Ma's scornful voice in her head. Ten minutes on the *motorino*, and she'd have it back in her pocket.

She stood up. 'Thanks, Carlotta,' she said, trying to contain a stupid, pointless panic rising in her, just because she didn't have her phone. Patted her neighbour's hand in a belated gesture of pity.

'What about the other one, though?' the old woman said slyly, detaining her.

'The other one?'

'The one that came after,' said Carlotta. 'Came yesterday. The kid. He came looking, too. White – sports shoes. Bright white.'

White shoes. And into Roxana's head came the image of a kid in low slung jeans she'd mistaken for a drug dealer. Hopping up and down outside the bank in white trainers.

*

Walking up the hill towards Bellosguardo, Sandro cursed himself for an idiot, for not bringing the car. His breath was laboured, and the humidity was intense as he climbed towards the grey-lidded sky. It was a bloody long way.

Time to think? How could anyone think, in heat like this? He paused to lean against a low wall, and looked back.

The patchwork of roofs spread out before him, intensely red in the strange, lowering light, and it occurred to Sandro that this was where you would come to see the façade of every church in the city. He ticked them off for a while, waiting for his breath to ease, Santa Maria Novella, Santo Spirito, Santa Croce, took in the aggressively pointed bulk of the new university development on the north of the city, the muddle of light industrial units and pylons where the city dissolved into ugliness at Sesto. Thought of the secret places hidden under the red roofs, the loggias and marble porticoes. The dusty streets around the synagogue, the grimy bars, the dumpsters. The Carnevale.

Nearly there. Sandro mopped his forehead, pushed off from the wall and doggedly walked on: he had no idea if his heart was up to this, at his age. Never having had any kind of check-up, just assuming that, if there was a weakness there, thirty years of police work would already have finished him off. Did he exercise? If walking very slowly counted. Did he drink? Yes. Smoke? No. But it didn't always work like that, did it? There were risk factors, of course he knew there were, but even so. Sometimes you got no warning.

It wasn't the climb, either. The horrible feeling, hardening to stone somewhere below his ribs, didn't come from mere exertion of his ageing muscles; he wasn't frightened of what his heart might do, he was frightened of something else. Risk factors. Did these include climbing on a piece of packing case to peer in at a cracked and filthy window round the side of a derelict porn cinema?

The street had been empty. Liliana and her little van had disappeared around the corner, leaving no more than a bluish tinge to the air. The Carnevale was boarded up, the fencing smooth and impenetrable, new pine and padlocks and signage with a drawing of an Alsatian. Above the glaring wood, the dirty façade looked even bleaker and uglier than ever; how could it have survived so long? Only the complacency of the city's surveyors and assessors, the academicians and bureaucrats who refused to allow even a new shutter to be erected, could have allowed this canker of a place. Sandro had skirted the pine boarding, round to the alley – no more than a man's width – that ran alongside the cinema.

The flank of the building was big and blind – a characteristic of theatres generally, Sandro acknowledged. A high, almost blank wall with the stinking alley underneath it – and it had stunk. Dog faeces and urine, intensified by the heat and the confined space. Moving along it with extreme reluctance, Sandro had came to a door and stopped. A plain, small door in the blackened wall, and the lock and doorknob were shiny with use. Sandro had taken the single step back that the space allowed. Narrow, featureless and dirty, the door could not have been more banal – but it was something else. It was the real point of entry, it was the secret life of this building. That had been when it had started up inside him, the slow tightening of that obscure and dangerous muscle: fear. He had pushed the door; it had resisted. Of course.

Further along the alley, something had gleamed on the ground, some stinking liquid, and there had been a pallet propped against the wall. Beyond it, a couple of metres up, he had noticed a small makeshift window of the sort inserted illegally all over the city, on the cheap and out of sight, to provide the bare minimum of light and ventilation. Holding his breath, Sandro had moved on.

Stopping below the small, high, broken window, the pallet at his feet, a feeling of aversion as strong as he had ever experienced had come over Sandro. There was a protruding overflow pipe of some kind to the right of the window, offering itself as a handhold: Sandro had set his foot on the pallet, tested it, reached up and taken hold of the pipe. As he had pulled himself up in the cramped space, the sudden sense of his own sagging weight, his singular uselessness and vulnerability, had pressed in on him like gravity, a choking sensation that he had had to fight to overcome, to continue upwards, inching until his face was there, his arm already aching, the ridiculous old man that he was turning out to be.

And at first, he had seen nothing anyway. The glass was filthy and behind it all was dark.

The pane had been cracked and a triangular segment had fallen away. Gingerly Sandro had pushed at it with his free hand, dust on his fingertip, and the old dried putty had given way, the glass moving inwards. He had eased his head sideways so as to see in without blocking the light.

What was there? Almost nothing. But Sandro had had the terrible sensation of being about to fall, whether backwards or forwards he didn't know, and of wanting, suddenly, urgently wanting to be back at home with Luisa in his kitchen and not here: the last place he had wanted to be was here, or perhaps worse than here was the next step, to be inside this building against whose wall he was so unwillingly pressed.

He had glanced into a small, empty room. A mattress on the floor in one corner, the dirty inside of a duvet, thin with age, bundled on it, shadowed and crumpled. Stained: worse than stained. An old cooker that might have come out of a dumpster, askew in one corner. Something on the wall. All up the wall. And the smell.

Head down now and plodding in the grey heat of the hillside with the rhythmic saw of the cicadas resonating among the trees, Sandro found himself pinching his nostrils against even the memory of the smell he'd left below him in the city. The ammoniac secretions of that alley and something thicker, dirtier, coming up at him from inside the Carnevale. Still climbing towards Bellosguardo, not far now, he heard a voice calling him from higher up; he kept his head down just a moment longer, told himself to keep moving. He had thought that he would vomit, there in the alley, make his own sour contribution to the stench. He had swayed, his grip had loosened a moment on the piece of dirty pipe, his foot had slipped and clattered. But he had not fallen; he hadn't vomited.

'Hey, pal,' came the voice again, concern creeping in, and Sandro raised his head and saw his oldest friend standing in the lee of a building, the low, square shape of a farmhouse behind him.

He was drenched in sweat, quite suddenly, and Pietro's hand encountered a sopping sleeve.

'You didn't bring the car?' Pietro was aghast. 'Madonna, Sandro. What are you thinking?' From the far side of the hill, down towards Scandicci, there was an ominous rumble.

'I'm fine,' Sandro muttered, feeling the reassuringly regular thump of his poor old heart. He mopped his forehead, leaned against the rough brick. The city was hazed below him now; was that the light, or were his eyes doing something funny? He took a moment. Pietro remained silent, watching him.

'No need to ask why here, then,' Sandro said when he began to feel more normal, although the light was still strange and thick. Pulling out the newspaper. This was the farmhouse in the picture, with Galeotti's car in the foreground, the body under its sheeting. Car and body gone, now.

'No,' Pietro said shortly. 'The girls are cursing me. This job. Now another murder. And we were hoping to get away.'

'It's connected,' Sandro said. Both had their eyes on a bleached stretch of road towards the mulberry trees.

Pietro looked at him curiously. 'They found a cutting in his pocket,' he said. 'About Brunello's body being found. But you didn't know that.'

Sandro nodded towards the trees. 'Come on,' he said, and together they set off, towards the crime scene. Pietro's car was parked in the shade of the farmhouse: his own vehicle. They walked past it and carried on.

'Where's Matteucci?' Sandro said. 'Your shadow?'

Pietro chewed his lip. 'He's not so bad,' he said. 'Just young. Following something up this morning. I'll tell you about it.'

The short row of manicured mulberry trees, and a view down towards the white tower blocks of Scandicci, glittering in a distant shaft of sun cast down from a heavy sky. Meadow grass and the dried heads of wild iris: the cicadas, he realized, had fallen silent.

'Storm coming,' he remarked.

'Oh, yes,' Pietro said. 'The forecast was crazy, this morning. They said there was a mini-tornado on the Po plain last night. A lot of damage.'

Below them lay the foothills of the Alps, visible on a good day. This was not a good day: a thunderhead a couple of kilometres high was spread across the entire western horizon, darkening by the minute.

They stood quite still. 'Better out here,' Sandro said, feeling his head clear. 'Sometimes you need to get out of the city.' But he felt exposed; what was the rule about lightning? Don't stand under a tree.

There was a silence. 'Oh,' said Pietro suddenly. 'We found Brunello's car. It had been towed away on Monday when the street-cleaning vehicles came through. It had been by the river, just down from the bank; where he always parked it for work, according to the woman.'

'What woman?' Sandro was alert, thinking of Roxana Delfino.

'What's her name? Goldman: his second-in-command.'

Another silence. 'Yes,' Sandro said slowly. 'About her. About Marisa Goldman. Did she tell you where she was, that weekend?'

Pietro eyed him warily. 'She did,' he said. 'She was away with her boyfriend. On his yacht.'

Sandro nodded. 'Well,' he said. 'You might want to corroborate that. With the boyfriend, to begin with.'

'Oh yes,' Pietro said, with just the faintest trace of a smile. 'I'll get Matteucci on to it.'

'Someone saw her. Standing on the doorstep of Brunello's apartment, at seven that Friday night. After she was supposed to be gone for the weekend. After he was supposed to be gone, too, for that matter.'

Pietro nodded. 'The traffic wasn't as bad as usual, you know. That Friday night. I didn't want—'

'You didn't want to mention that to Irene Brunello?' Sandro said. 'To suggest that her husband might have been doing something else that night?'

Pietro shrugged. 'He might have been packing, for all I knew,' he said. 'The fact that his car wasn't logged through the tolls until eight-forty-five, even though he left work early – well. I was going to wait until I had more information. Before telling anybody.'

Even me, thought Sandro. Claudio Brunello wasn't his client, nor was his wife. Why should Pietro tell him?

'The two tumblers,' he said, remembering. 'On the draining board in Brunello's flat.'

And then he remembered where he'd seen Galeotti's letterhead: lying on Marisa Goldman's desk.

'You mind if I talk to Marisa Goldman first?' he asked, knowing this would be a big favour.

Pietro gave him a sharp glance, then sighed. 'Christ knows, this murder's tying me up. All right,' he said. 'But do it now.'

Sandro exhaled. 'So,' he said. 'The car. You found the car.'

'Goldman and Brunello?' Pietro turned to gaze without focusing across the glittering valley, gave a slow nod. 'Could be right. Maybe.' He turned back to look at Sandro. 'The car was clean, or near enough. No violence, no bloodstains, it had obviously just been sitting there since Saturday afternoon, then some helpful *vigile* ordered it to be towed out of the way of the street cleaners. Clean enough, except for just one thing: a scrap of paper in the passenger footwell. *Josef C*, and a number written on it.'

'Ah,' said Sandro, and felt it loosen, the intractable tangle of this damned case, one thread coming free, at last. 'So the person who called him was Josef. Josef C is Josef Cynaricz. My Josef, Anna's Josef. Not Goldman, or Galeotti.'

Sandro thought of Brunello, the scrupulous bank manager, sitting inside his holiday house while his wife prepared the children for the beach. Josef C repeating to him, 'Take the number, write down the number.' Even though it would have appeared on the phone, Brunello was old-school, like Sandro. He wanted it written down.

Pietro said nothing, then nodded quickly.

'He called Brunello out on the first day of his holiday. A young man he knew only as a low-grade customer, who maybe once came in and asked for a loan, no more than that? He must have had something important to say.'

'Must have.'

They'd reached the bloodstain, and both stopped and looked down.

'And now Galeotti.' Pietro looked at Sandro through eyes

narrowed against the sky's glare. 'You didn't know about the cutting he had in his pocket. But you thought there was a connection. Between Galeotti and – who? And Brunello?'

'Not Brunello,' said Sandro. 'Josef.'

Pietro took a step back, watching him, and Sandro went on, 'Galeotti was the agent for the apartment my Josef was "borrowing". Only I think Josef believed he was going to get to keep the place. Someone let him think that. Maybe Galeotti, or maybe Galeotti was doing it as a favour to someone else. Galeotti's just the middle man, isn't he? The agent, doing favours to get favours. Keys to empty apartments are part of his currency.'

Pietro nodded cautiously. 'Still,' he said slowly. 'Murder? Over a borrowed apartment?'

Sandro nodded too. 'I know,' he said. 'But I can't help thinking – it's connected. Perhaps whoever was doing the favour – whoever was trying to keep Josef happy—' He stopped, unable to follow his train of thought. Was it the heat? He started again. 'I heard Galeotti was a crook,' he said. 'And I heard he had some big deal going down.'

Pietro let out a quick, astonished laugh. 'How'd you know this stuff?' he said, shaking his head a little.

Sandro examined his expression. 'It's true, then?' he asked.

Pietro chewed his lip. 'We went down to his office last night, a place on the Via Romana. We talked to the girl. Secretary-cum-receptionist, more or less the only other employee. He kept her pretty much in the dark, and she didn't seem too bright to start with, but she said he'd been involved with a big deal for the last couple of months, very secretive about it because it wasn't in the bag, a lot of to-ing and fro-ing, she said. Some big backhanders involved, you know how it works. The buyer's in cahoots with the agent, they get the place cheap and slip him some money on the side. In this case who knows – maybe someone else was involved, someone the seller trusts.'

Sandro frowned. The only trustworthy bloke he'd come across in this whole business was Brunello, and he was dead.

Pietro sighed. 'A month or so back it was all on, then it was all off, then it was back on again. Something kept blocking the sale. And, if I remember right, she said he'd gone off Friday night all keyed up for a big showdown, and he came in on Monday full of something. She was in shock when she heard he was dead. Total shock.'

'He was the kind of man – I don't know,' said Sandro. 'Cocky. Full of life.'

And there was that nagging regret again. For the loss of even a man like Galeotti, with his gleaming car and his crisp collars.

'You met him?' Pietro asked.

'I told you, didn't I? This place we were looking to buy, in San Niccolo.' Pietro looked sympathetic, and Sandro shrugged. 'Not much chance of that now. What with one thing and another.'

Pietro's hand came up to Sandro's shoulder. 'It's good to see you, Sandro,' he said. 'You know? Sometimes it's hard to do this without you.'

Sandro said nothing. Instead, he squatted, and Pietro came down beside him. There were chalk marks on the road and the blood had turned black. It would disappear, eventually.

'Last Friday night. Galeotti was expecting big news last Friday night,' said Sandro softly, almost to himself. Then he remembered something, took the paper out of his pocket. The sweat had dried on his forehead; he felt almost human again.

'Says here, you've got a suspect,' he said.

Pietro looked at him, a slow smile spreading across his face at last, running his hand through the grass at the verge. 'Well, there's the thing,' he said, and he pulled out an ear of wheatgrass. 'We have.'

'Not my Josef?'

Pietro shook his head. 'Not your Josef, no.' Still smiling. 'You remember that little weasel Gulli? Nasty little dealer from Campo di Marte, prone to violence?'

Sandro nodded. He remembered Gulli as clear as day the last time he'd seen him, being marched into the courts of justice in Piazza San Firenze, between him and Pietro on a charge of aggravated burglary. Twenty-five or so then, but skinny as a kid, hard, thin arms under Sandro's hand, stonewashed jeans, slicked hair. White trainers.

'Yes,' he said. 'I remember Gulli.'

'We've got a witness.'

'Saw him do it?'

'Good as,' said Pietro ruminatively. 'Old woman at the soft drinks stall at the bottom of the hill on the *viale*, saw him go past about two on a Vespa, saw him turn up the hill; she even says she saw something like a tyre iron strapped to the back of the moped. Recognized him. Must be tricky for him, plenty know Gulli, he's done enough people enough bad turns, considering he's still under thirty. It seems he mugged the old girl's daughter three years back and did only six weeks for it; she held a grudge.' Pietro spread his hands, dropping the piece of grass. 'Galeotti's body was discovered at just before three and he was barely dead then.'

'All right,' said Sandro, thinking hard. 'So where's Gulli now?' Pietro stood up with sudden, enviable ease. He was, Sandro couldn't forget, five years his junior. More creakily, he followed.

Pietro's smile faded, but not by much.

'We'll find him,' he said. 'Kid like Gulli never goes too far from home.'

'What's the motive?' Sandro asked. Something about this wasn't right. 'What was it, just a mugging? A bit off the beaten track for that.'

'And he wasn't robbed,' said Pietro. 'Mobile gone, yes. But a full wallet. Man had seven hundred-odd euros on him, as well. Untouched.'

'Cash backhander, no doubt,' pondered Sandro, momentarily sidetracked. 'Lot of cash. Not like Gulli. Unless—'

'Unless Gulli's taking a step up the career path. From violent burglar to hit man.'

'Incompetent hit man: that would figure,' Sandro murmured. It had always surprised him how stupid criminals like Gulli could be. 'Bad luck he was recognized.' He paused. 'I wonder where Gulli was on Saturday afternoon?'

He could see Pietro chewing the inside of his cheek gloomily. 'In custody, as a matter of fact,' he said. 'I checked arrest reports, first off, to make sure he wasn't inside and it was mistaken identity. Because Gulli's been inside more than out, this last ten years.'

Nothing to lose: prison was like home to the likes of Gulli. Get paid plenty to hit someone; the worst that happens is you're inside another fifteen years. They had no concept of the span of a life, these kids. Of what it might be like to wake up when you're forty and know it was all gone. The best of it, anyway.

Pietro sighed. 'He was brought in for trying to pickpocket Saturday morning, released without charge Sunday morning. But we'll find him. There'll be DNA, it'll stick, too.' But he sounded demoralized.

'So where are you looking?' Sandro wanted to keep on this trail. 'Who might have asked him to hit Galeotti?'

'Gulli's gone upmarket,' said Pietro thoughtfully. 'He's been seen in some very smart places.'

'Smart places?'

'That bar, by the British Consulate. San Niccolo, up here even.'

The sweat was beading again on Sandro's upper lip. 'Listen,' he said. 'Listen. What have we got? A crooked estate agent, a banker, a porn cinema up for redevelopment. A lowlife like Gulli.'

Where, he thought, where had he seen Galeotti's name? His letterhead.

'Ah,' said Pietro, and now a wind got up, fierce and hot, flattening the grass, sweeping across the hillside down to Scandicci. 'There's something—' he said. 'The cinema, you said? There was something I had to tell you. About Brunello.'

'Yes?'

'The ash, on his feet. Celluloid: burned film, old film. Old ash, too, not recently burned, more like dust with traces of the ash in it.'

Film. Sandro had known all along, it seemed to him: had known even before he raised himself up on that pallet. Pietro was still talking, but Sandro's mind was already elsewhere.

'The lesion on his leg – a burn, they say, inflicted post-mortem, thought there might be a connection with the ash but—' A pause. 'Sandro? Are you listening?'

A big property, up for redevelopment: it was staring him in the face. The Carnevale.

'You know what I'd like to know?' he said. 'I'd like to know who was selling that building, and when that deal went through. And I'd like to know what the Guardia found in that bank.'

Pietro snorted. 'Right,' he said. 'And I'd like early retirement and a Testarossa. Dream on, Sandro.'

'Oh, I don't know,' said Sandro. 'There could be a way.'

*

Luisa heard the wind sweeping over the roofs as she stood at her wardrobe, trying to decide what to wear. And trying not to think about the things that frightened her.

That girl with her great belly. That was the most important thing, and the most urgent. Luisa knew better than anyone that it wasn't so easy, that little skip from eight months gone to holding the baby safe and new in your arms. There were things that happened out of sight, a cord twisting, too much of this chemical or that, an enzyme malfunctioning. She'd seen the girl trying to batten down, to keep herself safe against everything that was going on, but sometimes that wasn't enough.

The wind came then, rattling down the street, blowing something ahead of it with a clatter. Something else came loose overhead with a scraping sound.

Giuli. What had that expression been, on the girl's face last night as she left to go home? Trying to smile as she said goodbye, but she'd only looked haunted, bewildered. Had the man, Enzo, whoever he was, had he said something? Done something?

Luisa reached into the wardrobe: what was the weather going to do? Linen. It would be crumpled in ten minutes with this humidity. She pulled it out anyway, dressed herself with habitual meticulousness. Bathroom. Scent on her wrists, a scrap of make-up. Reaching towards the mirror, Luisa saw she was too thin in the face: her mother had always told her it was a danger, in old age. But she couldn't eat, in this heat.

Dropping a cotton ball into the wastebasket, she saw it. Leaned down under the sink, pulled the basket out and peered inside. Nothing more than a scrap of thin shiny plastic with some blue letters on it, something clinical about it. GRAV – and the rest was missing. Not a whole wrapper, but a shard of one. Luisa puzzled over it, and looked further in, and there was a small sheet of printed paper, concertinaed to fit in a packet, like a packet that might contain pills. Sandro? She unfolded it and saw that this would be nothing to do with Sandro. It was a set of instructions from a pregnancy testing kit.

Slowly Luisa pushed the paper into her pocket. So that was what Giuli had been doing in the bathroom all that time, last night.

And the face she'd left with? The news Giuli had received had not been the news she wanted. Feeling a sudden chill of the kind a fever might give you, Luisa locked up carefully, pulled the shutters closed and secured them. The wind was gone again as suddenly as it had come, but you never knew.

The stairwell was clammy and stifling. Luisa let herself out on to the street and was startled by how dark it had grown, like doomsday. Who would want to go shopping on a day like this? Plenty would; Luisa had been in the business long enough to know that, even when across the world towers were falling, someone would be in Frollini, asking her for a pair of gloves in just the right shade of cream. The door closed behind her, and Luisa looked at her watch: it was nine o'clock in the morning and it looked like dusk.

Anna Niescu: there was a limit to Luisa's power over the unborn. Giuli: she had to trust that the girl – the woman – was strong enough, and clever enough, to deal with the news she'd received, and to manage a bit of love in her life. But Sandro: that was another matter altogether.

And it was back, the wind, gusting up the street, gathering strength, sandblasting her with dirt from the street, forcing her to tug down her skirt. Luisa turned into it, feeling it pull at her, behind her something crashed to the ground and then the wind was gone again and her hair fell back into place.

Anna; Giuli. They were the young, they would have to manage. But Sandro. She'd been trying to tell herself this case was just a missing fiancé, but it wasn't. A man was dead. A husband, a father, beaten to death and dumped.

She had trained herself during Sandro's thirty years in the Polizia dello Stato to assume that he was safe. To rationalize: he was thorough, he was careful, he had good reflexes. He would come home.

Until he didn't.

CHAPTER TWENTY-FIVE

DASHA HEARD SOMETHING FALL from the scaffolding opposite the *loggia* and leaned out further. The wind excited her: let the whole place blow down, she thought. A bucket that had been used to mix plaster had blown off and was dangling from a shred of frayed rope.

She was looking out for him. She knew he'd come, sooner or later. He'd been there yesterday and the day before, but Dasha wasn't going to tell anyone. Her own father had been a violent alcoholic who used to sleep in the street outside their apartment block when her mother threw him out. They would step around him on the way to school.

You'll be fine, she wanted to say to Anna Niescu, you'll toughen up, like the rest of us. The old woman'll keep you on, find you some cot a friend of hers is throwing out. You'll be fine without him. She squeezed her eyes shut, thinking about what kind of life that would be, for Anna, for the child. There was worse, out there; the Loggiata was a roof over her head at least. She opened her eyes and looked back down.

The street below held a line of cars, dusted with pollen and something else sticky that came off the lime trees in an adjoining walled garden. A walled garden, an alley, a row of blue dumpsters, overflowing as they awaited the morning's collection. That's where he would hide, coming to find Anna. She'd thought of chucking a bucket of water over him, as you would a cat, only something'd stopped her. Didn't want him to know she'd seen him, although she had, three times: she'd almost told the girl, Giuli, whose dog-eared card she fingered in her pocket from time to time, only then she'd decided against it. Softer than she looked, with her boyfriend and her job.

How long would he keep on coming back? In the end, he'd give up and disappear, off to find an easier life. Or someone would get him. Whoever was after him would get him and it would all be a whole lot simpler. Let her just think he's done a runner. Simpler.

They were all on his side, weren't they? These people coming looking, detectives and that. They all thought they knew what was best for Anna, they wanted to believe in her fiancé, they wanted a happy ending. But what if they'd got it wrong?

He wasn't coming today. Maybe it was all over already. Dasha turned her back on the street, perfectly cool. She didn't feel the heat, that was what came of being born in the Caucasus; like a lizard, you just soaked up the heat, after a winter on those plains. She could hear Anna, singing breathlessly inside, her little lungs squeezed up inside her so she could barely speak any more. Then there was another noise, a tinkle, a bell or an alarm. She came to the glass door and pushed it open.

'All right?' she said, and the girl's lips stopped moving. She seemed dazed with something, sleeplessness perhaps. Dasha had heard her moving about, unable to settle, until the early hours. Now she had a hand in her pocket, as if she'd just put something away, and there was a flush on her cheek.

'Yes, all right?' Anna repeated the words back to her, the other hand moving to her stomach. 'All right. Just need a lie-down, for a bit.'

*

Forcing herself to take things one at a time Roxana called Cellini from the home phone twice, and twice found his line engaged. She left a message. She could hear how it sounded, too: crazy old ladies with nothing better to do than imagine intruders. She tried to sound considered, thoughtful.

I think it was Josef; I think he'd come to find me but I don't know why. Serves me right for having my name and address in the book, I suppose. And paused, as if his answerphone might be in a position to reassure her, No, don't worry. *And then someone else came, after him. Maybe* – and she heard her voice falter – *Maybe he was looking for him. Carlotta said he wore white trainers. The second guy.*

She went through to the back and they turned towards her in mid-conversation as if *she* was an intruder, Ma amused, Carlotta peering across her, the Persian between them on the fence even less welcoming, its tail fiercely upright.

'Ma,' she said warily, 'I think you should get that handyman back out here. There's so much needs doing.'

The two old women exchanged a look. 'Fine,' said Ma comfortably. 'He's a nice young man. I don't mind.'

'Today,' said Roxana.

Climbing on to the *motorino*, Roxana told herself, that would do it, a handyman on the premises would surely deter this – this guy in the white trainers, whoever he was. Could he be after Josef? Wasn't she being – hysterical? Some feral kid, that'd be all. She squeezed her eyes shut, trying not to exaggerate the danger. They'd be all right; she wouldn't be gone long.

And she needed her phone.

The Via Senese was choked with cars heading the other way, south to the seaside. Friday: she could see anxious faces hunched over steering wheels as the holidaymakers peered up at the dark sky. The storm was coming down from the Alps, chasing them. If there was one thing worse, they were thinking, than boiling to death in the city in August, it was getting to the beach just as the weather broke.

She left the Vespa carelessly in the street outside the bank. The closer to the centre she'd come, the emptier it seemed, Roxana's sometimes the only vehicle in the street, the bar she'd lunched in days ago shuttered up. It didn't mean the traffic wardens had gone too, but Roxana didn't plan on being inside too long. A wind had got up, a weird mixture of scalding Saharan gusts and colder air sucked up from somewhere else, and for a moment Roxana had a vision of some great massing swirl of air currents overhead, portending disaster.

She punched in the access code at the side door without thinking, only in the pause while she waited for it to work did she wonder whether the numbers might have been changed already. She was surprised by the exhilaration she felt at the thought. And then the muted buzz indicated that the code had been accepted and the door slid back and, with only a moment's hesitation, Roxana went inside.

It was as if the place was already abandoned, as derelict as the Carnevale: a musty smell, as from an old cellar or the rowing club's boat house as you passed, a whiff of the river. Somebody had been back, after they'd left. There was a strip of plastic tape across the door to Claudio's office. Roxana peered over it.

Empty shelves, already gathering dust. The desk was still there, lonely at the centre of the room, and the computer.

Roxana had a sudden, powerful sense that she shouldn't be there. She took a hasty step backwards, away from the open doorway, and for a second she couldn't remember why she *was* there. The phone: and then she struggled to remember where she would find it. Not Ma losing her marbles, this time; Roxana had a glimpse of what that kind of confusion must feel like. Pull yourself together.

She threaded past the empty workstations. When she'd started at the bank, there'd been a couple of other tellers on a job-share, half the week each, and a part-time secretary. It had all dwindled without her noticing. She pushed open the door to the tiny kitchen, the only bright space in the bank with its frosted window facing south, a little patch of normality. The electric ring, the microwave, the coffee machine. A socket, and in it the charger to her phone, the wire leading off behind the cabinet. She reached down and pulled on the cord: the phone came up from where it had been hiding behind the toaster. She heard something else fall.

Two missed calls: Ma, Maria Grazia. She listened to the second message: *Coming home, should be back tomorrow on the train. Hope you're all right. Meet me at the station?* Absently she peered down to where whatever it was had fallen, and hung up. It would be nice to see her. A new start; she could tell her the bank was finished. They could plan – she leaned down. There was something down there. It looked like some correspondence. An envelope. Delicately she fished with her fingers, but the space was too narrow. Pulled open the drawer and took, at random, a kitchen knife, and poked. Got it: eased the envelope up with the point of the knife. She put it in her handbag.

MM Holdings, it said. This was the account into which Josef paid his weekly takings, and this was the name on those envelopes she'd seen littering the lobby of the cinema. She slit the envelope and stared down, frowning. A form letter, confirming the discharge of a debt against the property: it had been copied to Tyrrhenian Properties. She looked at the date on the letter and the signature, then thrust it all down into her bag. Slowly she turned and walked to the door.

Back past the workstations, out to the silent, dusty lobby: Roxana knew where she was going. She ducked under the tape and into Claudio Brunello's office.

Slowly she seated herself behind her dead boss's computer and switched it on.

What if someone caught her? The Guardia? The police? Or whoever it was who had killed Claudio? She told herself, she couldn't think about that.

Even as she typed in Claudio's user name and code – she'd observed him do it often enough, taken it as a sign of the trust he placed in his employees – a part of her brain was wondering, *How much would you need to know about Claudio to guess it?* The name of his first-born child and the date of her birth. Even Roxana knew that you were supposed to be an awful lot more cryptic than that, and a lot less sentimental. Was it his soft heart that had killed Claudio?

MM Holdings. It came up quickly, everything she wanted, plain as day. It was a very old client, and a lot of the early business was summarized; this must have been done when computerization came in twenty years earlier. Some scanned-in microfiche records, deeds and contracts – MM Holdings had been operating under that name since 1967, when it had been formed as a limited company. The directors were listed. Of the founding three, only one remained, the other names had changed three or four times. In surprise Roxana pushed the chair back. Good God, she thought, as she stared at the name. Her. Really?

A current account. The account had been exceptionally active until the late nineties. After that takings had fallen off dramatically, dwindling to less than was required to finance the account's operation. The sell-off must have come just in time. She wondered why it hadn't been negotiated sooner; then she saw. A loan taken out against the property a year ago would have had to be repaid before the sale could go through: this was the same debt discharged in the letter she'd found stuffed behind the cupboard. Discharged last Friday. Roxana clicked on the mortgage file for detail, and as she did so she heard something, a small, familiar sound, and she was so absorbed suddenly and the sound so familiar that Roxana overrode it in her head.

Something wasn't right. She peered at the figures. Something was wrong. And then there was another sound and she looked up.

'Oh,' she said. 'Oh.'

*

They were both in the front of Pietro's car, with the air-con on. It seemed safer there, somehow, the sight of sheet lightning coming down somewhere over by Pistoia had put the wind up both of them.

'Jesus,' Pietro had said, awed by the spectacle, the whole sky lit briefly like neon over the Pisan plain. 'Perhaps it's just as well we're not going to the seaside.'

Inside the car it was very hot in spite of the air-con, and horribly humid. From behind the windscreen the sky looked black, but it still wasn't raining. 'We can't stay here,' said Pietro, starting the engine, glancing up at the trees. 'Under a tree, on the top of a hill? I'll take you over there.'

They parked up on the street outside Marisa Goldman's gate.

'It's not money, then,' said Pietro, nodding at the villa's expensively pale façade, at the outhouses and the roses, glowing fluorescent in the strange light.

Sandro shook his head. 'You don't know that,' he said. 'Appearances aren't everything.'

'She was here all along,' said Pietro ruminatively. 'Do you think – could a woman have done it?'

Sandro had taken out his wallet and was sorting through it. Had he kept the card? Probably not. He raised his head, focused on Pietro. 'Depends on the woman,' he said.

'Nice car,' said Pietro, nodding at the handsome machine standing on the driveway. A customized Cinquecento, a kept woman's car. 'We could get forensics to pull it in. If she moved him in that? A woman?' He was deeply dubious: the car looked like no more than a toy.

'Yes,' said Sandro, 'just not yet,' and returned to his task. Patiently he sorted through old receipts, the card for a *rosticceria* around the corner from home, a reminder from the surgery for his prostate check. Damn. He got out the phone and without expectation scrolled through the numbers, but there it was. Giorgio Viola.

As he waited for the connection, he summoned up the man, his pale, sweaty despairing bulk behind that desk north of the station, his defeated look as he walked away from the bank and along the river last night, Sandro watching him through the long lens of the birdwatcher's camera.

'You might ask,' he said as an aside, hand over the mouth-piece, just while he remembered, 'a guy who takes pictures of birds, down on the river, not far from the African market. You might talk to him.' Pietro looked bewildered, but before Sandro could explain further, Giorgio Viola answered his phone.

It took five minutes of patient explanation before Viola softened even fractionally. Damn, thought Sandro, why aren't I better at this? It wasn't as if he didn't sympathize with Viola. How could he convey it, that he was on his side? That they were on the side of – what? Of the defeated, the not quite competent, the stupidly soft-hearted. Only the more he wanted to be sympathetic, the gruffer he sounded.

'I'm only trying to find the father of this woman's child,' he said eventually, in despair. 'I don't want to do any insider trading. The last thing I want to do is get you into trouble. Just give me a leg-up here.'

There was a silence, the chink in Viola's frightened obduracy. And then he spoke.

'There was the transfer of a considerable sum.' Sandro held his breath, hearing the man's fear, his voice quick and breathless. 'Brunello transferred just over a hundred thousand euros from the bank's reserves, initially into his own account, just before close of business on Friday. His own authorization.' And then Sandro could almost hear the man clamp his mouth shut.

'He was defrauding the bank?'

'I didn't say that.' Viola's voice showed that he still felt unsettled. 'I don't know. I just pointed it out to the Guardia, we don't know yet. But to do that last thing on a Friday night – I don't know.'

'You said initially? Initially into his own account? And where subsequently?'

He could see Pietro, head cocked, listening intently.

'I don't know. They don't know yet. It looks as though there have been attempts – to conceal the eventual transfer. The Guardia di Finanza are the experts – there are so many ways, you know. To launder money, to disguise the disbursement of funds. They're taking their time – look. Look. I have a pension, if I play my cards right. Please. I can't say any more. The Guardia will share the information with the authorities in due course. Won't they?'

Like hell – and he wasn't the authorities, anyway. But the man's manifest terror defeated him, he let him go. 'You're one of the good guys,' he said, and as he hung up he heard Giorgio Viola sigh, a small, unhappy sound that somehow encompassed all they shared.

They sat in silence in the car a moment: this was how he and Pietro had spent their every waking hour, side by side in the front seat of a stale-smelling vehicle, adjusting the air-con or the heating, saying nothing. Watching, or thinking, or preparing to get out and deal with something they didn't want to deal with. A little over a hundred thousand euros: Sandro's mind wandered over the figure, imagined Brunello in his office, Friday night, on the way to the seaside to his wife and children. Transferring money – for what? Hold on. Hold on. He turned to Pietro.

'So he was stealing,' said Pietro, suddenly despondent, before Sandro could say anything.

'That's what it looks like,' said Sandro slowly. 'Just over a hundred thousand euros.'

'A lot of money,' said Pietro, leaning his head back.

'Yes,' said Sandro thoughtfully. 'Or perhaps not enough. If you were going to disappear and spend the rest of your life on the run, say. Not enough.'

He could feel Pietro's attention.

'Can you find out who owns that place?' he said abruptly. 'Who owns the Carnevale? Or rather, who owned it?'

Pietro shrugged, still watching him. 'Easily done,' he said. 'A phone call.'

Sandro frowned down at the mobile still in his hand, looking at the cluttered little screen. An icon was blinking at him. Would the magic phone Giuli had been so keen on – what seemed like an age ago – would that explain things to him patiently, like the old fool he was? Somehow he doubted it. At random he checked his messages, and there it was. He held the phone to his ear.

Roxana Delfino, sounding hurried and anxious. Telling him she thought Josef Cynaricz was the man who'd been out to her house, telling him she thought somehow the man needed her help, that he'd come to her for help. And another man had come after him, a young man in white trainers. A man her neighbour really hadn't liked the look of.

Thoughtfully he flipped the phone shut and turned to Pietro. 'You might send Matteucci down to Roxana Delfino's place at the Certosa,' he said. 'She's in the phone book.'

'Delfino? The girl in the bank?'

'Sounds very much like Gulli's been out there. You'd think he'd stop wearing those white trainers.' He frowned. 'So Gulli's after – Roxana? No. After Josef. Off his own bat? I doubt it. And how'd he know where to look? How'd he know Josef had been out there?' He put a hand to his head, perplexed. 'You think you could – I don't like to ask. But I think it's just her and her mother. I don't like to think—' He stopped.

Pietro nodded. 'We'll get someone out there,' he said, looking up at Marisa Goldman's villa. 'What about this?' he said.

'I need you to let me run with this, only for an hour or so,' said Sandro. 'Do you trust me? Give me a morning.' He peered through the windscreen: it looked more like nightfall than morning.

'I trust you,' said Pietro, and he leaned across and opened Sandro's door for him. 'Get going.'

CHAPTER TWENTY-SIX

OH, SHIT, THOUGHT GIULI, tearing around the sweaty room in the half-dark, oh shit, oh shit.

It was ten minutes since Dasha had called her, and she couldn't find her keys. She heard Luisa's voice in her head, *Turn on the lights, might be an idea.* She wanted to cry, but the time for crying was past.

At the Women's Centre the charge doctor had sounded merely bored when eventually, an hour or so back, out of some last vestige of self-respect, Giuli had roused herself to call in sick.

'Feeling rough,' she had managed. 'I think it's something I've eaten.' An excuse transparent through over-use, and they had both known it.

'No problem,' the doctor, a woman she'd never liked, had said. Giuli had heard the idle calculation in her tone: give her one more chance, maybe, we can get a replacement, plenty more where she came from. Ex-junkie, ex-hooker, waste of space.

The worst of it was, she reminded herself of her own mother, a woman dead more than twenty years but when alive often to be seen lying motionless with self-disgust, face down on the bed. Mumbling incoherently.

You've come so far, Luisa would say. *This is nothing. This isn't the end of the world.* Giuli tried to hear Luisa's voice as she lay there with stupid tears leaking from her eyes but it didn't make it any better. *You've found a man, you've started to hope for something, for a day and a half you wondered if you might be pregnant. And you're not. You probably never will be: but since when did you want a baby anyway? Get over it.*

What would Enzo think, if he could see her? Face swollen with crying, reckless with despair. He'd run a mile.

And the thought of going into the Women's Centre and seeing those women, pregnant or aborting or begging for contraception, abusing the unborn with drugs or happy and hopeful – well. She couldn't do it. She had felt poisonous, her head full to bursting with rage and disappointment.

And then Dasha had phoned. Giuli had stared down at the phone and the unfamiliar number, letting it ring a good long time until she picked up. Straight away she had been able to tell something was wrong: Dasha's Italian had turned ragged, her accent heavier. Not the bored, guarded girl Giuli had last seen.

'Hold on,' Giuli had said sulkily, initially resentful of the girl's intrusion. 'Talk more slowly. Who called her?'

'Not called,' Dasha had said. 'Sent text message. Him. He sent the message asking her to come to him. She showed me.'

'Josef?' The words had drawn Giuli upright, off the bed. She had rubbed at her face. 'Josef sent her a text message. After all this time?'

'You knew he was around,' Dasha had said angrily. 'I knew, you knew. I don't know why he didn't try before. I begin to think, perhaps he is a good guy. He will leave her in peace. To be safe, just want to know she is all right, that is why he is coming every day, here.'

'Every day?' Jesus, Giuli had thought. Under our noses. 'You've seen him today?'

'Not yet,' Dasha had said. 'Maybe I won't see him, if he is meeting her. If he has changed his mind, if he wants her after all.'

Giuli had crossed to the sink, taken her flannel, soaked it and pressed it to her face a moment. Something hadn't been right about this.

'Why wouldn't he come to the hotel? Just walk right in.'

'I don't know.' Dasha had sounded angry. 'Maybe because he knows we would send him away. Maybe he knows the old woman don't like him. Since a long time, something with his dirty job and that woman who employ him. Some old problem, between those women.'

'Woman? A woman runs the Carnevale?'

'I don't know everything about it. I think yes.' Dasha's voice had turned stubborn and frightened.

'It's all right,' she'd said, conscious that Dasha could clam up at any moment. 'It's not your fault, Dasha.'

'My fault? Who said it is my fault? Is these men.' She spat out some of her own language, unmistakably a bad word, or series of bad words.

'Yes,' Giuli said, trying to stay cool. 'I know.'

'I should have kept her here,' she said through something that sounded harsher and more painful than tears. 'I should have called the old woman and we could have made her stay. But – I didn't know. I didn't know she would – maybe not come back.'

'Where's the old woman now?' asked Giuli. Thinking of the bad business between her and whoever ran the Carnevale. Whatever woman.

'Out,' said Dasha. 'I didn't tell her. She would be angry. She went out, to talk to someone, she said. Had coat on.'

'Coat?'

In this heat.

There was a weary exhalation. 'You can't talk to her. She don't listen. She hate everyone, except maybe Anna.' And an angry sniff, as though to hold back tears. 'That baby is coming soon. She was walking so slowly, to the lift, like it hurt her.'

How could you let her go? Giuli couldn't say it: Dasha might go for her, or shut up for good.

'All right,' she said carefully. 'It's all right. There was nothing you could do. You called me, that's the main thing.'

There was a silence, but Dasha didn't hang up.

'You saw the message,' she said.

Dasha cleared her throat. 'Yes.'

'Can you remember what it said?'

'She showed me first his name, at the top of the message. Showed me that it came from him: Jo, it said.' Dasha sighed. 'So proud of this mobile he give her. His number the first in there.'

Giuli waited: in the pause she became aware of her own breathing, of her own body functioning calmly now that the situation required it. No more panic or self-pity. Good.

'Then.' Her voice was tight. 'It said, *Darling. I'm so sorry. All is ready now* – something like that. Prepared, ready, something like that. *We can start our life together.*' Dasha made a sound of fierce contempt. 'How could he suggest that place? I don't understand that.'

'What do you mean?' said Giuli, feeling a flutter of panic. 'What place?'

'The – the cinema. The Carnevale. He said, *We meet there, please, I will explain.*'

'Perhaps – perhaps—' Giuli felt numb with fear. 'Perhaps he wanted to come clean. I mean, tell her the truth about everything.'

Dasha laughed harshly. 'Truth,' she said. 'Not always what you need.'

The Carnevale. The place had been a fixture all of Giuli's life, its grubby façade and its small crowd of men on the streets outside, smoking as they waited to go in, their gaze sliding over any woman who passed.

'You go after her,' said Dasha. 'Yes?'

'Yes,' said Giuli.

*

Sandro half expected a liveried butler to come to the door: what he hadn't expected was Marisa Goldman, looking like this.

Skinny to begin with, she seemed as if she'd dropped another four kilos, a line etched down the sides of her mouth, and she was haggard under the tan. She was wearing some kind of tunic over dark linen trousers that made her legs look very long and lean. It occurred to Sandro that he didn't like trousers on women. Old-fashioned, Luisa would say, but then again she never wore them, either.

'It's you,' Marisa Goldman said without preamble. 'All right, come in.'

Stepping across the threshold and into the air-conditioned interior, Sandro felt a sudden perverse regret at the abrupt disappearance of the humid outside air, the smell of roses and jasmine.

She showed him into a spacious ground-floor *salotto*. Cool and stale and surprisingly empty, the long windows shuttered. There was furniture, all right – three rectangular beige sofas, a sideboard, coffee tables – but every surface seemed too bare, too unadorned. Perhaps that was how the rich did things: he didn't know, or greatly care.

Marisa Goldman jerked a hand carelessly towards the nearest sofa, and he sat. She remained standing, arms folded across her concave stomach. There were bracelets piled up her slim brown forearms and she wore many rings, silver and gold, and a big square aquamarine on one little finger. The rings seemed to Sandro all to disguise the lack of one ring in particular, but then he was being old-fashioned again.

She didn't appear frightened. He'd expected her to be hostile or scared or both. But she seemed indifferent.

'You went to see your boss on Friday evening,' he said.

'Can I get you anything?' she said. Could she be more glacial? 'A glass of water? A coffee? I have some beer.'

Beer, at this hour? He looked more closely at her and understood that she'd been drinking herself.

He repeated the statement and abruptly she sat down, too close to him. Her face seemed like a mask, her fingers like bones under the rings, an empress exhumed in her finery.

'You went to see him, although you'd told everyone you were going away on the Thursday night. Out of the city. Where was it you were supposed to be going?'

'My – my lover has a yacht. We sailed to Elba. He has a cottage there on the cliffs. A private beach.'

Marisa Goldman disdained the word fiancé then, did she? Being of more elevated birth than little Anna Niescu, or Giuli.

'You didn't go to Elba,' he repeated patiently. 'You were here.'

'It's a beautiful craft,' she said, turning away from him and walking to the window with considered elegance, and he wondered if she was actually mad. 'Built in Genoa in 1932 for the Aga Khan's son, teak decks and Frette linens and a staff of six. The cottage isn't much.' She gave a tiny shrug, her back still turned to him. 'A simple place. But I don't really like sleeping on the boat.'

His phone gave a little peal to indicate the arrival of a text. The look Marisa Goldman threw him over her shoulder didn't deter him from opening the phone and looking. Too soon, surely, for Pietro to have found anything out? It was from Giuli, and he stared at it for too long, because he couldn't understand it. Sent in haste, full of fumbled abbreviations.

Josef's boss at Crnvle a wmn. Josef hs txtd Anna, askd hr 2 meet.

What did that mean? Josef's boss a woman? Suddenly Sandro's head felt ridiculously overstuffed: too many suspects, too many blind alleys. One thing at a time, please. A woman. He had a woman in front of him.

Asked her to meet? *Josef asked Anna to meet him?* He couldn't even think about that.

He looked at Marisa Goldman. He thought of those photographs in her office, the straight back, the tendons in her hands gripping the reins. The gun over her shoulder. He thought of Claudio, battered under the dusty trees.

The big villa seemed very quiet suddenly.

'Do you have staff here?' asked Sandro, partly because he wanted to know, and partly because the direct approach did not seem to be working.

Her big, pale, green-gold eyes were turned on him. 'A housekeeper and a maid and a gardener. The housekeeper and the maid are on holiday.'

'Did you send them away?' he asked gently. 'Did they tell Irene Brunello that you weren't at Elba after all, that you'd been here all along, and you sent them packing before they could tell anyone else?'

And abruptly the green-gold eyes brimmed with tears. He could hear Luisa's voice, tough and contemptuous, in his ear. *Don't fall for it.*

'Was Irene Brunello trying to contact you here, too, since Claudio didn't come home on Saturday evening. And you didn't answer, you didn't pick up.' His voice was soft but not gentle any more. Her face, turned towards him in the window's pale filtered light, was very still, the brimming eyes did not overflow and she said nothing.

'Do you know Sergio Galeotti?' he asked. Her lip just turned downwards, dismissive, the ghost of a shrug. 'He was an estate agent,' he said, helpfully. 'You had some of his material on your desk the other day. He'd just sold the Carnevale cinema, as a matter of fact.' Sandro still had no proof that this was so. But he had little to lose.

Marisa Goldman seemed to shiver in disgust.

'Does that offend you?' He spoke as softly as he could. 'The mention of that cinema? It's nothing to do with you, then, the Carnevale? It's run by a woman, did you know that?'

Her expression darkened, turned mutinous, and Sandro hastily decided to change tack.

'Listen,' he said. 'I know you had a relationship with your boss. Let me guess. You were bored, or between boyfriends, his wife was busy with the children. You found yourselves alone one evening.'

He tilted his head, appraising her. 'Let me guess,' he said, 'it would be, I'd say, three years ago, something like that? You were probably just a bit prettier, a bit fresher, three years ago. Let's say. Women reach their prime at a different age, I'm sure you know that. The skinny ones, in my experience, get there a bit earlier than the rest.' He knew he was sounding coarse; he didn't care.

She was looking at him with fury now, but the indifference was gone, she was engaged. The truth was building inside her, and soon she wouldn't be able to keep it quiet. Not yet, though.

'And on Friday you went to see him. What was that about? Was it about a property deal, was it about your rich boyfriend, was it about money?'

A faint flush appeared on her sallow cheek.

'Money. Did you need money from him?'

And he knew that was why she'd gone to see him. But triumph remained stubbornly elusive, because Claudio Brunello was dead, and he had no idea where Josef was, and he still couldn't see where Marisa Goldman fitted in.

'Was it something to do with the sale of the Carnevale?' he said. 'It had been on the market for months, hadn't it? Something was stopping the deal going through.'

She stalked back across the room towards him, a wraith in her dark linen. 'I have nothing to do with a pornographic cinema,' she enunciated, imperious and clear as a bell. 'Nothing, do you hear? My family—' and she snorted, 'if we owned two thousand square metres in the centre of Florence, believe me, we would have sold it years ago. Just like the rest. Sell when it's worth nothing, then wring your hands as plebs like Galeotti get rich. That's how it works in my family.'

Sandro said nothing, just watched wide-eyed as she leaned down to look him in the face.

'I asked him for money. All right. I did.' And then she sat hard down beside him, too close, hands clasped on her narrow knees so tightly the tendons stood out white.

'Why did you need it?' asked Sandro quietly, but he knew already: the absent maid and the lifeless house told him.

'I needed it because I need somewhere to live. That's why I was talking to that little creep Galeotti, too.' She wasn't meeting his eye. Sandro looked around the room.

'Somewhere to live? This place not good enough for you?'

'He's left me,' she said then, and all the fight seemed to go out of her. 'Are you satisfied now? Paolo's left me. I'm just a squatter here, they all know it now, that's why I sent them away. When I saw the maid gossiping with Irene Brunello it was the last straw.' Her head bowed. 'I've got till the end of the month, when Paolo gets back from the boat.' Her head came up again. 'So I went to Claudio and asked him for money. He could get it through the bank, it would be so easy. He could call it a loan, on favourable terms. So easy.' Her eyes were wide, distant. 'The great advantage of a small bank. Discretion.'

'How much did you ask for?' He put the question carefully, and still it seemed to surprise her.

'What?'

'Was it a hundred thousand euros, a little more perhaps?'

She frowned, bewilderment turning to offence. Perhaps a hundred thousand wouldn't be enough for a woman like her. 'I didn't mention specific sums,' she said, trying to stand on her dignity.

Sandro could feel his theory, his house of cards, struggling to stay upright. 'Did he know what you were going to ask?' he asked, willing it to stay in place. 'Had you spoken to him during the day, so that perhaps he might – make arrangements?'

Her frown deepened.

'What? No. I didn't – I didn't even know myself. That I – that I would be able to do it. To go over there and ask him. I only said – could I meet him? He didn't even want to do that. He said he needed to get to Irene and the children.'

Damn, damn. Sandro put his head in his hands, thinking furiously. He should have asked Viola, when exactly did Brunello move that money? Because if Claudio Brunello had had no idea she was after money, who was it for?

But Giorgio Viola had told him, of course he had. Last thing, he had said, he'd moved the money on Friday at the very end of the working day.

But he persisted: there was something there, there was some rage buried inside Marisa Goldman, and all he had to do was access it. She could have done it. She was desperate enough. Might she know Gulli? She might: they all knew someone like him, these slim-wristed, crisp-shirted, fragrant men and women, they all had someone to do their dirty work for them even if it was just slipping them a wrap of cocaine.

He tried another tack.

'Saturday morning,' he said. 'Did you call him? Did you ask again? Did you say you'd tell Irene if he didn't do something? Is that why he came back into Florence, is that why he lied to his wife about where he was going?'

With some connection he'd made but couldn't articulate, Sandro was reminded of that scrap of paper Pietro had found in Brunello's car. Josef's name and mobile number. He'd been so sure it was Josef who had called the bank manager.

Josef's mobile: he'd had it Saturday morning. But when he'd staggered out of Liliana's lock-up on Tuesday, he'd asked if he could borrow hers. Sandro's head ached with it all.

'In God's name,' Marisa Goldman said now, and she looked at the end of her tether. 'What kind of woman do you think I am? Blackmail? No.'

As if it wasn't already blackmail, thought Sandro, just to ask Brunello. She didn't even need to mention their affair. Or whatever it had been.

'He said no, and I went home and locked myself in my room and cried. For three days. Satisfied? You can ask the servants about that, when they're back from their surprise holiday. Irene started phoning me on the Sunday.'

'You didn't answer.'

Marisa didn't even look up. 'She wouldn't leave a message, but of course my phone recognizes Claudio's seaside number. I just listened to it ring and didn't pick up.'

Poor Irene Brunello, going out of her mind with worry. But then again, Marisa Goldman wouldn't have been able to help with that.

'So you didn't phone him on Saturday.'

She shook her head savagely. 'You're crazy. I didn't talk to him after that Friday evening. I asked him for money and he just said, no. He said, his family needed his money.' Her mouth was set and sulky. 'He was quite cool about it. He said, if he thought I really needed it, he would have found a way to help me, from his own pocket, what I was suggesting was blackmail – all that. He said, if you feel you must tell Irene, then tell her.'

Sandro leaned forward, observing her intently.

'He – moved some money,' he said. 'Last thing Friday. Claudio moved a little over one hundred thousand euros at close of business Friday night.'

Slumped back into the sofa's cushions, Marisa Goldman stared at him oddly. Let out a small, confused laugh. 'Claudio? After all that upright stuff he gave me, about how he could never abuse his position?' She folded her arms across her narrow body, and let out the laugh again, but it sounded no more certain. 'All along he was fiddling?' Her frown intensified, her whole face contracted, and she had become old and angry.

'You didn't phone him on Saturday,' repeated Sandro. Trying to make sense of it, the surge of facts hammering to be allowed in.

'The way he looked at me. I could have killed him. But I would never have spoken to him about it again.'

She caught a look on Sandro's face.

'What?' And then she laughed. 'You think I did it? You think I had something to do with Claudio's death?' Flung her head back. 'I suppose if I'd known he'd been screwing the bank over all along, I might have been furious enough.'

Her laugh grew louder. And Sandro just sat there and waited for it to stop.

And then it did stop, quite suddenly, and Marisa sat up, her eyes bright for the first time since she'd answered the door to him.

'He transferred the money at close of business? That's what you said?'

Sandro nodded, his attention fixed now by the glitter in the green-gold eyes. She could have been beautiful, he thought, unwillingly. 'Yes,' he said.

She stared back. 'Claudio wasn't there for close of business last Friday. He left at five, last Friday. He was angry about it, it was my fault, he said. He told them it was because of the holiday, but the truth was he knew I was coming over and he needed to factor in extra time. He didn't want to be late leaving for the seaside.' Her shoulders were straight. 'He wasn't there.'

*

Rounding the corner of the narrow street, Giuli saw the place, standing mournful and dirty behind its pine hoarding and felt a little throb of something like revenge. At the sight of a sad, aged flasher in a grubby raincoat, too old to shock anyone any more. And then that small satisfaction was gone and Giuli was still staring at the Carnevale's dead and dusty windows, a knot of hard fear forming under her ribs.

The street was empty, and suddenly almost dark. It must have been close on eleven, but the sky seemed to be coming right down on top of the city, thick and grey. She'd come past the bank where Brunello had worked, glancing quickly inside as she passed. Some kind of official sticker had been plastered on the door, informing the clientele of an investigation, invoking the appropriate section of whatever law they'd needed to seal the place off. There'd been a light on behind the smoked glass. Giuli had hurried on and turned the corner.

Reaching the new boarding outside the cinema, Giuli stopped and looked back along the street. Was it empty, after all? It was one of those streets where no one seemed actually to live; the centre of town was full of them. Owned by foreigners who were never there, the odd *fondo* still used for storage or garaging, the occasional old woman on a controlled rent. A crumbling bit of frontage that, on closer inspection, was a semi-derelict church. Quiet, but not quite silent: somewhere not too far off she could hear voices, or perhaps one voice, raised in complaint. The metal shutter was not quite closed on a *fondo*. The knot in her stomach loosened fractionally at the thought that she wasn't alone.

A door was cut into the boarding: close up, you could see that the pine was already beginning to discolour. Giuli rapped hard on the wood. Nothing happened, but then what did she expect? This wasn't the place's entrance. She tried to think. The tongue and grooved door was padlocked. Josef wouldn't have a key to it, either; the door would have been put in for the new owners or their representatives. Tyrrhenian Properties. There was an artist's drawing of modern apartments stapled to the pine, along with the name of the developer. The people who bought those apartments were not going to be told what the site had once been, were they?

There must be another door. Walking to the corner of the building, Giuli felt her reluctance grow, slowing every step. There was something wrong here.

Would you invite someone you loved to meet you in such a place? If you knew anything at all about little Anna Niescu, would you bring her here? Josef had gone to such lengths to keep her away, so why bring her here now?

He needed to hide. Could that be it? This place was out of sight. Had he been in here all along, hiding in some secret corner as the demolition men moved in?

The board was brought up close against the edge of the building, where it stopped, and then there was a long stretch of blank side wall down a narrow alley. It smelled: no worse, perhaps, than most of the city's alleys, but it was not inviting. Piss and garbage, but there was another door. She banged on it again, then again. Then again, feeling her knuckles bark and skin against the flaking paint.

'Anna,' she called, loud then louder. 'Anna!'

The sound echoed strangely in the cramped space, bouncing back at her. She thought she heard a cry back in the street, far back where she'd come from, so thin it might have been nothing more than an echo, or an animal. The building sat tight, providing no answers. Further on she saw a pallet leaning against the wall, above it a small plain window, as though someone had stood on it to look in. Or climb in? Not Anna, not that little barrel of a body: again Giuli felt the fear. She stood on the pallet.

No one inside. It looked like a dirty, abandoned kitchen. With extreme unwillingness, Giuli pressed her lips to a hole in the dirty glass and called Anna's name. Hissed it, as though now she didn't want to be overheard. No answer. And abruptly Giuli understood that the place was empty. She jumped down from the pallet, the narrowness of the alley and its stink getting to her at last, and, choking, she came back out in the street.

Which was no longer empty. A couple had turned the corner, leaning into each other. The sight of them turned Giuli's stomach: couples. The sentiment of it, the dependence seemed to her nothing but weakness. She just needed to find Anna and she could tell her that. You, me, Dasha, we'll manage the kid. Leave Josef. But her heart sank at the total failure of her mission. What could she do now? She pulled out her phone. Call Sandro, or Luisa. That was all she could do.

No signal here, though. This city: there was no knowing where you'd find your signal, or lose it. The river was the only safe bet. Feeling her head clear just fractionally, Giuli had a plan: she hurried south, every step taking her away from the Carnevale was a step in the right direction. She came past the *fondo* whose shutter was not quite closed and heard something shuffle, a mew.

She passed the couple. The man's hand was tight on the woman's shoulder, and Giuli looked away.

CHAPTER TWENTY-SEVEN

THE CITY WAS DEAD. Luisa stood at the door of Frollini, her cheek against the glass, and looked out into the street.

She couldn't relax: something was wrong. Everything was wrong.

The street was dark and deserted. The bags on the few tourist stalls that had bothered to set up under the arcaded straw market were being whipped and flung about by the wind, and there was not a potential customer in sight. Luisa turned her head slightly to look down the street towards the Ponte Vecchio, for a glimpse of sky. It was a nasty yellow with a bank of darker cloud pushing up over the southern hills.

In the shop window before her, Luisa's display of mannequins, in expensive nylon parkas trimmed with fur, pouted blankly, hands on hips. At their feet was an artful tumble of cashmere scarves and lace-up suede boots. It was madness, she knew that, but it was how it was done. Autumn–winter stock had been in the windows since the July shows, staring out at the palely sweating tourists. There were people who bought the stuff, too, in among the bargain hunters who wanted only to know where the sale rail was. For the first time since she had started on the shop floor in 1969, Luisa wondered about the business she was in. It had never looked so much like foolishness to her, and perhaps she was getting too old for it.

Giuli hadn't answered her phone when Luisa had called, perhaps an hour back. Giuli didn't want to talk about it, whatever *it* was. She knew she shouldn't, but she'd called the Centre, knowing Giuli was on duty this morning.

'Called in sick,' the woman who answered the phone had said, her voice expressing at once indifference and cynicism. Luisa had thanked her politely, rung off, called Giuli again.

Giuli might be throwing up out of morning sickness, or lying in the dark unable to get out of bed with the old, old trouble. She wished she'd just got a look at this Enzo, to know whether he was worth it or not. To know whether they could rely on him to get Giuli out of this, one way or the other.

She tried closing her eyes and thinking, for the hundredth time, of that apartment to the south of the city. Her touchstone, in the August sun: the long balcony, the view of hills, the wide, spacious rooms under their pall of dust and rubble. One day, she repeated silently like a mantra. One day. We could buy a new bed; they say you need one every fifteen years. Her kitchen table in that bright space.

At the cash desk, Giusy sighed and shook out her paper with a crack and Luisa opened her eyes again; the spell was too weak.

Beppe from menswear was standing on the stairs, arms folded. 'What's the point?' he said, bad-tempered under his carefully maintained crew-cut and trimmed sideburns, wasted on an empty shop and two middle-aged women. Fond though he was of them. 'The place is dead. Who's going to come out, in this weather?'

'Look,' said Luisa, calculating, 'we don't all have to be here. We can rotate. Coffee break, yes?'

Thinking, fifteen minutes, down to Giuli's flat in the Via della Chiesa, bang on the door till she has to let me in. She looked around for her jacket – she'd left it down in the stock room. But Giusy was already out from behind her till, laying down her paper, reaching for her bag.

'Thought you'd never ask,' she said, her heavy-lined eyes already looking past Luisa to the street. 'I'm desperate for a coffee. Bit of a late one last night.'

Giusy and her husband had no children, never wanted them, or not enough. They liked going out, instead: tango classes, dinner dances, clubbing, though sometimes Luisa did wonder if it wasn't taking its toll. Giusy was getting old, just like the rest of them.

Beppe rolled his eyes. 'Just you and me then, Lu,' he said, taking in her expression with an amusement Luisa felt unable to share.

'Don't be too long,' she said shortly to Giusy's retreating back. The door swung shut after her, letting in a gust of wind that was surprisingly cool, drawn down from some new weather system circling the city.

Luisa shivered and out of instinct moved behind the unprotected till. Always keep the cash desk manned.

'You all right?' said Beppe, but Luisa didn't answer. She was looking down, at the newspaper. 'Lu?'

She stared at the photograph: estate agent slain, it said. She looked up at Beppe.

'Oh, yeah,' he said curiously. 'Nasty one, that. Nothing to do with – with your Sandro, though, is it?'

Luisa stared back at him. 'I don't know,' she said slowly.

'Nasty one,' repeated Beppe, who for all his tailored jackets, sleeves pushed up just so, for all his nice aftershave and knife-sharp sideburns, still kept up with the boys he'd run with as a wild teenager, boys from the grimier end of Sesto in the industrial flatlands. 'I heard it was a hit.' Modified his language. 'I mean, someone had him killed. He'd got mixed up in something nasty.'

'Had him killed,' she repeated dully. 'He's the man who showed us the flat.'

But Beppe wasn't looking at her any more, his sideburns turned towards the window.

'Is this a customer?' he said.

The figure peering through the glass door with her little claw of a hand reaching to push it open was both familiar and unfamiliar. In a faded green gabardine coat perhaps thirty-five years old, shrunken with age, she was of a type, the old women who couldn't quite believe Frollini wasn't the old-fashioned haberdashers it had been in 1952, with wooden cabinets and hand-finished cashmere and stacks of lace-trimmed nighties. She was someone's mother or grandmother, come to give them grief on an already dismal day. At the till Luisa shaded her eyes to get a better look.

Good God, she thought, stepping around the till, just as her phone began to ring in her bag. It's old what's her name, Capponi. Serafina Capponi. From the Loggiata.

Hastily she gestured to Beppe to let her in, and with weary resignation he leaned down to pull the door towards him. In the moment that he stood between her and the old woman, Luisa snatched up her phone, gripped suddenly with another of those moments of panic that had been dogging her all morning: Giuli, said the screen. It was Giuli.

'Darling,' she whispered briefly into the mouthpiece, 'look, it's difficult.'

The signal was terrible, and Giuli was talking fast. Something about Anna.

'I'm in the shop,' she spoke through Giuli's fractured monologue, 'got a customer. Are you all right?'

Then suddenly, as the old lady approached Luisa, who was smiling apologetically and nodding and holding up a finger to ask her to wait for just one minute, the voice on the mobile was clear.

'Anna's gone walkabout, I'm worried about her. She could be – the baby could have started, and she's gone to meet Josef.'

Luisa looked from the phone to Serafina Capponi trying to establish some connection, concentrating at the same time on the fact that at least Giuli sounded all right. Alive: herself. On the case, as the girl would say.

'I'll call you back,' said Luisa, a snap decision.

There was something about Capponi's ancient chimpanzee face, dark eyes staring up at Luisa from under the headscarf, over the gabardine buttoned to the chin. Beppe was looking, bewildered, from Luisa to the new arrival, and back. Then he stepped away, retreating to the haven of menswear up the polished iroko stairs.

'All right,' said Giuli, taken aback, and Luisa, like a mother, registered and approved the beginnings of sullenness already checked.

'Five minutes,' Luisa said. Giuli hung up first. Luisa turned to the old woman who owned the Loggiata.

'Signora Capponi.' Slightly inclined her head, waiting for this unexpected customer to speak.

She wasn't here to ask for woollen vests and trimming ribbon: the brown eyes examined Luisa intently. There was a movement on the stairs, and Beppe was gone: the old woman put a hand to her chin, loosened the knot in her headscarf, just a little. Luisa spread a hand to indicate the small, velvet-covered footstool where customers sat to try on shoes. Serafina Capponi looked at it with hostility, but she sat. She kept her coat on.

'She was a good girl,' she said unexpectedly.

'Anna? Was?' Luisa felt a tightening under her ribs at the use of the past tense. 'Where's Anna, Signora?'

The woman's mouth tightened.

'Serafina?'

It was the name her mother would have called her. Luisa remembered her saying, *Hard as nails, Serafina Capponi. No children, and it made her hard as nails.* Did it do that to me too, wondered Luisa? She didn't feel hard, though; she felt as soft and helpless as the inside of a sea anemone.

The old woman's head turned, slowly, she looked at Luisa as if she hadn't seen her before, and when she spoke her voice was rusty. 'It's a long time since I was last in here,' she said deliberately. 'I suppose you have forgotten that I was once one of your respected clients?'

Luisa inclined her head. 'Not at all,' she said, truthfully.

'I remember your mother,' the old woman said.

'Yes,' said Luisa, detecting prevarication. 'Where's Anna?'

Serafina Capponi shrugged obstinately, drawing her shrunken shoulders up to her neck like an old tortoise. 'She was a good girl. I had to protect her from that man. It's not the money.'

'What money?'

'Her parents left her their money – well, adoptive parents, of course she had no real parents. She had them, and now she has me.'

Luisa's head was hurting with the low glare of the light from outside. 'Do you know where she's gone?'

'He must have been after the money. It was my duty to protect her. He worked in that filthy place.'

The mouth turned down, a waterfall of grimy wrinkles. Capponi's husband would have been one of the Carnevale's most loyal customers, in its heyday. So what? All Luisa's dislike of the place had suddenly fallen away; it was nothing more than a shabby little backstreet cinema. There was more at stake than that. 'He worked for that bitch. That old bitch.'

And then Luisa leaned forward: she didn't know if it was more than thirty years with Sandro but something had fine-tuned her to notice such things. That note of venom, that new piece of information. *He worked for ...*

'Who?' she spoke softly, hardly wanting to alert the woman.

Serafina Capponi's lip twitched, though Luisa didn't know if the contempt was for her, or someone else.

'The old bitch, Margherita Martelli. A dirty business, they tried to hide it, of course they did. Just used her initials for the name of the company, so I believe.'

Luisa stared at her. 'The *edicolaia?*'

She was astonished by the sheer, poisonous fluency of the woman who'd sat mumbling at the reception desk in her crumbling, inestimably valuable hotel. Serafina Capponi might be decrepit on the outside, but she'd been all there in the head, all along. It was why you should always treat the elderly with respect, was Luisa's fleeting thought, though she felt something more ambiguous than respect for the old witch in front of her.

'Why did you come here, Signora?' she asked quietly, wanting to separate truth from malice. 'Why do you come to me, now? Are you worried about Anna?'

Capponi's chin set, resentful at the directness of the question, and Luisa sensed that like so many of her kind – counting their money, watching their assets decay, fretful over the future and nursing hatreds – Serafina Capponi's conscience was a dusty, tangled, old spider's web of contradictions.

'You came for her, didn't you? With that husband of yours, that policeman. So he can just find her, if he's a policeman. That idiot Russian told me she let her go. To him – that place. She must be found, she must be brought back.'

'A private detective now,' said Luisa quietly, but Serafina Capponi waved her away impatiently.

Luisa saw that her fondness – if you could call it that – for Anna would be something like her feelings for her ruined and beautiful *palazzo*: an asset that needed protecting, that threatened to get away from her.

Capponi leaned forwards and whispered, 'And while your husband is about it, he can make sure everyone knows that Margherita Martelli's money comes from that dirty cinema. She thinks she can just pocket the cash and come out of it clean?'

So that was why the old woman was here: the need to claw back the only thing that represented a future, Anna and her child, and the need to exact revenge on an old enemy at the same time, for the crime of realizing her assets while Capponi sat and watched hers crumble.

'She could keep it quiet, she could hide her dirty business, but we know. Those of us who've known her since she was a grasping little kid.' She drew herself up. 'She can't even see they are cheating her, all of them, she will never see the real money. Too senile, too soft. The estate agent. Cheating her.' She pronounced it with contempt. 'And that boy.'

What boy? Anna's fiancé?

'She sold it,' said Luisa. 'It's been sold, hasn't it? The cinema?'

Serafina Capponi's eyes filmed over, and for an instant Luisa wondered whether she wasn't gaga after all, if this wasn't just addled, toxic ramblings, until she saw that crafty glint. All an act.

'I don't know,' said the woman carefully, undoing the top button of her gabardine.

'You do,' said Luisa, feeling the ache in her knees and ignoring it.

'She's got connections,' said Serafina Capponi. 'Old Margerita Martelli has family, you see.'

And glimpsing triumph in the old woman's eyes, Luisa wondered at the decades of hatred, wondered what ancient feud

– a childhood game? A husband led astray? – had provoked this unburdening. She'd waited all this time.

'Family where?'

The hands were in the lap, the narrow shoulders raised defiantly in an attitude of moral superiority.

'She needs him, you see. She's not all there any more, not since that heart attack last year. He deals with everything for her. In the bank.'

'In the bank.'

'We know, you see. The young ones, they think they can be invisible, they think there are ways of keeping things from us, with their mobile phones and their computers. But we know.'

'She has family in the bank?'

And Serafina Capponi's head turned, her monkey eyes fixing on Luisa.

'Claudio Brunello was related to her? Margherita Martelli owned the Carnevale and Claudio Brunello managed it for her?'

The woman clicked her tongue in disgust. 'Not him,' she said impatiently, 'not him. The other one, of course. That boy.'

*

Ma, thought Roxana as she felt his arm close around her shoulder. *Ma, I think I've done something stupid.*

She'd had that same thought submitting to her first kiss. Was that why she'd never had a proper boyfriend, not one she'd trusted?

In the alley he was fumbling with the lock now, turning his face to smile at her, one hand still holding tight to hers. Roxana felt only anxiety. Was it that there was something wrong with her? Physical contact a problem?

But there were so many things wrong. This alley, to begin with.

Ma, I think I've done something stupid.

In the bank, Roxana had looked up from the computer screen to Val's face as he appeared in the door, then back at the screen, trying to make sense of it. He'd beamed at her, his face alive with excitement, and bemused, she'd smiled back.

'How did I know you'd be here?' he'd said, smiling, and she was confused. Holding out his hand to her. He hadn't been wearing the bike helmet, or the leathers, but grown-up clothes. A fine striped shirt, a sports jacket, loafers. Maybe he really had sold the bike, then, just as Marisa said.

Now he turned to her in triumph as the door opened in the alley and a cavernous, cool gust of air billowed from the dark interior of the cinema. 'After you,' he said, and manoeuvred her in front of him. She could feel his arm, his arm strong from rowing, skiing with his wealthy friends, brooking no resistance. The door closed behind them.

How did he know she'd be there? He couldn't have known.

He'd come to where she sat at Claudio's desk, from the little kitchen. Had he known she'd left her phone behind? Impossible. So what had he been looking for in there?

'Listen,' she'd said urgently, 'there's something wrong here. Did you know old Mrs Martelli owned that place? The Carnevale. She must have been Josef's employer.'

Something had flickered across his face. 'Know?' he'd said. 'Of course I knew. She's my mother's cousin. Second cousin, actually.' He had tapped the side of his nose. 'Of course,' he'd gone on, 'it's not something they talk about. Not a particularly pretty business.'

Roxana had glanced down at the screen, aware of his hand still held out to her. 'They borrowed money,' she'd said. 'She borrowed money against the Carnevale last year. The letter – this letter says it was discharged on Friday. It was paid back on Friday.' She had looked up.

Valentino's eyes had still been bright, trusting, wide. 'Come on,' he'd said, almost laughing now. 'I've found out all about it. I'll show you.' Like a boy, like the friend she hadn't had since Maria Grazia left, actually not really since *scuola superiore*. And she'd got to her feet and taken his hand.

'Hold on,' she'd said, almost laughing herself, 'I came here for my phone. Let me get my bag.' He'd bowed, a little impatiently. She'd got the bag.

Ma.

On the street they'd passed a woman going the other way. A pale, sharp-chinned and skinny girl-woman with spiky reddish hair who gave them a fierce look. Did Roxana know her? From the neighbourhood, for sure. There'd been something about that blazing look she'd given them, like, how dare they? And she had pushed past, hurrying somewhere. Looking for someone. That had been when she'd started to get anxious herself, that was when the weight of Val's arm around her shoulders, pulling her in against him, had started to get uncomfortable.

'So, what have you found out?' she'd said as they locked up the bank behind them, Val giving the Guardia's pasted sign a contemptuous glance. 'Can't you tell me?'

'Surprise,' he'd replied, with that unwavering smile.

But now, as he closed the door behind them in the cinema and they were in the clammy dark, she didn't feel surprised. She felt a kind of awful certainty. He turned to face her, her back to the door. She could smell his aftershave, and knew it was expensive.

'Val,' she said breathlessly. 'Tell me what's going on.'

'Come on,' he said. 'You know.' His voice was soft: Roxana wanted to put her hands to her ears. She struggled to stay steady, feeling herself unbalanced by his proximity.

'Where are we?' she said, trying to sound normal. 'Where have we come in?'

And then abruptly he moved back from her, pushing his back to the door. 'You want to see?' he said. 'We're round the back: this passage leads to the private rooms. Not much use for them these days, business hasn't been any good at all, really. Josef wasn't even covering what she paid him, showing old stock to five old men a day.'

Instinctively Roxana put a hand to her abdomen, feeling it clench. It was so hot in here suddenly, as though the air had been shut off somewhere.

'And there's Josef's palatial apartments, obviously. Could give you the guided tour.'

'He's got a *fidanzata*,' she heard herself saying. 'They're having a baby.'

Valentino made a soft, disgusted sound. 'Oh yes,' he said. 'That bloody *fidanzata* of his was the cause of all the trouble, really, getting pregnant. Without her he'd have kept his nose out, done what he was told, I could have kept him quiet.'

'Quiet?'

'I didn't even think he knew enough Italian to understand, it was months ago. Galeotti and I discussing business after Tyrrhenian Properties' first visit, the division of monies, if you see what I mean? A certain price offered, a certain compensation, you know? And old Auntie Margherita none the wiser.'

He thought Josef wasn't even human, thought Roxana. You could say anything in front of him.

'He heard us. And when she got pregnant he started dropping hints. All that stuff about needing an apartment. We strung him along.' Turned his head towards her, but his face was dark. He was sweating, under the aftershave, the strong reek of him overcoming the sweet, expensive scent, an undertow of something else too. 'So. You want to see?'

He put a hand to the wall and she heard the empty click of a light switch. Nothing happened.

He clicked his tongue. 'Damn,' he said carelessly. 'Forgot about that, no lights. Still. This stuff we can manage in the dark.'

Roxana edged sideways, her hand moving out towards the door, feeling for the handle. 'What stuff?' she said, trying to keep her voice steady.

And Val just tilted his head so she could see he was watching, in the almost dark, where her hand was going: he didn't move, just watched.

'You want to leave?' he said softly. 'Come on, Roxi. We're waiting for someone – they'll be here soon. Once I have his woman, he'll come.' He nodded, almost reasonable. 'However long it takes.'

'Once you have her? Have who? Who will come?'

Val's eyes gleamed in the dark, and she knew that whatever plan he'd hatched, it was not a sane one.

'I sent her the message, you see,' he said. 'From his phone, telling her to come here. Someone will tell him.' He shifted in the dark, evasive. 'He's still here only because of her, and that child of his. He'll find out she's come here, someone will tell him, and sooner or later he'll come to me.' His voice was fervent with lunatic self-belief, or something stronger.

Sooner or later? Roxana knew in that moment that they would never leave, she and Val locked in the dark together forever. He was nuts enough to keep her here for as long as it took.

'And while we wait – there are things we can do. Don't you want to see? You do.'

'See what?' Roxana clutched the bag to her stomach.

He leaned down until his face was touching hers, as if he was about to kiss her. She didn't flinch, though his breath was hot and sharp and chemical. Drugs.

'I know you do. You want to see where it happened.'

CHAPTER TWENTY-EIGHT

*F*OR *CHRIST'S SAKE.*

    Why all this walking? What had possessed him to set out on foot? Because when you really needed to be somewhere fast, you had to take a damned cab, and when you really needed the cab to arrive in the two minutes they promised, it was nowhere to be seen.

Sandro paced on the corner of the *viale*, staring this way and that for a white cab, call sign Roma 86. The row of huge umbrella pines was being tossed and flung by the wind overhead. And then the rain began. Huge fat drops to begin with, evaporating almost before they hit the hot tarmac, each one diminishing his chances of the cab arriving on time, or at all.

Sandro could have called Pietro to beg a lift, but Pietro was on his way out to check on Roxana Delfino and her mother. He'd even texted Sandro to say he was on his way over there now; a call had come in from out that way about an intruder, and Pietro wanted to be on the safe side, he was picking up Matteucci and they were off.

Was Gulli the one they should be after? At least he was a nasty piece of work, at least they had him for Galeotti's murder.

But Sandro was after someone else.

'He wasn't there? He wasn't at the bank after five that night?' he'd repeated after Marisa Goldman had said it again, insisted. 'You weren't there, and Brunello wasn't there?' She'd shaken her head, almost smiling, avid.

'So only Roxana Delfino was there,' Sandro had said slowly, and in his head he scanned that gloomy bank of cashiers' workstations, silent and virtually empty.

'And Valentino, of course.' And Marisa smiled, polite, bored.

Valentino. Valentino – and then Sandro grasped who she meant. That – that boy? The boy she'd sent looking for Roxana, and Sandro remembered only a whiff of aftershave, an expensive shirt. The photograph of a Triumph motorbike pinned over his workstation. A nervous, shifty expression on his face as he eagerly – too eagerly – left to find Roxana. Boy, how old would he be? Thirty?

He rode a Triumph. There was a lesion on Brunello's leg. Surely not? A burn from a motorbike exhaust? Only a madman could have got the body of the bank manager on the back of a motorbike. He'd have to be – a madman. Or high on something? Hauled the body pillion as far as the African market, then given up?

And then Luisa had phoned. He'd seen Marisa Goldman watching him like a hawk now, alive again, as he had spoken. Had seen her not quite understand whom he could be talking to, the combination of impatience and fondness and longing in his voice clearly quite alien to her.

And then, Luisa had got the words out. 'Serafina Capponi at the Loggiata,' she said. 'Came and told me, just to stir, perhaps, maybe because she's really worried and doesn't know what to do.'

'Worried?'

'About the girl.'

And he had heard the dead echo of worry in Luisa's own voice, something chiming in his memory, something wrong. Concentrate.

'The woman who owns the Carnevale, an old *edicolaia* called Margherita Martelli, the cinema's been in the family for years, the building was theirs before it was a cinema. Anyway, she has a nephew or something, I don't know. Nephew, grandkid, cousin. A boy working at the bank.'

And it had fallen into place. The boy, Valentino. And even as he had hung up, the phone had rung again, and this time it had been Giuli. She had sounded like she was in a wind machine, and looking out through Marisa's big, double-glazed windows he had glimpsed the mature trees beyond her rose garden swaying violently.

His mind had been racing. How do we get hold of this kid? This Valentino. Find him. And what Giuli had been saying had taken a while to come through.

'I'm here, I'm outside the Carnevale and she's not here, but there's something wrong. I know there is.'

'Hold on,' Sandro had said, 'hold on.' He had put a hand over the receiver, seeing Marisa Goldman looking at him resentfully. 'Is it all right if I have a conversation?' he had said, suddenly enraged by her. 'I'll be gone in just a minute, out of your hair. You have an address for your colleague Valentino, by any chance? A phone number?'

And her mouth set in a hard line, Marisa had turned and stalked away.

'Giuli,' Sandro had pleaded. 'Again. Tell me again.'

'Josef sent her a text message, finally. Sent Anna a message telling her to come and meet him at the cinema. Dasha saw the message. She told me.'

There had been a tremendous crash of thunder, then: Sandro hadn't been able to tell whether he was hearing it over his own head, or down the line, or both. Both.

'Jesus,' Giuli had said, awed and frightened. 'That was close.'

'But he doesn't have his phone,' Sandro had said. 'He asked Liliana – oh, never mind. He didn't send that message.'

'She's not there, anyway,' Giuli had said. 'I banged and banged. No one's there.'

The sky was black now. From up the hill Sandro could hear a rushing, a pattering. He could have asked Marisa Goldman for a lift. Damn, why hadn't he? Because he couldn't stand another minute of her, that's why. He could see the rain coming, a sheet of it moving down the hillside. And then the taxi was there, creeping under the rain, and he put out his hand.

'You know the old Carnevale?' he said. 'Take me there.'

*

The old woman came back in, her currant eyes glittering with malice and satisfaction. She took off her coat: Dasha saw sweat patches under the arms. Took off her scarf and edged Dasha out from behind the reception desk. 'You go and clean,' she said with hostility. 'What are you good for, anyway? Get to the rooms.'

Dasha stood there a long moment, feeling her youth against the woman's age, hating her long and hard. 'In a bit,' she said at last, and saw Serafina's eyes narrow. 'Breath of fresh air first.' And shaking her cigarette packet in her employer's face, she turned to saunter towards the lift.

The wide, dim entrance hall was cool. Once down there, Dasha felt no urge to get outside, into the heat. She lit her cigarette, drew in the smoke. She wanted to escape; she wanted to kill Serafina Capponi. But Anna might need her. Anna.

And besides, where could she go? Inhaling, she heard something, held her breath until it came again. A tiny scratching at the main door. She stepped towards it, right up to the wide arched door with its smaller door inset, turned her ear towards the sound. Someone was trying to get in. She pulled it open sharply, and he fell inwards.

Stepping back, Dasha regarded him on the floor in the light that fell through the door before it swung shut again. Jesus.

Josef scrambled to his feet, putting out his hands to her: she jumped back, arms up, cigarette still in one hand. 'No,' she said sharply. In the gloom the bruising was less visible, but she couldn't ignore it. His throat dark and mottled, one side of his face turning yellow and scabbed. He stank.

'Please.' He was almost sobbing. 'I don't know what to do. I don't know where to go any more. I need to see her. I need to know she's all right.' Then he flung himself at Dasha and wept, hauling at her while she stood stiff as a board. She pushed him off, took a drag, then threw the cigarette down.

'You imbecile,' she said, arms crossed. 'You text her to get her to meet you, then you come here instead? You think in this heat, in her condition, she should be wandering all over town?'

And he stared at her.

'No,' he said. 'What? No.' Shook his head slowly. 'He took it. My *telefonino*. He took it.'

Then put both hands to the sides of his head as if to crush his own skull.

'Where?' he said. 'Where has she gone?'

*

'The girl,' Giuli had said. 'I'm worried about Anna. I think she's – she could be in trouble. That baby.'

'Stay calm,' Luisa had said. 'As soon as I can come, I'll be there. Stay calm. We'll find her.'

Leaning over the hot stone of the parapet and looking down into the river, staring, trying to get some air after the Carnevale's fetid alley, trying to think straight, Giuli heard the rain come, sweeping down the length of the river. Below her, the creeper-covered awning of the rowing club shivered like an animal in the sudden wind, and the narrow boats moored along the bank clattered against each other. A few big drops, the wind that blinded her and pulled at her hair, flattening the ripples on the water's surface, then suddenly it was roaring in her ears, a miniature tornado that swept along the embankment and continued past. She turned to watch it go, rubbing her eyes: it was real, she saw the twisting wind move up the side of a building, catch a satellite dish and gleefully wrench it from its moorings. The crash of shutters.

It wasn't him. That was what Sandro had said. It wasn't Josef who'd texted her; it was whoever had Josef's phone. Catch a rabbit to catch a fox: he'd got Anna. Anna the little rabbit, someone had her, the lure to catch Josef, a little rabbit panting in a snare. How could he be sure that Josef would find out? He must be nuts, whoever he was. Or perhaps he knew Josef better than the rest of them.

Think.

And then the rain came in earnest, rushing at her in the wake of the wind, hitting her side on, then it was overhead and coming straight down, and in a second Giuli was drenched. She ran, away from the river, back towards the Carnevale.

CHAPTER TWENTY-NINE

IN THE DARK ROXANA thought she might be sick. Everything in her strained to keep it at bay. She tried not to breathe through her nose, but she couldn't put her hand to her mouth for fear of alerting Valentino.

He was holding her hand painfully tight and tugging her now, away from the door.

'In here,' he said.

There was some kind of corridor ahead of them, dark as a cellar. She couldn't stop herself resisting, looking back over her shoulder to the feeble grey light that filtered around the door. Left on the latch: she could just bolt, if his hand wasn't so tight around hers. She felt choked, something big in her throat at the thought of where he might take her. Anything but further in; she could almost feel the labyrinth of rooms spread around her, a web that might catch her and hold her. She took a step, then another.

They must be somewhere behind the auditorium, deep inside the building. There were no windows.

'They'll be here soon,' said Val, taking something out of his pocket and looking down at it. Roxana realized he was talking to himself. 'Give it an hour.'

'Val,' she said, hating the wheedling sound in her voice, trying to ingratiate herself. Pretend this was normal.

'Pregnant, though,' he said, talking to himself. She saw his mouth turn down in an expression of distaste. 'Messy. We can just shut her in here, keep her quiet. Yes.'

Roxana didn't know what he meant: didn't want to know. That chemical smell seemed to ooze from his pores as Valentino came closer to her in the confined space. His breathing was shallow. It must be drugs: why was she so naive? Why hadn't she known? Because she'd allowed herself to think, Well, Val's not so bad. He's just a boy, he's just a spoiled boy, he could be good at heart. Bantering with his friends in the bar, off rowing after work.

He hadn't gone rowing, though, had he? After work on Saturday, he hadn't gone rowing. Waving to her in his singlet, heading this way. She had turned away but then turned back: she'd watched him go towards the river but never get there because he had turned down the alley beside the Carnevale instead. And on Friday night he said he'd passed Marisa outside Claudio's house: on the way home? Or on the way back into the city?

Overhead there was a strange rushing sound she couldn't identify, a clatter far above them, and a wind that seemed to make its way inside, a cool swirl of air brushing Roxana's ankles, a rustling ahead of them as it moved through the building.

'Was it true?' she said out loud. 'About Marisa and Claudio?'

'She shagged him a few years back,' he said peremptorily. 'Scheming bitch.'

'But you saw her on his doorstep?'

'I saw her. Wanting her dues. She's been dumped, and while she's looking around for the next meal ticket she thought she might touch him for a payment. I know women. Leeching bloody women. Bleed you dry.'

'Where were you going?' asked Roxana. 'Last Friday night?'

Why was she asking? Because she wanted to know? To keep him talking? It occurred to her she would probably never get to tell anyone. *Ma. I've done something stupid.*

'Going?' Again that look, as if he didn't recognize her. Would that make it easier for him? Then he smiled, wide as a shark. 'Friday night? I was coming here to meet Galeotti, give him his commission, tell him the deal. Of course. I moved the money – no more than borrowing it, really, in Claudio's name, then transfer it – via another account, of course, I'm not stupid – over to the Carnevale and the sale can go through. Easy enough to write the letter saying the property was no longer encumbered, copy it to them, just to speed it all up. Galeotti thought it was genius.'

I bet he did, thought Roxana.

'Last piece of the jigsaw, sale goes through Monday.' Then his expression darkened. 'Fucking Josef,' he said, and as he tilted his head back she saw him muse, coldly. 'Fucking thieving little gypsy scum. Hiding in his little hole, listening to every word.'

'The money,' whispered Roxana, knowing she should just keep quiet. Val turned his head and regarded her. 'You stole that money. To pay off what had been borrowed against the business. You stole it in Claudio's name.'

Who had authorized that first loan, taken out a year ago? When old Mrs Martelli had had her heart attack?

'The old cow,' he said. 'Nagging at me, where had the money gone, she'd let me take out the loan against the business and I'd been supposed to invest it for her, I'd told her I knew my stuff. Then when she had her heart attack I thought, well, it'll be mine soon enough anyway, who's going to know? I started spending. I don't know how you can live on what they pay at the bank.' His lip curled a little. 'You don't really have a life, though, do you?'

'When they made the offer on the cinema you had to come up with the money, pay off the loan.' Roxana's voice came out in a whisper. 'Thought about selling the bike back then but it wouldn't have been enough. Three thousand, the thieving bastards paid me for it.' He snorted contemptuously. 'It would have been paid back, when the sale went through, Tyrrhenian Properties' payment to me would've easily covered it. I thought my luck was in when he left early Friday, wrote the letter, made the preliminary transfer, all while you were staring out the window in the kitchen. We shut up shop and I went off to close the deal.'

Only you left Claudio's computer switched on, thought Roxana.

He sighed, self-pityingly. 'I'd have got all the money back where it should have been before Claudio was back from holiday – if only that little gyspy snitch had kept his mouth shut. Claudio thinks I'm so dumb: he's the dumb one. Was. No grasp of technology, the older generation.' Roxana just stared.

'Of course,' he said, almost pensive, 'the way it turned out, I didn't even need to pay it back. Guardia as thick as pig shit, they'll never track it down. Just looks like Claudio needed it for the bitch.' He wasn't sure, though: Roxana heard a note of bravado. But the Guardia weren't all stupid, and Sandro Cellini wasn't stupid. She said nothing.

'Come on,' he said, and tugged hard, shoved her in front of him, into the dark.

And then something cracked and burst overhead, a deafening bang as though a bomb had gone off and Roxana, who had always been afraid of thunder, stopped stock-still.

'Move, bitch,' said Val, and viciously he shoved her.

The thunder died away and the rushing replaced it, then the hard patter of torrential rain. Things began to drip, far off in the building: Roxana couldn't move, thinking of the building's warren of rooms. Not pretty, was that what the builder had said?

'You want to see, or don't you?'

I don't, she said silently. *I don't, I don't.* But out of some instinct, she moved, his palm in the small of her back. Against her shoulder she felt her handbag, and pressed it tight against her, trying to make it invisible. Her mobile? He wouldn't let her touch it.

'Dumb little shit,' said Val, almost conversational now. 'Josef had Claudio's card, had his numbers, but Josef dialled the bank first, didn't he? I knew then. You remember, me taking that call Saturday? Thought I recognized the voice, and the way he hung up so fast gave it away: he'd dialled the wrong number. I did callback, and knew it was him. Now why would Josef be calling Claudio on a Saturday morning? Because he'd overheard us, Friday night? I thought he was out with his girl but he must have got back and been hiding there, listening. Blackmailing bastard, thought it had worked once with the flat and would work again this time, only with more information? Like, how I'd managed to shift the money around before the boss was even on the autostrada to the seaside, and it was hardly even illegal.' He chewed his lip. 'Or maybe he heard me say how we could just cut the little gypsy loose, now, stop all that pretence about the luxury apartment we'd move him and his girl into.' He chewed his lip. 'Of course, I didn't know all that then. All I knew then was he was trying to get Claudio. So when I finished work Saturday, I got all dressed up in my rowing kit and off I went to find little Josef and set him straight. Only they were both there. Two birds, eh?'

Roxana just concentrated on locating herself. Left, then on. It was not completely dark after all: there was light from somewhere, though she didn't know where. A room with padded chairs around the side, like a waiting room. It disgusted her, she didn't know why. A smell. What did people do here?

Valentino chuckled at her shoulder, as if he knew what she was thinking. 'Go on,' he said urgently. 'It's here.'

And she was on the threshold of another room, a room so small it was inhuman, with a tiny dirty window high in a corner.

A lopsided cooker at the end of bed with a rail, and something spattered above it.

A strap hung from the rail. The kind of thing you might use to attach luggage to a car, or a moped. Or a motorbike.

And before she could even let the breath out that she'd been holding, he pushed her, those strong oarsman's arms propelling her across the room, on to the stinking bed, her bag beneath her, her head striking the wall so she saw stars. And as she tried to steady the spinning behind her eyes, she felt his hands, as hard as iron, felt the strap tightening around her wrists as he yanked them over her head.

'Honeymoon suite,' said Valentino.

*

Luisa paced the square metre of floor in front of the door, Beppe watching her.

'Jesus, she's taking her time,' she said again.

Beppe raised his eyebrows; it wasn't like Luisa to give in to anything like impatience, or profanity. She had her back to the door. 'You can just go,' he said. 'If you need to go.' She gazed at him: it would be breaking the habit of a lifetime.

'You're sure?' she said, and Beppe nodded.

'I'm going,' she said.

*

Soaked to the skin, Giuli had just retraced her steps and reached the steel shutter of the lock-up when the hail started up, startlingly violent, white pellets hurtling from the sky. And then the taxi rounded the corner, creeping along the street, the hail bouncing from its roof with a deafening rattle. It stopped just short of where

Giuli stood, hunched under the onslaught, and as she stared, Sandro climbed out.

Then a sound behind her, an awful kind of low grunt, like an animal, made her turn. An animal? She remembered that mewling earlier: had it come from here? The shutter was raised by a metre, maybe a bit more. She kneeled and shoved it up further.

'Oh, Jesus,' she said. 'Oh Jesus, God in heaven.'

Anna Niescu was in there.

Crouching among vegetable crates, like an animal who'd crawled inside somewhere to die. Her face was so white it was luminous, and her eyes were filmed, as though she was looking at them but couldn't see them. She was leaning forward.

'I couldn't – I couldn't—' The girl turned her head and gazed at Giuli, pleading, the words came with difficulty. 'I didn't know it would be like this. He's waiting for me, do you know? He's come back for me, only I – I had to stop.' Her voice lowered, to an urgent whisper. 'The baby's coming. It's coming. I couldn't – not in the street. The shutter was up and I – I'm sorry. Am I in trouble?' And then her face changed, her eyes stared, focused on some terrible inner effort.

Giuli felt Sandro come up beside her, heard him say something under his breath but she didn't hear it. She couldn't hear anything for the rushing in her own ears. As they watched, Anna made that terrible sound again, the sound that had brought them in here, a cow sound, a moan from low down in her throat. She shifted, and with the movement Giuli saw that there was blood on Anna's skirt.

Anna's mouth moved, but she didn't seem to be able to say words.

'She's having the baby,' said Giuli through numb lips, looking into Sandro's face for help.

Sandro was staring at the blood. 'I can't – ' he said, 'I don't know if I can—' And swayed just enough to galvanize Giuli into something like sense.

'Get an ambulance,' she said.

He was still staring. 'Josef,' he said. 'Did Josef come?'

She shook her head. 'A man and a girl,' she said impatiently. 'I saw a man and a girl. That's all.'

As if hypnotized, Sandro went on staring, then abruptly his eyes came into focus. 'Ambulance,' he said.

On her knees, Anna turned her head and her eyes met Giuli's.

'All right,' Giuli said. 'I'm coming.' And she took the two steps, three, four, towards the kneeling girl, and the blood. 'It's all right, Anna,' she said. 'It's going to be all right.'

Chapter Thirty

'I ALWAYS THOUGHT I could do it,' said Valentino, reaching under the bed for something. She heard it scrape. His voice was musing, almost conversational.

'Of course, with the two of them, I had to be fast. You have to be fast, take them by surprise. They were in here: I let myself in, and I heard them. Got Claudio on the back of the head, before he even turned around.' He nodded to himself. 'That little Roma Josef was trickier. I got his phone off him but he was like a pig, fast and slippery. I got him down though. Superior strength and all that. I train, you know?'

She said nothing.

'Getting Claudio out of here, that was the hard bit.' He laughed briefly, in admiration of himself, and straightened up, holding what he had retrieved from under the bed in his lap.

'Didn't know how far I'd be able to get him on the back of the bike,' he said airily, daring her to gasp at his boldness. She swallowed, sick. 'Left it till the early hours, like three or something, left them both here, went out for a bit of R & R. Had a good pizza actually, out in San Frediano, picked up some coke, for the ride, you know. Both dead, so I thought.' He scratched his head. 'Josef wasn't breathing, I'd swear it, though I tied him up just to be sure. Still there when I came back to get Claudio. How was I to know?'

Valentino tilted his head from side to side. She could feel the weight of him against her legs.

'You see, I couldn't really leave Claudio – the body – here. Why would he be here? Draw attention to the place. Josef – well, he lived here. Someone might have broken in, a struggle, you know. Just leave him here for the developers to find, why not?'

'But he wasn't dead.'

Roxana was past caring whether she should keep silent or talk. Too late to worry. Underneath her something sharp was digging into her through the fabric of her bag and she tried to think what might be in there. She wanted to cry, thinking of her mobile, of Ma.

Valentino made a small growl in his throat, a warning sound. 'Soon will be,' he said. 'I set that little piece of shit Gulli on to him but he kept getting to places too late. Out at yours, for example, when you said there'd been someone, a prowler, I knew straight away. I told Gulli, I think he's gone out to find her, to spill the beans, he's a bloody liability out there.'

'Why didn't he just go to the police?' said Roxana, almost groaning. If only.

'Kid like Josef? No way,' said Val. 'An illegal, a Roma? They like to stay out of the system.' He sucked his cheeks. 'Gulli, Jesus. Can track down Galeotti for me and put him out of the picture, in five minutes flat, bang on the car door, cracked skull, gone, but can't find a skinny Roma on the run.' She thought there was just a trace of admiration for Josef in the words. 'Had to be done. Galeotti was losing his bottle, when he saw in the paper Claudio was dead. He knew, you see. I shouldn't have told him about the money, how I got it. '

'Boasted,' said Roxana, with what felt like the last fight she had in her. And as his head turned slowly to fix on her she saw, reflected in his pupils in the darkness, the sudden gleam of something.

'Genius,' he said, almost dreamily.

Genius, thought Roxana? Not even smart enough to keep your mouth shut. And at once she understood that he would be caught, but it would be too late for her.

Val's eyes were on her as he spoke levelly. 'I've killed animals. Just hit as hard as you can. I knew I could do it.'

And then, in one hand, he raised what it was in his lap and she saw it, and as it came down towards her at the last minute she twisted, raised her forearms and it came down, glancing off her hand with a horrible cracking. A length of metal; what was it? A piece of piping. Almost fainting with the pain, she could keep herself conscious only by focusing on the need to identify it. And Roxana felt herself go limp, and as the arm came up again she could only turn over to let it fall on the back of her head, and felt, as if by a miracle, one hand come free and under her. And inside her bag, reaching, reaching, for something, grappling: mobile, mascara, all the small, smooth, harmless things women keep in their bags, when they need something sharp. Nailfile.

Her hand came out, hoping it would be strong enough, sharp enough, the cheap nailfile she'd used since she was sixteen, bought for *centesimi*, and she lunged, one hand still trapped behind her, and the little piece of plastic and metal went in, somewhere, she didn't know where, somewhere soft. It wouldn't be enough, was all she could think, she put all the force she had behind it and still it wouldn't be enough.

But on top of her Valentino made a shrill, gasping, horrible sound, of outrage, of pain. Of fear. And then, with the tiny pulse of hope that sound gave Roxana, the weight on her shifted, the smell of aftershave and chemical sweat with it. There was abruptly more light as his body lurched sideways off her and she heard the clatter of the piping. Had he let it go?

She scrabbled away from him on the bed, trying to see: his hand was at his face. His eye? Had she blinded him? At the thought she almost dropped the nailfile: she didn't want to have blinded anyone. Now he'd kill her.

'Bitch,' he said through his hands, and his voice clotted with fury. 'Bitch. That could have been my eye.'

And then from far off in the echoing labyrinth of the building Roxana heard it: someone banging to catch their attention, *bang, bang, bang.* Or to break something down? Then a bellowing shout, words she couldn't make out. Without pausing to think, she lurched towards the sound, propelling herself off the bed, but then she was on the floor and Valentino was on top of her again, on her back this time with his hand on her mouth, his hot sharp breath in her nostrils as he pulled her round and under him. He pressed his cheek against hers and hissed, spitting, into her face, *Shut up shut up.*

Someone had come. The possibilities crowded in on her as she struggled to breathe under Val's hand and she felt the pressure build in her head: all the possible rescuers; hopeless, doomed, little Josef, a pregnant girl. Then she heard a rough shout: a man's voice. A door banged, followed by a loud curse and her heart sank as she realized he was moving further away, whoever he was. It couldn't be Josef after all, the cinema was his home, he would know where he was going, and this was a man lost and crashing through the building's blind corridors.

Something dripped on her from his face: sweat, she thought, but then although her mouth was clamped shut against it she tasted blood, and she began to buck underneath him, to thrash and kick as though she knew in that instant that her life depended on it, on not giving in, on not being good. And simultaneously she bit down on his hand and blindly kicked upwards, between his legs. Connected.

He howled, fell off her, and Roxana, on her knees, tried to get up, fell. Got up again, her knees bleeding from something, and stumbled away from him until her back was against the wall. Dizzy, she didn't even know where the door was.

Wherever he'd got to, at the sound of Valentino's howl the hopeless, futile blundering of this man who might be her rescuer but might, Roxana considered only now, be coming to finish her off, abruptly stopped.

'Who's there?'

And the voice, hoarse and urgent, reached her through the blind passageways and partitions of the hideous building, she knew that voice.

'Where are you?'

Help, she meant to scream, but nothing emerged, no more than a whisper, as if she'd lost breath and voice at once. Opened her mouth again and this time it came, the air whistled back into her lungs, her larynx opened like an instrument and she bellowed, she didn't even know what. *Here.*

At her feet Valentino was curled in a foetal position, whimpering. Pressed against the wall, Roxana looked down on him as if from a great height, and knew she should do something else. She should get something heavy and hit him hard before he got up again.

She didn't move.

Is he coming?

There was nothing else she could do.

*

In the stinking dark Sandro's hands were bleeding from the splintered wood of the cheap pine door he'd broken down. There'd be a price to pay for the damage, Tyrrhenian Properties would exact it, he'd known with dull certainty as he pounded away at the wood with his battered knuckles. But mostly he could only think, I'm too late. Again, as always, too late.

He'd nearly dislocated his shoulder as the boarding finally gave way under his weight. Astonishingly, behind the hoarding the glass door to the cinema's littered lobby had stood ajar. Three doors led off the back of it, one a double set leading into the auditorium. He'd decided against that one, taken another at random and found himself in the muffled darkness of a corridor, walls padded with fake leather, sticky carpet underfoot.

Confined spaces had never been one of Sandro's phobias – or at least he'd never thought so. But in that corridor, straining for a sound, any sound to give him a clue that he was there for a reason, he felt the certain signs of rising panic, an inability to fill his lungs or expel air from them, a drumming in his skull.

The walls were coated with something gritty, and Sandro didn't like to touch them but had no choice, and the greasy carpet clung to the soles of his shoes. The first door he pushed at was a cupboard, and he cursed. He didn't want to go further into the building – there was no light. He kept moving in the dark and when he came to another door he opened it and stepped through.

Pitch black: Sandro blinked and waited in vain for his eyes to adjust. But at least there was some air in here, some elusive draught from somewhere, and he let the door to the suffocating corridor close behind him. He shouted in the thick darkness, and as he waited he thought he did, finally, hear something, a scuffling, and a soft ugly thump in answer. Emboldened, he moved into the room, sniffing for a way through, like a trapped potholer following a breath of air from the outside. And banged his shin hard and painfully on something. He cursed again, louder and more profane this time, *cazzo, cazzo*, blinking not so much at the pain as in furious disgust at his own clumsy incompetence.

With his hand pressed against his shin in a pointless attempt to dull the pain, he heard the scream. And didn't know whether it was a man or a woman, almost gagging against the layered smells, fresh pine and latrine and old sweat. For a moment Sandro thought he might choke on it and die right there but his heart kept on thumping steadily, against all reason.

'Who's there?'

A silence and then he heard her cry out, he didn't know whether it was the same voice, but he could tell this time that it was a woman, and turned towards the sound. Tripped and stumbled through the cluttered blackness of the room, feeling that draught freshen and pick up as though, miraculously, it was leading him towards the sound. There was another door. Another corridor, so dark, so dark he had to put out his hands and feel his way.

She shouted again. *Here.*

And a door gave under his hands and he was in there with them. Some thin grey light in here, though barely enough to see in the few seconds Sandro had to gather himself that at his feet a crouched form was struggling upright.

'Watch out,' a woman's voice said sharply, from somewhere else, and Sandro could only think, as the shape on the floor launched itself at him, *Oh, Jesus. I'm too old for this.*

413

*

Giuli heard the ambulance's siren from a long way off, getting louder. She heard the rattle as the shutter came up and saw Luisa standing there.

'Oh my God, Giuli,' she said, staring. 'Oh my God. Oh my God.' In a voice Giuli had never heard Luisa use before, tremulous under huge pressure, a dam holding back some great flood.

It's all right, Giuli wanted to say, only she didn't know if it was. There was blood on her hand, and on her jeans. Heard the siren become deafening and abruptly stop, then saw the ambulance men crowd into the space with their bulky jackets and a bag of something and a cylinder of something else.

And then one last face appeared, a narrow, battered face belonging to a man with dark eyes and an expression of anguish and fear and desperation who edged to the door frame and stopped, and stared. Josef.

Beside her Anna lay half-collapsed on her front, still warm, still breathing, holding tight and alive to Giuli's hand and making a small sound, over and over again. Giuli heard all this and saw all this and felt all this but really she heard and felt and saw none of it. All she saw was the child, the new child in her lap, her free arm around it, the child warm and bloodstained and covered with some waxy stuff, its eyes glued shut, its body folded and naked as a puppy's, on the skull the skin still transparent with newness. And the child – the new girl, the new being among them – opened her mouth, and made herself heard.

CHAPTER THIRTY-ONE

Saturday

H E HAD APPEARED ON the Saturday morning, nine o'clock, which would have been a decent hour on any other day. At least they'd slept well, like the dead, for the first time in what seemed like months. But they hadn't set an alarm, and the sound of the street bell woke them.

As she padded through the flat to answer the intercom Luisa registered the new cold in the air as a benediction. Summer would end.

'Who?' she said, not understanding. Then she got it, and put a hand to her breastbone. Please God. Not Giuli, now. She buzzed him in.

She stood at the top of the stairs in her nightgown and slippers, aware of her face crumpled from sleep, her unbrushed hair. She listened to the slow climb of footsteps and it occurred to her that this was a brave step for the boy to take.

Boy? The man who raised his head to hers as he climbed the last flight was about forty. And she needn't have worried about her hair; Enzo, Giuli's *fidanzato*, looked as though his mother cut his for him. An open face: kind.

He stopped on the landing, hesitant. '*Permesso?*' Polite, too.

'Is Giuli all right?' she asked, unable to keep the anxiety out of her voice. Remembering the astonishment in Giuli's face as she held the bloodstained bundle in her lap, could it only have been yesterday afternoon? It might have been too much for her.

But Enzo's face split in a shy smile even at the mention of her name and Luisa saw it all in that instant, and relaxed.

'Yes,' he said, ducking his head then raising it again to meet her eye. 'I – I – she didn't call me, all yesterday.' The ghost of that anxiety clouded his open face. 'But last night – then last night—'

Luisa nodded. They'd been at the hospital, waiting uselessly on plastic seating, not relatives, barely friends, to be told everything was all right with the baby. And then Giuli had started up and said, there's something I've got to do.

'So she's fine,' said Enzo, looking down again. He stood there waiting to be invited over the threshold, holding a bike helmet between his hands. He mumbled. 'I've come to ask you – to ask you—'

'Come in,' said Luisa.

*

The stocky nurse who'd dressed the five-centimetre laceration on one side of Sandro's neck where Valentino Sordi had gouged him with manicured fingernails clearly also thought that, at sixty-something, Sandro was too old to be spending his Friday nights like this.

Sitting in Pietro's garden now with his old friend opposite him, Sandro still didn't know if he'd have been able to do it without Roxana Delfino's help: perhaps best not to dwell on that. It had seemed an eternity before she did come to his aid, that much was for sure: the younger man writhing like a snake, smaller than him but furiously energetic and alarmingly strong, Sandro had registered immediately. Also weirdly, maniacally unfocused in his movements, though: not a fighter. Valentino Sordi might have honed his body for leisure but he didn't know what fighting was, and fortunately for him it turned out that Sandro, for all the weight and slackness and age he felt dragging against him, still did.

Even as Roxana unfroze and flung herself on Sordi's back, he'd felt it come back to him, that trick of twisting an opponent into submission with the right grip on the wrists and a sudden shift of one's weight, and as Valentino went down underneath them he'd remembered, on a hot summer's night just like this, perhaps ten years earlier, bringing down a drug-addicted car thief as he tried to flee into the gardens of some apartment blocks in Sesto Fiorentino, cuffing the boy and rising in triumph to meet Pietro's eye in the dark.

It hadn't been Pietro who'd finally arrived, with a feebly wailing siren, at the Carnevale. Sandro hadn't recognized the uniformed officers of the Polizia dello Stato standing uncertainly in the littered lobby as Sandro sat, sweating and dishevelled and, of course, too old for this, beside the sullenly silent Valentino Sordi, bound at the wrists with a plastic tie and bleeding profusely from a jagged wound just below his eye. He supposed he would have to get used to not recognizing members of the Polizia dello Stato.

And Pietro had appeared, in the end, at the police station, with news of Gulli, and Roxana Delfino's supposedly helpless elderly mother.

'Unbelievable,' his old friend mused now, raising a beer to his lips at the garden table. 'Two old biddies? Had him cornered in the back yard.'

It had rained again that morning but now, at five in the afternoon, the sky was clear and the temperature in Pietro's pretty garden, lowered by thirty-six hours of storms, was deliciously cool. Sandro could smell roses.

'Hardly even need to go to the seaside, if it's like this,' Sandro mused. He felt wrung out: all those women. All those women depending on him. But he also felt at peace.

And it turned out that two old ladies – Roxana Delfino's elderly mother and her even more doddering neighbour – had not needed his help, nor anyone else's. They had felled Gulli with a rusty spade when they spotted him lurking behind their gardens, then tied him up with washing line, for good measure. Wouldn't have held him for long, but then Pietro and Matteucci had arrived.

'Matteucci turned almost human,' said Pietro reflectively. 'Couldn't stop laughing when he saw the little ratbag trussed up in white nylon line. And he switched on the charm for the old dears.' He let out a sigh. 'I suppose I can put up with him.'

Pietro's daughter Chiara came out with a tray of coffee, smiling shyly, set it down and went back into the kitchen, where she and her red-headed mother were still going over Sandro's case, awestruck. They just couldn't get over it. Signora Martelli had owned the porn cinema, all these years, sitting there in her news-stand, pronouncing on other people's sins.

'Someone has to own those places,' Sandro had said. 'It's not always who you expect.' And in fact, now that it was gone, he almost felt affection for the Carnevale, symbol of a simpler age, and doomed.

They poured the coffee. No sugar for Sandro, on a health kick now, although, as Luisa might have pointed out, if he was serious he'd leave out the coffee, too.

'He'd never have got away with it,' said Pietro. 'That's the crazy thing. The Guardia might work in mysterious ways but they would have traced the money in the end, Jesus, it's their job. Hell, I think even that fat guy, Viola, would have got to the bottom of it, in the end.'

Sandro shrugged. 'Sure. Valentino's trouble was that he thought he was smart, smarter than everyone else. Maybe the drugs, too – he was on so much shit, that's what his friends are saying now. Getting more and more obnoxious, thought he could do anything, even hauling Claudio Brunello's body across town in the middle of the night, strapped to his back on a motorbike.' Shook his head. 'I'm astonished he even got as far as the African market without someone seeing him, or flipping the bike.'

'Explains the lesions on poor Brunello's leg, though, doesn't it? Burn from the bike's exhaust. And the rope marks on the wrists.'

'Then he went and sold the bike, thinking that would cover his tracks.' Pietro laughed shortly. 'Amateur stuff. Gulli, see, he's a professional, knows the odds, knows the tricks, but young Valentino?' The smile that crept across Pietro's face was wry. 'Uh-huh.'

Sandro was still thinking. 'Of course, you're right, he'd have been caught out, the movement of the cash would have been traced in the end, and for my money Viola would have got there before the Guardia. He's a smart guy. That wasn't my case, though, was it? I had to find Josef. And Valentino could easily have got to him before me. Almost did.'

The coffee was good. The smell of coffee, and roses after the rain, and a view of the hills up to Fiesole. There was nothing more you could want, thought Sandro. He yawned.

'Luisa OK?' Pietro shook his head at the thought. 'And Giuli. *Mamma mia.* Turns out she's cool under pressure, that girl. Delivering a baby in a thunderstorm?'

'She says she just caught it,' said Sandro. 'Right place at the right time.'

'Well,' said Pietro, 'that's a skill in itself, isn't it? Not too bad at that yourself. Matteucci, now, that's a different matter.'

And he looked sidelong at his old friend, and together they laughed.

*

Roxana and Maria Grazia sat on the porch. Ma and Carlotta were next door, thick as thieves, fussing over the handyman, who'd made a reappearance in the wake of all the drama.

'All they could go on about was the mess,' said Roxana, smiling. 'So cross, they were, about having to use the washing line, and the stupid boy falling into one of Carlotta's big geraniums, and another bit of the fence had gone. So they got him back. The handyman.'

Maria Grazia sat up to get a better look into next-door's garden. 'I think they've got an ulterior motive,' she said. 'He's quite good-looking, isn't he?'

Roxana laughed. 'A bit young for them,' she said.

Maria Grazia shoved her good-naturedly. 'Not them, you idiot.' Roxana didn't even blush.

'You lot,' she said. 'You never stop.' She felt as though she was on a different plane altogether. Work, her single status, Ma: none of it a problem any more.

Other priorities: she was working through them. Disposing of them: conscientious, methodical, Roxana had that talent at least. The bit she couldn't stop rerunning in her head had been not being able to move: watching Sandro Cellini and Valentino struggle as if in slow motion at the centre of the room. It had seemed like an hour, but had probably been thirty seconds, and then she'd flung herself on the thrashing monstrous shape they made together, not knowing which one of them she was clawing at.

He'd collapsed under them quite suddenly in the end, like a child, as though, as with everything in his privileged life so far, Valentino Sordi simply couldn't be bothered. Sandro Cellini had told her afterwards, still breathing heavily with the effort, that it was a chemical thing: addicts fight like that – like animals with a limitless supply of energy, then suddenly the fuel runs out and they stop dead.

They'd taken him away in a police car, handcuffed. Cellini watching from the lobby of the Carnevale, feeling his age, exposed in the flat light after the storm.

Valentino. Stupid, superficial, narcissistic Val, and she'd always thought killers were made of different stuff, of something tougher and fiercer and sharper. Turned out vanity and greed and stupidity could make a murderer too: that was the reality. Thank Christ, was all she could think, thank Christ I never fell for it. He might even have taken me home, for a joke or something, or to make sure I didn't cotton on. I might have slept with him. There'd been that fraction of a second after all when she'd thought, could I? She rubbed her eyes. No. Never.

'You all right?' said Maria Grazia sharply.

Roxana let out a long breath and in her mind's eye Valentino, wherever he was, sitting in some remand cell somewhere, dwindled to nothing. Ash on the breeze, along with Marisa, Roxana's job, the bank, that old life led in the half-light. Yes.

'I think so,' she said.

'So,' said Maria Grazia, eyeing her warily, 'what's next, then?'

'I don't know,' said Roxana, who had had a job of one sort or another continuously since she was fifteen years old. At peace. 'Something'll come up.'

CHAPTER THIRTY-TWO

Autumn

'I T'S PERFECT, DON'T YOU think?' Anna beamed.

'Perfect,' agreed Luisa.

Giuli looked at her. 'But—' she said, and at the sound of her raised voice, the baby, who'd been asleep on her shoulder, squirmed, her fingers splaying against Giuli's arm. Giuli closed her mouth.

But, she'd been going to say. This is your place. This is your apartment, yours and Sandro's, the dream place, the iron balcony, the view of the hills.

Anna's nest egg, the money left her by her adoptive parents, it turned out, was not a couple of thousand euros, after all.

'Oh, no,' Anna had said. 'I told you, didn't I? The farmhouse, twenty hectares of land in the Casentino – well, it's not Chianti but it was quite a lot of money. I put it in the bank, of course, when I came to the city, to work for Signora Capponi. I didn't want to live alone, you see?'

Giuli had just nodded, wordless. It had been more than enough for this place, the third-floor apartment in San Niccolo in need of work. It had been Luisa who'd suggested it.

The baby squirmed some more, properly awake now. Josef, who'd been sticking a screwdriver into a damp patch in the kitchen, came towards her with his arms out, and Giuli handed the baby to him. He still couldn't quite meet her eye, she thought. Was he good enough for Anna? Anna thought so. Was he after her money?

Luisa, having taken a look at him, didn't think so. 'Leave them be,' she'd said.

Where the baby had been lying against her shoulder, the sweat was cooling now, a damp patch under her chin where the baby's mouth had been. It was all right, though.

*

In bed a long time later, in the comfortable cool after more rain and with the street outside quiet for once, Luisa rolled over and set her cheek against Sandro's chest. She heard the thump of his heart. Nothing need change, she thought. Nothing.